A Place Called Rainwater

BOOKS BY DOROTHY GARLOCK

DOROTHY GARLOCK

A Place Called Rainwater

DOUBLEDAY LARGE PRINT HOME LIBRARY EDITION

WARNER BOOKS

An AOL Time Warner Company

Warner Books, Inc., 1271 Avenue of the Americas, New York, NY 10020

An AOL Time Warner Company

Printed in the United States of America

ISBN 0-7394-3150-1

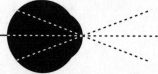

This Large Print Book carries the
Seal of Approval of N.A.V.H.

FOR THE MIX FAMILY OF NORTHWOOD:
AMOS, karate champion
LORAINE, exceptional mother and music teacher
JACOB and LOGAN, who make life a joy for
Grandma—
but only for a half day at a time

A Place Called Rainwater

Thad's Song

I'll sing you a song 'bout my sassy girl
If I can remember the tune.
She's little but mighty—a diamond, a pearl,
And I'm goin' to marry her soon.

In this oil boomtown she's made a mark.
Runs the hotel her auntie began,
But there's danger for her where the streets are
   dark.
Out there waits a murderin' man.

Is he the attorney who harbors a grudge
Or the rich man who owns half the town
Or someone who works in the oil and the sludge?
I must, for her sake, track him down.

Oh, Jilly Justine, I'll watch over you
Whether you like it or not.
Whatever hazards I have to fight through
With all the strength that I've got.

Oh, Jilly Justine, I'll be faithful to you,
Though you may say that I tease.
You can taunt me and doubt me; I will be true.
To my heart only you hold the keys.

—F.S.I.

Prologue

Jefferson City, Missouri, 1903

"Get out, you worthless slut!"

"Please. Please let me stay. I'll work hard. I'll do anything—"

The young girl dropped to her knees and clasped the old man so tightly around his skinny legs that he stumbled backward. After grabbing the back of a chair to regain his balance, he lashed out with a large, bony hand. He slapped the girl with such force that she fell to the floor and lay there sobbing.

"Don't you dare touch me, you . . . goddamn bitch! I mollycoddled you for months while you carried that wretched creature. You had new shoes and dresses, a coat and scented soap. I put food in your mouth and allowed you to loll in bed until an hour past daylight. You never did another tub of washing after you *took.* When I look at what you've given me in return, I want to kill you."

"I . . . didn't do . . . anything to cause it. Can't you understand that?"

"Are you saying it's my fault that that brat came into the world with the mark of the devil on it?" He reached down and grabbed a handful of rich auburn hair and turned the girl's tear-wet face to his. "I had to plow you for months before your trashy puss could generate enough heat to fertilize my seed." He threw her head from him. It hit a table leg with a loud crack. "All this time wasted . . . for a flawed brat I'll be ashamed to show in public."

"Judge, these things happen in the best of families. Only God knows why." The doctor reached down and helped the girl to her feet.

"I've not heard of it and I've been on the bench twenty years. You told me that birthmark would go away. It's been a month, and if anything it's . . . redder."

"I thought it probably would fade, Judge. I've not seen anything like it before. I've written to dozens of other doctors around the country, and they all tell me that it can't be removed. The baby would bleed to death."

"It would be a blessing! It's the mark of the devil." The judge looked at the young girl as if he'd like to cut her heart out. "I should have her locked up in a place where she'd never see the light of day again."

"I can't go along with you having her locked up, Judge," the doctor said firmly. "You can't place the fault with her. What happened is a freak of nature. Some babies are born simpletons with big heads, crooked spines or deformed legs. This child has a different deformity, but it doesn't mean that he won't be bright."

"All I wanted from the bitch was a son. Look what I got! One that's marked for all the world to see." The judge's angry voice could be heard from the attic to the cellar of the large mansion on the south side of Jefferson City. The cook in the kitchen and the maid scrubbing the back stairway shuddered at the thought of being on the receiving end of his wrath.

"I'll take him away, sir. You won't have to see me or my baby ever again. No one will know who fathered him."

"Are you mad? That scrap in there, sorry as it is, has my blood. It's probably the only offspring I'll ever have. I'd see it dead before I'd give it to you. It'll not be raised to be a weakling. It's got the devil in it, and I'll see to it that it torments you for the rest of your life."

Courage she didn't know she had bubbled up in the young girl. She lunged at him with balled fists and would have hit him if the doctor hadn't grabbed her arm. Angry unguarded words spewed from her mouth.

"He's not got the devil in him. You have!" she shouted. "He's a helpless little baby, not an *it*. I'll take him far from here. You can find some other fifteen-year-old girl to suffer your disgusting pawing and slobbering and . . . rape when you can get that puny *thing* that dangles between your legs hard enough."

"Shut your lying mouth!" The judge's voice was equally loud. He trembled with anger. Stooped and gaunt, with sparse gray hair and dried skin that stretched across his bony face, he looked every one of his sixty years. Saliva ran from the corner of his mouth.

"I want the doctor to know that the second week I came to work here you grabbed me by the hair, pushed me up the stairs to your room, locked the door and whipped me with your belt until I took off my clothes. You said if I didn't spread my legs for you, I'd go back to jail and rot there."

Bolstered by the doctor's presence, and with the heartbreaking knowledge that she was going to have to leave her baby behind, the hatred she had kept bottled up came boiling out. At their first meeting, the judge had seemed to take pity on her when she had been falsely accused of lifting a purse. Later, he had held that accusation over her head throughout the months he had pleasured himself on her young body in an attempt to impregnate her.

"Liar. You followed me around like a bitch in heat thinking I'd marry you!"

"Marry *you*?" she said scornfully. "I'd not marry you if you were the King of England, you skinny, decrepit old bastard," the girl shouted. "I never went to bed with you without strop marks on my behind. You made me want to puke, and I often did after you'd violated me. I despise you, I wish I'd killed you in your sleep!"

"Get out! Get out, you ungrateful bitch, or I'll call the police!"

"I won't go before I see my baby and . . . and tell him good-bye." The girl stood her ground. The doctor secretly applauded her courage.

"Judge, it won't do any harm to let her see the baby, and you don't want to involve the police in this." The doctor kept a tight hand on the girl's arm.

"Agnes," the judge shouted. "Bring the . . . brat. Maud, get her suitcase." He turned to the doctor. "She's taking out of here only what she brought in."

When the stout woman came down the stairs with the tiny bundle in her arms, the girl broke away from the doctor and snatched the baby from her. With a motion of his head, the judge sent the woman to stand in front of the door.

The girl turned her back to those watching her and, with tears streaming down her face, cuddled the sleeping infant to her.

"I don't want to leave you, little man, but there's nothing I can do," she whispered. "I've no way of taking care of you. If I don't leave, he'll have me jailed. Know that your mama loves you. I'll be back . . . someday."

She placed kisses on the child's head and on the red mark on his tiny face before he was taken from her embrace.

Without looking back, the young mother picked up the suitcase and walked out the door. The doctor followed her down the path. He took the suitcase, placed it in the boot of his buggy, then helped the sobbing girl up onto the seat.

September 1911

The buggy moved slowly past the big fenced-in mansion where the judge sat on the porch watching a boy in knee britches and a billed cap kick a ball.

"He's growing up. He's eight years old now." The woman held tightly to the hand of the man beside her. "When I last saw him, he was only three. That time I followed the woman who took him to the barbershop and got a good look at him. I wish I could see him up close again and tell him who I am."

"It would just open old wounds for you, honey. The boy may not know anything about you. If he does, he's been poisoned against you. He seems happy and well cared for. I think you should leave well enough alone."

As they watched, the boy raced across the yard to where a small puppy squatted beside the walk. He drew back his foot and kicked the small animal as he had kicked the ball. The dog yelped as it flew through the air to land with a thump on the brick walk. It lay there yelping in pain.

"Oh, dear God!" the woman gasped and began to cry.

Apparently giving no thought to the injured puppy, the boy ran across the yard to the ball. He laughed and yelled something to the man sitting in a high-backed wicker chair. When the kicked ball went up onto the porch, the boy followed. The tall, gaunt man in a long black coat stood and said something that caused the boy to leave the ball and come to stand in front of him.

The lad snatched his cap from his head and held it beneath his arm during their brief conversation. Then, ignoring the still-yelping puppy, the man pushed the boy ahead of him into the house.

Chapter 1

Rainwater, Oklahoma, 1929

"You ill-mannered lout!"

The glob of brown tobacco juice had hit and splattered as Jill was sweeping away the water she had used to scrub the well-worn boards on the hotel porch. Appalled, she glared at the man on the bench. His thin lips stretched in a grin, revealing stubs of tobacco-stained teeth. Then, to express his indifference, he extended his muddy boots out in front of him, crossing his legs at the ankles.

Jill's temper flared. "You . . . jackass! Get off this porch and stay off."

His grin widened.

"Are you deaf as well as uncivilized? Get!" She made a shooing motion with the broom.

"This is a public porch."

"It's no such thing. It belongs to the Byers Hotel. The bench you're sitting on belongs to the hotel. If you're too lazy to go to the end of the porch to spit, you're no longer welcome to sit on it."

"Ain't yore bench. It's Justine's bench. Justine's porch. Justine's hotel."

"That may be, but I'm running this hotel now and I'm telling you to leave."

"Or what?" He switched the chew of tobacco to his other cheek and puckered his lips as if to spit again.

"Don't you dare!" Jill shouted. "Spit on this porch again and I'll call the sheriff."

"Go ahead. Sheriff ain't goin' to arrest me for spittin'. Ask Justine if she wants Skeeter Ridge to get off her porch. Me and Justine's just like that." The two fingers he held up were pressed together.

Jill leaned her broom against the side of the building. The man was dirty, with streaks of grime on his face, hands and forearms where the sleeves of his shirt were rolled up to the elbows. His britches and boots were caked with red Oklahoma clay. The neck of a flat bottle of whiskey protruded from his hip pocket.

"I don't care if you and Aunt Justine are *just like that.*" She mocked his gesture with two fingers pressed together. "I'm in charge here now. I have just scrubbed this porch, in case you haven't noticed, and I'll not stand for a good-for-nothing loafer spitting on it. I'm telling you to go."

He gave her another impertinent grin. "Make me."

Jill picked up the bucket and turned as if she were going back into the hotel. Instead she whirled around.

"This is probably the closest thing to a bath you'll get all summer," she shouted as she tossed the dirty water in the man's face.

He came up off the bench cursing and balled his fists.

"Ya . . . goddamn . . . bitch!"

Jill dropped the bucket and grabbed the broom.

"Back off or I'll wrap this broom handle around your neck." Grasping the straw end, she swung the handle at his head. He escaped by dodging down the porch steps.

"Ya goddamn she-wolf!"

"Call me that again, you filthy braying jackass," she shouted, "and I'll bust your stupid head. You and your filthy habits are not welcome on this porch." Her angry words were accompanied by a jabbing motion with the broom handle.

"What ya need is a strop on yore butt."

"Lay a hand on me, you belly-crawling worm, and I'll put holes in you big enough for the sun to shine through."

Attracted by the commotion, two roustabouts paused on the walk to watch. Fresh from an oil rig, in oil-soaked clothes and with grimy faces, they shouted with laughter.

"Skeeter, ya goin' to let that little wildcat run ya off? She ain't no bigger than a good-sized chigger."

"That yore summer bath, Skeeter? Ya'll need another'n 'bout Christmastime."

"What'd ya do to get her so riled up?"

"He spit on my clean floor, is what he did," Jill yelled. "If he does it again, I'll do more than douse him with water. I'll break this broom handle over that knot on his shoulders."

"Wow, Skeeter! That little wildcat is madder than a wet hen. Ya'd better watch yore step."

"Ya just wait, ya little split-tail. Justine'll set ya straight about a few things." Skeeter wiped the water from his face with the sleeve of his shirt.

Jill ignored him and vigorously swept the water from the porch, flinging it as far as possible toward the street. She had been in Rainwater for only a few weeks and doubted there was a dirtier town anyplace on the face of the earth.

The town had been just a wide spot in the road until a wildcatter brought in an oil well a half mile from town. Now, three years later, a dozen pumping wells surrounded the town and a dozen more were being drilled. Rainwater had doubled, then tripled in size until now it housed almost five thousand oil-hungry souls and was still growing.

The unpaved street that divided the two rows of buildings was hard-packed clay. The crude structures that had been hastily erected along Main Street had gradually been replaced by sawed-lumber buildings. The new boards were darkened with oil carried by the wind from a gusher before it was capped. The well, not far from town, had been cheered by the citizens of Rainwater even as they were being coated with what they called black gold.

Jill waited until the three men ambled on

down the street toward the stores, pool halls, eating places and speakeasies where bootleg whiskey was as easy to come by as a cup of coffee. All were eager to part the roustabouts from their money. The sheriff had more than he could handle with fights, thieves and robbers to spend much time arresting bootleggers.

Everyone knew that it was just a matter of time before Prohibition would be repealed. The law was not working as intended and was instead making millionaires out of a few big-time operators in places like Kansas City and Chicago.

Jill picked up the bucket and went back into the small lobby of the hotel, then on through the kitchen. When she pushed on the screen door to go out onto the back porch, a black and white shaggy dog jumped up, moved a few feet away and waited expectantly.

"Are you still here?" she snapped.

The dog's tail made a half wave, then sagged between her hind legs. Jill hung the bucket on a nail.

"Go home." The mongrel looked at Jill with sorrowful eyes, then lay down and rested her head on her forepaws.

"Suit yourself. But don't expect me to keep feeding you. A few bread scraps doesn't make us lifelong friends," Jill grumbled, then went back into the kitchen and slammed the screen door.

"Mercy me. What's got your tail in a crack?" It was always a surprise to Jill to hear the melodious voice that came from Radna, the bronze-faced woman who sat at the table peeling potatoes. None of the Indians she had ever known had such musical voices, nor spoke so precisely.

"A nasty old man spit a glob of tobacco juice on my clean porch."

"Well, now, isn't that a surprise?" There was lilting laughter in her voice.

"I gave him a bath with my mop water."

"I bet he loved that." The dark eyes continued to smile at her.

Jill giggled. "I couldn't have surprised him more if I had sprouted wings."

"That must have been Skeeter Ridge."

"How do you know that?"

"He's harmless. He's been sitting on the porch for years. Thinks he owns it."

"I set him straight about that, I think." Jill went quickly down the hall and looked out the door to see if the man had returned.

"Aunt Justine hardly touched her breakfast," she said when she returned to the
kitchen.

"We're losin' her. You best prepare yourself. Justine's going downhill fast."

"Have you known her a long time?"

"Many years. She was here when I came
to the area just before the war. At that time
Rainwater was just a spot on the prairie.
The hotel, a store, a saloon and a few other
buildings that didn't amount to much. It was
a place to come to on Saturday night."

"You didn't live here in Rainwater?"

"No. My man and I lived out on the
prairie. He died about that time and I came
here to help Justine."

"Was he an Indian?"

"Cherokee like my daddy. Lovely man but
just couldn't leave the booze alone."

"I don't see how Aunt Justine made a living here. There couldn't have been many
travelers through the town in those days."

Radna gave her a sideways glance. "She
had enough business."

"Was this a whorehouse?" Jill bluntly
asked the question she had wanted to ask
since her arrival.

"Not exactly." Radna didn't seem to be

surprised by the question. She glanced at the door to Justine's bedroom to make sure it was closed. "Justine took in . . . unfortunate girls from time to time and they had male friends who came to call," she explained in a low voice. "If they chose to give Justine a little money to pay for a girl's room and board, no one thought much about it."

"Aunt Justine . . . didn't—"

"How do I know, girl? She was still a good-looking woman ten years ago. Almost as pretty as you—bigger, more bosom. Men like women with big titties."

"Then that lets me out."

Jill studied Radna. Although it was impossible to guess her age precisely, she seemed to be in her middle or late thirties. Her hair was thick and black. She combed it back and tied it at the nape of her neck with a ribbon. Not much taller than Jill's five feet three inches, she was thin but muscled from hard work. Her eyes were dark brown, her skin free of wrinkles. Only her work-worn hands told of a lifetime of hardship. She was always cheerful, although she often sang sad ballads in a throaty contralto as she worked. Now, as she sliced the potatoes, she sang a few lines of a song about a letter edged in black.

"Where did you go to school, Radna?" Jill asked.

"An Indian school. The Cherokee Seminary at Tahlequah. They took me though I'm one-eighth colored. Mama was a beautiful quadroon. I've not tried to hide it." She looked directly at Jill to gauge her reaction when she made the announcement. "My daddy was a teacher and loved my mama to distraction. My, they were a handsome couple. She teased him about naming me Night Bird or some other Indian name. He threatened to call me Topsy or Jemima. I don't know how they settled on Radna."

"Are you their only child?"

"No, I've a brother around somewhere." Radna moved the chair back and got up from the table.

"No children?"

"Had three. Two never breathed at all. One lived two days."

"I'm sorry. It's hard to lose a loved one. Especially a baby."

"It's all right. They never lived long enough for me to get acquainted with them." Radna poured water over the pota-

toes she had peeled. "I hear one of your hotel guests stirring around. You'd better get
out there or he'll scoot out the door without
paying."

Jill was standing behind the counter
when the drummer came down the stairs
carrying a large suitcase. She hadn't liked
him when he came in, and she doubted her
opinion of him was going to change now
that he was leaving. His line was too
smooth for her taste.

"Hel-lo. How are you this morning?" He
smiled, showing a gold-capped tooth.

"Fine, thank you. Did you find your room
satisfactory?"

"For a place like this, it was adequate. At
least it was cleaner than it was the last time
I stayed here."

"And when was that?"

"About two years ago. The town has
changed."

"Do you come through Rainwater often?"

The mustache on his upper lip twitched.
He leaned on the counter, bringing his face
closer to hers. His hair smelled strongly of
brilliantine.

"Would you be waiting for me if I did?"
His bold eyes moved down to her breasts.

"No. I'm just making polite conversation and waiting for you to pay me. That'll be seventy-five cents."

"I'd pay two dollars for another night, if you know what I mean."

"I know what you mean." Her voice lashed out at him like a whip. "I suggest you bring a tent the next time you come to town. This hotel will be full."

Jill's eyes, which could shine with laughter or turn as cold as a frozen pond, gave him a dismissive stare. She lifted her brows as if he were beneath her contempt. They were dark, with lashes to match that contrasted with her blue eyes and blond hair.

"I'm a paying customer, sweetheart, and don't you forget it," he said with an unabashed grin.

"You're a cheating, low-life, rutting stud, is what you are. How many children is your wife taking care of while you wander about . . . if you know what I mean?" Jill looked pointedly at the wedding band on his finger.

"Well, it was worth a try." Showing no embarrassment at all, the drummer backed away, placed his coins on the counter, picked up his heavy case and without a word walked out the door.

"I guess we don't have to worry about him coming back or about you taking care of yourself." The voice, followed by a low laugh, came from the hall, and Radna pulled a heavy iron skillet out from behind her skirt.

"Were you going to hit him with that?"

"If I had to. I've done it before."

"How long ago was it that this was a whorehouse?"

"Four or five years ago. And don't let Justine hear you call it that. She considered it a rooming house for young ladies."

"Yeah, sure. What did everyone else call it?"

"A whorehouse." Radna's laugh was like tinkling bells. "But not to Justine. That aunt of yours has a heart as big as all outdoors. A lot of people in this town are indebted to her. As far as I know, she never turned anyone away who was sick or needy."

"When she wrote to Papa and asked if her namesake could come and help her out until she could get on her feet, he had no idea her hotel had been a place of ill repute or that his eldest sister would probably never get on her feet. He didn't want me to come, but Eudora, my stepmother, persuaded him that at almost twenty-one, I was old enough to make my own decisions."

"Is Justine's name Jill?"

"No. My name is Justine Jill Jones. All the kids in our family have names starting with the letter *J.* Mama's name was Jane and Papa's is Jethro. My sisters and brothers are Julie, Joe, Jack, Jason and Joy. In the town where we grew up, we are known as the *J*'s."

"Isn't that something?" Understanding was in Radna's voice. "It sort of binds you all together."

"Back on the farm it was one for all and all for one. If you ever messed with a Jones, you were in deep trouble with all the Joneses. My brother Joe is over near Tulsa. Eudora said she would write to him and tell him that I'm here and to come see me when he got over this way."

Sudden spontaneous laughter erupted from Jill.

"Well, kiss my foot! What's tickled your funny bone?" asked Radna.

"You," Jill said and giggled. "I'd like to see you in action with that skillet. Are you sure you can swing it?"

"You bet! Ask Justine. I backed her up a few times when we had to get a drunk out of here."

"I'd better go see about her." Jill came from behind the counter. "She might have heard the ruckus on the porch."

"Oh, she heard it, all right. Not much goes on here in the hotel that Justine doesn't know about."

Justine Jones Byers settled in the chair beside the window looking out onto the side street. A year ago she'd had the energy of a twenty-year-old, but now she had to exert a major effort to negotiate the few steps to the chair. The thick wavy hair she had colored with henna was thin now and streaked with gray. The bright jewelry she loved lay forgotten in a bureau drawer.

As a bride, she had come to Oklahoma in 1907, the year it was admitted to the Union as the forty-sixth state. She and her new husband had lived in Bartlesville, Ponca City and Pawhuska before settling in Rainwater. Ralph Byers had been a dreamer, a man who had flitted from one business to the other seeking recognition and hoping to strike it rich.

Justine never did find out where he had found the money to build the hotel and didn't really want to know, but she suspected he had won it in a poker game. The hotel had provided them with a meager living, but it had given Ralph the prestige he needed so badly.

He had been mayor of the small town of three hundred citizens when he stepped out in front of an ice truck and was killed instantly. He would have been pleased to know that almost every person in the town attended his funeral. Later that same year the Byerses' little three-year-old girl died of whooping cough.

Since that time Justine had had many opportunities to remarry, but Ralph had been her one and only love. And she had found satisfaction helping her "girls."

Justine turned from the window when Jill came into the room. She had not been one bit disappointed in her namesake, just surprised that her brother, Jethro, had allowed his daughter to come. Most people considered Oklahoma a land of wild Indians, outlaws and empty prairie land. Justine loved the openness, the rawness and the variety of people who lived in the state formerly known as Indian Territory.

Jill reminded Justine of herself at age twenty. Although she hadn't been nearly as pretty as her niece, she'd been just as ready to command the world with a buggy whip. Jill's wavy mass of wheat-colored hair ended just below her jawbone, accentuating her high cheekbones and the pure cream of her skin. She had a generous mouth, full-lipped and red, with a charming uplift at the corners. Her slim young body moved with vibrancy, yet with the grace of wind on prairie grass. It was her personality Justine admired the most. Her niece had backbone and a mouth to go with it. She'd not be pushed around.

"Did I hear you calling someone buzzard bait?" Justine wheezed when she spoke.

"I can think of a lot more names to call him. His name was Skeeter-something-or-the-other and he spit on my clean porch."

"Skeeter Ridge. He knows better than that. I'd have whopped him alongside the head."

"I bathed him with my dirty mop water."

Justine smiled. "Good for you. I've run him off that porch more than once."

"Not to hear him tell it." Jill noticed her aunt's hands lying loosely in her lap. "When is the doctor coming again?"

"That old quack?" Justine scoffed. "Old fool admitted that he didn't know what the hell was wrong with me. Just losing strength, he said. Well, Christ Almighty. I already knew that."

"Aunt Justine, why don't we go to Tulsa? The doctors there may be able to operate or . . . something." Jill squatted down beside her aunt's chair.

"Honey, they can't do any more for me than Dr. Russell. I want to stay right here. This is my home. Besides, I don't think I could stand the trip."

"Are you sure? Doctors can do great things now."

"There is nothing they can do for me. Old Doc isn't the smartest man in the world, but he was honest with me. He didn't know what was causing my trouble, but he'd heard of a case like mine. Creeping paralysis, he called it. I've already lost the strength in my hands—can't hold a water glass. It's affected my arms, my feet and my legs just like he said it would. I'm at peace with what's to come and thankful that I'm not in terrible pain." She looked first at the limp hands lying in her lap and then at Jill. "I regret that I'm so much trouble."

"When you take care of someone dear to you, it's not trouble." Jill patted Justine's hand.

"I'm so glad you're here." There was a tear in Justine's voice.

"I'm glad, too. Can I get you something?"

"You can brush my hair. The brush is over there on my dresser."

Jill fetched the hairbrush, moved behind the chair and drew the brush through her aunt's hair.

"That feels good." Justine sighed contentedly. "I've not been able to brush my own hair for months."

"When you feel up to it, I'll bring in a pan of rainwater and wash it." Jill stroked the gray-streaked hair from her aunt's scalp to the ends. "Would you like for me to make you a couple of pigtails?"

"Ralph used to call me his little squaw when I braided my hair."

"It must have been wonderful to be so much in love as you were."

"When I first saw him, I knew that he was the one I wanted to be with for the rest of my life. I went after him and never regretted it for a minute." A little laugh caught in her throat. "Don't ever settle for second best, honey, when it comes to choosing your life's mate. Get a man who'll want you to stand beside him and not behind him."

"I've not seen anyone yet that I'd want to spend the rest of my life with."

"You will." Justine chuckled and her eyes lit up. "It'll happen when you least expect it."

"Aunt Justine, do you really think I should go to the town meeting tonight?"

"It's a merchants' meeting. You've got as much right to have your say as any of them. This hotel may not be fancy, but it's been here a lot longer than most businesses and it's important to the town."

"I'll go and listen, but I doubt if I'll say anything."

"I used to enjoy the meetings." Justine's body was losing its strength, but her mind was sharp. "How many paying guests did we have last night?"

"Eight with the three on the weekly rate."

"You wouldn't have any trouble renting out more on a weekly basis. It's sure money. But you have to leave at least seven rooms open for travelers or Byers wouldn't be considered a hotel."

"I'm learning about the hotel business. Aunt Justine, why have you not offered meals?"

"Martha, who owns the restaurant across the street, nursed me through a time when I didn't know if I wanted to live or die. I don't want to take any of her business. Besides, it would be too much work for Radna."

"You think a lot of Radna, don't you?"

"You bet. She was the nearest thing to kin I had until you came. I wish she could find a good man who would appreciate her," Justine said wistfully. "A woman isn't complete without a mate."

"There are plenty here to choose from."

"Radna makes no bones about her colored blood. That narrows the field considerably."

"I'd never have guessed it and was surprised when she told me. I thought she was only part Indian."

"She is . . . mostly. She loved her mother and won't deny her blood."

"Aunt, will Martha be at the merchants' meeting? I don't want to be the only woman there."

"I expect she will. She and Flora Hadley usually go. Why don't you go over and ask her?"

"I think I will."

"Call Radna, honey. She'll help you get me up from this chair, and I'll lie down."

Chapter 2

Jill felt confident in a freshly ironed blue print dress with a ruffled oval neckline and a calf-length full skirt, but she was glad for the company of the big woman who ran Martha's Restaurant. They made their way down the wooden walk bordering the unpaved main street of Rainwater. This was the busy section of town. They had to pass through it in order to reach the schoolhouse, where the meeting would be held.

Day or night, there was activity on the streets of Rainwater and even more on Saturday night. Jill wondered if everyone in the entire county had come to town. Loitering on the walks were roustabouts, loafers, roughnecks, men looking for work and gamblers looking for a card game where they hoped to fleece a greenhorn out of his week's pay. Welders, riggers and drillers, in overalls made stiff by wet clay and oil, mingled with men in broadcloth suits who had angle-parked their cars along the street.

Jill was careful not to make eye contact with any of the men she and Martha passed on the street. For the most part the men were hardworking and missed the families they had left back home. But there were some rowdies in the crowd who roamed the street. A man leaning against a porch post called out as the two women passed.

"Hey, Skeeter. Isn't that the little wildcat who chased you off the hotel porch?"

Jill gave the man a scornful glance, then recognized him as one of the roustabouts who had witnessed her temper tantrum that morning. She couldn't hold back a grin. The man laughed and tipped his hat in a respectful manner.

"This li'l wild . . . cat can ch . . . hase me off her porch any day." The man who spoke fell in step with Jill.

"You're drunk, Bert. Beat it," Martha ordered sharply. She was a robust woman with a don't-fool-with-me attitude.

"Shome on, Marthy. I ain't sheen a woman this purty since I come to Texas."

"This isn't Texas, Bert. It's Oklahoma. Now skedaddle or I'll lay a fist alongside your head."

"Be nice, Marthy, I ain't goin' to hurt 'er. Jist wanta look at 'er."

"Are you ladies going to the meeting at the schoolhouse?" A tall man wedged himself between Jill and the drunk. "May I walk along with you?"

Jill thought he was another masher and jerked her elbow from his grasp. When she looked up, he had put his fingers to the brim of his hat.

"You need a little help getting through that crowd, ma'am. Hunter Westfall at your service. Will you allow me the pleasure of escorting you?"

"Thank you," Jill murmured, then turned her eyes away from the narrow, clean-shaven face and light tawny gold eyes. He was a handsome man and prosperous, judging by the cut of his black suit and tan felt hat.

"We need more places where the men can go to get off the streets. Don't you agree?"

"I guess so. Why don't they go home?"

"You haven't been here long, have you?

Home might be a tent out at the rigging or a tarpaper shack thrown up as a bunkhouse." He chuckled. "They need to come to town once in a while and let off steam."

"Most of them are decent hardworking men, lonesome for their families." Jill was surprised to hear a belligerent tone in Martha's voice.

"You are right there, ma'am. There are a few, however, who spoil it for the others."

"Do you know the reason for the meeting?" Jill asked.

"I think the mayor has some grandiose ideas for turning Rainwater into a thriving metropolis." Hunter smiled down at Jill. His eyes stayed on her profile long after she had looked away.

The two-story frame school building was newer than Jill had expected. A dozen men sat on folding chairs when they entered the room where the meeting was to be held, and Jill, glad that she had made an extra effort to look nice, became the focus of their attention.

"Gentlemen, you know Mrs. Caine. This is Miss Jones." Hunter took Jill's elbow and steered her forward. "She is taking over the management of the Byers Hotel for her aunt. As you know, Mrs. Byers is not well."

Jill tried to keep her mouth from dropping open in surprise as the man whom she had met a mere five minutes ago explained her presence.

"Miss Jones, this is our mayor, Orvis Henshaw," Hunter said smoothly. "He is the owner of one of our dry goods and grocery stores."

"How do you do?" The man stood and Jill offered her hand.

Hunter continued with the introductions. "Mr. Langley from the barbershop; Mr. Stevens, the owner of another one of the grocery stores; and Mr. Burns, here, is the druggist. Mr. Fields and Mr. Grover are the proprietors of the recreation parlors, and Mr. Holder and Mr. Parson, along with Mrs. Caine"—he nodded toward Martha—"run our eating establishments." Hunter continued around the room and included the two men and one woman who had come in during the introductions. One of the men was a lawyer with a huge red birthmark on his face and one was the city treasurer. The woman ran the bakery.

"How do you do?" Jill said to all. "I'll not

remember all your names, but I'm glad to meet you." She sat down quickly beside Martha.

The meeting started with the mayor expressing his appreciation to those who came. He was a robust man in his mid-forties with thin hair parted in the middle and a thick mustache with the ends waxed to turn upward.

"There are two things I'd like to discuss tonight. The main one is how we are going to keep our town alive after the boom. We've enjoyed the boom since the gusher came in out on Kelly's place. I'm not an oilman, but from what I've seen and what I've read about other boomtowns, our oil will last only a few years. I'd like to have some type of industry ready to take its place when it's gone."

"There's no reason to think the town will die any time soon," Hunter interjected quietly. "The wells surrounding the town will be pumping for years."

"That may be, Westfall, but how many men does it take to keep wells pumping when the derricks are gone and the tanks are built?"

"There is equipment to be moved, oil to

be transported, pipelines to be built. And don't forget the possibility of gas wells here in this area. Oklahoma's natural gas is in demand now. Think about the demand as the population grows."

"I hadn't heard there were plans for a pipeline." The comment came from the lawyer behind Jill.

"Rainwater isn't Tulsa, but a cross-country pipeline isn't out of the realm of possibility." Hunter's compelling eyes paused on Jill as he surveyed the room. His manner was daunting, if for no other reason than his air of self-confidence. His features were calm, his lips unsmiling. Sideburns framed his face and thick brown hair waved back from his forehead.

"Does anyone else have anything to say on this subject?" the mayor asked.

"I agree with you, Orvis." Mr. Burns, the grocer, lifted his hand to get attention. "When the boom passes, my business will be cut by half, if not more."

"You'll still have business from the ranchers. And another thing that will keep the town going is the railroad. The tracks won't be removed just because some of the wells are capped." A hint of impatience was evident in Hunter's voice.

"I'm not sure the ranchland around here will survive the oil boom." The lawyer spoke again. He was a man in his mid-twenties. Jill felt a wave of pity. He would be nice-looking without the blood-red mark, the shape of a palm, that reached from the corner of his eye across his cheek to his nose.

"The 101 Ranch over near Claremore seems to have adapted to modern-day ranching and farming." Jill noted a muscle jumping in Hunter's jaw, even as he responded quietly.

"There are more oil wells out there on the prairie than prairie dog holes. A law should be passed to make the oil companies more responsible for the land they spoil." The lawyer appeared to be enjoying the argument. "They lease a few acres of land and ruin a hundred with overflow and leaking tanks."

"The owners don't have to lease," Hunter argued smoothly. "Let those who want to make a piddly living off the grass keep it."

"If a ranch doesn't lease, a company will set up a derrick nearby and, using the whip-stocking technique, drain off the oil from under his land. Who can tell where the oil is coming from out of a fourteen-thousand-foot hole?"

Jill watched and listened closely. Hunter Westfall had an air of power that only money could engender. She was curious about him. The others, except for the lawyer with the birthmark, seemed to kowtow to him.

"We don't seem to be getting anywhere with this." The mayor's words brought Jill back to the matter at hand. "My other concern is our streets. We need to do something about them. Every time it rains we have a quagmire. We can't afford pavement, so I suggest we grade and oil them. We have four companies drilling near here. They should be willing to donate the oil."

"I'll take care of Main Street, Orvis. I'll have a couple of my men drag it to soften it up, then apply the oil. It will mean blocking it off for a couple of days until the oil soaks in."

"Thanks, Mr. Westfall. That'll go a long way toward holding down dust.".

"By the way, Mayor, do I need a permit to build a dance hall? I own a chunk of property south of town. I've been thinking about developing it into an amusement park of sorts, with a dance hall, a roller-skating rink and a few rides."

"The county license to run the hall, the rink and the rides will cost you five dollars each."

"Better think about it, Mayor," the lawyer said. "Christian folks in this town won't want that park open on Sunday."

"We'll take that up when the time comes, Madison." The mayor stood. "I guess that's all, unless someone has other business they want to discuss."

Jill stood beside the door and waited for Martha, who had made a beeline for the woman who had come in late, a short, heavyset woman with a pleasant face. She noticed the young lawyer eyeing her, but he didn't make an effort to speak to her. After chatting with the woman for a few minutes, Martha brought her over and introduced her to Jill.

"Flora runs the bakery," Martha explained.

"Hello, Jill. I've been wanting to come over for another visit with Justine. The last time I was there you had gone uptown and I missed you. How is she?"

"She stays in bed most of the time."

"Ah, law." Flora's homely face showed concern. "This has been comin' on for a while. I'm glad she's got some of her folks with her."

"Let's go while the oil king is busy bending the ear of the mayor." Martha urged Jill out the door. When they got outside, she said, "I think you've got a beau if you want one. It seems that Mr. Westfall has taken a shine to you."

"What are you talking about?" Then, "Oh, no. He was just being nice."

"Mr. Westfall is never nice unless it's going to benefit Mr. Westfall."

"Listen to Martha, honey." Flora glanced over her shoulder to see if anyone was behind them. "He's had a number of women come to visit, then suddenly you don't see them around anymore," she added in a low voice.

"Why did you call him the oil king?" Jill asked.

Martha answered, "He owns more than half of the wells around town and is trying to buy up the other half by putting pressure on the small companies."

"The mayor seems to like him."

"He has no choice. He could pull out and take his business to Tulsa or some other place."

"His wells would still be here."

"He owns the water well-drilling business, a truck line, two gas stations and other companies that employ a lot of people in town."

"Where does he live?"

"He spends a lot of time in Tulsa, but he owns that big square brick house two streets over from the hotel. It doesn't look like much on the outside, but they say it's very nice on the inside. He has a colored couple working for him."

"The one who stands up to him is Mr. Madison. He's such a nice man. Pity he has that *thing* on his face." Flora clicked her tongue against the roof of her mouth. "He would be a fine catch for a girl if she could look past that horrible red mark."

"It doesn't seem to bother him," Jill said.

"He's probably used to it."

"I don't know how Mr. Westfall plans to run a dance hall," Flora said, looking at the men idling on the street. "There's only one woman for every four men in town and most of them are attached. He'll have to bring in a bunch of loose women to dance with the men. The first thing you know, they'll open a whorehouse." She whispered the last two words.

It was almost dark. The streets were even more crowded than they had been before. Flora said her good-byes and turned toward her home behind the bakery. Jill and Martha proceeded down the walk past the stores. Men loitered on the street, leaned against the parked cars or sat on the edge of the plank walk. Music came from the recreational parlors and loud voices from the pool hall.

Beneath a streetlight at a crossing, two brawny men were leaning over the hood of a car engaged in a contest of arm wrestling. The men who gathered around them were shouting encouragement and making bets. Before Martha and Jill realized it, they were hemmed in by the crowd.

"Here's the wildcat." The voice was loud and close to Jill. "How about a kiss for the winner, wildcat?"

Jill shoved at the body of a half-drunk, whiskered man. "Get out of my way."

"Fun is fun, but that's enough," Martha

said crossly when another man threw out the suggestion of a kiss.

"Ah, come on, wildcat. You'll not miss one little kiss and old Sully'll strain his guts out to win."

The crowd was pushing Jill and Martha closer and closer to where the two straining men were bent over the hood of the mud-splattered, topless car, and anger began to replace Jill's panic. She turned and lashed out at the man behind her.

"Stop pushing me, you mangy polecat!" Anger made her voice loud and shrill.

"Whoa!" The grinning man threw up his hands in surrender but didn't budge an inch. "Simmer down, little sweetheart. No one will lay a hand on you. Promise Sully a kiss and I'll split my winnings with you if he wins."

"I'd sooner kiss a warthog! Get out of my way, or I'll slap your jaws!"

Hoots of laughter from the men followed her words. She looked around for Martha and realized they had been separated and that she was as much of the show as the contestants.

"Slap my jaws, honey. I ain't had 'em slapped since I left home."

"Say you'll kiss old Sully if he wins, wild-cat," a man yelled, then he bellowed glee-fully. "She nodded, Sully. She'll kiss ya!"

"I did no such thing. I will not!" Jill shouted, then balled her fist and hit the man nearest to her on the jaw.

"Wow! The wildcat's got a temper! Hey—" His words were cut off when Jill's other fist landed on his nose. Her foot lashed out and struck another man on the shin. Having been raised on a Missouri farm with three brothers, Jill knew how to use her fists and her feet.

"Filthy hogs! Low-down, pig-ugly var-mints! Get away from me."

Jill was too busy yelling and lashing out to see that roughneck after roughneck was being shoved aside by a tall, dark-haired, sun-browned man with long arms and a fierce scowl on his face.

"Jill." The voice reached her at the same time the man did. "What the hell are you do-ing out here on the street brawling like a common slut?"

"Now, wait, mister. She's not—" When the man she had just hit opened his mouth to defend her, the front of his shirt was grabbed in a huge fist and he was pushed so hard that he staggered into the group behind him.

"Stay out of this!"

Angry eyes moved back to Jill. The hand that had gripped the shirt came out to latch on to her arm.

Jill was unable to believe who was standing over her with rage radiating from him. Dark brows were drawn together above green eyes. As she watched, his frown deepened and the muscle in one lean cheek jumped in response to his clenched teeth. Further thought was snatched from her as suddenly she was sandwiched between two tall men.

"Get your hand off her!" Hunter Westfall's voice was not loud.

"Or what, dude?"

"One word from me and these men will break both your arms and your legs," Hunter answered quietly.

"No!" Jill suddenly came to life. "He's a friend from home." Pride forced her to add, "Sort of."

"Jill," Hunter said patiently, "a gentleman doesn't call his friends sluts."

"He didn't understand what was going

on." Jill pulled on the hand still clamped to her arm.

"You don't do your own dirty work. Is that it, dude?" The tone of voice was clearly insulting.

"Not if I don't have to."

"Well, send your bully boys in. After finding Jill here making a spectacle of herself, I'm in the mood to tear up a few of your dumb-ass flunkies." His teeth snapped together.

"Thad Taylor, you shut up!" Jill shouted. "Thank you, Mr. Westfall, for thinking that I needed help. Thad is a friend of . . . my folks from back home. Come on, Thad, or I'll slap you into tomorrow."

Hunter hesitated, looking from Jill to the big angry man beside her and wondering what claim he had on her. He seemed to be pretty sure of himself.

"Are you sure you'll be all right?" Hunter asked gently.

"Yes, thank you."

Jill turned, lifted her chin and, mustering the fragments of her self-possession, locked her gaze with that of the tall, angry man and refused to look away.

"Are you ready to go?" Martha touched her arm.

"I'm ready. More than ready."

With Thad, silent and simmering with rage, walking beside her, they headed for the hotel at the end of the street.

"You're dumb as a cob," Jill fumed. "Don't you have brains enough to know when to back off?"

Not another word was spoken until after Martha said good night and crossed the street to her restaurant. Jill and Thad had gone up the steps to the hotel porch when Jill turned and lifted a hand to slap him. He caught her hand in midair.

"Slap me and I'll slap you back."

"That was going to be for calling me a slut!"

"You were acting like one."

"I was not! I was defending myself. Besides, how do you know what I am? I've not seen you for three or four years. And what are you doing here anyway?"

"I apologize for calling you a slut. But you sure as hell were acting like one out there, brawling on the street corner with a bunch of roughnecks."

"It wouldn't be any of your business if I was a slut. You have no claim on me."

"You think not? If you'd've sunk that low, it would've broken the heart of the best friend I ever had, and that would be my business, little *Miss Wildcat.*" He grasped her upper arms with large, strong hands. "And why were they calling you that?"

"Get your hands off me," she snarled. Then, ignoring his question, she asked again, "What are you doing here?"

He dropped his hands to his sides. "Joe got a letter from Eudora telling him that you were here. He can't get away right now. I came on ahead to see what you're up to. From the looks of things, it's a damn good thing I did."

"From the looks of what things, Thad Taylor?" Jill refused to move. She stood on the step above him, her face level with his.

"Good goddamn! Do I have to spell it out for you? And who was the dressed-up dude coming to your rescue like a highballing freight train? Is he your . . . protector?"

"No! He's a very nice man."

"Ha! No man is nice when it comes to a woman he wants."

"Speak for yourself. Not all men are like
. . . that."

It was hard for Jill to believe that she was
standing on the hotel steps in Rainwater,
Oklahoma, talking to the boy she had
known all her life. The Taylor farm in Missouri was a mere half mile from the Jones
farm. Thad had been several grades ahead
of her in school. He was the best friend of
her older brother Joe and had been in and
out of their house ever since she could remember.

Thad had grown into a big man and was
much better-looking than he had been
when he was younger, not that it mattered
to her how good-looking he was. He was as
bossy as Joe and Jack, her brothers. And
Jill had other memories associated with
Thad Taylor that, at times, were too painful
to recall.

"How is Joe?"

"He's all right. He's laying pipeline. He'll
finish the job in a week or two and be up
here."

"You're staying until then?"

"Damn right. We're not leaving you here
in this wild place by yourself. There's no
telling what you'll get into."

"For crying out loud! I've been here al-most a month and nothing's happened to me."

"Luck. Just plain luck. What's that dude to you?"

"Nothing. I just met him tonight."

"I don't think much of a man who would hire bullies to do his fighting for him."

"Maybe he wouldn't've had to hire them. Maybe they'd have done it because they like him."

"If you believe that, you'll believe cows can fly. The way I see it, they'd have given it a try or lost their jobs. I saw the gold watch fob on his vest, the ring on his finger and the five-dollar hat on his head."

"There's no use arguing with you. You're as bullheaded as ever." She turned to go into the hotel. "Good-bye. It was nice see-ing you again . . . I think. I've got to go in and tell Aunt Justine about the meeting."

"Yeah, she said that's where you'd gone. Good thing I went to walk you back." In-stead of leaving, Thad followed her into the hotel.

"You've talked to Aunt Justine?"

"Sure. We had a visit. She's glad I'm here." He headed for the kitchen. "I'm hungry as a wolf. Aunt Justine said Radna would hash up something for me to eat when I got back from seeing about you."

"*Aunt* Justine?" Jill turned on him with an angry glare. "I'll not allow you to stay here and freeload off my aunt."

"Freeload? I rented a room."

"Rooms are seventy-five cents a night." She lifted her chin and looked down her nose at him even though he was a head taller. "That will soon add up to real money if you stay very long."

"She gave me a weekly rate." A look of smug satisfaction covered his face. "And"—he paused—"I'm going to give you some help around here to pay for my meals."

"Help around here? Sheesh! We'll just see about that." She gazed into his eyes, astonishingly green and luminous, and drew a quivering breath.

"Go talk to your aunt." He was now good-naturedly amused by her anger.

"I'm the manager of this hotel. Aunt Justine put me in charge and no one gets a weekly room rate or hires on to help around here unless I say so." With that, she tossed her head, dismissed him and spoke to the man sitting behind the counter.

"Everything all right, Mr. Evans?"

"Right as rain, miss. When ya wasn't here, the young feller wanted to see Mrs. Byers. Hope it's all right that I let him in."

"I don't think you could have stopped him with a steam engine, Mr. Evans. He's a bull-headed Missourian."

"Rooms are all full, miss."

"What room did you give Mr. Taylor?"

"Mrs. Byers said give him the little 'un up on the third floor. And she said that he could have it for a dollar a week if he lent ya a hand around the place."

"A dollar? Well, we'll just see about that."

Casually, with an outward calm belying both the ache behind her forehead and the dancing devils in her stomach, Jill headed for her aunt's room.

Chapter 3

Justine was propped up in bed against a stack of pillows. Light from the single bulb that hung from the center of her room gave her skin a yellowish cast. She was smiling.

"Were you surprised . . . to see Thad?" Justine's eyes were brighter than usual.

"I sure was. I haven't seen him for three, maybe four years. I want to talk to you about him, Aunt, but first let me tell you about the meeting."

Jill pulled up a chair, trying to put off the unpleasant subject of Thad Taylor until she had cooled down. She told her aunt about meeting Mr. Westfall on the way, but left out the part about the drunk bothering her and Martha.

"The mayor is concerned about what the town will do when the oil plays out. One man, a lawyer, argued with Mr. Westfall about how the oil wells were ruining the land for grazing. The man had a red birth-mark on his face and wore glasses."

"That would be Lloyd Madison. He doesn't care about the land. He hates Hunter Westfall because he's everything that Lloyd wants to be. If Hunter said white was white, Lloyd would say, 'No, it's black.'"

"Mr. Westfall is going to oil Main Street."

"Oh, my. They did that once before and . . . oil was tracked up onto the porch and into the lobby. It was a mess to clean up."

"I can scrub the porch. It's the carpet in the lobby that will be hard to keep clean."

"Honey," Justine said, with a distressed look on her face, "Hunter Westfall runs things around here. He doesn't make a show of it and most folks don't even think about it. Be careful of him." Justine paused to catch her breath. "Be especially careful of Lloyd Madison. He's smart; he's hard as nails and ruthless as a rutting steer. If you see him coming, head the other way. Don't have anything to do with him. Promise me, now."

"Of course I promise. Mr. Westfall was nice to me and Martha."

"Hunter is a businessman. He's nice as . . . pie when he wants something. He wanted to buy the hotel. . . . When I refused, he backed off." She paused to take some deep breaths. "He knew that I was sick and thought he'd get it soon or later anyway. I bet he was surprised when a young, pretty girl like you showed up to run it for me." Justine's face was flushed, and her quavering voice caused Jill concern. "Now tell me, were you surprised to see Thad?"

"We can talk about Thad Taylor later, Aunt Justine."

"Tell me now, Jill. I can't put things off like I used to do."

"Thad's from back home—"

"He told me. We had a long visit while he was waiting to go walk you home." Justine tried to move her hands. Jill lifted them up onto her chest. "He told me about the neighborhood ball games at Jethro's and that Jack wanted to play professional baseball." Justine paused again, looked toward the picture of her late husband, then back to Jill.

"Jack still loves to play baseball."

"Thad told me that Jethro's new wife is real nice. I'm glad. He was almost crushed when your mother died, leaving him with a houseful of youngsters to raise." She paused, then said, "Thad reminds me of the boys I knew back on the farm in Missouri."

"Aunt Justine, Thad isn't a boy. He's Joe's age or older . . . at least twenty-five or -six. He said you gave him a weekly rate and that he'd work for meals. I wish you hadn't done that."

"You need a man around here, honey. You know what? Radna was trying to help me out of that chair. He came in and lifted me as if I were light as a feather and carried me over here."

"How did that happen?"

"He was just passing the door."

"Of course he could pick you up. You don't weigh much more than a feather," Jill scoffed.

Justine sighed. "I feel so much better with him here."

"We have Mr. Evans—"

"How much can a one-legged man on crutches do, honey? Thad said he'd stay until Joe comes."

"He and Joe are thick as thieves. He'll be here as long as Joe's here." Jill stood up. "I've worn you out. Can I get you anything before I go?"

"No, dear. You can turn out the ceiling light. Thad said that tomorrow he'd fix the light here by the bed."

"Good night, Aunt."

After Jill closed the door, she stood for a minute and fumed. *Thad would fix the light by the bed.* Darn him! He was wasting no time making himself useful and endearing himself to Aunt Justine. She went down the hall toward the kitchen, then paused when she heard Radna's voice and Thad's deep rumbling laughter.

"I sure do like this cornbread, Radna. Will you marry me?"

"Watch your mouth, boy. If I said yes, you'd wet your drawers. You'd better work your charm on Jill or you'll be out of here on your ear."

"Yeah, she's a mouthy little spitfire and has the guts to go with it. She was no more than knee-high to a duck when she flew into a couple of tough kids for making fun of her brother's limp. I had to pull them off her.

Even with a bloody nose, she came up scratching and spitting like a pussycat."

"She's not afraid of dirtying her hands. She works hard here."

"I don't doubt that. All the Joneses are hard workers. Julie Jones was in school when their mother died. She quit and took over the raising of the younger kids. Jill had a good teacher."

"I'm glad there's something about me that you approve of." Jill leaned against the doorjamb, a rebellious look on her face.

Thad looked at her with an unabashed grin. "Have you still got your tail over the line, kitten?"

"You didn't waste any time getting in good with Aunt Justine, did you? Now you're working on Radna."

"I'd forgotten how bullheaded you are, little sis. I thought you'd be glad to see someone from home. Aunt Justine was." His green eyes gleamed with amusement.

"I'm not your sister, Mr. Taylor. Justine Byers is not your aunt. It was low of you to go in there and butter her up in order to get yourself a cheap place to stay."

Across the green eyes that had been liquid and warm with amusement spread a steely, cold glaze. For moments that pulsated with tension, they stared at each other. Jill remained perfectly motionless.

"She set the price for the room," Thad said, with only a touch of anger in his voice. "If she'd said five dollars I would have taken it. Someone's got to keep an eye on you. Joe asked me to do it, and I intend to do just that, whether you like it or not."

"I don't like it."

"That's too bad. Mrs. Byers said I was welcome."

"Of course she would. You got to her before I did."

"Radna says the only man around here is that old man out at the desk."

"That *old man* at the desk lost his leg in the war. I doubt that he's ten years older than you are. If you'd been through what he has, you'd look old, too. Aunt Justine said that he can work here as long as he wants, and I agree."

"I wasn't suggesting that you fire him. But he's limited as to what he can do."

"Amazingly smart of you to realize that. Mr. Evans is at the desk all night and if he needs help he rings for me or Radna."

"Pull in your horns, Jilly Justine. I'm here

to make things easier for you. He can ring for me now."

"Bull-foot, and don't call me that silly name!" Jill looked away from Thad's smiling face, opened a cupboard door and spoke to Radna. "Laura and her mother will be here tomorrow to do washing. Do we have enough soap?"

"Tomorrow's Sunday," Radna replied.

"Oh, gosh. I've got my days mixed up."

"Have I upset you . . . Jilly Justine?"

Jill spun around. Thad was smiling, his white teeth cutting a gash in his sun-browned face. His hair, full and thick and black as midnight, framed an intriguingly handsome face. Tanned skin stretched over high cheekbones. But his eyes irritated her, clear green knowing eyes, laughing eyes, secret eyes.

"You flatter yourself, Mr. Taylor."

"My brother Roy had a terrific crush on you, did you know that?"

"Another one of your made-up stories. Roy and I were friends. He liked Ruby Mae from the time we started school."

"Ruby Mae had eyes for Jack. Roy liked you more. Thank goodness he got over it.

He's over in St. Joe now. He met a nice *quiet* girl, and before long I'll be an uncle."

"Give him my congratulations when you see him, which I hope will be soon."

Thad's laugh rang out. "Don't get your hopes up, honey. I'm staying here."

"Only until Joe gets here, then you're *out!*"

Without waiting for him to retort, Jill left the kitchen and went back into the lobby, where she stopped to speak to Mr. Evans.

"Have you had to turn many away tonight?"

"Only one so far. He was with the sheriff and I took him to be a lawman. I sent him down to Mrs. Jenson's rooming house."

"I wonder what he's doing in town."

"They come through here every once in a while on their way to Tulsa."

"How is Mrs. Evans?"

"Fine. She wanted to come sit with me awhile, but I don't like for her to go back alone late at night."

"There's a small couch in a room upstairs. I'll ask Aunt Justine if we can bring it down. We can move the counter out a little to make room for it and put it behind a folding screen. You and Mrs. Evans could take turns taking a little nap during the late hours. That is, if she wants to stay with you."

"She'll want to, miss. She ain't fond of spendin' the nights alone. I thought maybe you'd not need me now that the young man is here."

"We need you, Mr. Evans. Thad won't be here long. You know how these fly-by-night roughnecks are: Here today and gone tomorrow."

"He seems like a nice fellow; said he's from your hometown."

Several responses came to Jill's mind, but she said, "I think I'll sit on the porch for a while."

On her way to the door, she stopped to speak to one of their weekly roomers, who sat in the lobby reading a newspaper.

"How are things at the barbershop, Mr. Boise?"

"Fair to middlin', miss. New crews comin' in means more hair to cut. Mr. Langley is right pleased."

"I met him tonight at the meeting."

"He said he was goin'."

"I'll let you get back to your paper."

Jill stepped out onto the porch. The

bench on one side of the door was occupied by a man and his wife, who were on their way to visit relatives in Bartlesville. After exchanging a few pleasantries with the couple, Jill went to the bench on the other end of the porch.

She enjoyed being here in Rainwater and liked the responsibility her aunt had given her. It troubled her that Aunt Justine had taken some of her authority away when she rented the room to Thad and hired him to help her. She didn't want his help. She could see the writing on the wall. Before long, *she* would be helping *him.*

Thad had charmed her aunt.

Now that she thought about it, Thad had always been a charmer when it suited his purpose to be so. Jill giggled as she remembered his telling Birdie Stuart, a city woman whom none of them had liked, how the floor at a country barn dance was made slick by using fresh cow manure. Thad and Joe hadn't wanted Birdie to go to the dance, and Thad convinced her that it was the custom to dance barefoot in the fresh manure in a brand-new barn and that, if she went, that was what she would be expected to do.

The story had been the talk of the neighborhood for the rest of the summer. Thad had been only eighteen at the time. Now, seven years later, he could probably charm the bark off a tree if he set his mind to it.

What also lay heavy on Jill's heart was that she owed that boy of eighteen a debt of gratitude that she could never repay.

A young couple came out of the hotel and stood on the porch. The man put his arm around the woman with him and pulled her tightly to his side. She laughed up at him and he dropped a kiss on her forehead; then, arm in arm, they crossed the street to Martha's Restaurant. Jill wondered if they were on their honeymoon.

Once in a while a truck went by with several men in the back. They yelled good-naturedly to their friends on the walkway, who yelled back. She heard someone call out something about "wildcat," but she couldn't make out the words.

The screen door opened and Thad came out onto the porch. He stood for a moment in the path of light from the lobby. He was no longer the boy she had known back in Fertile. His legs were long, his shoulders broad, his hips slim. He was a man a woman could weave a romantic fantasy about . . . that is, if she hadn't known him all her life. Jill wondered why some woman hadn't caught him and put a ring on his finger.

She hoped that he wouldn't notice her and would walk down the street and blend in with the rest of the men loitering in front of the stores. She wasn't that lucky. He came to where she sat, slouched down on the bench, leaned back against the wall and stretched his long legs out in front of him, crossing them at the ankles. Folding his laced fingers over his midsection, he looked off toward the main part of town as if he didn't know that she was there.

Minutes passed without his speaking or acknowledging her presence. Jill became annoyed. If not for the fact that she would need to step over his legs, she'd go back into the hotel; but, on second thought, she'd be damned if she'd let him run her off *her* porch.

The silence between them deepened. As far as she knew, he hadn't even looked at her. With considerable effort, she managed to keep her mouth shut and stay quiet; she waited for him to speak. Finally, when he did, it was as if they had been holding a lengthy conversation.

"It isn't as rowdy as some of the places I've been."

"What isn't?" Jill's question was a reflex she regretted.

"The town. What did you think I meant?"

"How was I to know what you meant? But I imagine that if there was a place where lowlife gathered, you'd find it."

"That must go for Joe, too. We've been together since we came out here."

"Joe's got more sense than to hobnob with rowdies and troublemakers."

"And I haven't. I get the point."

"I never said that."

"You don't know anything about me. Stop jumping to conclusions." His tone reflected his irritation.

"What other conclusion can I jump to? You don't appear to have much to show for the past few years."

"Want to see my muscles?" He was back in the teasing mode.

Jill didn't retort; she had just caught sight of a tall man in a light-colored Stetson coming up the walk. Hunter Westfall turned in and mounted the steps to the hotel porch.

He opened the door to go into the lobby, then saw Jill at the end of the porch. She stood up as he closed the door and came toward her.

"Miss Jones?"

"Hello, Mr. Westfall." Thad refused to draw in his legs. Wanting to kick him, she stepped over them.

"I stopped by to make sure that you'd returned safely to the hotel and to apologize for the behavior of my men."

"It wasn't your fault. I was in the wrong place at the wrong time. I wasn't afraid, only angry."

"You'll not be bothered again. At least not by the men who work for me."

"That's mighty good of you." Thad's hand came down on Jill's shoulder in a proprietary manner. She felt his chest against her back. "We appreciate you looking after our little Jilly Justine." Thad extended his hand. "Thad Taylor," he said, as Jill's elbow jabbed his midsection.

"Hunter Westfall." Hunter took Thad's hand while looking at Jill's unsmiling face. "Are you related to Miss Jones, Mr. Taylor?"

"Almost. I've known her since she was in

diapers. Close to her as a brother. Huh, Jill?"

Jill ignored him. "The men had had a little too much to drink and didn't mean any harm, Mr. Westfall. I hope you weren't too harsh with them."

"If they didn't mean any harm, honey, why did you poke one of them in the nose?" Thad tightened his hand on her shoulder.

"Would you walk around the block with me, Miss Jones? I have a few things to discuss with you about the oiling of the streets."

"I'd love to, Mr. Westfall. Excuse us, Thad." Jill took the arm Hunter offered. "Oh, Thad, check the plumbing in the water closet on the second floor. It's been known to clog when the hotel is full."

"Sure thing, honey. Don't worry about it. I've already put rolls of that soft paper you have in the storage room in both the toilets. The woman in 206 asked for a chamber pot. Shall I take up a granite or a china or tell her to go down the hall?"

"I'll let you decide."

With her face flaming and her throat so clogged with anger that she couldn't speak, Jill let Hunter lead her down the steps and onto the walk. They turned away from the busy part of town and walked past the bank, the doctor's office and the small building that housed the telephone company.

Hunter held her hand in the crook of his arm pressed close to his side and matched his stride to hers.

"I've been wanting to meet you ever since you came to town. Tonight was the first excuse I've had. I was there at the station the day you got off the train."

"It was a long ride and I had to change buses twice to get to Kansas City so I could take the train."

"You don't go out much."

"I've been busy with Aunt Justine and learning about the hotel."

"It's a big job for a small girl."

"I can do it."

"This is a tough town. I've told the sheriff to keep an eye on the hotel."

"Isn't he supposed to keep an eye on all the businesses in town?"

"Of course, but you didn't have anyone but Mr. Evans in case of trouble."

"Thad will be here until my brother comes."

"Is Taylor looking for work? I could use a driller or a welder."

"I don't know what he does." Not wanting to talk about Thad, Jill asked, "When will the street be oiled?"

"In a couple of weeks. If we wait until it's hot, the oil will soak into the ground faster."

"I think it's hot now."

"Not like it will be later on. It's usually hotter than a pistol here the latter part of June."

They walked in silence for a while, then Hunter said, "I tried to buy the hotel from your aunt."

"She told me."

"Knowing that she was ill, I thought to take it off her hands."

"The hotel is her home. She wants to stay there until the . . . end."

"I can understand that. Will you stay on . . . afterwards?"

"I've not decided. I may go back home and teach, or may go to a teachers college so that I can teach the higher grades."

"How about getting married? That's the goal of most young ladies."

"Have you ever been married, Mr. West-fall?"

"Call me Hunter. No, I've never taken the plunge. Why do you ask?"

"Curious. Some people marry and divorce nowadays at the drop of a hat."

"You must be talking about movie stars. Most of the people I know take marriage seriously."

"You hear about the movie stars. I don't know many people who are divorced."

They turned a corner and ran out of sidewalk. Stepping down into the street, Hunter paused.

"It will be rough walking from here on. Let's cross the street and go back on the other side."

A few minutes later, Jill asked, "Are you serious about building a dance hall and an amusement park?"

"More than serious. I've plans under way."

"It will be quite an addition to the town."

"I got the idea from a fellow I met back East; the famous flagpole sitter Shipwreck Kelly."

"That's a funny name, even for a flagpole sitter."

"Kelly was a former boxer who fought under the name of Sailor Kelly. It was said that he was knocked out so many times that the crowd started yelling that Kelly was ship-wrecked again. The name stuck like glue. He draws a crowd wherever he goes."

"Will he come here?"

"I don't know. I can't get the park up and running for several months and by then it will be winter. Shipwreck doesn't like to per-form during cold, windy weather." Hunter stopped on the corner across from the ho-tel. "Would you like to walk down to the ice-cream parlor for a dish of their very good chocolate ice cream?"

"Thank you, but I should get back and see about Aunt Justine."

"I understand. This was a spur-of-the-moment thing. Will you go to the movie house with me on Wednesday night? A Greta Garbo movie will be showing."

"*The Flesh and the Devil,* with John Gilbert. I saw the movie before I came out here. But thank you."

Jill's eyes scanned the hotel porch for Thad as they approached it and she sighed with relief when he was not there. Hunter walked her up the steps to the door.

"Thank you for a very pleasant half hour." Hunter took her hand and held it firmly.

"I enjoyed it, too. Good night."

"Good night." He gave her hand a quick squeeze, then waited until she was inside the hotel before he went back down the steps to the street.

Jill looked at the big clock that stood in the lobby and was surprised to see it was ten o'clock. Two men were playing checkers at the table in the corner. Another man was watching the game. Mr. Evans sat on the high stool behind the counter, watching her. Jill was relieved not to see Thad.

Her relief was short-lived. He came barreling through the door with a thundercloud look on his face, took her arm and propelled her down the hall toward the kitchen.

"Let go of my arm, you bully! What the heck is the matter with you?"

He waited until the swinging door closed before he turned her around. His hands gripped her shoulders; his green eyes glared down at her.

"Why in hell did you go off in the dark with that slicked-up dude? Did you do it to spite me? If so, it's a dangerous game you're playing, little Miss Know-it-all."

"What in the world are you talking about?

Hunter is a well-respected member of this community, which is more than you are."

"So it's *Hunter* now. It was *Mr. Westfall* before you went walking out with him. You don't know him!"

"I know him as well as I know you. I've not seen you for years. You could be a completely different person from what you were back in Fertile."

"If I was, would Joe have sent me up here to look after you?"

"How do I know he sent you? I've not heard a word from him."

"You can bet your buttons that I'd not be putting myself through this if my best friend hadn't asked me to. I could be making good money—"

"Hunter offered to give you a job. He's hiring drillers and welders."

"I'd not work for that dressed-up jelly bean if I was starving."

"Why? Because he asked me to walk with him? It just goes to show how dumb *you* are." She attempted to move away from him, but he held her.

"It's a damn good thing for him that you turned and came back when you did. If he'd taken you any farther out of town, I'd have been on him like a hungry dog on a bone."

"You . . . you followed us!"

"Damn right, I did," he snarled. "I don't trust that bird any farther than I can swing a mule by the tail."

"I don't give two hoots and a holler how far you can swing a mule by the tail or if you trust Hunter Westfall or not. He's a gentleman. He asked me to go to the movie Wednesday night."

"Stay away from him. Hear? I heard things about him before I got here."

"I like him. He's gentle, refined and terribly smart. He's going to build a dance hall and an amusement park. His friend Shipwreck Kelly will be here. I don't suppose you know who *he* is."

"I've heard of him. He's the brainless jackass who sits on a flagpole for a living. Some friend!"

"Stay out of my business, Thad Taylor. You've no right to tell me what to do."

"Then grow up so I won't have to tell you what to do." When he spoke, each word was pushed from behind clenched teeth.

"That was a mean thing to say." She stared up at him. Defiance was written on her face. Her eyes were like a storm cloud blowing across the vast prairie, carrying with it rain, wind and lightning.

"You can make me so mad I could spank you." He gave her a little shake.

"Just try it and . . . and you'll be sorry!"

"Just behave yourself and we'll get along fine. When Joe gets here, he can have the job of riding herd on you."

She shrugged her shoulders and his hands dropped to his sides. After walking slowly to the swinging door, she turned to see him standing, hands on hips, staring at her. She stared back. Her face was calm, but her heart was pumping like a locomotive going uphill.

She managed to get to her room before the tears spilled from her eyes.

Chapter 4

By nine o'clock on Sunday most of the overnight guests had checked out. The next few hours were busy ones for Jill and Mrs. Cole, the woman who cleaned the rooms on Sunday. Linens on the beds had to be changed, the washbasins in each room cleaned, fresh towels put up, the rugs swept with the carpet sweeper and the floor around the carpet wiped with a dust mop.

Jill was up at dawn. She and Radna had cleaned the lobby before breakfast. After a restless night, she was tired. The events of the evening before had left her mind reeling. As hard as she tried, she couldn't understand why Thad had acted as if she were a twelve-year-old who didn't have sense enough to stay out of a fire.

For an instant last night on the street corner, she had felt a burst of gladness when she had seen him; but that had faded quickly when she realized that he had called her a slut.

Now she hated him! Maybe she didn't *hate* him, she thought, as she ran the dust cloth over the windowsills, but she thoroughly disliked him. How could she not dislike him, when he treated her like an out-of-control child and dragged out that old teasing name, Jilly Justine. Nobody had called her that in years.

Mr. Evans said that Thad had stayed in the lobby from midnight to three in the morning, giving him the opportunity to sleep for a couple of hours.

"Take it out of my pay, miss. I ain't wantin' to be paid for sleepin' on the job."

"We'll not worry about that," Jill assured him. "You didn't look like you felt good last night."

"I didn't, miss. It's a fact. But I feel right chipper today."

"That's a relief. We depend on you, Mr. Evans."

"The young fellow said that he could fill in."

"Thad will be here for only a short time,"

Jill answered quickly. "We can't depend on him."

In the quiet of the early dawn, she watched Mr. Evans go down the hall and into the kitchen, his crutches making a thumping noise on the wood floor. He came and went by the back door because there were fewer steps and it was nearer to his small house a block behind the hotel.

After breakfast Radna spent time with Justine, who usually had a visitor or two on Sunday. Radna gave her a bath, put her in a fresh housedress and fixed her hair. Jill poked her head in the door to find the two chattering away like schoolgirls.

When she had first come to Rainwater, Jill had feared that Radna would resent her taking over. On the contrary, Radna was relieved to turn over the responsibility to Jill. The small woman with golden skin and the educated voice continued to be a mystery. She lived in a room off the kitchen and often went out at night.

The town was quiet on Sunday morning. The people of Rainwater were either sleeping, going to church or nursing hangovers. Jill sat behind the counter waiting for the last two overnight guests to check out. The woman cleaning the upstairs rooms came down with an armload of sheets and towels. She carried them through the kitchen to the back porch. She and her daughter, Laura, a widow with a young child, came on Monday and again on Thursday to do the washing. Justine had known Mrs. Cole for many years; after the woman's husband died suddenly, Justine hired her, adding to the legend that Justine Byers's heart was as big as the town.

When the last of the overnight guests had been checked out, Jill went to the kitchen, where Radna was cooking dinner.

"Our handyman hasn't put in an appearance this morning. I guess he figures this is his day off and he can laze in bed all day."

Radna grinned. Her thick dark hair was held back with a ribbon that matched the red blouse she wore over the long print skirt that floated around her calves as she moved.

"He's in the wash house."

"What's he doing out there?"

"Fixing the washing machine . . . or trying to."

"For crying out loud. What does he know

about washing machines? I didn't know there was anything wrong with it."

"The wringer isn't working. Laura and Nettie have been turning the hand wringer. I asked Thad if he knew anything about engines."

"And he said . . . ?"

"Everything." Radna smiled broadly. Her eyes darted to Jill, then back to the greens she was washing.

"Of course. I should have known," Jill muttered on her way to the door.

She stood on the porch beside the pile of dirty bed linens and towels and noticed a bucket of water and an empty tin plate. Someone had fed the stray dog that had been hanging around. She was a little ashamed that she had forgotten to take care of the poor thing.

The wash house sat back twenty or more feet from the hotel. Justine had had it put there because she feared the heater that was needed to heat the water for the large commercial washing machine might cause a fire. She had invested in the appliance when the oil boom had brought more business to town.

The door of the frame building was open

and the window shutters propped back. As Jill approached, the black and white shaggy dog, lying just inside the doorway, looked up and growled.

"Calm down, Fertile." Thad's deep voice came from inside the building. "It's just the *boss* coming to see if I'm earning my keep."

Ignoring the dog, Jill stood in the doorway. Benches and tubs had been pushed aside to make room for Thad, who sat on the floor with the wringer from the washer between his spread legs. He had a wrench in his greasy hand and a smudge on his cheek.

"Fertile?"

"Fits." His dark hair tumbled over his forehead; his clear green eyes gleamed with amusement. "She's about to have a batch of pups. Besides that, she likes the name."

"She'll answer to any name as long as you feed her," Jill scoffed.

"She likes me."

"I'm not surprised. You're both dirty, hungry and lazy." Jill tried to keep the laughter out of her voice and failed.

Thad's laughter rang out. "But she's pregnant and I'm not."

Jill looked down at the shaggy dog. Her

eyes were on Thad. He'd always had a way with animals. Jill recalled seeing him ride into the yard back home with his dog at his heels. His horse, too, followed him like a dog when he wasn't on it. Thad always had time to pet their dog, Sidney, who went into raptures when he was around.

There had been a time when Jill herself went into raptures when Thad came to the farm. She had been fourteen and Thad five years older. To him, she had been the pesky kid sister of his best friend. To her, he had been as handsome as any hero she read about in the dime novels she had sneaked from Joe's room. Thad had teased her, pulled her hair and treated her in the same way as had her older brothers, Joe and Jack. It had been frustrating until she had grown out of the crush.

"Hand me that small wrench."

"Which one?"

"The smallest."

Jill stepped over the dog in order to reach the bench where the tools were laid out, selected the one Thad wanted and put it in his outstretched hand.

"Where did you find the tools?"

"In my tool chest."

"They're yours?"

"Uh-huh."

"Is that what you do? Work on motors?"

"That and a few other things."

"Like what?"

"Drill, rig or weld pipe—that is, when I'm not lawyering, doctoring or toe-dancing." His head was bent so that she couldn't see his face, but she knew he was laughing silently because his shoulders were shaking.

"I'd like to see that sometime," she said seriously. "Can you fix the motor on the wringer? Laura and Mrs. Cole will be here tomorrow to do the washing."

"I think I can have it ready by then if you'll stay and keep me company while I work on it."

"Sorry to disappoint you. I have better ways of spending my time. Radna is cooking dinner and will call you when it's ready."

Jill headed back into the hotel thinking what a difference a day made. Today Thad had been almost the boy she'd had the crush on so long ago.

It was the middle of the afternoon when Justine called as Jill passed the door to her room. It was left open so she could hear, as much as possible, what was going on. Jill turned and went into the room to see Thad standing beside her aunt's chair.

"Thad's going to take me out onto the porch. There's a cushion on the floor of the wardrobe. Will you get it, please, and put it in the chair?"

After Jill placed the cushion in the chair, Thad maneuvered the chair through the doorway and down the hall.

"I've been longing to sit on the porch, but I didn't want people to see me stumbling around. Thad must have been reading my mind. He suggested carrying me out there." Justine watched the doorway expectantly, awaiting his return.

"You should have said something. Radna and I would have figured a way to get you out there."

"I know you would have, dear, but as long as we have a big, strong man willing to help us, we should take advantage of it."

Thad returned and, without a word, scooped her up in his arms, carried her down the hallway and through the lobby to the porch. He placed her gently in the chair, moved the small footstool close and placed her feet on it.

"How's that?" He sat back on his heels and smiled at her.

"Thank you, Thad. It's grand to be out here." There was a trace of tears in Justine's eyes. "So many memories." She shook her head.

"I was here the day the ice truck hit Ralph. I knew before I reached him that . . . he was gone and my life would never be the same. I miss him still.

"It seems only yesterday that I was sitting in this very same spot in this very same chair when the first gusher came in. Oh, my. It was a sight. People ran out in the street to see what at first looked like a big smoke cloud. Then the cars began to go by as everyone who could get a ride wanted to go out to the well."

"I've seen a couple of gushers. They're able to cap most of the wells that come in before they blow." Thad had settled down on the floor of the porch and Jill sat on the bench beside her aunt's chair.

"Almost overnight, Rainwater woke from being a sleepy little prairie town to what it is now: cars and trucks coming and going at all hours of the day and night, people on the streets, the hotel full most of the time. Ralph would have loved every minute of it."

Thad got to his feet. "I'd better go put the motor back on the washing machine before the boss lady fires me. When you want to go in, send someone for me."

"Thanks again, Thad."

Just for an instant Thad enclosed Justine's delicate fingers in his. "The pleasure is mine. It isn't often that I get to carry a pretty lady." When he passed Jill on the way to the door, he winked.

Jill rolled her eyes. *Charmer, flatterer, conniver!*

"I think he likes you," Justine said after Thad cleared the doorway.

"Bull-foot. I'm Joe's sister. He liked Joe's dog, too."

"It could be more than that. A man doesn't tease a girl and give her the looks he gives you unless he's interested in her."

"Oh, he's interested, all right. He told Joe he'd look after me, and he'll do it if it kills him. He and Joe are as thick as eight in a bed. Joe would do the same for Thad's sister."

Justine smiled. "You don't know much

about men, honey." Her smile faded. "Why didn't you tell me that Hunter Westfall came calling last night and that you walked off with him?"

"I didn't think it that important. Who told you?"

"Not much goes on around here I don't know about. This place talks to me." She took several quick breaths before she continued. "We had a honeymooning couple above me last night, or else a man up there was determined to get his money's worth out of the woman he bought. The bed-springs squeaked off and on all night."

"Aunt Justine. How you talk!"

"You're blushing, honey. I was shocked, too, when we first came here. You'll learn that a lot of shocking things go on behind closed doors in hotel rooms. Radna can tell you that. There's not much she hasn't seen."

Jill saw the smile leave her aunt's face as she watched a man come up the walk. He bounded up the steps to the hotel porch. Jill recognized him as the man who had argued with Mr. Westfall at the merchants' meeting, the one with the birthmark on his face.

"Afternoon, Justine."

Justine grunted a reply.

"It's good to see that you're well enough to sit on the porch. Introduce me to the pretty lady."

"Jill's busy. I don't want you bothering her."

Lloyd smiled and extended his hand. "Hello, Miss Jones. Your aunt is a great kidder."

From the tone of her aunt's voice and the look on her face, Jill wasn't sure that her aunt was kidding.

"Hello, Mr. Madison. I saw you at the meeting."

"I wanted to speak to you, but you left before I could get away from the mayor."

"Is this a business or a social call?" Justine asked briskly.

"Both." He patted the paper in his shirt pocket.

"I don't do business on Sunday."

"Course you do. You don't close the hotel on Sunday." He turned to Jill. "How do you like our raw little town? We're doing our best to civilize it."

"That's going to take some doing."

At first Jill thought Lloyd Madison's face

was friendly and boyish in spite of the blood-red birthmark that flowed down over his cheekbone. On a closer look, his smile didn't reach the eyes that turned on her, analyzing, assessing through the wire-framed glasses. Like a dash of cold water, they poured over and touched her everywhere.

It was hard not to stare at him. It didn't seem to Jill that the man resented being stared at. Tall, thin, with wiry blond hair, he appeared perversely to display the thick, blood-red mass by turning his head in such a way as to keep it in full view.

"Jill, will you excuse us? He's determined to have private words for me before he goes."

"Of course." Jill stood up. "Nice meeting you, Mr. Madison."

"Call me Lloyd, Jill. We'll be getting to know each other better . . . I'm sure." He glanced at Justine when he said the last two words.

At the door, Jill looked back at her aunt's flushed face and was tempted to go to her. There was no doubt that she was irritated with the lawyer. Both seemed to be waiting until she passed through the doorway, so she reluctantly opened the door and went into the lobby.

"Pretty as a speckled hen." Lloyd removed his glasses and wiped the lenses with a white handkerchief he took from his back pocket.

"Stay away from her."

"Why? She's single. I'm single. My bloodline is as good as hers."

"Stay away from her. I mean it."

"Ah, come on, Justine. I waited damn near a month before coming to meet her. I wasn't sure she'd last that long. When I heard that she'd been seen with Westfall, I hotfooted it right over."

"You're too late. She's been spoken for."

"You mean . . . Westfall?"

"No, I mean her sweetheart from back home is here."

"That dirty roustabout who yanked her away from Westfall last night? I heard about him." Lloyd laughed. "I heard she threatened to slap him into tomorrow. It doesn't sound like she's very fond of him."

"Why did you come here? Get to the point."

"Every time I come to see you, you look worse. Last time I thought you were on your deathbed. I'm happy to see that you came out of your decline enough to sit on the porch."

"Horseshit! It'll be a cold day in July when you're concerned about my health." Justine's voice was heavy with sarcasm.

"Why wouldn't I be? It's been a while since I've seen you. Just before Jill arrived, wasn't it? By the way, how is that darky who guards you as if you were a virgin about to be ravished?"

"That darky is the best friend I ever had. You bother her and I'll blow your damn pecker off."

Lloyd's laugh rang out. "God, I love it when you talk trashy. It comes so natural." He pulled the paper from his shirt pocket. "I've got something here I want you to sign. We'll need a witness. I'll call Jill."

"What is it?"

"It's giving me power of attorney, the authority to look after your affairs."

"Are you out of your mind? I'll never sign that! I'd rather turn my affairs over to a mangy dog!" Justine was breathing hard and fast. "I want you to stay away from me."

"Watch it, dear. You could have a heart attack."

"It's what you want, isn't it?"

"No, not quite yet." He put the paper back in his pocket, leaned back and was silent until a car went by, leaving a trail of dust in its wake. "You will sign the paper. You owe it to me, you know."

"You've no right to stick your nose in my business."

"I've every right, and we both know it. God, you're even stupider than I thought you were."

"I don't owe you a damn thing!"

He laughed. "You think not? But enough of that. It was good of old Hunter to volunteer to oil the street."

"Old Hunter? I doubt he's any older than you are."

"Now, how would you know how old Hunter is?" Lloyd's eyes moved over Justine's flushed face before going beyond to the man coming up the steps to the porch.

"Hello, Skeeter," Justine said. "Come sit a spell. Mr. Madison was just leaving."

"Howdy, Justine." Skeeter stood hesitantly in front of her.

Lloyd got to his feet. With an amused

look on his face, he looked from Skeeter's down-at-the-heels boots to his dirty tattered shirt and up to his whiskered face.

"You do like the lowlife, don't you, Justine?" He shook his head as if in wonderment. "Why am I surprised? Water seeks it's own level, as the saying goes." He took a quick step and dropped a kiss on her cheek before she could flinch away.

"Get away from me!"

"I'll be going. Far be it from me to stand in the way of . . . romance. I'll be back in a day or two. Think over what I said about your . . . affairs. I will handle them, you know." He smiled down at her. "Take care of yourself, and if you need anything, phone me or, better yet, send Jill over. It's time she and I got better acquainted."

Justine's mouth was clamped shut and it stayed that way until Lloyd left the porch. He never merely walked anywhere but scurried, sprinted. Instead of turning, he seemed to spin around.

"Sit down, Skeeter."

"I don't like that son-of-a-bitch," he growled.

"Why?"

"Hell, he always acts like he's got some-thin' up his sleeve beside his arm."

"Forget him. Tell me the news."

"The darky that works for Westfall said that the gal that's been stayin' there ain't there no more. She flew the coop."

"What's new about that? His women come and go. Next week he'll have another one, and it's nobody's business but his."

"I hear he walked out with that prissy miss you brought here to run the hotel. If'n she's like the others, she'll be hightailin' it out."

"Godamighty, Skeeter. She just met him last night."

"I don't like her, either."

"I don't give a damn if you like her or not. Why were you up here on the porch making such a horse's ass out of yourself?"

Skeeter chuckled. "See how far she'd go, I guess. Didn't 'spect her to dump no dirty water on me."

"If you'd've spit on my clean floor, I'd a slapped the pee, wind and hockey out of you."

"That's why I never done it." He chuckled again. "Why're ya doin' business with that fellow with the devil mark on his face? He ain't the only lawyer in town. If this was back in the olden days, he and Westfall'd have a shoot-out on Main Street."

Jill came out onto the porch, but she stopped short and glared when she saw the man sitting on the bench. Her hands went to her hips.

"What's *he* doin' here?"

"He came to apologize," Justine said. Then, to Skeeter, "Get with it."

"Yeah, well . . ." He stood up and re-moved his hat. "I'm sorry I done it and won't do it no more." He slapped his hat down on his head. "'Bye, Justine."

"'Bye, Skeeter. Come again." Justine's shoulders slumped. "Honey, tell Thad I'm ready to go back inside."

Chapter 5

"Dinner is ready, Mistah Hunter." The soft voice fell in the quiet of the room.

"Thank you, Dinah. I'll be there in a minute."

Hunter shuffled the papers on his desk. He seldom worked at home; but, knowing that it was going to be a long, lonely day, he had decided to while away the hours by putting some figures together to see if adding a roller coaster to his amusement park would be profitable. It was definitely not as enjoyable as spending the hours in hot pursuit of sexual gratification with Carsie. But that wasn't to be.

He looked up when he sensed Dinah was still standing in the doorway. Her round dark face was creased with worry. If he had two loyal friends in the world, they were Dinah and Casper. They had been a part of his life for almost as long as he could remember, and he cared for them possibly more than he cared for any other living souls.

"What's the matter, Dinah?" Hunter went to her and placed his hand on her shoulder. She was a short round woman, the top of whose gray head came even with his chin.

"I ain't understandin' why dat girl just pack up an' go so quick-like. The other'n did that, too."

"What time did Carsie leave?"

"Was dark. Maybe nine o'clock. I come to tell her me'n Casper was goin' to bed. She comed downstairs with her suitcase. She said, real mad-like, that she was leavin'. And I said, what'll I tell Mistah Hunter?"

"What did she say to that?"

"She said, she said . . ." Dinah bowed her head. "Said tell yo to go"—she looked up and mouthed the word—"yo-self."

"I get the message, Dinah. You don't have to say it. You told me last night she left in a car. Did you see it?"

"No, sir. I heared it. Why'd she go like dat, Mistah Hunter?"

"When she came here, I told her that she

could stay and that we would enjoy each other, but that it was temporary." He sighed. "Women want their hooks in you so that you can't get away. I'll not tie myself to any woman. Carsie probably thought she'd not waste any more time on me."

"That other'n left sudden-like, too. Is yo mean to dem women up dere, Mistah Hunter? If yo is, I'll spank yo 'hind. I didn't raise yo to be mean to womenfolk."

Hunter chuckled. "I'm not mean to them, Dinah. I swear I'm not. They give me what I want, I give them what they want. Have you ever seen a bruise on any of them?"

"Nooo . . ." Dinah drew the word out. "Seen 'em cry a time or two."

"That's when they realize the party is over. None of them leave here broke, Dinah."

"I ain't knowin' why my boy don't get him a good woman and have him some kids."

"Maybe someday. Meanwhile, I'm hungry. What have you got for me?" Hunter placed his arm across her shoulders and they went to the dining room.

Business and sex were the two major factors in Hunter's life and he craved variety in both. He had never truly loved a woman, but he had been fond of many. He had discovered while in college that he had the proper equipment and a certain talent for using it to satisfy his appetite. Since that time he had seldom been without a woman for any length of time.

In a small town like Rainwater, however, it was wise to be discreet. The women who came to spend time with him were often passed off as sisters, nieces, family friends. When in Tulsa or Kansas City, he was free to treat himself to the services of experienced women in the best pleasure houses, where his desires and sexual fantasies would be satisfied for a while.

He loved sex, especially the moment when he entered a woman's body. It was the height of all sensations: hot, tight wet flesh surrounding him. Wonderful. Wonderful. He also learned from the females he bedded. Hunter prided himself on the fact that he had never forced a woman, and when he left them, they were completely satisfied.

As he sat down at the beautifully set table and to the meal Dinah had prepared, the only thought he gave to the absent Carsie was to compare her to Jill Jones.

Jill was like a prairie flower: untouched except by the wind. She would keep a man's attention far longer than an experienced woman like Carsie. He smiled while thinking about her hitting one of his men in the nose and kicking the shin of another. She had the refreshing look of innocence, but he was sure that once she was introduced to the pleasures of sex, she would be as wild as an untamed cat in bed. It had been a while since he had taken the time to seduce, then teach a virgin the art of sexual gratification.

Jill Jones would be a delight to teach.

In a law office above the bank on Main Street, Jill was also on the mind of the man leaning back in his chair with his feet on the desk. She was a little scrawny for his taste, he thought now as he viewed her once again in his mind's eye. She was pert, sassy as a young colt and not at all bad to look at, as Justine must have been all those many years ago. The little country miss would fit nicely into his plans, although he preferred women with large breasts, meat on their bones and little or nothing in their pretty heads.

Lloyd Madison's character had been forged not only by the permanent disfigurement on his face, but also by a father who was sixty years old when he was born. Over the years he had become so used to the blood-red mass that even if it were possible to have it removed, he would not part with it. He rather enjoyed having people stare at him. The mass that some called the mark of the devil made him unforgettable.

"You've got the mark of the devil on your face," his father had told him almost every day as he was growing up. "But you've got my brains. Use them as well as that appendage between your legs. Let no man or woman stand in the way of what you want." When the dried-up old bastard finally died, setting Lloyd free, he had just turned eighteen.

He had taken the old man's advice to heart: used the brains inherited from him and the money the old miser had held on to until the last breath. He got through law school, roamed a little, then headed for Oklahoma.

The devil part of Lloyd's character had taught him to be calculating, persistent and to search out details that would be beneficial to him, while presenting a persona of caring and decency. The traits had been far more rewarding than he had expected.

While in Rainwater, Lloyd had carefully crafted his image as the badly disfigured young man who spent his time and talent bravely fighting the oil companies on behalf of the laborers they employed, the small businessmen in the town and the ranchers whose land they leased.

Only with Justine Byers did he allow the real Lloyd Madison to surface, and he had a good basis for that. She was the reason he had come to this godforsaken place. And as long as she lived, he intended for her to be on *tenterhooks* wondering what he would do next. He wanted her to know first uneasiness and then outright fear.

He laughed aloud remembering when he had first presented himself to her. He'd been here in Rainwater a few weeks and was already established firmly on the side of the workingman when he finally caught her alone on the porch of the hotel.

"Mrs. Byers? I'm wondering if we have met before."

She peered up at him, and when he

turned his face toward her, she gasped, "Oh, my God!"

"So you do remember me." He sat down on the bench, placed his ankle on his knee and stared at her. "People usually do."

"Lloyd! Oh, my God. Lloyd."

"I hear that you're ailing. Well, don't kick off too soon. You and I have some settling up to do. Hear?"

"What do you . . . mean?" she stammered.

"You figure it out. Don't worry. I'll be here as long as you are and . . . longer. I'll be back to see you from time to time so you'll not . . . forget me."

He had left her then before the look on her face caused him to burst out laughing. He had managed to get her alone several times since then. Each time he had managed to convey his hatred without speaking of it. He was determined to make her a nervous wreck before she died.

Hunter Westfall, too, had made the big mistake of making an enemy of him. Plans had already been set in motion to ruin the oilman. Lloyd would enjoy every minute of it.

Was there anything in the world as sweet as revenge?

"Yes," he said aloud with gusto. "One thing!"

Utterly relaxed and satisfied with himself, Lloyd leaned his head back against the wall while he considered his next move. He entertained and then discarded several ideas.

Suddenly he smiled and sat up. His feet hit the floor with a loud thump. Why hadn't he thought of it before? It was perfect, absolutely perfect, and would kill two birds with one stone. It would take careful planning; all the elements would have to be in place for it to work the way he wanted.

After filing in his mind the steps he would take to implement his plan, he returned his feet to the desk, leaned back against the wall and was soon asleep. Last night had been a busy night and tonight would be just as busy.

With the help of Mr. Boise, the barber, and another guest who had volunteered his services, Jill had brought the small armless couch downstairs and fit it into the alcove behind the counter. The ornate Chinese folding screen she had found in a storage room stood in front of it, hiding it from view.

"What are you up to now?" Thad's voice startled her. She hadn't heard him come in. "Why didn't you call me if you wanted to move that thing? Are you one of these women who thinks she can do anything a man can do? You'll be joining the volunteer fire department next or running for sheriff."

"Questions. Can't you talk without them?"

"Not if I want to find out something. You didn't move that couch by yourself?"

"No, I didn't move the couch by myself. Mr. Boise and another man helped me," she replied crossly.

"So . . . you'd ask one of your paying roomers for help before you'd ask me." His brows were drawn together over piercing eyes in what could only be called a scowl.

"You are so darn nosy. If you must know, they offered to help me," she snapped. His scowl disappeared, but his taunting grin was more irritating.

He chuckled when he saw her eyes turn cold.

"What happened to upset your aunt?" He

had the habit of switching subjects without taking an extra breath.

"She's tired. And I don't think she likes that lawyer who came to see her today."

"What did he say to her?"

"More questions. I don't know. I don't eavesdrop on my aunt's conversations." Jill leaned over the counter and saw the black and white dog standing close to Thad. "What's that dog doing in here?"

"She's with me." Thad reached down and caressed the dog's head. "What time does your night man get here?"

"In about an hour."

"Go spend some time with your aunt. I'll stay here until he comes, then you and I will go for a walk."

Jill bristled at the orders. "I'm not going off in the dark with a . . . a polecat like you. You might strangle me . . . or sic your dog on me."

"Worse than that, I might kiss you." He was leaning with his elbow on the counter, his face close to Jill's; alarmingly close.

"I can think of nothing worse!"

His green eyes were alight with laughter and she fleetingly wondered if his lashes had always been so thick and dark. Leaning close to her as he was, he was intimidating. She realized that his strength and purpose were nothing to tangle with. Only a fool would try. She swallowed and suddenly became warm and breathless. She ridiculed herself for acting so juvenile and not telling him to go fly a kite.

"Well?"

"Well. A deep subject for a shallow mind."

"Very good, Jill." His laugh was a deep, pleasant sound; soft and intimate. He reached for her hand, covered it with his and pressed it to the counter. Her heart, some time ago, had leaped from her chest to settle somewhere in her throat. Now it began to pound, blocking off her breath. She tugged on her hand.

"Let go of me!"

"There's never a dull moment around you, Miss Wildcat."

"Stop . . . calling me that."

"Don't like *Miss Wildcat*? Okay, I'll call you *sweetheart* or *darlin'*." He gently pulled her from behind the counter. "Go on, now. See about your aunt, sweetheart. She needs cheering up. I'll be here until Mr.

Evans gets here, then Fertile and I will come for you."

"Aunt Justine wouldn't like that dog wandering around in the lobby."

"She won't wander. And Justine likes her. We just came from her room."

"Before taking her calling, you could have brushed the cockleburs out of her tail." Because she was nervous, words spilled out of Jill's mouth.

Thad spoke to the dog. "Don't mind her, Fertile. She's a frustrated, grouchy old maid and jealous because you're pregnant and she's not."

For long moments Jill couldn't speak, couldn't move. She could feel her mouth hanging slack. The *old maid* part hurt to the depths of her being.

"That was a stupid and unkind thing to say," she said on an incredulous gasp, then spun on her heels and stormed toward the door leading into the hallway.

"Jill," he said, with such authority that she halted in spite of her haste to get away from him. "Look at me, Jill."

Determined for him not to know of her hurt or think she was intimidated, she turned to stare at him from across the room.

Haughty disdain was evident in her expression and her stance.

"I'm sorry. I didn't realize how that would sound until it was out of my mouth."

Unable to speak, she nodded, turned and left the lobby. Before reaching her aunt's room, she paused in the semidarkness of the hallway and pressed her hand to her chest in the hope of calming her pounding heart. If Thad even considered her anything but his friend's annoying kid sister, he'd never have made such an outrageous personal remark.

Why did knowing that hurt so much?

Chapter 6

When Jill entered the room, Justine was lying on her side facing the window.

"Aunt Justine? Are you all right?"

"I'm all right, honey. Just tired."

Jill moved around to the side of the bed. "Want company for a while?"

"I'm not very good company."

Jill sat down and took her aunt's limp hand in both of hers, rubbing and massaging it as she had seen Radna do.

"The couch fit perfectly behind the desk. The colors on the screen came out nice and bright after I washed off the dust."

"Ralph bought the screen the first year we were married. We couldn't afford it, but that never bothered Ralph when he wanted me to have something."

"It's beautiful."

"He liked for me to undress behind it and throw my stockings over the top like he'd seen in a picture."

"Did you?"

"Of course. I'd have done anything he asked me to do."

Jill stroked her aunt's hand. After a long silence, Jill asked, "Was Mr. Madison's business with you upsetting, Aunt Justine?"

"No more than usual."

"He seems nice. Is he a good lawyer?"

"As good as they come, I guess."

"That awful thing on his face doesn't seem to bother him. He must be used to it."

"Yes," Justine said tiredly. "He's had to live with it . . . and other things."

"I've never seen a birthmark like that."

"It doesn't happen very often. They call it the mark of the devil."

"That's terrible. It must have been hard for him when he was a little boy."

"He got hardened to it. Don't feel sorry for him, Jill. He would scorn your pity and use it to his advantage."

"I get the feeling that you don't like him very much."

"I don't, but . . ."

Jill waited. Justine didn't say any more.

Several minutes went by before she spoke again.

"I shouldn't have brought you here."

The quiet words cut into the silence. It took several minutes for Jill to digest their meaning. Then she fought the sinking feeling in the pit of her stomach.

"I'm sorry if I've disappointed you."

"Oh, child. It isn't that. You've done far better than I expected you to do. There are things here that you'd be better off not knowing."

"Things that worry you? I wish I could help."

"You can't turn back the clock. No one can." Justine turned her hand over and tried to grip Jill's. "Thad promised me that he and Joe would stay here with you until it's . . . over and things are settled. That eases my mind a lot."

"I wish you wouldn't worry so. Would you feel better if someone else was managing the hotel?"

"No, honey. No, no, no. You've done just fine. Tomorrow I want you to call Bernie Shepard and tell him that I want to see him."

"He's the lawyer who came to see you right after I got here."

"Yes, he's old and doddering, but I trust his judgment. He came to Rainwater right after Ralph and I did."

Jill heard the thump of Mr. Evans's crutches coming down the hall. She turned to the open doorway of her aunt's room to see him and his wife standing there.

"Hello, Mrs. Evans, Mr. Evans." Jill got to her feet.

"Is Mrs. Byers awake?" Mrs. Evans was a short, plump woman who wore her hair in a knot at the back of her neck. The Evanses were a closely knit couple who were often seen holding hands and smiling at each other.

Justine turned her head to face the doorway. Jill adjusted the sheet covering her.

"Hello, Rose." Justine's voice was quavery.

"Elmer and I just wanted to say hello." Rose Evans came into the room to stand by the bed. Elmer stayed in the doorway.

"How are you, Rose? Are you working in your garden?" Not waiting for an answer, Justine said to Jill, "Rose and Elmer have a beautiful garden every year."

"Flowers?" Jill asked.

"Flowers and vegetables. Elmer and I put up enough vegetables each year to see us through the winter."

"We did that in Missouri, too. My sister used to crack the whip over us kids to make us help." Jill smiled, remembering. "I bet I've picked, washed and snapped enough green beans to fill a boxcar."

"Elmer has an uncanny way of making things grow. I swear he gets more beans per bush than anyone I ever knew. It's the same with okra and tomatoes."

"How is your rose garden doing?" Justine asked.

"Our roses have started to bloom. As soon as there are enough buds to make a decent bouquet, you'll have one."

"That would be nice," Justine said with a tired smile.

"We put the couch behind the counter, Mr. Evans. Now Mrs. Evans can stay with you, if she wants."

"That will be grand, miss," Mrs. Evans exclaimed excitedly. "I don't like to be home alone. I'd much rather be here with Elmer."

After the couple had left, Jill went back to her aunt's bedside.

"Have you known them long?"

"Since the end of the war. They were married just before he went over. When he came back, he was in terrible shape. Rose was waiting to take care of him. They've been together every day, almost every hour since. He gets a little pension from the government and they make do."

"Do they have children?"

"No. It's just the two of them." Justine sighed. "They'd be lost without each other. It was that way with Ralph and me. I hope that someday you'll find a love like that."

"It's the same with Julie and Evan. He looks at her first when he comes into a room, touches her every chance he gets. Before their baby was born, he practically carried her around on a pillow. I never saw a man as frantic as he was when it came time for her to give birth."

"But it turned out all right?"

"Oh, yes. And she's expecting again."

The shaggy dog came into the room, followed by Thad. Jill's heart jumped, but it was a momentary reaction. Then her chin went up defiantly.

The dog walked right up to the bed and nuzzled Justine's limp hand.

"I'd like to pet you, girl, but it's too much of an effort to lift my useless hand."

Jill lifted her aunt's hand and placed it on the dog's head. After a minute, the dog moved out from under it and went back to Thad.

"I'm taking your girl for a while," Thad said to Justine.

Jill refused to look at him.

"Go ahead. Turn off the light and close the door, please."

"Is there anything I can get for you, Aunt?"

"No, dear. Go and enjoy yourself with your young man."

"He's not my young man, Aunt," Jill said firmly. Her cheeks flamed when she heard Thad chuckle.

"Well, whatever he is. Enjoy being with him. And count your blessings that you're young and have your life ahead of you. Good night."

Jill turned off the lamp on the bedside table—the one Thad had fixed—and walked stiffly to the door, brushed past him and headed for the kitchen.

"Radna isn't here." Jill turned on Thad and spoke as calmly as her pumping heart would allow. "I'm not leaving Aunt Justine alone."

"She won't be alone. Elmer's wife will look in on her. Come on, you've worked all day and you need to get away from here for a while. Your nerves are strung tighter than piano wire."

"And whose fault is that?" Her words were spoken in a low, strained voice. She prayed that she'd not cry and disgrace herself.

"Not mine. I'm trying to make things easier for you and you're bucking me every step of the way." Strong fingers reached out and looped a curl behind her ear.

"I was doing just fine until you showed up."

"Ah, honey, don't be mad at me." He smiled tenderly. His searching eyes caressed each feature of her face.

His softly spoken words broke her resistance; but, determined that he not know it, she continued to hold herself stiffly and to glare at him.

"I'm not mad." *I'm hurt, dammit!*

"I'll make it up to you and buy you an ice cream," he coaxed teasingly.

"Are you sure you can afford it?" she

asked as she turned to go to the lobby. "You're out of a job."

"Oh, I've got a couple of nickels to rub together." With his fingers riding lightly on the small of her back, he ushered her through the hall and out into the lobby. Elmer and Rose Evans were sitting behind the counter.

"Mrs. Evans, will you look in on Aunt Justine in a little while? I won't be gone long." Jill's voice was not quite steady.

"Of course. Stay out as long as you like. I'll look in on her every little bit."

"Thank you."

Thad didn't touch her until they reached the walk. His large hand gripped her arm and moved down to draw her hand up into the crook of his arm. He pressed it tightly to his side as they walked to the corner and turned toward the residential part of town.

Without uttering a word, Jill walked beside him, telling herself that Thad Taylor was the most arrogant, infuriating creature she had ever met. He had used endearing words and smiles to soften her up and was probably snickering to himself about how easily she had surrendered. He thought that she was a frustrated old maid, hungry for a man's attention, and he was giving her a treat.

The more she thought about it, the madder she became and the faster she walked. They passed houses where families were seated on the porch and children played in the yard. Music from a Victrola came from a house on the corner.

"Slow down, sweetheart. We're not going to a fire." They had passed the last house in town and were walking along a hard-packed dirt road.

"Don't call me that."

"You don't like Miss Wildcat or Jilly Justine."

"You can call me Miss Jones; that's my name."

"Miss Jones, you're more fun than a barrel of monkeys." His laugh was a deep rumble that she could feel in the hand pressed to his side. They walked in silence for a few minutes before he spoke again. "I like to get away from the noise and the lights of town and look at the sky. I'm a country boy at heart. There are a million stars up there."

"Probably more than that. We can't see them all."

"Have you ever been out on the prairie at night?"

"I've not been out of town since I came here."

"Someday I'll take you out on the prairie where there isn't a tree or a light. The stars are bright and you can see from horizon to horizon. You feel like you're the only person in the world."

"Sounds lonely."

"I guess it would be after a while, unless you had someone with you who enjoyed it as much as you did. There are a lot of things for a man and his woman to do when they are alone like that." His head was tilted down toward her. She knew that he had that teasing grin on his face, but she wouldn't look at him.

"You would think of *that*."

"How come some fellow back home hasn't snatched you up and run away with you?"

"Being a grouchy old maid might have something to do with it."

"Hell and tarnation!" He swore softly. "I'm never going to live that down." He flung his arm across her shoulders and pulled her close to his side. "I let my mouth run away with me that time."

"You may have spoken before you thought, but the words were in your mind or you wouldn't have said them. They're partly true. I'm not married and at times I am grouchy, but I'm not envious of a dog because she's pregnant."

"I'm sorry I said that. If you'd have been pregnant and unwed when I got here, I'd have had to kill someone."

"This is not a subject I want to talk about, Thad." Jill had stopped. She tried to shrug his arm from her shoulders and failed, then swung around to face him. The dog stopped and looked up at them.

"You want to get married someday, don't you?" he asked.

"Of course. But not now."

"What kind of man are you looking for?"

"I'm not looking." She turned and started walking again.

The dog, satisfied that they were not going back, ran ahead to smell along the roadside.

Thad's arm remained protectively in place, fitting her shoulder nicely beneath his. Contrariness inside her forced her to keep her body ramrod stiff.

"I'm not looking," she said again. "But it wouldn't be any of your business if I were."

"I'd make it my business if I thought you were taking up with some trashy hell-raiser who wasn't worthy of you," he growled, then swore under his breath. "There are a hundred men in this town, besides that rich dude you walked out with, who would give a year of their life to get a girl like you alone out in the dark. I'm here to see that it doesn't happen."

"Are you one of them? Is that why you insisted we take a walk . . . in the dark?"

He laughed. "If you weren't so damn sweet, I'd shake you until the freckles on your nose rattled, then I'd kiss you until you didn't know which end of you was up."

"Try it, and you'll get a fist in your gut!"

Thad whooped with laughter. "If I'd known you were this much fun, I'd have come looking for you sooner."

It was a warm summer night with a slight breeze blowing from the south. Wrapped in the soft darkness, they continued to walk away from town. Jill's insides were in a turmoil. She kept pace with him, automatically putting one foot in front of the other. She wanted to put her arm around his back so that it wouldn't continue to bump into him, but she didn't dare. It would give him an even greater opinion of himself than he already had.

She was so absorbed with him, her brain became disconnected from her feet and she stumbled over a hard dirt clod in the road. Thad's arm tightened, pulling her to him. He took her arm and drew it behind him and wrapped it around his waist.

"Hook your fingers in my belt and hold on to me." He grinned down at her. "This is better. I was wondering how I was going to manage to get you to put your arm around me."

"Was it important?" she asked and tried to put a dry note in her voice.

"To me it was. I'm trying to get up the nerve to kiss you. I haven't kissed you since you were about fourteen. I bet you don't even remember it."

"No, I don't." She was pleased that she could lie so convincingly.

"Joe and I had found a bottle of Walter Johnson's bootleg whiskey and were more than a little tipsy when you and Ruby Mae

Farley came out to the barn. We saw you coming and decided that we were going to kiss you."

"Why didn't you kiss Ruby Mae?"

"It wouldn't have been any fun for Joe to kiss his own sister."

"I guess not. We knew you were out there drinking, but we didn't tell Papa."

"Was that the first time you'd ever been kissed?"

"Of course not." Another lie. Thad's kiss, even though it had been a brotherly peck on her lips, had been so wonderful that she had daydreamed about it for the rest of the summer. "And it wasn't the first time you and Joe had hid in the barn with a bottle of whiskey."

"How do you know that?"

"Jack told me that several times you and Joe waited until Walter Johnson was falling-down drunk, then stole his whiskey."

"That low-life jackass! I'm going to break Jack's head when I see him."

"It won't be easy. You've not seen him lately. Jack can take care of himself."

Thad chuckled. "Those were the good old days. Life was easy and a good time

was playing baseball on Sunday afternoon
or going to a barn dance—"

"Or drinking bootleg whiskey in the barn.
I wonder why it's called *bootleg* whiskey."

"I just happen to know that."

"Why am I not surprised?"

"Get lippy and I'll not tell you." Thad's
arm tightened on her shoulder.

"You'll tell me. You're dying to impress
me with how smart you are."

"All right, if you insist. Bootleggers got
their name because they smuggled illegal
whiskey in their tall loose-legged boots.
Back during or before the Civil War, whiskey
was heavily taxed. A lot of smuggling went
on and one way was in the boots."

"Aren't you the smart one."

"I'm glad you finally realize that." He
laughed softly.

"Don't be getting a big head over it."

Thad stopped and looked back. They
were almost a mile out of town. Ahead they
could see a faint light and hear the *chug-
chug* of a pumping oil well.

"We'd better head back, unless you want
to go on out to where that well is pumping."

"I'd like to see it, but not tonight."

"When Joe gets here with the car, I'll take

you out to see a derrick going up and to where you can watch a crew drilling."

"I never thought to ask how you got here."

"I hitched a ride. Several of them. Everyone knows about Rainwater. It's a hot little town right now." He looked around. "Where'd that dog go?"

"Maybe back home."

"She'd not leave me. Unlike some females I know, she knows a good man when she finds one."

"Bull-foot!" Jill snorted. Then: "Joe had better hurry up and get here."

"They should be here by the end of the week."

"They?"

"Joe and a friend of ours. We got into a little trouble the first month we were out here. Blue helped us out a bit and has been with us ever since. He's part Kickapoo Indian. He told us one night, after drinking a bottle of hooch, that his name was Randolph Frazier Bluefeather, but when he sobered up he swore that he hadn't said any such thing. I've never heard him called anything but Blue."

They started back toward town. Thad's

arm was still across her shoulders, hers around him. They had only gone a few steps when he stopped, looked back and whistled for the dog. A minute passed and he whistled again.

"She'll be back to the one who feeds her."

"Not if she's caught in a trap some- where."

"Maybe she's wandered off in search of romance."

"Do women do that in her condition?"

Jill was glad the darkness concealed her flushed face. Why had she said such a stu- pid thing?

"Here she comes," Thad said with relief and waited for the dog to approach. She trotted up to him with something hanging from her mouth. "What've you got there, girl? Drop it." Thad bent down to get a bet- ter look at what dropped from the dog's mouth. "God Almighty," he swore and backed away, pulling Jill with him.

"Turn around," he commanded, and with his hands on her shoulders he turned her to face the lights of the town. He dug in his pocket for a match, lit it and knelt down for a closer look at what the dog had brought to them. The gruesome sight caused his stomach to roil.

"What is it?" Jill demanded.

"Nothing for you to see," he managed to say in spite of the bile rising in his throat.

"What is it?" She tried to move around him. He blocked her way by holding her shoulders

"Don't look!"

"Dammit, Thad, what are you hiding from me?"

"Jill, don't—" He tried to move her away, but she pushed him aside and looked down. "It looks like a— Oh, oh, it's a . . . it's a . . ."

"It's part of a human arm and a hand . . . a woman's hand. Now are you satisfied?" he barked angrily.

Chapter 7

"Oh, God! Oh, good Lord—" Jill stumbled away. Her hands reached for Thad, clutching his shirt. With her eyes tightly closed, she could still see the long, white, slightly curled fingers at the end of the pale stump of a forearm. "Thad! I'm going to be sick."

"I'm here, honey. Take deep breaths. That's my girl. Open your mouth and breathe in deep."

Thad wrapped her in his arms, cupped her head with his hand and held her tightly and protectively against him. She clung to him, her arms around his waist, her face buried in his shoulder. She trembled and little mewling sounds of horror came from her.

"Is it . . . was it . . . ?"

"No doubt about it, sweetheart. It's what we think it is," he whispered close to her ear. "I'll take you back to the hotel, then bring the sheriff out here."

"Maybe . . . it isn't real. Maybe it's one of those things from a store window," she said hopefully.

"It's real, honey. It's the arm of a woman or a child."

"A child? Oh, my goodness! Could the dog have gotten it out of a graveyard?"

"The graveyard is on the other side of town."

"Is there more . . . of the body?"

"That's up to the sheriff to find out." With his arm wrapped tightly around her, they started toward town. Thad turned and spoke sharply to the dog. "No! Goddammit! Drop it." Holding tightly to Jill's hand, he grabbed the dog by the hair on the back of her neck and shook her until she dropped the thing she carried. Then he dragged her along until she went on ahead of them.

"Oh, I hate that dog! She was going to . . . eat it." Jill held tightly to Thad's arm.

"Don't blame the dog, honey. It was just food to her, and from the looks of her she's been hungry."

"Arms don't come off like . . . that, do

they?" The words stumbled from her trembling lips.

"No. It appears to me that it's been cut off. Don't think about it." He increased the pace until she was almost running to keep up with him.

"Slow down," Jill gasped. "I've got to get my breath."

"Sorry. I forget that your legs aren't as long as mine." Thad stopped and put his arms around her. She leaned against him, welcomed his strength and wound her arms around him. He was so dearly familiar. She felt safe and protected in his arms.

"Hey, now. Am I such an ugly fellow, that it takes something like this to get the prettiest girl in town to put her arms around me?"

"Stop teasing, Thad Taylor." Jill buried her face in the curve of his neck.

"I'm not teasin' about some of it."

"Just give me a minute."

"Darlin', take all the time you want."

"Oh, you!" She pulled away to look up at him, expecting to see a teasing grin on his face, but it was cold sober. "I'm all right now."

Back at the hotel, he stopped at the steps leading to the porch. With his hands on her shoulders he looked down into her face.

"Stay in the lobby with Elmer and his wife. I'll go down and talk to the sheriff and be back as soon as I know something."

"Thad, it's so . . . awful. She was murdered, wasn't she?"

"We don't know that, honey. But I don't think that what we saw came from a graveyard."

"You'll come back?"

"As soon as I can. Go on in. Don't say anything to anyone until we find out more about it." He hugged her to him, then held her away so that he could look into her face. "I hate to leave you, but I'd better go on down to the jail and tell the sheriff."

"I'll be all right. Go and do what you have to do."

"That's my girl." He framed her face with his hands, placed a brotherly kiss on her forehead, then gently pushed her up the steps and onto the porch.

Thad waited until Jill was inside the lobby before he headed down the street toward the town jail, where he expected to find the sheriff, or a deputy. The dog trailed along behind him.

*   *   *

Ira Page was a man who took his job seriously. Being sheriff of Rainwater County was not an easy assignment, although on this Sunday night it was relatively quiet. His jail consisted of three cells that usually held three or four prisoners each. Tonight, two of the cells held two men each. All four men had been drunk and rowdy and would be released in the morning. In the third cell was a knife-wielding half-breed Cherokee Indian with scars on his face from numerous barroom brawls. He had cut the thumb off a cardplayer he thought was cheating him.

The Cherokee was a dangerous man with a fondness for knives and was quite proficient with them. He was back in the cell block ranting and bragging about being a friend of Charles Floyd, the notorious outlaw more commonly known as Pretty Boy.

If true, the prisoner's friendship with Pretty Boy didn't impress Page. A short, thick-chested man with iron-gray hair, the sheriff observed the letter of the law. If his brother had been brawling in the pool hall, he'd be in jail. His dear old mother would be in jail if she had sliced off a man's thumb on the mere suspicion that he was cheating during a card game.

Page closed the door to the cell block to shut out, to a degree, the racket made by the prisoner and seated himself behind his desk. With his booted feet propped on the corner, his hat pulled low over his forehead, he dozed. That was the way Thad found him when he opened the door and came into the office.

The only move Sheriff Page made was to tilt his head slightly and silently eye the big, dark-haired man who filled the doorway.

"Are you the sheriff?"

"The badge says so. Who're you?"

"Thad Taylor. I'm helping out at the hotel."

"Hadn't heard Justine had took on anybody since she brought in that little gal from Missouri to help run things. What's on your mind? If it's not important, hold it till morning. I need a nap."

"I'd consider this more important than a nap." Thad's voice was tight.

"Well, spill it."

"Mrs. Byers's niece and I were walking out south of town. About halfway between town and that first pumping well, my dog—

she isn't really mine, just a stray that got attached to me because I fed her—came back from up the road with something in her mouth. It was part of a human arm with a hand on the end of it. From the look of it, I'd say it was a woman's hand."

"The hell you say!" The sheriff's feet hit the floor.

"It had been chewed on a bit, but it looked to me like the bone had been sawed. It wasn't a jagged break."

"Where is it?"

"Beside the road, right where the dog dropped it."

"How long ago?"

"Came here from there after I took Miss Jones to the hotel."

"Have you told this to anyone?"

"Not a soul. I told Miss Jones not to say anything."

"Good. Something like this could cause a stampede of curiosity seekers out there." He picked up the telephone. "Clara, get me Deputy Franklin." After a minute, he said, "Hello, Gus. How long will it take for you to get over here? No, there's no emergency. I just need to do something. All right. Five minutes." The sheriff hung up the phone and took his gun belt from a peg on the wall behind the desk. "Anything that's said on that phone is all over town before you can say doodle-dee-squat," he warned as he strapped on the belt.

"I know. That's why I didn't phone."

"Glad you didn't. Where're you from, Taylor?"

"Missouri originally. Been working down near Tulsa."

"You working for anyone up here?"

"Not yet. Haven't been here but a couple of days."

"What brought you here?"

"You're asking a lot of questions, Sheriff."

"I don't know you, mister. I need to know who I'm dealing with."

"You'll not be dealing with me on anything after I show you what the dog found. But as long as you asked, I'll tell you what brought me to Rainwater. My family and the Jones family live side by side back in Missouri. At her father's request, I came here to make sure Jill Jones had arrived safely and settled in with her aunt. Her brother will be along in a day or two."

"Good assignment, if you ask me. I've

seen the young miss. She's pretty as a covey of quail."

"Yes, she is. She's shaken up over what we saw."

The sheriff took a gas lantern and a powerful battery-powered flashlight from a closet.

"That the dog outside the door?"

"That's her."

"We'll take her with us. Here's Gus."

The young deputy wasn't very tall but was powerfully built. His features were heavy and coarse, but large blue eyes softened the bluntness of his face. He wore a red bandanna about his neck, a black Stetson hat and cowboy boots.

"What's up, Ira?" The deputy eyed Thad.

"Probably nothing. If that fellow back there gives you any trouble, throw a bucket of water on him." The sheriff went out the door and Thad followed.

After several attempts to coax the dog into the touring car parked behind the jail, Thad picked her up, got into the backseat and held her between his spread knees. The sheriff took the dark back streets to the edge of town, then turned on the road going south.

"Tell me when to stop," he called back to Thad.

Thad looked back to judge the distance from town. "Stop here," he said a little later. "The dog and I will walk."

The car's headlights forged a path in the darkness. Fertile ran on ahead, happy to be out of the car. Thad trotted along behind her, sure she would head for what she considered a tasty meal. He was right, and he grabbed the hair on the back of her neck before she could pick it up. He held her and waited for the sheriff to stop the car and get out.

Leaving the motor running and the lights on, Sheriff Page came with the flashlight to squat down for a close look at what was lying on the ground.

"Hell and damnation!" He picked up a small stick and turned the hand over. "Mother of Christ! Looks like someone cut the arm off with a handsaw. But I won't know for sure until the doc sees it."

"I hope you have something to wrap it in. I'm sure as hell not going to carry it back."

The sheriff went to the car and returned with a newspaper and the gas lantern. With a stick he rolled the hand over onto the paper and wrapped it up.

"Now let's see if we can find the rest of her."

Thad released the dog and trailed along behind her with the lantern. The sheriff followed in the car. A hundred yards from where they had picked up the hand, Fertile, roaming a dozen feet back from the hard-packed road, began digging in a sand dune. When a bare foot emerged, Thad held her back.

"Here," he shouted. "Bring a shovel."

Thirty minutes later, they had uncovered two legs, both cut off at the knee and again at the upper thigh, one forearm with a hand attached, two upper arms and a woman's naked torso, the breasts removed. Swallowing repeatedly in an attempt to keep from emptying the contents of their stomachs, the two sweating men, one digging with the shovel, the other with a piece of tin from the sheriff's car, dug until the mound was leveled.

All the body parts were accounted for, with the exception of the woman's breasts and her head.

"Dear God! What kind of a man would do

this?" Shaken, the sheriff turned his back on the eerie scene. The body parts laid out in the lamplight were such a gory sight that Thad, no longer able to control his heaving stomach, went a distance away and threw up.

"I've no experience in this sort of thing, Sheriff. I just couldn't hold it a minute longer."

"Can't blame you, son. I thank you for the help." Sheriff Page picked up the small spade they had been using. "I've seen a lot of dead bodies during my twenty years as a lawman, but nothing like this."

"How long do you think she's been here?"

"Not long. Another day and the smell would be a lot worse. I've got to go back to town and get the doc and the hearse. I need you to stay here until I get back."

"It isn't something I want to do, but I see the need for it."

"I'll be back as soon as I can. Turn off the lamp. I'll leave you the flashlight. We don't want a carload of drunks stopping to see what's going on. I'll honk the horn a couple of times before I get here and you can flash the light."

Thad watched the sheriff back the car into the ditch, turn around and head for town. He welcomed the darkness. It had seemed obscene to him to expose the poor naked body to the light from the lantern. With the dog close to him, he moved back from the road and watched the car's taillight disappear.

There was something evil in this town, or if not in town, close by. A man who would do such a thing to a woman had to be crazy mean. The remains Thad was guarding were those of a young woman, somewhere near Jill's age. It would take a monster, totally without human feelings, to use a saw and cut up a woman. Somewhere nearby there was probably a bloody mess and the missing head.

Thad looked toward town. As soon as the sheriff returned, he'd hotfoot it back to the hotel and stick close to Jill, Radna and Justine until the sick son-of-a-bitch who murdered the woman was found. When Joe got here, maybe he could persuade Jill to go back home. It was unlikely, though, that the stubborn little cuss would leave her aunt. Which meant that he would be staying here with her. Which also meant that he'd have to do something to earn some money. He didn't want his living expenses to eat up the money he had saved to buy the land he and Joe had their eyes on.

Who would have thought the skinny little spitfire he had teased all her life would grow up to be such a beauty? He had had the socks knocked nearly off him when he saw her on that street corner, fists flying, spitting like a cornered cat. Four, maybe five years ago, she had been just a cute kid, always full of sass. That was why it had been so much fun to tease her.

She was no longer a kid. Being with her seemed to knock his common sense out of kilter. Hellfire! He didn't know how to act around her. Treating her like the kid he used to know back in Missouri didn't work. He'd said things to her that he was ashamed of now.

Jill was a Jones, with the Joneses' work ethic, grit and honesty. The incident in the woods when she was fifteen had been a shock to her, as it had been to all of them, but she had bounced back to near normal within a few weeks. Since that time he'd had a protective feeling toward her as he would have had for a kid sister and had been worried about her when they heard she was here in this hell-raising town.

Keeping his mind on Jill so he wouldn't think of the pitiful pile of human flesh behind him, Thad wondered what Jill would have done if he had kissed her tonight. It sure as hell wouldn't have been a brotherly kiss. What he was feeling for her wasn't brotherly at all. It was what a man feels when he likes a woman, a lot.

Without being aware of it, a smile spread across his lips just thinking about how surprised she'd have been. When it happened, and he was sure it would, he'd have to guard his shins. She knew where to kick so that it would hurt. She was all woman! Thad's insides felt warm and melting just thinking about kissing her. Christ Almighty! His heart was thumping and goose bumps were climbing up his arm.

Headlights appeared down the road. Thad got up and, holding on to the dog, moved back from the road until the car had passed. He had no way of measuring time. It seemed hours since the sheriff had left. The night suddenly was terribly dark. A rain cloud was forming in the southwest. It was eerie sitting out here on the prairie alone with a corpse.

When two sets of car lights appeared on the road, Thad got to his feet. He had no guarantee it was the sheriff's car. God, he hoped it was. He sure didn't want to have to explain to a carload of roustabouts why he was a mile from town with the cut-up body of a woman. Drunk, they might hang him and ask questions later.

The lead car slowed as it approached and tooted the horn. When Thad was sure it was the sheriff, he stepped out and signaled with the flashlight. The other car, a long dark hearse, pulled up behind the sheriff. Thad was introduced to the doctor, a stooped old man with gray hair who was also the coroner, and to the undertaker, who was the owner of the funeral parlor and furniture store.

"Unless you want me to stay, Sheriff, I'm heading back to town."

"We shouldn't be too long here if you want to wait for a ride."

"Thanks, but I need a walk to clear my head."

"Go ahead, then. I'm obliged for your help."

"By the way, I'd appreciate it if Miss Jones's name was kept out of this," Thad said.

"I'll do what I can. Can't swear to it, though."

"I'll be at the hotel if you want me." Thad took off, walking down the dark road toward town. He spoke to the dog trotting along beside him.

"Tonight you earned your keep, Fertile. Tomorrow I just might go to the butcher shop and buy you a beefsteak."

Chapter 8

Jill entered the brightly lit lobby of the hotel, nodded to Elmer and went down the hallway to the bathroom. The two roomers on the ground floor also used the room. She was relieved to find the OCCUPIED sign on the door turned over so only the back was showing. Inside she groped for the pull chain to turn on the light.

Her mind was still trying to grasp the meaning of what she and Thad had seen out on that dark road. She gazed at herself in the small mirror above the washbasin for a long moment, holding on to the hope that there would be a logical explanation for what they had seen. She looked down at her hand, curled her fingers and shuddered.

Shaking her head in an attempt to banish the vision that danced before her eyes, Jill washed her hands, splashed water on her face and dried it on the roller towel. After smoothing her short blond hair with her palms, she left the bathroom.

Quietly she opened the door of her aunt's room, tiptoed inside and stood for a minute in the darkness. If her aunt was awake she would speak to her. After a bit of silence, Jill soundlessly backed out, closed the door and went to the lobby to wait for Thad.

Elmer and Rose were sitting behind the counter talking in low tones. Rose stood up.

"I looked in on Aunt Justine, Mrs. Evans. I'm going to sit over here and read the newspaper . . . before someone carries it off." Jill picked up the Tulsa paper left by one of their guests and went to the far corner of the lobby to sit down facing the door.

An hour passed. No longer able to use the paper as an excuse for being there, Jill folded it and placed it on the chair beside her. With her hands clasped in her lap, she stared out the window, knowing that the Evanses were probably wondering about her odd behavior.

There wasn't much activity on the street. The restaurant across from the hotel was dark. It closed early on Sunday night. An occasional car or wagon went by. Several men passed on the walk, going home or to a rooming house.

Thad, where are you?

She heard the mournful whistle of the Rock Island train as it approached the station from the north and again as it left town. Twenty minutes later two salesmen carrying large sample cases came into the hotel seeking a room for the night. Shortly after they went upstairs to their rooms, Thad came in from the hallway leading to the kitchen. He beckoned to her. She followed him to the porch.

As soon as they were outside, Thad took her hand, led her to a bench and pulled her down beside him.

"I had to wash. I couldn't touch you or myself until I washed. Not that I touched *it.* When we had to, we used an old newspaper the sheriff had in the car." Without conscious thought he had arched his arm over her head, put it around her and drawn her close. He was tired and shaken. He needed the comfort of being close to her. "It was a sight I hope never to see again."

"Did you find the rest . . . of her?"

"The sheriff and I dug up what was

there . . ." His voice trailed. Thad pressed Jill's head to his chest and spoke with his lips in her hair. "He'd cut her up with a saw," he whispered. "All of her was there except her head and . . . he had cut off her breasts . . . sliced them off."

"Oh, Thad—"

"We leveled the dirt pile but didn't find them."

"How awful." Jill stroked his arm in an attempt to comfort him.

"I stayed there with her while the sheriff went to fetch the doctor and the undertaker." Thad's arms tightened around Jill and unconsciously rocked her back and forth. "She was a young woman, honey. About your age." Jill heard the horror in his voice and could feel the shudders that passed through him. "The sheriff didn't think she'd been there very long."

"Poor thing. They won't know who she is."

"Whoever did this is a lunatic. No sane person could have done such a thing. I'm worried about you being here in this place where there is so much craziness." His voice became demandingly gruff.

"He may not have been from here."

"This lunatic knew what he was doing. He was handy with a knife. He may have done it before and may do it again. He's a sick son-of-a-bitch," he ground out angrily.

"I'm glad you're here."

"So am I. I'll not let you out of my sight until that bastard is caught!" He spoke with a strong tremor in his voice. "Don't buck me on this, Jill."

"I'll not buck you. But it's unreasonable for you to think you have to keep me in sight. I'm smart enough not to take any chances. Oh, Thad—what about Radna? She goes off somewhere at night. She's always back when I get up in the morning."

"We'll tell her. It will be all over town by morning. There's no way to hush up something like this."

"While I was waiting for you, I was thinking that you were with me both times when horrible things have happened to me: that time in the woods and now this."

Thad was silent for a minute, then he said, "Maybe I'm bad luck."

"No! You know better than that! You saved me then. I'll always love you for what you did." She pulled back, put her hand on his cheek and turned his head so that she could look into his dark face. "Hear me, Thad. I'll always be grateful that you were there."

"I just happened to be there, honey. I don't deserve any credit for doing what any man would have done under the same circumstance."

"You were just a boy. You tackled a man and could have been killed."

Time seemed to stand still, as did his heart. He gazed down at her parted lips. Was this the time? Should he kiss her? She answered the questions for him. His heart plummeted.

"No girl ever had better brothers than you and Joe and Jack." She spoke earnestly and stroked his cheek with her fingertips. "I hate it that you had to go with the sheriff. This has been horrible for you. Will you have nightmares?"

"Probably." He captured her hand in his. "We'd better go in and tell Elmer and his wife. We'll tell him to keep that shotgun under the counter loaded." Then, after they had stood up, "I'm not staying up there in the attic with you two stories below. I'll bring down a cot and put it up in the kitchen. I'll be near you."

"You don't need to do—"

"You promised not to buck me."

"I did? I don't remember that."

By midmorning the town was abuzz with the news about the cut-up body of a woman having been found south of town.

Mayor Henshaw knocked on Hunter Westfall's door while Hunter was at breakfast. Obviously shaken after just viewing the body, the mayor called Hunter out onto the porch and gave him a brief rundown on what had happened.

"I wish to God I'd never looked at it. Doc said she'd been treated badly before she was killed."

"In what way?"

"Her . . . ah . . . privates were, ah . . . damaged. Doc found bite marks on her stomach and buttocks. The bastard sliced off her breasts clean as a whistle. They been searching since daylight for her head."

"Jesus Christ! It would take a monster to do such a thing. Does the sheriff have any idea who she is?"

"We don't know who she is or who did this dreadful thing. Doc said that she was a young woman, slender and medium height."

"What's the sheriff doing about it?"

"Asking about missing women. He asked me to tell you to talk to your men in charge of the crews. Find out if anyone failed to show up for work and ask if one of their womenfolk is missing. Doc says the murderer was good with a knife and that there has to be a bloody mess somewhere because he didn't do it out where they found her."

"She could have been killed in another town and brought here."

"The sheriff seems to think that whoever did this wanted her found. The grave was shallow. A good stiff wind would have leveled that sand dune and uncovered the remains."

"Has the sheriff asked for outside help?"

"He was trying to get through to the U.S. marshal's office in Oklahoma City."

"Come in for a cup of coffee, Orvis."

"Thanks, but I'll get on back to the store. I just wanted you to know what was going on before you went uptown. This will stir up folks aplenty."

"I appreciate your coming by."

The mayor walked briskly down the walk toward town and Hunter went into the kitchen where Dinah was cleaning a chicken. Her knowing eyes searched his face. Something had shocked her boy.

"What done happen now? Yo is lookin' like yo seed a ghosty."

"The body of a murdered woman was found out south of town."

"Lawsey mercy!" Dinah dunked her hands in the washbasin and dried them on a towel. She clicked her tongue against the roof of her mouth and shook her head. "These is bad times. I ain't knowin' what dis world is comin' to. Who is she? Does they know who did it?"

"They don't know who she is. He cut off her head," Hunter said tightly. "If they find who did it, he'll be hanged before they get him to jail."

"Ah . . . lawsey!" Dinah's hands went into the air.

"I'm worried about Carsie. I wish she hadn't left so suddenly."

"Yo think it could be Miz Carsie?"

"I don't know what to think. Later this morning I'll call down to Tulsa and see if she's there. She may have gone home or taken the train to Kansas City."

"Is yo—" Dinah started to say something, but cut it off when she heard a knock on the back door. "It's Miz Hopper wid yore shirts."

"I'll get them."

Hunter opened the screen door and looked into a pair of large violet eyes beneath a head of dark curly hair. The girl, tall and slim as a reed, had wire hangers looped over her hand and hanging from them were his freshly ironed shirts. She held them out to him.

"I didn't bring back one of them. I'm trying to get a spot out." She spoke in a soft southern voice.

Hunter took the shirts, but for once he was completely speechless. His eyes fastened on the most beautiful face he'd ever seen.

"Lawd, chile, yo done a fine job." Dinah edged Hunter aside, took the hangers from his hand and hung the shirts on the knob of the door.

"Thank you. I'll bring the other shirt in the morning." The girl turned to go.

"Wait," Hunter said quickly. "Come in. No need for you to leave without your pay."

"Thank you, but my little girl is in the wagon. Dinah can pay me tomorrow."

Hunter had been so busy looking at the girl he hadn't seen the wooden wagon on the walk. He glanced at it now and saw a dark-haired child sitting in it on a blanket. Both the mother and the daughter were beautiful. How had it happened that he'd not seen her before?

"I'll watch her while you get your pay." Hunter went to the wagon and squatted down. "Hello, there." He held out his finger. The child grasped it and tried to put it in her mouth. He laughed and tickled her under the chin.

Tight black curls framed the baby's face. She had bright blue eyes, rosy cheeks and a soft little mouth. Her little dress was a faded blue check and her shoes had holes in the toes, but she smelled fresh, sweet and clean.

"You're just as pretty as a picture." Hunter wiped some drool off the child's chin with his handkerchief.

"She's teething." The soft voice came from above him and Hunter became aware again of the child's mother standing beside him. He stood and looked down into violet eyes, deep violet beautiful eyes, surrounded by long, spiky black lashes.

"How old is she?"

"A year and a half."

"She's a beauty," he said and meant it.

"Thank you. I think so." The woman took the wagon handle and turned the cart around. "Hold on, Mary," she cautioned.

"Is that her name? Mary?" Hunter stood on the walk, reluctant for them to leave but unable to think of a reason for them to stay.

"Mary Pat. Mary for my mother and Pat for my father."

"It suits her."

Laura smiled. She pulled the wagon around the side of the house and disappeared. Hunter stood there for a moment longer with a strange feeling stirring inside him, then went back up onto the porch. Dinah was frowning at him when he came into the kitchen.

"What's her name?"

"Laura Hopper. Now, Mistah Hunter, dat girl ain't one of dem play toys like Miss Carsie. Dat girl's had her a heap a trouble and what her needs is a marryin' man to help her wid dat young'un."

"How long has she been doing my shirts?"

"Month, maybe. Her mama brings 'um sometimes. Dey work at Miz Byers's hotel."

"Who's the baby's daddy?"

"Ain't got one. Her man got hisself kilt out on one of dem oil wells."

She wasn't married. Hunter felt a spurt of elation.

"Did he work for me?"

"I ain't knowin'."

"Where does she live?"

"Down dat road what goes by dey lumberyard. What yo wantin' to know dat for? Yo ain't a marryin' man, Mistah Hunter. Yo done tol' me dat and tol' me dat. So doan yo go be honeyin' up to no gal like she is. Yo know yo can get in dat gal's drawers if'n yo sets yo mind," she scoffed. "Her ain't got no business rompin' 'round up dere in yo bed when she got dat young'un to see to."

"You worry too much about whose drawers I get into, Dinah." He smiled fondly at his dear friend, pinched her cheek and left the room.

"Mind me, now," Dinah called. "Dat girl ain't one of dem fast women yo play wid. Lawsey me," she muttered to herself, "dat man be the beatin'est I ever did see when he sets his mind. Someday he goin' to meet a woman dat's goin' to turn 'im inside out an' upside down. I hope I's here to see it."

Lloyd Madison walked down the street toward the sheriff's office and met the mayor as he was turning to go into his store.

"Morning, Lloyd. You've heard the news?"

"About the . . . woman? I heard it at the restaurant. 'Bout ruined my breakfast."

"Terrible thing. Terrible."

"Any idea who she was?"

"It's hard to tell without a head. They're out there searching for it around that sand dune where they found the rest of her."

"It's hell of a note when a woman is killed like that. Won't do the town any good, that's sure. I'm on my way to volunteer my services to the sheriff. I had an investigative course in law school."

"I'm sure that he'll welcome any help he can get. This is a sad day for Rainwater. Last night over at the billiard parlor a fellow lopped off a man's thumb because he thought he was cheating—held his hand down on the table and whacked it off before he knew what was happening. Both of them were all likkered up."

"Was he arrested?"

"Sittin' in jail right now."

"That's a start. I heard the woman was cut up. Not many are that handy with a knife." Lloyd squinted down at the mayor. "Didn't we pass an ordinance closing the pool halls on Sunday?"

"Ha! Try to enforce it and you'd have a riot on your hands. What do you think men are going to do on Sunday? Twiddle their thumbs?"

"They could go to church."

"Bullshit!" the mayor snorted. "Use your head. They work all week and I don't fault them for playing a little cards on Sunday."

"The law is the law. They shouldn't be breaking it," Lloyd insisted.

"I suppose you won't want Westfall's amusement park open on Sunday."

"The council voted to close amusements on Sunday. The sheriff's job is to enforce the law."

"Lloyd, I've not got time to argue with you today. You'd do us all a favor if you'd talk to the council and get that stupid law off the books."

"Don't count on me to do that, Orvis." Lloyd started up the walk. "For us Christians, Sunday is the Sabbath and God said to keep it holy."

"And for the Jews it's Saturday. Do you want us to close the stores on Saturday?"

Standing on the porch steps of his store, Mayor Henshaw watched the young lawyer walk down the street. He was a good man, he had to admit, even if he was a radical about law and religion. He didn't seem to be as money hungry as some, just too damn straitlaced for his own good. Too bad he couldn't find a nice girl and settle here permanently. When the oil boom was over, Rainwater would need men like him if it was going to survive.

Sheriff Page was hanging up the telephone when Lloyd walked into the office.

"Howdy, Lloyd." The sheriff looked as if he hadn't slept for a week.

"Morning, Sheriff."

"What do you want, Lloyd? I'm warning you. Don't give me any hassle about the pool hall being open yesterday. I've got enough shit to wade through this morning."

The door to the cell room was flung open before Lloyd could answer. He stepped back out of the way as Deputy Franklin prodded two handcuffed prisoners into the room ahead of him. Both stared at the floor, obviously sick from their drinking spree.

"I'll take these two on over to the judge."

"Get them out of here before they puke on the floor. If they can't pay the fine, bring them back in through the back door. I don't want to look at them anymore today," the sheriff growled.

"Bad mood, Sheriff?" Lloyd asked as soon as the men were out the door.

"Goddamn right. You want to make something out of it?"

"No, just kidding, Sheriff." Lloyd held up his hands. "Sorry if my humor didn't sit right. Just trying to brighten things up a bit."

"Get to the reason for the visit, Lloyd. I've been up all night, seen things that turned my stomach, and I'm in no mood for kiddin' or small talk."

"I can understand that. I stopped by to see if there was anything I could do. I've had some experience in this sort of thing. Took a class while I was going to law school."

"An officer recommended by the United States marshal is coming up from Oklahoma City. He'll be in charge . . . once he gets here. And that's all right with me. You can talk to him then, if you've still got a mind to."

"That knife-happy fellow you've got in the back room could be someone to start with. Orvis told me the girl was cut up pretty bad."

"Cut up? Hell, she was butchered. Fellow that did it knew what he was doing. Bet my life he's done it before."

"There you are. A fellow that can whack off a man's thumb with one stroke has had some practice." Lloyd went to the door. "Good luck with your hunt, Sheriff."

"We'll need more than luck to catch this son-of-a-bitch," the sheriff answered without looking up.

Later, in his office, Lloyd polished his glasses with a clean white handkerchief and in his mind reviewed the events of the past few days with satisfaction.

So far, so good. Things were working out well. Very well, indeed.

*   *   *

Hunter Westfall had only two men working in his office in Rainwater. One was the bookkeeper and the other was a young man who acted as jack-of-all-trades. Perry Reade wrote letters, ran errands, took phone messages and even kept track of the women Hunter amused himself with. Conrad, the bookkeeper, kept meticulous records of the money that passed through Hunter's hands.

Both men were exceedingly loyal to Hunter, and he paid for their loyalty with generous salaries.

"Perry, see if you can get Carsie Bakken on the phone. She had a temper fit Saturday night and left while I was at the merchants' meeting. She's been gone two days and I've not heard from her."

"Shall I call Tulsa or Kansas City?"

"Call Tulsa first. She left about the time the southbound train went through."

Fifteen minutes later Perry came to the door of Hunter's private office.

"I called two numbers in Tulsa and the one in Kansas City. Miss Bakken isn't at either place."

Hunter sat quietly for a moment. "She wouldn't have stayed in town. She didn't know anyone here. Lord, I hope the woman they found wasn't Carsie."

"What makes you think it could be?"

"Just a feeling. She left Saturday night. You know how wild she is. She could have taken up with some deranged person and come to a bad end. The body was found Sunday night. Doc didn't think that she'd been dead long. And Carsie hasn't called. By now she would have been sorry she left and would be wanting to come back." Hunter put on his hat. "I'm going down to the funeral parlor to talk to Mr. Kyle and see if they are any closer to finding out who she was." At the door he turned to Perry. "I want you to find out everything you can about a woman named Laura Hopper. Her husband was killed out on a rig. I don't know when. She's got a child about a year and a half."

As soon as the door closed behind Hunter, Conrad said to Perry Reade, "That man goes through women like I go through a pack of cigarettes."

Perry shrugged. "So would I, if I had what he has."

On the street in front of the stores, Hunter nodded to a few people but didn't linger. He walked past the furniture store and entered a small adjacent building with dusty black curtains on the windows and four rows of chairs. Mr. Kyle, the undertaker, encouraged the use of one of the churches for funerals with over thirty mourners.

Hunter rapped on the door to the back room. After a brief delay, Mr. Kyle opened it. He was wiping his hands on a towel. Hunter made no apology for disturbing him but got right to his reason for being there.

"Are you any closer to identifying the body of the woman found out south of town?"

"No. It's kind of hard to identify a person without a head. I've got nine pieces of her in there but that doesn't tell us who she was."

"Oh, Lord." Hunter took several quick deep breaths. "Did you find any birthmarks?" he asked.

"Mr. Westfall, the sheriff has given me strict orders not to give out any information. I'm sorry."

"That's all right. I'm sorry I asked, Mr. Kyle. I should have gone directly to the sheriff. I'll do that now." Hunter put his fingers to the brim of his hat, left the funeral parlor and headed down the street. Dammit, if Kyle had said that there were no birthmarks on the body, it would have saved him from going to the sheriff.

Hunter saw Lloyd Madison leave the sheriff's office as he approached it. He was relieved that the lawyer headed in the other direction. Something about the man disturbed him, and it wasn't the red splotch on his face. It had to do with the way he sat back, listened, then jumped in to defend something or someone, regardless of right or wrong. It was as if his mission in life were to make Rainwater a paradise on earth, where good prevailed and evil was punished. Madison, Hunter was sure, would do everything he could to prevent him from building the amusement park even if it would be good for the town.

Sheriff Page looked at him with tired, bloodshot eyes when he walked into the office.

"This place has been as busy as a free whorehouse this morning," he growled. "I've had everyone in here that could walk on two legs."

"Morning, Sheriff. I know you've got a lot on your mind, but I just want to know if the body you found had a birthmark; a dark brown spot shaped like a butterfly."

"Why do you ask?"

"Mind if I sit down?"

"Have a seat. What's on your mind?"

"A lady friend from Tulsa has been staying at my house," Hunter said after he pulled a straight chair up to the side of the desk and sat down. "She up and left Saturday night while I was at the merchants' meeting. I haven't been able to get in touch with her and when I heard about the body . . . well, I'm worried about her."

"Hummm." Sheriff Page leaned back in his swivel chair. "Your lady friend had a birthmark?"

"Yes. Carsie had a dark brown spot shaped like a butterfly about the size of a half dollar on her lower abdomen." Hunter watched the sheriff swivel back and forth in his chair. When a minute passed and the sheriff didn't say anything, Hunter took out his handkerchief and wiped his forehead. "God, Sheriff. Say something. Tell me that there isn't a birthmark on that body."

"You saw it many times, huh?"

"I'll not beat around the bush. Carsie was a prostitute. A high-class one. She came to visit for one reason only and I saw her naked many times." Hunter looked the sheriff in the eye. He hated exposing his personal life, but it couldn't be helped.

"You'd recognize such a mark."

"The body you found . . . had one? Oh, Lord!" Hunter turned and looked out the window while he composed himself.

"The body had a mark," the sheriff said to his back. "You'll have to look at it to know if she was your lady friend."

"I don't know . . . if I can."

"You'll have to, and the sooner, the better. I'll go over with you to take a look." Sheriff Page got up and put on his hat. "Let's go out the back." He led the way past the cell block, where one prisoner lay snoring on a bunk, and out into the bright sunlight.

Hunter walked beside the sheriff. A part of him wished that he had stayed in his office and tended to his own business. The other part desperately wanted to know if Carsie had been the victim of a vicious killer.

"An officer from Oklahoma City will be here by late afternoon." It was the only comment the sheriff made until they reached the funeral parlor, where he knocked sharply on the back door.

Ernest Kyle opened the door and they

stepped inside. The sharp odor of embalm-
ing fluid stung Hunter's nostrils and his
heart began a mad dance in his chest. *God,
don't let it be Carsie.* He didn't love her or
even like her very much, but he had known
her body very well. She had been a willing
and daring partner in their sexual games.

"There's not much I can do with body
parts but keep them packed in ice." Kyle's
voice came to Hunter as if from a distance,
then the sheriff's.

"Mr. Westfall would like to see the
woman's lower abdomen. No use him seeing the rest of her."

"I've got her here in the back room where
it's cool. Ice melts so damn fast in this
weather. I had a hundred pounds brought in
this morning. Is the county going to pay for
it, Ira?"

The sheriff grunted something, then said,
"We'll wait until you uncover her."

"There's not really much to see." Ernest
switched on an overhead light.

In the middle of the room was a waist-
high table with a canvas-wrapped bundle
on it. The legs of the table had been lifted
on one end. A bucket sat on the floor beneath it to catch the water dripping from the

melting ice. The undertaker removed a clamp from the middle of the canvas and drew it back. He looked over his shoulder and motioned to the two men in the door-way.

Hunter approached and gazed down. His view was from the navel to the pubic hair. He closed his eyes when he saw what he feared he would see, then opened them again to be sure. The brown spot approximately two inches above the dark pubic hair left no doubt in his mind that it was Carsie, yet he was compelled to see more.

"May I see one of her hands?"

The undertaker pulled back a piece of the canvas. After glancing down at the curled fingers with long pointed fingernails, Hunter turned away and headed for the door.

"It's her." His voice came out with a croaking sound he didn't recognize himself. Hunter kept his back turned while the sheriff spoke to the undertaker.

"Not a word to anyone about that brown spot, Ernest. You and the doctor, me and Westfall are the only ones who know about it besides the killer. It may be a way to trip him up.

"It's a relief to know who she was, Mr.

Westfall," the sheriff continued. "Thank you for coming forward. Come on back to the office and I'll write down the particulars. The officer will want to talk to you when he gets here."

Justine was told about the murdered woman after Radna finished feeding her breakfast. Jill left the telling to Thad, while she stood in the doorway of her aunt's room so that she could keep an eye on the front desk.

"Ah, law. The poor girl." Justine's voice trembled. A scared look came into her eyes. She seemed to shrink down in the bed. "There's never been a woman murdered here that I know of."

"We don't know how she was murdered. I pray to God that she was dead before he started cutting her up." Thad had a hard time saying the words, just as he had a hard time getting out of his head the vision of those white limbs lying in the dirt.

When Justine tried to lift her hand, Thad took it gently in both of his big rough ones.

"You'll stay, won't you, Thad?" There was a pleading look in her eyes.

"Of course I'll stay. You couldn't get me

out of here with a winch and a towline," he said in an attempt to lighten the tension. "I'd be out of my mind to leave when I've got three good meals a day and three pretty women fussing over me."

Jill snorted, rolling her eyes to the ceiling, then said, "Because the man killed once doesn't mean he'll do it again. It may have been an accident and he was afraid to report it, so he . . . tried to dispose of . . . the body."

"He may have brought it from Tulsa or some other place," Radna suggested. Jill had thought her unshakable, but she had showed signs of fear when told about the murdered woman.

"I'm staying. I'm not willing to take the chance." Thad ran his fingers through his hair. "I'm not trying to scare you ladies; but a man who would do such a thing has got to be crazy, and you can't predict what a crazy person will do."

"I'll start wearing my pistol again," Radna said. "I used to wear one all the time."

"Good idea, if you don't shoot yourself in the foot."

This time it was Justine who snorted.

"Radna can outshoot any man in town. I've seen her in action."

"Is that so?" Thad cast an admiring glance at Radna. "It's a comfort to know I've got a backup. Are there other guns in the hotel besides that shotgun out under the front desk?"

Radna and Justine looked at each other. "I have a six-shooter under the mattress," Justine said. "I don't know why: I couldn't use it."

"I put it there," Radna said.

"Why do you have a gun, Aunt Justine?"

"Habit, honey. This was rough country when I first came here." Then: "Is Nettie cleaning the rooms?"

Radna answered, "She started cleaning as soon as the first guest left. Laura is in the wash house."

"The wash lady is here? I'd better get out there and be sure the washer is working." Thad stopped beside Jill as he left the room. "Stick close. I'll be right back."

Jill threw up her hands. "Oh, for goodness' sakes." Then she complained in low tones to her aunt, "He's carrying this stick-close thing too far. The next thing I know, he'll be standing outside the lavatory when one of us goes in there."

"I heard that." Thad had come back to stand behind Jill. His hands gripped her shoulders to keep her from turning and hitting him. "It's a good idea. Call out the next time you ladies have to use it and I'll guard that door with my life." Shaking with laughter, he followed Radna into the kitchen.

Chapter 9

"Oh . . ." Laura let out a cry of alarm when she looked up and saw Thad's large frame filling the doorway of the wash house. With a look of fright on her face, she hastily backed up to put herself between the big dark man and the wagon where her little girl lay asleep on a pillow.

"Sorry. I didn't mean to scare you. I'm staying here at the hotel and helping out for a while. I've been repairing the washing machine and the wringer. Is it working all right?" When she only stared at him, he said, "Ah, hell. I don't blame you for being scared after what has happened." Thad stepped out of the wash house and yelled, "Radna!"

"What? What's wrong?" Radna came running out onto the porch. The door slammed behind her, scaring the dog, who scurried under the porch.

"Come out here and tell this girl she doesn't have to be afraid of me."

"Is that what you're yelling about?" Radna stepped off the porch and came down the slat-plank walk. She looked up at Thad and winked. "A girl would have to be out of her mind not to be afraid of you."

"You're not."

"I'm not young and pretty."

"Ha! You're sure not old and *ugly.*"

"Are you flirting with me?"

"You bet! The girl is scared of me, Radna. Tell her I'm harmless."

"You want me to lie? Oh, all right."

Thad enjoyed his exchanges with Radna. She was bright and always had a witty comeback. He followed her into the wash house.

"Laura, this is Thad Taylor. He's from Justine's hometown back in Missouri. He's helping out here for a while. He's harmless but a big flirt. Take everything he says with a grain of salt. If he gets fresh, threaten to tell Jill. That'll cool him off because he's crazy about her." Radna's head barely came to Thad's shoulder. She tilted her chin to look up at him. "You didn't think I knew that, did you, *Buster*?"

"Doesn't surprise me a bit." Thad couldn't help but return her grin. His eyes found the girl backed up to the wagon. "Is the washer working all right?"

"I've not started it."

"I fixed the wringer. It worked when I put a dry shirt through it."

"Is Mary Pat asleep?" Radna went to the wagon, bent down and smoothed the dark curls back from the baby's forehead.

"She's tired. We were up early this morning." Laura's voice was barely above a whisper. Her eyes went anxiously to Thad as he moved into the room.

"I'd think that she'd fall out of the wagon."

"I have to tie her in when she's awake. She doesn't like that very much."

"I'd not like to be tied down, either." Radna looked up at Thad, who stood behind her gazing down at the sleeping child. "Mr. Handyman, can you fix a little pen for her out in the shade? Before long it'll be too hot for her in here."

"Sure. I'll pound some stakes in the ground and get some chicken wire. My friend back in Fertile made a pen like that for his boy who was about the same size."

"And she needs a bucket of sand to play in." Radna picked up the child's little hand and placed it on her palm.

"Is she walking?" Thad asked.

"Running is more like it," Laura said with pride. A smile lightened her violet eyes. "I have to get as much done as I can while she's asleep."

"Here's the rest of it." Mrs. Cole crowded into the wash house with an armload of bedsheets. Laura went to meet her and relieve her of the bundle. "I'll be finished in there in another hour and be out to help you."

"Let me know if you have trouble with the wringer." Thad backed out the door, went to the hotel porch and scratched the dog's head while he waited for Radna, then followed her into the kitchen.

"That girl out there is as skittish as a wild colt. I was afraid she was going to fly out the door."

"Since her husband was killed, Laura hardly shows her face in town. When she does, every horny male who gets a look at her beats a path to her door."

"Why would they do that? She didn't look like a loose woman to me."

"She's not a loose woman." The tone of Radna's voice made that perfectly clear. "She's a nice girl with heavy loads on her shoulders. One of them is keeping food in that baby's mouth and the other is being sinfully beautiful, which draws men like flies to a honey pot. Didn't you notice?"

"Now that you mention it, she is pretty."

"Oh, Lord. You've got a worse case than I thought." Radna filled the dishpan with water from the teakettle and then dropped in a bar of P&G soap.

"What do you mean by that?" He looked at her with a puzzled expression.

"You're so smitten with Jill you can't see beyond your nose."

"Of course I like Jill. Love her, even. She's like a little sister to me—"

"Don't give me that sister hockey, *Buster.* You're nuts about her. But back to Laura. I don't know why she married a no-account like Bradley Hopper in the first place. Some say that he forced her and got her pregnant. She's never said. Anyway, one night he got stinking drunk, climbed a derrick up to the crown block and fell fifty feet to the ground.

Killed him deader than a doornail. I think that God did it as a favor to Laura."

"Holy smoke! I'd better go out there and take another look at her. If she's that good-looking and doesn't talk much, I might be missing out on something. I like a woman who doesn't give me a lot of sass, not like a certain pint-sized, black-haired, smart-talkin' female I know."

After Mr. Evans and his wife came to take over the front desk, Jill fed her aunt, then she ate supper at the kitchen table with Radna and Thad.

"Did you hear any news about the murder when you went to the store?" Radna asked the question while she filled their glasses with iced tea.

"Nothing new except that an officer is coming up from Oklahoma City. The sheriff isn't giving out any news, so the old news is being hashed and rehashed. Everyone has an opinion on who she was and who killed her."

"I suppose they think it was a crazy Indian that did it." Radna sat down and pushed the plate of cornbread across the table to Thad.

"How'd you guess?"

Radna rolled her eyes. "Any fool would know that an Indian would have taken her scalp, not her whole head."

"What else are they saying?" Jill asked.

"That it was done by someone who escaped from the insane asylum."

"I can believe that."

Thad helped himself to a serving of cornbread. "Radna, you make darn good cornbread. My mama would love you. Are you spoken for?"

"I thought you were going to marry Laura." Radna saw the hand that lifted the fork to Jill's mouth hesitate.

"She turned me down." Thad's eyes, shining with amusement, were on Radna and didn't see the loss of color and the stunned expression on Jill's face.

"Poor Thad. I guess it's up to you, Jill."

"I'm not so desperate that I'd take someone's leftovers," Jill said sharply. "I don't play second fiddle to anyone." She got up and took her plate to the dishpan.

"Hey, you can't be finished. You didn't eat much."

Thad's chiding voice irritated her. Jill's lashes momentarily screened her eyes. A blush colored her cheeks, so recently pale, with flattering color. Her mind not understanding the sinking feeling in the pit of her stomach, Jill ignored him.

"I'll sit awhile with Aunt Justine," she said to Radna and left the kitchen.

"What got into her?" Thad's brows lowered over his puzzled eyes.

"Oh, Lord," Radna exclaimed. "Men are so dumb."

Jill managed not to be alone with Thad for the rest of the evening. As soon as Radna came to sit with Justine, she went to her room, undressed and washed, using the small basin on her washstand. When finished, she put on her nightdress and turned off the light. Instead of getting into bed, she raised the window shade and looked out at the star-studded sky.

All day she had suffered a growing homesickness for the peace and quiet of the farm back in Missouri. Her eyes filled with the tears she had kept at bay since supper.

There were so many people in this place that she couldn't step out onto the porch, either front or back, without seeing someone or someone seeing her. She couldn't walk down the street without some man in oily clothes wanting to talk to her or walk beside her.

She was lonesome for her family.

Visions of home flashed before her eyes. She wondered what her sister Julie was doing. Did Jack and Jason, her brothers, miss her? Was her daddy cutting hay? Thad was dear and familiar. Was that the reason she'd begun to have romantic thoughts about him?

Trying to think of him objectively, Jill realized that he was an exceedingly attractive man with a way about him that would endear him to any woman. He was protective, amusing, and when he talked to a woman he gave her his full attention, as if she were the only woman in the world.

Laura must have been impressed. Of course, he was teasing about her turning him down. He was far too smooth to try to court her on such a short acquaintance, but Radna must have had some basis for saying that Thad wanted to marry Laura.

He had spent a couple of hours making a pen in the shade of the wash house for Laura's little girl. When he was finished, he lifted the child over the fence. He and Laura watched the little girl toddle around enjoying her new freedom. How could a woman not fall in love with a man who was as handsome, kind and gentle as Thad?

What in the world was she thinking of? She wasn't in love with Thad. He sure wasn't in love with her.

Impatient with her thoughts, Jill went to bed, hoping that she might switch off images of Thad with Laura. Rather than being dispelled, they seemed to intensify as she lay there. She tossed restlessly as visions of the beautiful dark-haired children Laura and Thad could have filled her mind. Her body was tired, but her mind refused to shut down.

Finally, when she fell into a fitful sleep, she dreamed of being lost on the prairie and being found by a man with a long knife. His white hair stood up in spikes all over his head and his eyes glowed like fire. More frightened than she'd ever been in her life, she screamed and ran through high grass that twisted around her ankles.

A large man ahead of her blocked her way. She couldn't get around him. Her feet became so heavy she could hardly lift them. The man with the knife reached for her. His hand touched her shoulder. She awakened and sat up with a cry of fright. A dark shadow loomed over her.

"No! Get away!" she shrieked and lashed out at the hard body with her fists.

"Jill, it's me, Thad." His hands gripped her shoulders. "Wake up, honey."

"Thad?"

"What scared you, sweetheart?" He sat down on the edge of the bed and pulled her into his arms. "Was it the fire bells? They woke me and I heard you cry out."

Jill's breathing was short and shallow with fright. It felt so good to be against his chest, enclosed in his arms. Her arms locked around him as if she were being swept out to sea. She couldn't seem to get close enough to him. She burrowed her face in the curve of his neck and gulped for breath. He was warm and solid and . . . safe.

"You're all right." His voice was soft and raspy. "Sweet girl, you're all right." Her breasts, soft against his naked chest and the wetness of her tears on his neck, were now causing his heart to do funny things. It had taken off like a runaway train when he heard her cry out.

"I was so . . . scared—"

"Don't cry, honey. You're safe here with me." His hand caressed her back and pressed her to him.

"I didn't hear the fire bell," she whispered when her heart slowed enough so that she could speak. "I had a bad dream. A man . . . was chasing me with a knife."

"You cried out. It scared me to death, sweetheart." He brushed the damp hair back from her face.

"I'm sorry I woke you."

"I'm not a bit sorry, honey. Do you want me to turn on the light?"

"No. I'm glad you're here."

"I'm glad I moved that cot down, blocking the hall. Anyone trying to get to you would have to climb over me."

"I'm . . . homesick, Thad." The words came out on a sob. Her voice was a ragged whisper and so sad that it tore at his heart.

"Ah . . . honey. This is the first time you've been away from home. It's natural to be homesick."

"I miss Papa and Julie and . . . the kids."

"I'm sure they miss you, too."

"I . . . don't like it here."

"I'm not crazy about it, either," he whispered with his cheek against her hair.

"I can't leave."

"No, we can't leave. We've got to think of your aunt. She may not be with you much longer. She's alone except for Radna, and she needs you. You can hold out awhile longer, can't you?"

"I have to. And I'll not let her know that . . . I wish I was home."

"That's my girl. Joe will be here in a few days." She lay against him, docile and unmoving, lifeless as a rag doll. "He'll be bringing Blue with him. He's the Kickapoo Indian I told you about. With three of us here, there isn't a chance anyone could get to you."

"I'm not worried about that," she murmured. "I don't like being with so many people. It's like someone is watching me all the time."

"That's because you're so pretty. Everyone wants to look at you."

"I don't believe . . . that."

"I believe it. Now, whose opinion is more important?" he teased.

"Do you think Laura is pretty?"

"Yeah. She's pretty."

Jill tried to pull back, but his arms held her tight. "I'm all right now. You can go back to bed."

"Don't you like it here in my arms?" he whispered.

"I don't want to be a . . . bother."

A low masculine growl purred in his throat and he pressed his lips to her forehead.

"You're anything but that."

Thad didn't want to leave her. He wanted to lie down on the bed and hold her for the rest of the night. The feeling he had for her now was tenderness. She was no longer the sassy Jill he had known most of her life, nor the one who had ripped into a gang of rough men on the street corner. The woman he held so lovingly against him was his Jill, the girl who was beginning to mean the world to him.

"I want to hold you. Go to sleep, little love." He cuddled her in his arms, holding her firmly against him, kissing the top of her head.

Minutes passed, or it could have been half an hour, before he was sure that she was asleep. He reluctantly eased her back down on the pillow. The light from the moon came through the window and shone on her face. Thad stood for a long moment looking down at her. She murmured something and wedged her palm beneath her cheek.

Thad didn't want to stop looking at her. This was the first time since he had come to Rainwater that he had been able to look his fill without her knowing it. He liked her large eyes, closed now, with thick lashes lying on her cheeks. He liked the tangle of blond curls that stuck to her cheeks. He liked her sassiness, her spunk. He especially liked her full expressive mouth, the way the corners tilted up when she smiled. He wanted desperately to kiss her.

Little sweetheart, you could break my heart.

He left her with a kiss placed lightly on her soft lips. Then, feeling guilty for taking advantage of her vulnerability, he went back to his cot in the hallway, leaving the door to her room slightly ajar.

Morning came, and with it the news that during the night Lloyd Madison's house had burned to the ground and at two o'clock in the morning he had moved into a room at the hotel.

When Justine learned that Elmer Evans had checked him in and given him the big upstairs corner room, Jill feared that her aunt would swoon. Her face turned white and then red with anger.

"I don't want him here!"

"He paid for a whole month, Aunty."

"I don't care. Get him out!"

"I don't . . . understand—"

"Thad! Thad!" Justine yelled.

Thad came running in from the kitchen to see Jill standing helplessly beside her aunt's bed with a bewildered look on her face.

"Thad, they rented a room to that . . . to that—" Justine's breath caught in her throat and she couldn't finish, so Jill helped her.

"Elmer rented the upstairs room to Lloyd Madison, the man whose house burned last night. Aunt Justine doesn't want him here."

"Well, in that case, we'll tell him to go."

At that moment a knock sounded and Lloyd Madison appeared in the open doorway.

"Morning," he said cheerfully. "May I come in?"

"No! Get out!" Justine shouted.

Lloyd ignored the outburst and held his

hand out to Thad. "I'm Lloyd Madison. I don't believe I've met you."

"Thad Taylor." Thad accepted his hand with a puzzled look on his face.

"How are you this morning, Miss Jones?" Lloyd smiled down at Jill.

"All right. It was a mistake to rent you the room, Mr. Madison," Jill said firmly. "We would appreciate it if you'd vacate it immediately."

"I can't do that, ma'am. I rented it for a month, paid in advance, and have a receipt."

"We'll return your money."

"It isn't quite that simple. My house burned last night and I have nowhere to go."

"It's my understanding that there are several rooming houses in town."

Thad watched Justine while this exchange was going on. Her eyes were on Jill. She had not looked at Madison after seeing him in the doorway. The mild-mannered man with the birthmark on his face had not really acknowledged her.

"The hotel is the logical place for me. It's near my office and my favorite restaurant is across the street. You're in the business of renting rooms, are you not?"

"We can do without your business, Mr. Madison," Jill insisted.

"I'm sorry you feel that way, because I'm here for the month. According to the law, there isn't any way you can make me leave unless you file a complaint with the sheriff. Then you'd have to give him a damn good reason for not wanting me here."

Jill looked at her aunt. Justine's eyes were on the wall opposite her bed.

"Aunt Justine?"

"He knows the law. Damn him." Her lips barely moved when she spoke.

"All right, then, that's settled," Lloyd said cheerfully. Then, to Justine, "You're looking good, Mrs. Byers."

Justine spoke without looking at him. "Go to hell."

Jill gaped at her aunt.

Lloyd laughed. "In a bad mood this morning? I'm the one who lost almost everything last night. It's a good thing I keep an extra set of clothes in my office." He grinned at Thad, then looked down at Justine. "Ah . . . women. Their moods change like the wind.

Now that I'm living here, I'll be in often for a visit, Justine. We can talk about old times."

"Get out!"

Lloyd lifted his shoulders in a noncommittal shrug and left the room. Thad followed him out into the hall.

"What's that about?" Thad asked as soon as they reached the lobby.

"The lady doesn't like me."

"That's as plain as the nose on your face. Why?"

"Well, it's kind of a long story—"

"I've the time."

"To make it short, her husband, Ralph Byers, was a crook that my father, a judge, dealt with rather harshly. Her dislike of him has filtered down to me."

"Mrs. Byers is ill and shouldn't have to suffer your presence. Why don't you just move out? Your money will be refunded."

Lloyd removed his glasses, wiped the lenses carefully with a handkerchief and put them back on.

"By the way, I forgot to ask last night if the hotel has laundry service."

"Are you so thick-skinned that you'd stay where you're not wanted?" Thad asked harshly. To his amazement, Lloyd laughed.

"It isn't a matter of having a thick skin. This thing on my face has conditioned me to endure curiosity, suspicion, revulsion and even hatred. My own father couldn't stand to look at me. Justine doesn't dislike me as much as she lets on. Give her a day or two and she'll get over her mad about me being here."

"Don't bet on it."

"What's your position here?"

"Let's just say that Mrs. Byers wants me here. I'm her bodyguard, so to speak."

"That so? And to keep an eye on Jill, I presume. Can't say that I blame you for that. She's a lovely girl. Word of warning: Watch her around Hunter Westfall. He can get under a woman's skirts quicker than a duck on a june bug. How long are you staying?"

"Until I'm ready to leave," Thad answered tersely.

"By the way, I told the night clerk that I insisted on having the only key to my room. Tell the cleaning lady to leave clean towels on the table in the hall. I'll let her in on Saturday to sweep." He went to the door and turned. "And . . . tell Justine that I'm still waiting for her decision on that legal matter we talked about."

Thad followed him to the door. "Stay away from Mrs. Byers's room."

"And if I don't?"

"I'll beat the shit out of you."

Lloyd let out a whoop of laughter. "You'd hit a man wearing glasses?"

"Hell, yes. I don't give a damn if you've got one eye, no arms and two wooden legs. If you bother her, I'll cram your head up your ass. She's a sick woman. Stay away from her."

"Jesus! You do have a mean streak. I'll have to be careful, won't I?" The grin on his face was more like a smirk. He went out onto the porch.

Thad heard him speak to the man sitting on the bench.

"Are you glued to that bench, Skeeter? Christalmighty! You'd better get in there and calm down your lady friend. She's in a snit."

Lloyd whistled happily as he went down the steps to the walk. He had not had so much fun since he'd watched his papa trying to screw the cleaning girl and failing to get the job done. He'd laughed himself silly that night.

The days ahead were going to top that. Right now he had to put the sad look back on his face and go sift through the ashes that had once been his house.

Chapter 10

"Does the sheriff think Mr. Westfall did it?"

"I've not heard that, but people are saying that he could have been the one. She was staying at his house."

Jill and Thad were sitting at the supper table, the food eaten, the forks and knives together on the sides of the plates, the iced tea glasses empty. Thad answered Jill's question while eyeing the small helping of potatoes still on her plate. He had decided not to say anything more about her lack of an appetite and the fact that she was already so thin a good stiff wind could blow her away.

"I can't believe that Mr. Westfall would go to the meeting, then come here and go walking with me before going home and killing a woman."

"Stranger things have happened."

"He's the one who identified her. How could he do that without seeing her . . . head?"

"The sheriff wouldn't say how he identified her. Just that he had."

"The *Rainwater Reporter* has put out two extras in two days. Yesterday's edition was about the body being found by you and the dog. Today's paper speculated about who she was and the reported arrival of Officer Hurt from Oklahoma City. I'm glad he's staying here at the hotel. I'm also glad they didn't mention me."

"The sheriff promised he'd try to keep you out of it."

"Aunt Justine said that in all the time that she's been here they've only put out one other extra. That was when the bank was robbed. They didn't do it when the gusher came in. There was no need to tell about it. The wind blew oil all over town."

"The *Tulsa World* has a reporter here. A murdered woman, especially one who was cut up, is big news, right along with the trial of that fellow for teaching we came from monkeys and Lindbergh flying an airplane across the ocean. The folks down at the

Mirror didn't want to be scooped by a big city paper."

Jill got up and carried the plates to the dishpan. She'd offered to clean the kitchen so that Radna could sit for a while with Justine before she went to sleep.

"Aunt Justine seems frightened since Mr. Madison moved in. She doesn't like being alone." Jill poured water from the teakettle over the dishes. "She asked me to lock her door when I left the room."

"Did you?" Thad bent over to put the butter into the icebox.

"Yes, but I didn't want to. What if we had a fire and had to get her out of there in a hurry and I'd lost the key?"

"I could get skeleton keys for me and Radna. But if Madison wanted to get in, it would be easy enough for him to get a key. I'll keep a close eye on him and your aunt's door."

"I wish Joe would come."

"Ah, honey. Don't worry." Thad came up behind her, gripped her shoulders and pulled her back against him.

"I have an uneasy feeling, Thad."

"Don't be afraid." His arms crossed beneath her breasts; his nose got lost in the loose curls above her ear. When his lips pressed against her temple, her heart jumped out of rhythm. "Don't you trust me to take care of you as well as Joe or Jack?" he whispered in a soft, raspy voice.

"Of course I do. It isn't that I'm afraid for myself." For an instant Jill allowed her head to fall back on his shoulder, closing her eyes and leaning against his strength. Then she forced herself to move away and rushed into speech to mask her confusion. "There's something about Mr. Madison that bothers me. He's friendly to everyone, but it's obvious to me that there are two sides to him. Mr. Boise thinks he's God's gift to the workingman. He said that he was always going against the big oil companies, trying to get more money for the workers."

"The only *big* oil company in town is Westfall's. The rest of the wells are being drilled by wildcatters. The fellow down at the hardware store, where I got the latch to put on your window, seems to think Madison doesn't give a fig for the workers but is out to do everything he can to cause trouble for Westfall. He said that at the council meetings he's against everything Westfall is for."

"You asked him about Mr. Madison?"

"Not exactly. I just drew him out a bit." Thad flashed his endearing, lopsided grin.

"At the merchants' meeting Mr. Madison was the only one to speak up against the amusement park. The mayor kind of shut him down. I wish I knew why Aunt Justine doesn't like him."

"She'll tell you when she's ready for you to know." Thad picked up a dish towel and started drying the dishes.

"You don't have to do that," Jill protested.

"I want to. I like being in here with you like this. It's like we were old married folks living in our little house out on the prairie."

She glanced up at him. His shimmering green eyes were busy exploring every feature of her face. His smile was lazy and satisfied. Her belly felt warm; her heart thumped; her senses splintered.

"If that were the case, you'd be washing dishes and I'd be sitting over there in the rocking chair watching you." She suddenly felt deliciously reckless and smiled into his eyes.

"You'd be boss?" he asked with mock horror.

"Of course. The smartest one is always the boss," she said with a sassy grin.

"I'd be boss. I'm bigger than you are." A rumble of laughter came from him.

"I notice you didn't say smarter."

"I was getting around to that."

They were laughing into each other's eyes when Jill glanced over his shoulder to see Lloyd Madison's silhouette filling the doorway. The smile left her face so quickly that Thad turned. His eyes followed hers.

"The rooms back of the stairway are private family rooms, Mr. Madison," Jill said coolly. "If you need something, you can speak to Mr. Evans at the front desk."

"I'm sorry, Miss Jones. The hotel is so homey, I didn't realize that there were places in it where guests were not welcome."

"You're welcome to use the porch and the lobby."

"Well, yes. I'm aware of that." Lloyd smiled shyly and managed to look embarrassed. "I was looking for you."

"Well?"

"I came to ask if you'd walk uptown with me. We could get an ice cream or some popcorn."

"No, thank you. I have work to do."

"It's early. I can wait until you're finished."

"No, Mr. Madison. I'm not interested in going out with you."

"Why not? I haven't heard that you're going out with anyone special." He glanced at Thad standing beside Jill with a dishcloth in his hand, then, with a lift of his brows, dismissed him.

"I can set you straight on that, Madison." Thad spoke before Jill could open her mouth. He looped his arm across her shoulders. "Jill is spoken for. She's my girl. And I'm possessive as hell of what's mine."

"Is that so?" Lloyd spread his feet, rocked back on his heels and crossed his arms across his chest. His face was set in a condemning expression. "I'm considered a good catch, Jill. As a lawyer, I will earn considerably more than a day laborer."

"What you earn may be important to some women but not to me." Jill looked Lloyd in the eye and leaned closer into Thad's embrace.

"After a few years of drudgery you may change your mind."

"I think not. I'm proud to be Thad's girl, Mr. Madison."

"Then why did you walk out with Westfall the other night?"

Jill's face reddened. Her blood was churning, yet so far she had been able to hold on to her temper. Now it was about to break out and spew all over him. When she spoke, her words were sharper and her voice louder than usual.

"I don't have to explain my actions to you."

"No. No, you don't," he said in an apologetic tone. "I was just curious. Some women would think Westfall handsome. Being rich is also in his favor. You should be careful of him, though. Most people think that he killed that prostitute who was staying with him."

"Talk is cheap, Madison." Thad's hand tightened on Jill's shoulder. "If the sheriff and the officer they brought in agreed with *most people,* Westfall would be in jail."

"If folks get riled up, he won't make it to the jail." Lloyd moved back out of the doorway. "Guess I'll walk uptown and see in what direction the wind is blowing."

Thad went to the door and watched Lloyd saunter past Justine's room and out onto the porch through the lobby. When he turned, Jill was beside him. He looked down into her worried eyes.

"He gives me the creeps and it has nothing to do with the thing on his face. Somehow, I can't even feel sorry for him because of it."

"I think we set him straight about you being my girl."

"Thank you for saying that."

Thad's eyes scanned her face, lingering long on her mouth, sliding down her throat to the neck of her dress. In his temple ticked a racing pulse. His breath was warm on her face and in his eyes she saw the signs of an internal battle being fought. He dragged his gaze away from her, afraid that he had allowed too much of what he felt for her to show.

"It's no more than what any gentleman would have done in order to save a damsel in distress." The old teasing grin was back and he winked at her.

For an instant her eyes flashed like lightning as she glared up at him. Her heart was heavy with the hurt that he would make light of his saying she was his girl, even if it was a lie to protect her from Lloyd Madison.

"You're no gentleman, Thad Taylor." She

managed to speak lightly, trying to appear nonchalant. "But you are a pretty good dish dryer. So get busy."

Radna sat close to Justine's bed. The two women talked in low tones.

"He wants me to be afraid of him. He knows that I can't even lift my damn hands to defend myself!"

"He won't hurt you. He knows that if I didn't kill him, Thad would. He just wants to keep you scared."

"He's doing a damn good job of that."

"And you're letting him." Radna arranged the pillows behind Justine so that she could sit up a little straighter. "Bernie Shepard didn't stay long today."

"Long enough. I told him that Lloyd wanted me to give him control of my affairs."

"And what did he say to that?"

"He snorted and said that Lloyd had known that I'd not do that. Bernie called it mind games he was playing with me. He said that I'd better have an airtight will. He's going to look things over and be back in a day or two with a paper for me to sign while I can still move enough to put an X on it. He said he'd bring Judge Broers and several others to witness it. The judge's wife, Patsy, and I are old friends."

"Did you tell him anything about Lloyd?"

"I had to. He's one of the few men in town that I trust. He's been in Rainwater almost as long as I have."

"I remember when you and Ralph built the hotel. I thought you were just pouring your money down a rat hole. Shows you what I know. It provided you with a living when Ralph died."

"I want this place sold as soon as I'm gone, Radna," Justine said earnestly and looked pleadingly into the eyes of her friend. "And I don't want Lloyd Madison to get his hands on a penny of it."

"I'd not worry about that. Bernie knows what to do."

"But Lloyd's smart and he knows the law."

"Yeah, but Bernie knows the law, too. Stop worrying. You've got me, Jill and Thad, and soon you'll have Joe Jones. If he's half the man Thad is, he's a corker." Radna lifted her brows. "Flitter, Justine, why couldn't I have met a man like Thad when I was younger?"

"Because you've always had some good-for-nothing booze-hound hanging on that you felt you had to take care of. You don't leave any time for anyone else."

"Jesus! I'm sorry I asked."

"It's true."

"I'm the only person in the world that cares if he lives or dies, Justine."

"Did you ever stop to think that he made his own bed and you should let him lie in it?"

"Many times. But that doesn't mean that I can walk away from him. Let's talk about something else. I think that Thad likes Jill a lot."

"Of course he does. He told me the night he came here that she was like a little sister to him."

"Sister, my hinder. He may have thought that the day he got here, but his attitude changed the minute he got a good look at her. He watches her like a man starving for a drink of water. He can't keep his hands off her."

"I've seen men like that and so have you. Most of the time it means they're desperate to get their rocks hauled."

"This isn't like that. If it was, he'd have

turned handsprings when he saw Laura Hopper. You've got to admit that you've never seen a more beautiful girl than Laura. I don't think Thad even noticed."

"Oh, he noticed. Most men go into instant lust when they see Laura. Thad just hides it better than most."

"What a terrible burden for a girl to bear," Radna said with a deep sigh.

"I've seen plenty of men go into full erection when they looked at you," Justine said with a cocked brow. "Even Bernie Shepard gave you the eye before he was married."

"That was when I was young and women around here were scarce as hen's teeth."

"Not that scarce."

"Are you about ready to sleep now?" Radna stood up and stretched her arms over her head.

"All right, change the subject when you think I'm going to mention that good-looking lawman who was head over heels in love with you."

"It wouldn't have worked and you know it. I'd have dragged him down and he'd probably have lost his job. Now . . . are you ready to go to sleep?"

"Are you going out there tonight?"

"It's a perfect time. Sheriff Page is so busy with the murder, he'll not be paying attention to me."

"Be careful, Radna."

"I'm always careful."

"You know what I mean?"

"I know. Do you think I've given Thad enough time to kiss Jill?"

"I have a feeling that if he wants to kiss her, he'll make the time. I wish to hell I could handle that gun under the pillow."

"You won't need it. Thad sleeps on the canvas cot in the hallway."

"What's to keep him from coming in the window?"

"Him? You mean Lloyd Madison?"

"Or anyone."

"Do you want me to sleep in here with you?"

"No. You have things you want to do. I can still yell loud, if I have to."

"You don't have to tell me that. Back in the old days you could yell loud enough to raise the dead if someone was rough with one of your girls. I've seen a few suckers leaving here in the middle of the night carrying their pants in one hand and holding their tally-whackers with the other." Radna's laughter filled the room. "You were behind them with that old blunderbuss, yelling so loud you woke up everyone on this side of town."

"Lord! That seems a lifetime ago. Don't let Jill hear you saying anything like that. That's a part of my life I don't want my family to know about."

"You were some woman in those days. Your family should be proud of you." Radna laughed again and tossed her head. The thick dark hair, tied back with a ribbon, bounced on her slender shoulders. She moved like a young girl who owned the world: her head back, her shoulders straight.

Radna hasn't changed all that much since I first met her, Justine thought, watching her as she went to the door. *She's still a damn good-looking woman. She's used her little dab of Negro blood as a shield between her and any decent man who wanted her. Lord, I wish she could find a good man who would take care of her after I'm gone.*

"I'll lock the door and give Jill the key. She'll be in to turn out the light."

After the door had closed behind Radna, Justine slowly turned her head and looked toward the bureau at the picture of her late husband.

"Another long, lonely night ahead, my love. Help me to get through it."

Hunter Westfall sat at the desk in a dimly lit room in his house. He stared down at the papers he knew needed his attention, but he couldn't concentrate. The past two days had been the most hellish of his life.

When things were not going well for him, he had always been able to relax and enjoy himself with a woman—one for whom he didn't have to have much, if any, consideration, one who enjoyed the bed games as much as he did.

The weight of guilt he felt for bringing Carsie here had almost brought him to his knees when he saw the butterfly on the body he had played with for over a period of a week and a half. She had been a lusty, full-of-life woman when he left her Saturday to go to the meeting. She didn't deserve to die like that. He prayed that she had been dead before the monster began cutting her.

His last conversation with her had played over and over in his mind the last few days. As hard as he tried, he couldn't ferret out a reason for her to be so angry with him that she would leave so suddenly.

They had been at the dinner table. Dinah had prepared a delicious meal and he had brought out a bottle of his best for an after-dinner drink.

"This meeting is important, or I wouldn't go," he explained and playfully pulled Carsie down on his lap. Dipping one of her full breasts in his liquor glass, he sucked on the nipple beneath the thin material.

"Lover! That feels good. I'd tell you that you're the best lover I ever had, but you've already got an inflated opinion of your abilities."

"This is a hell of a time to have to go to a dull meeting." He tipped his glass and let the whiskey trickle down between her breasts.

"Oh . . . you just filled my belly button! Stay here, lover. You'd have more fun with me." She wiggled on the hardness of his erection beneath her bottom.

"I'll be back about nine. We'll have all night and all day tomorrow . . . after we go to church."

"Church, my foot!" Carsie laughed. "If I know you, we'll stay in bed all day."

"It's what you want, isn't it?"

"Sure it is, lover. I have a few new tricks to show you. Don't you dare stop along the way." She wiggled on his hardness again.

Hunter laughed. "Better stop that or I'll have to go change clothes."

"I don't want the edge taken off this." She rocked back and forth on his lap.

"If it were, there would still be plenty left for you."

"That's what I like about you." She put her arms around his neck and kissed him with an open mouth. "Morning, noon or night, you're ready and randy as a billy goat. I heard that a goat can do it every hour on the hour all day long. Have you ever tried it?"

Hunter grinned at her, then nipped her lower lip. "No, but I'd like to . . . with you. I'd need to rest for a week before going on a marathon like that. Now get that sweet butt of yours off my lap so I can get going."

"I'll be waiting."

The last time he had seen her was when he took his hat from the hall tree, bent and kissed her on the lips and walked happily out the door thinking about the night ahead.

Lord, he wished he'd come right home

after the meeting instead of going to the hotel to inquire about Justine Byers's niece. Carsie might be alive if he had. An impulse to show up the dark-haired man who had been so high-handed on the street corner had led to his asking Miss Jones to go walking with him.

Something had happened between the time he left the house and his return about three hours later that put Carsie in such a rage that she told Dinah to tell him to go fuck himself. Had someone called? Dinah hadn't heard the phone ring, but then she wouldn't if she had been out in the rooms where she and Casper lived.

Hunter had told the officer everything he could remember about the last time he had seen Carsie, including what she had said to Dinah.

Hunter poured a jigger of whiskey from the bottle on his desk. He had drunk more the last couple of days than he had for weeks. After downing the drink in one gulp, he turned out the light, swiveled his chair and stared at the darkened windowpane. Thoughts of Carsie vanished when he remembered a pair of violet eyes set in a calm beautiful face.

He had thought a lot about Laura Hopper since meeting her on Monday morning, and he now knew much more about her. Perry had written down everything he had found out about the beautiful girl. She was twenty years old and had been married to Bradley Hopper for two months when he fell off a Westfall derrick and was killed.

Laura's daughter had been born four months later, which meant that she had been pregnant when she married. She had lived with her parents until her father died suddenly. Now her mother cleaned rooms at the hotel and they both did the hotel laundry. Laura ironed for a few special customers. He, Hunter, was one of them.

The young mother didn't socialize or go to church, Perry discovered, although her mother attended the Baptist church service. He had noted that Laura kept close to home and seldom went to town.

The one little bit of information that interested Hunter the most was the fact that Laura's husband had been killed on one of his derricks. It gave him an excuse to call on her and try to become better acquainted.

Right now he wasn't sure of his intentions

toward Laura Hopper. He needed someone in his bed to play with, but he wasn't sure that Laura was that kind of playmate. Of course, he wouldn't know that unless he spent some time with her.

He needed a diversion badly . . . something other than business. He turned back to the desk and turned off the light. There was nothing he loved more than a challenge.

Chapter 11

The light of dawn was coming in through the east windows and birds were chirping in the big ash tree beside the back porch.

Suddenly Thad awakened and his feet hit the floor.

He knew instantly that someone had come into the hotel lobby. He tilted his head and listened to the low murmur of male and female voices. The man was speaking to Mrs. Evans, who for the past few days had taken a turn at the desk early in the morning.

Thad eased up off the cot and, not bothering to put on either boots or shirt, went quietly down the hallway to where he could see into the lobby.

The tall man standing at the desk wore denim britches and a shirt bleached to a faded blue by many washings. Heavy boots, planted firmly on the floor, supported a body as sturdy as an oak tree with broad shoulders and a head of shaggy sun-bleached blond hair.

"This is a decent hotel." Thad spoke gruffly as he crossed the room on his bare feet. "We don't allow roughnecks and wild shidepokes in here."

Alarmed, Mrs. Evans stepped back from the desk.

The man turned toward the voice and a smile creased his tired face.

"God, Thad. You'll have the woman thinkin' I'm Pretty Boy Floyd."

"You're too damned ugly for her to think that."

Thad turned to the front desk. "Mrs. Evans, this mud-ugly son of a gun is Joe Jones, the black sheep of the Jones family." He grabbed Joe by the back of his neck and they danced around each other like a couple of bear cubs. "Glad to see you. You're a day or two early."

"Blue and I beat it right up here when we heard you found the body of a murdered woman. Scared the hell out of me. Is Jill all right?"

"She's fine. Same old Jill; full of sass. You know I'd not let anything happen to our little sister."

"Did you know that you're in all the papers? The Tulsa paper said that you were a roustabout looking for work and that you and your dog found the body. What in the hell were you doing out in the country late at night, and when in hell did you pick up a dog?"

"It's a long story."

Joe turned and spoke seriously to Mrs. Evans. "I've been keepin' this son of a gun out of hot water since he was knee-high to a short frog. As soon as I turn my back, he's in trouble up to his neck."

"I'm not in trouble, but you will be if you wake up everyone in this hotel." Then, "Where's Blue?"

"Sleepin' in the car. We got here a couple hours ago."

"Drive all night?"

"Left at sundown yesterday. Broke a fan belt and had two flat tires. Good thing I had a couple extra tubes. A certain clabberhead I know used the last of the patches and didn't replace them."

"You can't blame that on me."

"Maybe not, but I'm sure as hell goin' to try." Joe whacked Thad on the shoulder. "What did Jill say when she saw you?"

"I don't remember her first words, but somewhere in there she yelled, 'Thad Taylor, you shut up.'"

"Sounds like her."

"Come on back to the kitchen and I'll make you a cup of coffee."

"First I'd better get Blue. He might come stumbling in here and scare hell out of the lady."

While Thad was filling the teakettle, Radna came from her room wearing a loose, Indian-style dress. Her hair was plaited in two loose braids. She moved so quietly that she was beside Thad before he knew she was in the room.

"What's going on? Why are you up so early? Who were you talking to out in the lobby?"

"Shoot, Radna. I was trying to be quiet. Does anyone or anything move around here that you don't know about?"

"Not if I can help it."

"You haven't had much sleep. I heard you come in just after the clock struck two."

"Yeah, I had a wild night out on the town."

Thad set the teakettle on the stove and threw his arm across her shoulders. "You worry me, girl."

"Girl? Hell, *Buster.* I'm old enough to be your mama."

"You don't look it."

Joe and Blue came in the back door. Joe paused in the doorway when he saw Thad with his arm around an Indian woman.

Joe Jones was a handsome young man. His blond hair was soft and wavy, his eyes sky-blue. His well-muscled body was hard and strong. The grin on his face was so contagious that Radna couldn't help but return his smile.

Thad crossed the room in quick strides to hold out his hand to Blue.

"Lord, Blue, you look like you've been run on a rim for five miles."

"Hell damn. I'm 'bout dead, that's why. Young pup hit every dadburn bump between here and Ponca."

"Both of us would have been dead if I hadn't squeezed him out from under the wheel," Joe explained. "I went to sleep and woke to find that he'd decided to take a shortcut across the prairie. 'Bout jarred my guts out." Joe's smiling eyes went past Thad to the woman who stood beside the stove.

"This is Radna, good friend of Aunt Justine and Jill and now my best girl. I've asked her to marry me." Thad grinned at the astonished look on Joe's face.

Radna rolled her eyes. "Pay him no mind. This boy's got about as much sense as a drunk hoot owl. I take it you're Joe, Jill's brother."

"That's right, ma'am."

"Are all the Jones kids as pretty as you and Jill?" Radna asked.

"No, ma'am. I'm the prettiest by a long shot."

Radna laughed. "Modest, too."

"Yes, ma'am. Modest and pleasant and pretty and smart."

"Bull-foot!" Blue muttered. "He's 'bout as pleasant as a boil on the butt."

"This galoot beside me is Randolph Bluefeather, usually called Blue. He's got a mite more sense than Thad, but you'd never know it."

"That wouldn't take much."

"We knew him a year before we learned

the Randolph part of his name. If you want to make him mad—and you will because he's an ornery cuss and stubborn as a Missouri mule when he gets his back up—just call him Randolph."

"I'll remember that."

Blue acknowledged the introduction with a nod of his head when she didn't offer her hand.

Radna stepped to the doorway and looked down the hall.

"Everything's fine. I never heard a peep out of her all night," Thad said when she turned back. "The door is locked and I've got the key in my pocket."

"Well then, I'll wash up and fix breakfast. Fire up the oven, Thad, if you want biscuits."

Thad showed first Joe and then Blue to the lavatory in the hall and told them about turning over the OCCUPIED sign on the door when they went in and reversing it when they came out.

After washing his face in the wash dish Radna kept in the kitchen and running the comb through his hair, he knocked gently on the door to Jill's room. When there was no answer, he knocked again, then opened the door.

In the light coming through the window, he could see that she was sleeping soundly, her tousled blond head pillowed on a bent elbow. Leaving the door open a crack, Thad went inside. The sheet covered only her legs and hips. He gazed down at her soft breasts showing plainly beneath the thin nightdress and felt a strong surge of desire.

Feeling like a cad for looking at her while she was sleeping, he gently pulled the sheet up until it covered her breasts before he eased himself down on the side of the bed. He looked at her for a long moment. Her mouth was slightly open, her long lashes lay on her cheeks. He reached out to brush her hair away from her face with his fingertips, but drew back for fear that he would awaken her.

Would she be outraged to know that he longed to hold her warm and naked in his arms, kiss her in a hundred different places, make long, slow love to her? He had known after he'd been here two days that he wanted to live with her for the rest of their days, wanted to make a family with her.

As he sat there, he thought about how

angry he and Joe had been when they learned that she had come alone to the rough town of Rainwater. But if she hadn't come here, he might have discovered too late that she was the woman for him. She might have stayed in Fertile, married someone else and been lost to him forever.

"Honey." Thad placed his hand on her shoulder. "Wake up."

Jill's eyes opened. "Thad—?" Startled, her senses swimming in a pool of confusion, she reached for him.

"Everything is all right," he said, quickly taking her hands in his. "Joe is here."

Jill sat up, holding the sheet to her. "Joe is here? Where is he? When did he get here?"

"He's in the kitchen and he got here in the night but waited until dawn to come in." Thad laughed, delighting in her joy. It was hard not to wrap her in his arms and hold her warm, sweet little body tightly to him. Instead his hands slid up her arms for an instant before he stood up. "Get dressed, sugarfoot. Radna's cooking breakfast. Do you want me to bring some water so you can wash in here?"

"I brought some in last night. Oh, Thad, it's been so long since I've seen him."

"He's still as ugly as ever."

"Oh, you! Get out of here so I can get dressed."

Thad turned at the door for one last look. Their eyes caught. She was smiling broadly. He winked at her before he left the room.

When Thad returned to the kitchen, Radna was stirring a skillet of gravy, and Joe was talking to her as if he had known her forever. Blessed with the gift of gab, Joe never had any trouble carrying on a conversation with the young and the old, male or female.

"We had planned to go on down to Healdton. There's a big oil boom down there. Then Pa wrote that Jill was here in Rainwater. I don't think he realized how rough an oil boomtown can be or he'd not have let her come."

"Justine may not have mentioned that to him. She was anxious to have some of her family with her."

"Thad and I decided that we'd better put off going to Healdton and that he'd better come on ahead while Blue and I stayed to finish the job we were on." Joe caught a glimpse of Thad in the doorway. "He wasn't much use anyway. He'd got the big head after helping to put out a little old oil well fire. He jumped at the chance to run up here and look after my little sister."

Radna realized that there was a deep and abiding affection between these two men that allowed them to tease each other.

Thad lingered in the doorway. "Don't believe a word he says. He blows so much hot air that every time he opens his mouth I get an ear ache."

Blue, behind Thad, gave him a not-so-gentle push and they both came into the kitchen.

"You'd better not pick on me," Thad warned. "Radna will scalp you with that butcher knife."

"Hell damn, Thad, you lettin' a woman do your fightin' now?" Blue said. And then to Joe: "I told you we shouldn't have let him come up here without one of us come along to be nursemaid."

Blue, some years older than Joe and Thad, seemed rather short when compared to them, but he was thick in the shoulders and chest. His complexion was smooth and dark; his eyes, black as midnight, had deep crinkled grooves at the corners, from squinting at the sun.

Other lines that experience had made marked his face, too. The black, silver-streaked hair that framed his Indian features was brushed straight back, looped behind his ears and chopped off bluntly at the nape of his neck. He was an unlikely companion to the two young men, but the three were obviously fond of one another.

Radna opened the door of the oven. "Biscuits are done. Pour the coffee, Thad. The rest of you take a seat."

"Joe!" Jill came flying through the door and launched herself at her brother. "Joe, I'm so glad to see you."

"Hello, little sis." He caught her and lifted her off her feet.

"Oh, its been so long!" She kissed his cheek again and again.

"I'm glad to see you, too. Let me look at you." He set her on her feet and held her away from him. "Damn! What happened to you? You've grown up and got bumps." Joe looked over her head at a grinning Thad. "If I'd known that, I'd not have let Thad come up here."

"You can't make me mad today. I've had

bumps for a long time. You've just never noticed." She thumped him on the chest with her fist and threw her arms around his neck. "I've been homesick, Joe."

"So have I, brat," he said and hugged her again. "Were you surprised to see Thad? I knew he'd look after you until I got here."

"Thad? Oh, Radna and Aunt Justine think that he's as handy as a pocket on a shirt. The problem is, he thinks I'm still fourteen."

Joe's eyes swept over her again. "I doubt that. Huh, Thad?"

"She definitely does not look like she did at fourteen. I remember how skinny she was. She was waspish then, too."

"Thad Taylor, you hush up." Jill lifted her chin and spoke again to her brother. "I'm eager for Aunt Justine to see you. Everyone back home says that you look just like Papa did when he was young."

"Eat breakfast first." Radna plopped the pan of biscuits down on the table. "While you're eating, I'll get her ready. Give me the key, Thad."

"Ready for what?" Joe asked. "And what's this about a key?"

"Ready to meet her handsome nephew. What else?" Radna had to tilt her head to look up at him. "Justine's got pride she hasn't used yet. She was a damn good-looking woman in her day. She'd not want you to see her until she's made presentable. Thad will tell you about the key."

After putting a cup of coffee, a couple of buttered biscuits and a jar of strawberry jam on a tray, Radna prepared to leave the room.

"Come on, Princess Laughing Water," Thad said. "I'll open the door for you."

Radna giggled. "Some day, Thad Taylor, a woman is going to tie you in knots."

"I think you're right, princess."

Joe looked at his sister and lifted his brows.

"She likes him. Aunt Justine dotes on him," Jill said.

Joe introduced Jill to Blue, who had been standing quietly behind his chair during their reunion.

"Blue, in case you haven't guessed, this is my little sis. I've got two more at home. She's the middle one." He threw an arm around Jill. "Brat, when we first came out here, green from the farm, this fella saved my bacon, and Thad's, more than once."

"How do you do?" Jill held out her hand.

"Thanks for being a friend to these two know-it-all country boys from Missouri. I know it hasn't been easy."

"Hello, lady. It isn't so bad now that they've had some sense knocked into them."

"You'll have to tell me about it. While I was growing up, they sometimes teased me until I cried. I need new information to hold over their heads."

"I never did. It was Joe." Thad came back into the room as she finished speaking.

"It was you, too, Thad Taylor. Don't try to deny it."

"Blue, tell her about the fat girl who had a crush on Joe and set up camp near the well where we were working and how the men razzed him about his bucket of lard." Thad cocked a knowing grin at Joe and pulled out a chair for Jill to sit down.

"If he does, I'll tell about how dumb you were to pay two dollars for a bottle of bootleg whiskey. When you discovered it was a bottle of well water, you jumped four roughnecks to get your money back and 'bout got your guts stomped out. You would've, too, if me and Blue hadn't taken pity on you."

"Tell her, Blue," Thad said, "how you and I saved him from getting his head cracked open when he got into a fight with a driller who called him a stupid Missouri jackass because he let a pulley slip and ruin forty feet of casing."

"He called me more than that. But I fought him because he said he hadn't met a Missourian yet that was worth the powder it would take to blow out what few brains he had. That made me mad! I could have handled him, too, but when his two buddies jumped in—"

"Well, I can see that you and I will have some interesting conversations," Jill said to Blue as she passed him the biscuits.

"Be careful what you tell her, Blue, she's been known to make a mountain out of a molehill." Joe smiled fondly at his sister. He couldn't get over how pretty she was.

"Excuse me, Miss Jones." Lloyd Madison stood in the doorway. "I'm sorry to interrupt your breakfast, but would you tell the cleaning lady to leave me a towel?"

"There's a roller towel in your room, Mr. Madison, and the bath towel was left on the table in the hall at your request." Jill spoke briskly and not at all kindly.

"It wasn't there."

"It was. I made sure of it."

"Well . . . it could be that one of the other hotel guests took it." Lloyd's eyes were going from Joe to the Indian sitting at the table. He came forward and held his hand out to Joe. "You must be Jill's brother. I heard that you were coming. Lloyd Madison, attorney at law, and temporary guest in your aunt's hotel."

"Pleased to meet you." Joe stood up and shook hands.

"Your aunt has been looking forward to your coming and will be pleased that you're here. She isn't well, you know. The doctor says she has creeping paralysis. I'm glad you got here while she is still coherent."

"I knew that she wasn't well."

"What in blazes—" Jill started to speak but was cut off by Lloyd speaking to Joe.

"You've been working down near Bartlesville and Ponca City."

"Among other places."

"A good friend of mine has a field at Ponca City. I hear it's really producing. Perhaps you know my friend. His name is E. W. Marland."

"Heard of him."

"Almost everyone in Oklahoma has. He's the founder of Continental Oil Company. If you decide to go back down there, I'll send a letter—"

"Excuse me, Mr. Madison," Jill interrupted, a look of pure hostility on her face. "Joe's breakfast is getting cold."

"I'm sorry, Jill. Truly I am. I'm interested in Joe's opinion of the field, since he just came from there. Glad to have met you, Joe. We'll have to get together again. I'm eager for news of E.W. I'll let you folks get to your breakfast. I've things to attend to at the office."

As soon as Lloyd left the room, Jill sputtered, "Of all the nerve!"

Thad got up and went to the door to look down the hall. When he returned and sat down, Joe gave him a quizzical look.

"What's that all about?"

"*That* will take some telling." Thad shook his head in a silent signal while Jill was looking away from him.

"He's got the mark of the devil on his face. I've only seen it one time before," Blue remarked.

"It doesn't bother him a bit," Jill said heatedly. "I think he's proud of it."

"What's this about Aunt Justine? Is she crazy or something?"

"She's no more crazy than you and I. She wants us to lock the door to her room to keep *him* out. She's scared to death of him."

"Why?" Joe paused in putting gravy on his biscuits.

Jill waited for Thad to answer. "We don't know why . . . yet."

"So much has happened. I don't know where to start." Again Jill looked to Thad.

"Let them meet your aunt first, then we'll tell them as much as we know."

"More coffee?" Jill asked.

"I'll get it, honey." Thad put his hand on Jill's shoulder to press her down in the chair. He got up, carried the coffeepot from the stove and filled the cups.

Honey? Not brat or squirt or tadpole? Not Jilly Justine? Joe looked down at his plate and tried not to grin. *Holy hockey! Thad has fallen for my little sister.*

Chapter 12

Justine was sitting in the chair beside the window when Jill and Joe came into her room. Her hair was combed back from her face and she had on a thin blue robe trimmed in white lace. Radna had helped her to look as nice as possible for the meeting with her nephew. Thad had carried her to the chair and then he and Radna had left the room.

"Oh, my. Oh, my." It was all Justine could say when she saw Joe. Her eyes teared. "Come let me look at you. You're the spittin' image of Jethro the last time I saw him."

"Hello, Aunt Justine." Joe squatted down beside the chair and took the limp hand that lay in her lap in both of his. "I'm told I look like my pa. It makes me proud. He's the best man I know."

"Seeing you brings back so many memories. Jethro was handsome and the girls were wild about him. It almost killed him when he lost Jane. Is he happy now?"

"I'm sure he is. Eudora, his wife, fits right into the family. The kids all like her or Pa wouldn't have married her."

"I'm glad he found someone. It's lonesome being alone. I'm glad you're here, Joe."

"I'm glad, too, Aunt Justine. We'll stay just as long as you can put up with us."

"I'm so grateful to have some of my family with me." Tears rolled down her cheeks.

"Now, now, don't cry," Joe said soothingly. "I regret that we didn't come sooner."

"Did you hear about the girl that was murdered here?"

"It was in the papers. That's one of the reasons why Blue and I hotfooted it right up here."

"Radna said you had a friend with you."

"Yes. Thad and I met him a few years ago."

"I'm worried about Jill being here in this rough town. I shouldn't have asked Jethro to send her. I just wasn't thinking straight."

"Don't worry. Blue and I are here now. No

one's going to hurt our little sister, you or Radna."

"Thad's been sleeping in the hall outside our doors."

Joe chuckled. "A man'd be a fool to tangle with Thad. When he's got his back up, he's mean as a gunnysack full of rattlers."

"I can believe that," Jill said, thinking of the gang he was willing to tackle the night he arrived.

"Room number three has two beds, Jill. Put Joe and his friend there. They'll be near."

"We're not going to put you out, Aunt Justine. Blue and I can pay—"

"I'll not hear of it! Thad'll not pay, either. You're my family and this is my home. I don't give a damn if this hotel makes any more money or not." She looked up at Jill. "I'm going to have to lie down. I can't stay up as long as I used to."

"Do you want me to get Thad, or will you let Joe take you to bed?"

Joe stood up. "What do I do?"

"Pick her up and carry her."

"Well, what do you know? I've not carried a pretty lady to bed in a long time."

"You rascal. That sounds like something Jethro would have said."

Joe carefully scooped his aunt up in his arms, carried her to her bed and gently placed her on it.

"Thank you, Joe."

"You're very welcome."

"Jill has been awfully good to me. I feel guilty that I never did anything for Jethro's children when they were young."

"We got along just fine."

Jill moved her aunt's hands to her chest and pulled the sheet up over her legs.

"Would you like to sit up straighter?" At her nod, Jill said to Joe, "Put your hands beneath her arms and lift her. I'll put some pillows behind her."

When it was done, Joe went to the door. "I'll be back in later, Aunt."

"Make yourself at home. Lordy, I wish I was able to show you around. Rainwater was a nice little town—before the gushers."

After Joe left, Justine's eyes caught Jill's. "Is *he* gone?" she whispered. Jill knew that the *he* was Lloyd Madison.

"He left about an hour ago."

"Tell Joe to be careful of him." Her eyes pleaded. "He'll hurt him if he can."

"He came in while we were eating break-fast and talked to Joe about the oil field down at Ponca City. He said that one of the owners was a friend of his."

"Bull-foot! Don't believe a word he says. He's warped."

"Aunt Justine!" Jill chided gently. "How do you know that? He couldn't be warped and be a lawyer. I'll admit that he irritates me, but that doesn't mean that he's—"

"Evil. Believe me, Jill. He's evil, conniving and . . . dangerous." She closed her eyes and said, "You stick close to Thad and Joe. Don't let him get you alone."

"Thad told him that I was his girl. That took some of the wind out of his sails." Jill giggled softly.

"He hates me." The words came softly.

"Are you sure, Aunt Justine? I can't think of what you could have done to cause him to hate you."

"He does. He's just waiting for his chance to get even." Justine's eyes remained closed. "Leave the door open when you leave. If you should see it closed, get Joe and Thad. *He* will have closed it."

"Don't worry. Thad's at the desk. If he comes in, Thad will keep an eye on him. I locked the upper door. If he comes into the hotel, he's got to come by the front desk and we'll know it."

Justine's eyes opened. "I'll be kind of glad when it's over," she said tiredly, and her eyes sought the picture of her husband on the bureau.

"You don't mean . . . ?"

"It's exactly what I mean. When it happens, promise me that you'll leave here with Thad and Joe. Go home, Jill. Bernie Shepard, my lawyer, will handle things here."

"Don't talk about that, Aunt."

"I've got to talk about it. It's inevitable. Promise."

"Of course I promise. There wouldn't be a reason for me to stay." Jill bent and kissed her aunt's smooth forehead. "Get some rest. One of us will be within calling distance at all times."

Jill left the room and went to the lobby, where Thad was tying up the long ends of the sweet potato vine that almost filled one of the side windows.

"The roots of this thing have filled a gallon jar and it keeps on growing."

"We always had one of those at home, but it never got this big."

"I remember. One time Joe and I got to scuffling and turned over the jar it was in. Julie ripped into us because water went all over the parlor carpet. There, that's done. The newspaper is here. Want to look at it with me?"

"Anything in it about . . . the woman?"

"No. They're still looking for the rest of her. Hunter Westfall has offered a hundred-dollar reward, so you can bet there are men out there looking."

"Aunt Justine is scared of Mr. Madison," Jill blurted. "I don't know what to do to ease her mind."

"Did Joe talk to her?"

"Not about that."

Thad took her hand and drew her behind the counter. "What do *you* think of him?"

"He's nice enough . . . at times. But he gives me a creepy feeling. It's like he's a cat and we're mice and he's playing with us."

"I've got that feeling, too. He knows when to push and when to back off."

"I wish Mr. Evans hadn't given him a room."

"We can't blame Elmer. I'm going to nose around and see if I can find out what started the fire that burned his house." He still held her hand. "I'm on pretty good terms with the sheriff."

A drummer came down the stairs and paid for his lodging. He was a slick-looking little man with small black eyes and a wide mustache on his upper lip. He eyed Jill while she was getting his change.

"Thank you and come again."

"I'll do that, pretty lady." He waited for a reply, but when she turned her back to him and put his key in the box, he shrugged and went to the door. He placed his hat carefully on his neatly combed hair, picked up his heavy valise and left.

Thad chuckled. "He asked me last night if you were married. When I told him that you were not, but that I was working on it, he offered to show me the samples of the line he was selling. Something every young woman needed and would be pleased to have, is the way he put it."

"And . . ."

"And, although I would have liked to have seen them, I declined."

"Hummm . . ."

"Aren't you going to ask me what he was selling?"

"I'm afraid to."

"I wasn't going to tell you anyway. You'd slap me."

"Ladies' underwear?"

"More intimate than that."

"Then don't tell me."

Radna came down the stairs carrying a mop. She stopped when she saw Thad and Jill standing close together and conversing in low tones.

"How come you two aren't fighting? It makes me nervous when you're civil to each other."

"We'll fight again soon. It's such fun making up. This is make-up time." Thad flung an arm across Jill's shoulders.

Jill looked up into green eyes bright with amusement. His hair, black and shiny, hung down over his ears. She suppressed the urge to push it back and thought, *He needs a haircut.*

"We were talking about the salesman who just left." Jill moved out from under Thad's arm.

"The duded-up little jelly bean left a calling card in his room. I suppose he thought you'd be the one to clean it and be shocked."

"What did he leave?"

Radna put her hand in her apron pocket. "I'll show you later."

"Excuse me, ladies. I think I'm wanted elsewhere." As he moved behind Jill, Thad's hand squeezed her waist and then moved slowly across her back.

Radna waited until Thad had disappeared down the hall before she came to the counter.

"He needs a haircut." Jill spoke her thoughts.

"I rather like it long. He's a damn good-looking man."

"Not as good-looking as Joe."

"Yes, he is. In a different way. Joe's pretty. Thad's not only good to look at, he's got that rugged, powerful masculinity that attracts a woman, confuses her, angers her and makes her achingly anxious to go to bed with him."

"Well, glory! Does he know that you think he's so special?" Jill hated the fact that a blush covered her cheeks.

"Of course not. Thad doesn't even realize the effect he has on a woman. I'll tell you this: The woman he takes to bed will know she's been on a wild ride before the night is over."

"Shame on you!"

"The strongest urge in the world is to survive, and the next strongest is to procreate. God gave some men an extra dose of the latter and the looks to go with it." Amusement played over Radna's face as she viewed Jill's flaming cheeks.

"What did the salesman leave?" Jill asked after a moment of silence.

"The slimy little pervert thought that you'd clean the room, find this and be shocked. He left it lying on his pillow." Radna pulled a sanitary napkin out of her pocket. "He's a Kotex salesman."

"I wouldn't have been shocked. Well, maybe I would've, finding one in a man's room," Jill confessed with a little laugh. "I've been using them for a couple of years. My sister Julie told me about them and bought me my first box."

"If he was sending a message, I don't know what it is. But no use wasting it." Radna put it back in her pocket. "I've finished upstairs. Everyone is gone except Officer Hurt from the city. He comes in late and goes out early. Nothing in his room but a couple of clean shirts and a dirty one."

"Aunt Justine told me to put Joe and Mr.

Blue in room three. It has two half beds. She's relieved that the boys and Mr. Blue are here. Their friend isn't what I expected. What do you think of him?"

"The Indian? Oh, I guess he's all right for an . . . Indian."

Without waiting for a reply, Radna went down the hall into the kitchen and out onto the back porch. The *Indian* they had been talking about was sitting on the edge of the porch plucking the feathers from a chicken.

"What are you doing?" The female voice held more than a hint of annoyance. Radna hung up the wet mop and came to look down at him.

"What's it look like? I ain't pickin' my nose and I sure as hell ain't suckin' eggs."

"Where did you get that? We don't have any chickens. Old Mr. Worth's chickens wander over here once in a while. That looks like one of his."

"All white chickens look alike."

Anger now made Radna's cheeks grow warm. "You killed Mr. Worth's chicken! That old man lives from hand to mouth. You can get right over there and pay him for it."

Blue looked up at the woman standing with her hands on her hips glaring down at him. His intense gaze held hers, making him aware that she was a fine-looking, feisty woman who could make this trip to Rainwater rather enjoyable.

"Indians are expected to steal. It's our heritage," he said quietly.

"Damn you. That old man depends on those chickens for eggs to trade at the store."

"Me dumb Indian. Me not know that. Me want eat chicken." Blue went back to pulling long feathers from the wings.

"Well, dumb *Indian* or not, you're going to pay Mr. Worth for that chicken."

"No. I'm going to eat it . . . after I cook it. My tribe, the Kickapoos, cook meat. What your tribe do?"

"My father was a Cherokee chief. My mother was a quadroon from New Orleans."

"Are you bragging or complaining?" he asked in a bored tone of voice that served to irritate her more.

"My father's people cooked meat. Some of my mother's ancestors came from Africa. I don't know how they ate their meat. But I do know that they were far more civilized than yours."

"I never heard that folks in Africa ate raw

meat, but if that's the way you want it, I'll save the chicken's head for you. You can work your voodoo magic with it before you eat it."

Radna's temper flared. Acting on pure impulse, she lifted her foot and kicked him in the side with the toe of her shoe. His hand lashed out and fastened around her ankle, holding it firmly. She had to hop on one foot to keep her balance.

"Let go of me, you thievin' blanket-ass!"

"Not until you apologize, little spittin' squaw."

"Go to hell."

"I probably will, but not now."

"Turn loose of me, or my knife will find your rotten gizzard."

"That'd hurt." Blue looked up at her, his Indian features void of expression.

"Damn right it would!"

"What's going on?" Joe came out of the wash house, followed by Thad.

"She kicked me."

"He won't let me go." Radna and Blue spoke at the same time.

"Thunderation, Blue. Why'd she kick you?" Thad stood in front of them with a serious look on his face.

"Damned if I know. She may have broken a rib. I'm not turning her loose until she apologizes. Among my people a squaw would be tied to a stake over a red ant hill for kicking a warrior."

"Warrior, my hind leg! You're no more a *warrior* than that chicken." Radna exploded in rage and tried to step on his hand with her other foot. "I'll apologize to you when there's a man on the moon, you dog-eatin' savage!"

"See what I mean? She's dangerous. She threatened to cut out my gizzard, Joe. And I never ate a dog in my life," Blue finished seriously.

"What started this . . . battle?" Joe was trying not to laugh. Blue had met his match at last.

"He's a thievin' red blanket-ass!"

"I'm a white blanket-ass, too," Blue corrected with indignation. "My white forefathers would be ashamed and never rest in peace if I didn't acknowledge them."

"What did he steal?" Joe had a hard time keeping his face straight when he looked at Thad, who was grinning broadly.

"Mr. Worth's chicken." Radna yanked on her foot, then turned furious eyes on Joe.

"You brought this mud-ugly crow-bait here. Tell him to turn loose of me or I'll bust him in the mouth." She doubled up her fist and prepared to swing.

"Turn her loose, Blue. She looks mad enough to bite the head off a snake."

"Oh, all right, but it's on your head if she . . . hurts me."

"I couldn't hurt you with a ball bat," Radna shouted.

The instant her ankle was released, she raked all three men with a searing glance and, with chin raised, went into the kitchen, the screen door slamming behind her. As she leaned against the table, swear words she'd often heard but seldom used came bubbling out of her mouth with every breath.

At first she was too angry to notice the sacks on the table or the bag of sugar and the one of coffee that lay beside them. On the floor, propped up against the kitchen cabinet, was a fifty-pound sack of flour.

"What in the world?" she exclaimed after she looked into one of the sacks and found cheese, canned goods, raisins and crackers. In another sack there were several packages of meat, a sack of red beans and one of pinto beans. Before she could look into the third sack, Joe came into the kitchen from the porch.

"I apologize for Blue," he said quickly. "He loves to tease and gets carried away sometimes. He also likes to play the dumb Indian when he thinks folks expect it. He didn't steal the chicken. He bought it at the meat market. I was with him."

"For all that's holy! Why didn't he say so instead of letting me think . . . ?"

Joe lifted his shoulders in an I-don't-know gesture.

"Did you buy all this?"

"Blue and Thad pitched in. It's the least we can do. We eat like a swarm of locusts."

"Am I expected to cook it?"

"We don't want to cause more work for you. If you'd rather not cook, Blue will. He's a good cook."

"I'll not let that Kickapoo savage in my kitchen. I'll cook, but I've got to wash my hands first."

Radna filled the washbasin. After washing and drying her hands, she took the pan to the back door, opened it and tossed the pan of water on the man who sat on the edge of the porch with his back to her.

Blue came off the porch spitting obsceni-
ties. Water ran off his head and down over
his face.

"Uh-oh! Sorry, Randolph. I didn't see
dumb Indian sitting there."

When Blue leaped up on the porch,
Radna dropped the pan and, with squeals
of laughter, dashed through the kitchen to
Justine's room and slammed the door.

Chapter 13

Hunter had put in five of the most miserable days of his life.

Carsie's remains were still in a coffin at the funeral parlor. A burial date had not been set. It had taken a dozen telephone calls to locate her brother in Denver, Colorado. The man was sincerely grieved when told of his sister's tragic death. When asked what he wanted done with the remains, he confessed to being flat broke and didn't have money for burial expenses. He was vastly relieved and grateful when Hunter offered to assume that responsibility.

On two different occasions Hunter had talked with Officer Hurt: one time at the police station with Chief Page present, and the other time when the officer came to his house.

Officer Hurt had spoken at length with Dinah and Casper, after Hunter had told them to be forthcoming and tell the officer everything, even if it was uncomplimentary to him. After his interview with Dinah and Casper, Officer Hurt spoke again with Hunter.

Now, in the quietness of his study, Hunter played that interview over in his mind.

"How often did Miss Bakken visit you?" Officer Hurt asked.

"Three times this past year. Carsie was involved with several men. As far as I know, I am the only unmarried one. She was biding her time, thinking that I would marry her, but I had made it clear to her before she came here the first time that I would not even consider it."

"How did you meet her?"

"I met her in Kansas City. She was very beautiful and skilled in giving sexual pleasure. She was completely uninhibited and enjoyed sex."

The officer's face never changed expression, but Hunter suspected that hearing that a woman enjoyed sex was foreign if not repugnant to him. Hunter hated exposing his and Carsie's private life to this man and hoped that he was professional enough to keep the information confidential.

"In other words, she was a whore who enjoyed her work," the officer commented dryly.

"I didn't think of Carsie as a whore and she didn't think of herself that way. She considered herself a mistress, a companion, a paramour, a sexual playmate."

"What's the difference?"

"A whore is paid for each act. A mistress is supplied with food, lodging and an allowance for her services. She is given the respect of a substitute wife." Hunter recited dispassionately what he considered to be the definitions. Then he added, "Marion Davies is Randolph Hearst's mistress. Do you consider her a whore?"

The officer refused to answer, and his eyes caught and steadily held Hunter's. He waited and finally Hunter began to speak again.

"After I left to go to the meeting Saturday night, something happened to make Carsie angry enough to leave the house. I've racked my brain trying to figure out what it could have been and have come up with nothing."

"No telephone calls?"

"I checked with the telephone operator and she didn't remember plugging into our number."

Officer Hurt nodded. "She said you had."

"If you knew there were no calls, why did you ask?"

"My job. When Miss Bakken was here before, did she leave suddenly?"

"No. When it was time for her to go, I took her to the train." Hunter rubbed his hands wearily over his face.

"And paid her at that time?"

"Yes. I gave her some money."

"Did you give her any money while she was here this time? Would she have had money when she left here?"

"I had not given her any money. She may have had some. She didn't seem to be short of ready cash."

At that, Officer Hurt stood up and reached for his hat. Hunter walked him to the door. The two men shook hands and the officer left.

"Supper is ready." Dinah's voice broke into Hunter's thoughts.

"Thank you, Dinah. I'll be right there."

While eating his meal, Hunter admitted to

himself that he was dissatisfied with his life and had been for some time. He was thirty years old. For the past ten years he had worked to build his companies; he enjoyed his money and what it could buy for him. He had a fine house, the respect of the town's merchants and could have any kind of sexual pleasure money could buy. Yet, what did it amount to?

Besides Dinah and Casper, who cared for him for himself, instead of what he could do for them? The sex no longer excited him as it used to. He had never been with a woman who had caressed him because she loved him and wanted to please him. He wondered how it would be to have a woman who was totally his because she wanted to be, one who would love him through good times and bad.

There were women like that. He'd had glimpses of them from time to time. He believed Jill Jones was a one-man woman. He had enjoyed walking out with her, but he had not felt one-tenth the attraction to her that he had felt toward Laura Hopper, although he and Laura had exchanged less than a dozen words. He wanted to see Laura again and talk to her. Maybe then he would understand why she was constantly in his thoughts.

As terrible as it was, he couldn't let what had happened to Carsie stop him from getting on with his life. He had cooperated in the investigation in every way he could and would continue to do so. He would, however, regret to his dying day that, because of him, Carsie had come to Rainwater and met such a tragic end.

Hunter finished his meal, went to his room and put on a clean shirt. He inspected himself in the mirror to be sure he was well groomed, and left the house.

It was that short span of time between late evening and dark. Hunter walked quickly down the street, turned and headed toward the outskirts of town. He knew exactly where he was going and wanted to get there before dark. He had seen the house several times while in his car going or coming from one of his oil wells.

He passed the ruins of Lloyd Madison's small house and noticed Madison's Ford roadster parked on a side street. Within the stone foundation only a blackened bathtub and an iron cookstove were visible. He wouldn't think the man would find anything of value left, but he couldn't blame him for searching. The fire was assumed to have been started by a short circuit in the electrical wiring. Madison had been playing cards at the billiards parlor at the time, and the fire had had a good start before it was discovered.

Hunter's excitement built as he neared the small, neat house where Laura Hopper lived with her mother. Like so many in town, it had two doors leading off a porch that stretched across the front. A stand of hollyhocks grew just inside the fenced yard; a barrel filled with blooming petunias stood nearer the porch. When Hunter opened the gate, a cat scurried beneath the porch.

Behind the house, still visible from the road, was an outhouse surrounded by more hollyhocks, a neatly tended vegetable garden and a clothesline that reached from the corner of the house to an iron post. Laura was taking white shirts off the line. Hunter walked around the house and found breathing difficult as he watched and waited while she stripped the line and turned toward the house.

"Oh." Laura let out a little gasp when she

turned and saw Hunter. She hugged the garments to her and took a couple of steps to the side when he approached her.

"I'm sorry I frightened you. I guess, under the circumstances, every woman in town has a right to be cautious." Hunter took off his hat. "I'm Hunter Westfall. We've only met one time before. . . ."

She stood still; her only movement was when her eyes darted once behind him, then back to his face as though cataloging every detail.

"I know who you are." Her lips barely moved when she spoke. "Your shirts aren't ready."

Her large violet eyes studied his face. Hunter suddenly felt shy and uncertain, a sensation he'd not had for many years.

"I didn't come for the shirts. Dinah said you'd bring them Monday morning." She was still, watching him; and he knew that if he made a move she would dash away like a startled fawn.

"Then why—"

"I want to talk to you about something else."

"All right."

Her softly spoken concession effectively

gave him the courage to say, "I can wait until you take the clothes in the house. Then maybe we can sit down." He nodded toward the stoop attached to the back of the house.

"All right," she said again and made a wide circle around him and hurried into the house.

Hunter stood where he was, just pivoting to watch her. She was everything he had remembered and even more beautiful. She was slim and as graceful as a willow switch and so beautiful it almost hurt his eyes to look at her. The gingham dress she wore was faded from many washings, but it outlined her softly rounded breasts, hugged her waist and danced around her bare calves. She was barefoot. He hadn't noticed until she stepped up on the porch.

He was enchanted by her.

She was out of the house in a minute or two. Hunter had not moved. She stood on the stoop looking at him and waiting. As he came slowly toward her, his hat in his hand, she sat down on the edge of the porch. She had made no effort to make herself more presentable. She was still barefoot, her hair a tangle of dark curls. His eyes stayed on her face as he approached. Her skin was a warm ivory, a perfect background for her magnificent eyes.

She was beautiful, but there was something else about her that drew him like a magnet, some quality that he couldn't name.

"May I sit down?"

When she nodded, he sat down on the edge of the porch, leaving a space of four or five feet between them.

"Mary Pat is asleep." This appeared to be an apology for not inviting him into the house.

"Does she walk?"

"Oh, yes." She turned to look at him. "She's a year and a half."

"I remember you telling me that. But I don't know much about children that age."

"She walks and is . . . quick. I have to get as much done as I can while she sleeps."

"Do you work at night?"

"I iron sometimes. I hang out the white things when the wind isn't stirring up the dust."

Hunter listened intently to her every word. His mind searched for a way to keep her talking.

"I came to speak to you about your husband's death."

"Bradley? He's been dead for two years."

"He died before your child was born?"

"Yes." She looked straight ahead. Hunter stared at her profile. Calm, cool and lovely was the only way to describe her.

"I'm sorry."

"Why? Did you know him?"

"No. I'm sorry because it must have been terrible for you." When she didn't say anything, he continued: "I learned only a few days ago that he died while working on one of my rigs."

Her head swiveled around slowly. "He wasn't *working.*"

"It's my understanding that he climbed to the crown block of the derrick and fell eighty feet. It's a policy of our company to pay compensation to the widows of men killed in our employ. I can find no record of you having been paid. I'd like to remedy that."

"Why?" She seemed to say that often. "Bradley wasn't working. He hadn't worked for a couple of weeks. He was drunk. It just happened to be your derrick he fell off of."

"Yet it *was* our derrick."

Laura stood up. "You have no obligation to pay me anything. It wasn't your fault he was drunk or that he climbed your derrick and fell."

Hunter got to his feet. "I do feel obligated. It's what we would have done for any of the other employees. It can't be easy to support a child alone."

"We get by. We don't need your charity." She spoke coolly, with a haughty tilt of her chin, and stepped up onto the porch as if to go back in the house.

Hunter began to panic.

"Please, Laura—I mean, Mrs. Hopper—I'm sorry if you feel what I was offering was charity. It's a company policy—"

"Was the company policy in place two years ago? A policy that paid a widow if her drunken husband went to the oil well in the middle of the night, climbed the derrick and fell off and killed himself? If it was, I would have been notified at that time."

"It had not happened before."

"I'll have your shirts ready by Monday morning." Dismissal was in the tone of her voice.

"Laura, I'm sorry if you feel insulted by

my offer. I only wanted to compensate you for your loss."

"How do you know it was a loss?"

The question dumbfounded Hunter for a moment. "I don't know that, but—"

"Good night, Mr. Westfall."

"Laura, stay and talk to me for a while."

"About what?" Her hand was on the handle of the screen door. "Do you want to talk about the real reason you came here?"

"Oh, Lord." Hunter groaned and twisted his hat around and around in his hands. "Was it that obvious?"

"To me, yes. I've heard everything from 'my mother sent me over' to 'I found a dollar on your doorstep and it must be yours.' Your excuse is a new one."

Hunter's eyes smiled into hers. "It's no wonder that you're leery of men."

"Women are in short supply here in Rainwater."

Sweetheart, women like you are in short supply the world over.

"Will you accept my apology?"

"Accepted. I have work to do, Mr. Westfall."

Her hand was on the door handle and he

was desperate to keep her talking. He said the first thing that came to mind.

"After what happened, you shouldn't be here alone."

"Mama went to prayer meeting. She'll be back any minute."

"The woman who was murdered had been staying at my house." It was dark. Hunter couldn't see her eyes, but he could feel them on his face.

"I heard that."

"I suppose it's all over town. She was a friend."

Fool! Of course she was a friend: I wouldn't have had an enemy staying at my house. Lord, I wish I could take back the last ten years of my life and start fresh with a girl like Laura.

"She was very pretty. I saw her one afternoon when I brought a shirt I had mended."

Hunter fumbled for words. His first thought was that Carsie would not have been friendly or even nice to a girl as pretty as Laura. His second thought was that it must have been the shirt Carsie had ripped off him one night when she couldn't wait for him to get undressed.

"You did a good job replacing the buttons."

"Thank you."

He didn't know exactly how much Dinah paid her for doing his shirts. He made a mental note to tell her to increase whatever it was.

"May I come back some evening?"

"Why?" There it was again.

"We could take a walk. Get acquainted. I'll pull Mary Pat in the wagon." His smile faded when she slowly shook her head.

"I'm usually busy evenings."

"If you don't want to go for a walk, we can go for a ride in the car. I'll show you the wells my company is drilling." She silently shook her head and he said somewhat desperately, "Are you afraid of me because of what happened to Miss Bakken? Mother of God, Laura. I'd never hurt you."

"I'm not afraid of you."

"Then what is it? Why won't you spend some time with me?"

"I don't know you, Mr. Westfall, and I'm not sure if I even like you."

"Why?" It was his turn to ask.

"I said that I'm not sure why. It's something about the way you live."

"Are you in love with someone?" He held his breath while he waited for an answer. It seemed to him that she was weighing a decision. Finally she shook her head and his shoulders slumped in relief. "Would you mind if I came back tomorrow night and we sat here on the porch for a while? You might find out that I'm just an ordinary man when you get to know me."

She lifted her shoulders in a noncommittal gesture, but he took it to mean that she was agreeable. He put his hat on his head, hoping to hurry away before she changed her mind.

"Good-bye, Laura. I'll see you about this time tomorrow night."

She was still standing beside the door when Hunter turned and walked away. When he reached the road, he saw a woman coming toward the house. No doubt it was Mrs. Cole, Laura's mother, returning from her prayer meeting.

"Evening, ma'am." They met and Hunter tipped his hat as she hurried past, almost running toward the house.

Hunter was sure that he had never had anything in his life affect him like his meeting with Laura Hopper. He was elated that tomorrow night he would be coming back to see her. Lord, he wanted to give her everything. But he'd have to be careful. She had pride and spirit.

Pretty girl, you are a treasure.

He chuckled to himself. The little dickens! She had known that the reason he gave for calling was a pretext. His feet seemed lighter and he was surprised to discover that the tempo of his heartbeat had increased. He was not aware of the grin on his face or the fact that he had fallen head over heels in love.

His steps slowed as he reached the ruins of Lloyd Madison's burned-out house. The idea struck him that in the short time he had been with Laura, he hadn't thought one time of how she'd be in bed, which was the usual way he considered a woman. He didn't even want to think about that now. He wanted to think about how he could make life easier for her, protect her and Mary Pat from anyone who would hurt them.

Hunter was so engrossed in his thoughts that he didn't see the man beside the car on the side street. Pure hatred shone in the eyes of the man who stared at him.

"It didn't take you long to latch on to another woman," the man muttered. "Enjoy yourself, Mister Big Shot. Your world is about to come tumbling down."

Chapter 14

Jill sat on the edge of her aunt's bed.

"Come out onto the porch with us, Aunt Justine. Thad or Joe will carry you." Justine closed her eyes and was so still that it alarmed Jill. "Aunt Justine. Are you all right?"

"I'm . . . all right."

"It's a lovely night. There's a nice breeze."

"You don't have to stay in here with me. Find Thad. He'll take you for a walk. Just lock the door when you go out."

"I'll not go out and leave you alone. Joe, Thad and Mr. Blue are on the porch. Radna, too, if she hasn't gone off somewhere."

"I'm here. I'm not going anywhere to-night." Radna had paused in the doorway, then came into the room. "What's she nagging you about now, Justine?"

"She wants me to go out to the porch."

"Joe or Thad will carry her." Jill spoke to Radna, but her eyes remained on her aunt's face. "We'll bring out a chair from the lobby."

"Why not, Justine?" Radna took a house-coat from Justine's wardrobe. "Aren't you tired of lying in that old bed and looking at these four walls? I'd jump at the chance to have a hairy-chested bucko carry me."

"Has *he* come in?"

"I've not seen him," Jill replied, knowing that her aunt was referring to Lloyd Madison. "Don't worry about him, the hairy-chested buckos will be with us." A giggle burst from Jill's mouth, bringing a smile from Justine.

"They're on the porch. I'll get them." Radna was not giving Justine a choice.

"It's a lot of trouble."

"Ah, poot. It's no trouble, but what if it is? They've got to pay for all that food I cooked up for them." Radna was on her way out the door.

Joe came in while Jill was putting the housecoat on her aunt. "Are we going somewhere?"

"We're going to the porch and see the

sights. Put your hands under her arms, Joe, and hold her up while I tie the belt."

Joe held his aunt upright while Jill tied the sash around her small waist, then eased her back down on the side of the bed.

"Get your hands off my woman." Thad's voice was loud and threatening.

Jill frowned at him. "You're like a bull in a china shop, Thad."

"Can't help it, darlin', I have to be loud to get this farm boy's attention." He bent and scooped Justine up in his arms. "Ready to go dancin', sugar?"

"Not if you don't Charleston," Justine said haughtily.

"Of course I do the Charleston. I shimmy, too."

"I don't doubt that for a minute," Jill said dryly.

"I was going to carry her," Joe complained, trailing Thad out the door. "She's *my* aunt."

"No one carries this woman but me. You can carry Jill."

"Jill? Why would I want to carry my *bratty* sister? I've been lugging her around since she wore nasty diapers."

"Hush complaining, Joe, and help me get a chair out of the lobby."

Jill followed Thad as he strode down the hallway with a giggling Justine in his arms. His treatment of her aunt was endearing him to Jill more and more. He knew just what to do to raise her spirits.

Blue appeared. He and Joe carried a padded chair to the end of the porch and Thad eased Justine down into it.

"How's that?" He leaned close to her and whispered, "I'd rather sit in the chair and hold you on my lap."

"A few years ago I'd have taken you up on the offer, bucko," Justine whispered back. "You've got the blathering tongue of the Irish, Thad."

He backed up and gave her a stricken look. "Is that why you fell in love with me? I thought it was my good looks."

"Don't let him turn your head, Aunt Justine." Joe straightened his aunt's feet the way he'd seen Jill do. "He's used that blathering tongue to romance girls all the way from Missouri to central Oklahoma. They all fall for it . . . until they find out he uses the same line on all his girls."

"Pay him no mind, Aunt Justine," Thad

said. "He's jealous because the girls don't pay as much attention to him as they do to me."

"Both of them are full of hot air, ma'am." Blue snorted in disgust. "The only girls I've seen running after either of them looked as if they'd come out of their mamas backwards and no one noticed."

"I'm so glad you're here, all of you. You, too, Mr. Blue. Having my family with me is more than I deserve." A tear choked Justine's voice.

Jill arranged her aunt's hands in her lap, then sat down on one side of her. Joe sat on the other side. Jill patted her aunt's hand, but her mind was still on what Joe had said about Thad romancing girls. She looked up to see him towering above her, his eyes on her face, his lips smiling. She had half believed that he cared for her in more than just a sisterly way. How foolish she had been. Thad liked women. All women. He liked to make them happy. He was one of those people whose confident, unruffled presence attracted them.

Jill was relieved when he moved, but then he turned and sat down on the bench close beside her . . . too close.

"There's room here for you, Blue. It gives me an excuse to sit close to Jill and put my arm around her." Thad moved until his hip and thigh were pressed to hers. He sent a sideways glance at Jill, teasing her with his smile, and snaked his arm across her shoulders.

"When did you need an excuse to snuggle up to a pretty girl?" Blue grunted, and went to sit on the porch steps.

"You can move over now." Jill gave Thad a bump in the ribs with her elbow.

"You'll regret this, Blue," Thad threatened. "I've done plenty of favors for you." He moved, but just slightly away from her. His arm remained behind Jill, his hand capping her shoulder.

"It's been a while since I was out at night," Justine said. "Martha has new lights in her café."

A truck went by and a loud male voice yelled, "Hey, pretty little wildcat!"

"What was that about?" Joe asked.

"I haven't told you about the night I got here and found our little sister on the street corner—"

Jill's elbow lashed out again and connected with Thad's ribs. He grunted. She had meant for it to hurt. It did, and she was glad. *Our little sister!* The remark put her firmly in a category she didn't want to be in. She was more angry at herself than at him for thinking that it could be otherwise.

"Why'd you do that?"

"Because you've got a big mouth!" Jill would have gone to her room, but she didn't want to upset her aunt.

"I was about to ask you to walk down to the drugstore for an ice cream."

"Don't bother. I wouldn't go anywhere with you if you were the last man alive!"

"Why are you mad? I was kind of proud of the way you were taking up for yourself on that street corner."

"You sure as heck didn't show it," Jill sputtered. "You came in there swearing like a sailor, knocking people out of your way. I've not forgotten that you called me a sl—"

"Don't say it." Thad quickly put his hand over her mouth. "I told you that I'm sorry I said that. I'm sorry, sorry, sorry. I even told Joe that I was sorry. That took some doing on my part to admit anything to him."

"Sorry doesn't cut the mustard with me, mister. You can be sorry until the cows come home and I'll still remember what you said," Jill insisted.

"I don't want you to be mad at me. Come on, let's go for a walk." His hand began stroking her upper arm. His green eyes were focused on her profile.

"No." She tried to bump his hand from her arm.

"Pl-ease." The murmured plea in her ear was like a soft caress.

"No. I'm staying here with Aunt Justine. I told her that I would and I am." She didn't dare move her head an inch for fear that her face would collide with his.

"Go walk with him." Radna came out of the shadows at the side of the porch. "Joe and I and Randolph will take care of Justine."

Blue let out a snort and looked over his shoulder, a frown pleating his brow, which caused Radna to needle him further.

"That is, if Randolph isn't planning to go on the warpath tonight and take a few scalps."

"If I do, that mop of yours will be the first to hang from my belt," Blue threatened.

"Go on, honey," Justine said, unaware of

the byplay between Radna and Blue. "I'll be fine."

"I'll take Aunt back to her room when she wants to go."

After Joe made his comment, Jill jumped to her feet. "It's easy to see that I'm not wanted or needed here. I can take a hint. You want to get rid of . . . me." At the end she was striving to keep her tone level and her lips from trembling, but her traitorous voice betrayed her on the last word.

Not understanding the reason Jill was as mad as a hornet but feeling that he must have been the cause of it, Thad stood up, mentally kicking himself for having caused the pain reflected in her voice. More than anything he wanted to cradle her face in his hands, bring her head to his shoulder and comfort her. He wanted her to look at him with laughter in her eyes instead of the pain he saw there now.

"They're not trying to get rid of you, honey. It's me. They think the only way to get rid of *me* is if you go with me."

"Horse hockey!" Jill's hurt had been replaced with an unreasonable anger. "And don't be *honeying* me, you big, ugly clod-hopper!" Glaring at him as if she'd like to run him through with a saber, she stomped down the hotel steps. Thad hurried after her, catching her on the sidewalk.

"Slow down, honey. I wanted us to go for a walk, not a run."

Jill turned on him with a balled fist. "Stop calling me that, or I'll hit you in the nose."

"You don't want me to call you honey?"

"No, I don't. You say it as if you were talking to a six-year-old. Save it for the stupid girls who chase after you."

"Joe was just making that up. He's the one girls go for." Thad cupped her elbow with his hand and refused to let go when she tried to wrench it away. "If we're walking down through town, I want all the men who stare at you to know that you belong to me."

"I don't belong to you, Thad Taylor. Get that through your thick head. *I'm not your little sister!*"

"I thank God for that, you stubborn little imp."

Jill was afraid to look at him, afraid that the taunting gleam in his eyes would goad her into hitting him and that once again she would make a spectacle of herself on the street for the men to gawk at.

Had she looked at him, she would not have found a teasing glint in his eyes but loving concern.

A number of men were loafing in front of the billiard parlor. One of them, Lloyd Madison, broke from the group and came up the sidewalk toward them. Thad, with his hand firmly attached to Jill's elbow, steered her across the street to avoid him.

Jill stopped. "Let's go back. Lloyd Madison's going to the hotel, and Aunt Justine's on the porch."

"Joe and Blue will take care of it. I told them the whole thing about your aunt being afraid of him. If he says one thing to upset her, Joe will break him in two."

"I wish I knew why she's so afraid of him and why he takes such pleasure in needling her."

"Does Radna know anything about him?"

"If she does, she isn't saying. If Aunt Justine doesn't want her to say anything, she won't. They've known each other for a long time and I think they've come through tough times together."

They were on a dark street now, one without sidewalks. The houses were set far back from the road. Some had no electricity. Jill could see lamps like the ones they had used at home before Evan, her sister's husband, brought out the electric line. It went past their place, so her father had hooked on. And how exciting it was to have lights at the turn of a switch!

"Where's your dog?"

"She was under the back porch when I went in to supper. She'll probably have her pups there."

"What are you going to do with her when you leave?"

"I'll find a place for her or take her with me. I couldn't very well desert her now. If not for her, I'd not have had my name in the paper." Jill looked up at him and burst out laughing. He grinned back at her, his eyes drinking in the sight of her smiling mouth, her bright, laughing eyes. "It was tough finding that girl, but you came through it just fine. I was proud of you."

His praise was like a warm healing balm. "Do you think they'll find whoever killed her?"

"I don't know, honey—" The endearment slipped out. Thad glanced down at her, but she didn't seem to notice or remember that she'd told him not to call her that. "When I went down to the creamery to get milk for Radna, the man there said people are beginning to think that maybe Mr. Westfall killed her. She had been staying at his house."

"If he had, he would have put her someplace where she wouldn't be found so soon. Didn't you say that a good stiff wind like the one we've had for the past few days would have leveled that sand dune?"

"I think it would. They've not found the rest of her, her clothes or her suitcase."

"Poor woman." Jill shivered, giving Thad an excuse to put his arm around her, drawing her close to his side.

They had reached the schoolhouse. Thad led her onto the playground where a section of swings stood silent and unmoving in the moonlight.

"Are you afraid out here, honey?"

"No, I'm not afraid—and my name is Jill."

"Well, glory be. I thought it was Josephine."

Her head jerked up. She felt his laugh against her shoulder that was wedged beneath his arm. Without seeing it, she knew that mischief danced in his green eyes.

Pride surfaced.

"I don't like for you to call me honey, lumping me with all the girls you call that. I don't like for you to call me *little sister.* I'm not your sister and I'm not six years old!"

"Oh, Lord," Thad muttered on a breath of a whisper. His hands closed about her upper arms. He looked down into the face turned up to his. She was serious. She thought he was belittling her, treating her like a child. She was so sweet, so pretty and so precious to him, and in trying to keep from showing his feelings for her, he had made a complete idiot of himself.

"Honey— Oh, there I go again. I don't think of you as being six years old. I don't think of you as being my little sister." He drew her close to him, and when she offered no resistance, his arms slipped around her. He cradled her head in one of his hands and pressed it to his shoulder. "I think of you as the prettiest, sweetest and spunkiest girl I've ever seen. I don't know if I can stop calling you *honey,*" he whispered with his mouth against her forehead. "I think of you as *my* honey."

She pulled away from him, holding a handful of his shirt to steady herself while her eyes searched his face to see if he was teasing. His brows were drawn in a worried frown.

"No, you don't. You think—" Her voice stumbled to a stop. She choked back the lump that rose in her throat and turned her eyes away from him, only to have them swing back of their own accord. She was acutely aware of the warmth radiating from his broad chest and his body made firm and muscular by hard work.

"Right now I'm thinking . . . about kissing you. I've wanted to since the night I got here."

"All the time?"

"Off and on. Right now the thought is eating a hole in my brain and making my heart do handsprings."

"You're teasing me." She didn't want to smile at his foolish words, but she did. Her face shone, sweet and pale in the moonlight. "Is that one of the glib lines you use on girls that Joe and Blue talked about?"

"No, ma'am. That's one I've not used before, nor will I ever again with anyone but you."

"Promise?" She kept her voice light, teasing.

"I'll swear on a stack of Bibles as high as

my head. I'm going to kiss you. What are you going to do about it?"

"Nothing," she said breathlessly. "You're bigger than I am."

"Remember that," he teased.

He moved his hands up the sides of her neck to frame her face. With his thumbs locked beneath her jaw, he tilted her head and put his mouth to the sweet, soft one that was driving him crazy. He kissed her soft mouth without passion, almost as if comforting a child.

Jill pulled away, confused by the shafts of pleasure his lips sent along her spine. He pulled her back to him and claimed her lips again. His lips pressed recklessly hard, giving hers no choice but to part.

Lord of heaven, help me! She's so sweet. I've been waiting for this all my life.

The pressure of his mouth hardened— seeking, demanding, willing her to recognize her own need, forcing her head back as his lips moved hungrily over hers. Her head was spinning helplessly from the torrent of churning desires racking her body. The intensity of these feelings were strange to her, and she was powerless to control them. His warm, wet tongue caressed her lips, heightening the sensation. When he lifted his head, their eyes locked: green onto blue, both unwavering. Her ragged breath hissed through wet, throbbing lips.

"Thad . . ."

"It's all right, sweetheart. It's nothing to be frightened about." He kissed her trembling mouth again with incredible gentleness.

"Why . . . did you kiss me?"

"Because I wanted to. I wanted to kiss you with your arms around my neck."

"You didn't tell me."

He brought his hands down to clasp hers and guide them upward. When they were moving of their own accord, he wrapped his arms all the way around her so that his hands rested on the sides of her breasts.

"I wanted to kiss you with your breasts against me, and I wanted to hold your hips in my hands." His hands moved down and his palms rested against her buttocks.

He lowered his head and a sweet, wild enchantment rippled through her veins as his lips moved over hers with warm urgency and molded them to his in a devastating kiss. Her senses responded with a deep, churning hunger for his touch, and she rose on tiptoe, arching to meet his height, her fingers clinging to his shoulders. He held her small, soft body tightly against him, lifted his hands and dared to stroke the sides of her breasts with his fingertips.

"Good Lord! Sweetheart. Help me to stop. It's like I'm starving for you."

"Do you kiss all girls like that?" The question tumbled out of her heart through her lips.

"The only girl I have is you. The only girl I want is you," he said almost angrily. He broke the embrace and led her to the swings, lifted her and sat her down. "Hold on," he muttered huskily.

Jill sat in a daze while Thad moved behind her and pushed. His hands on her shoulders were strong and warm. What had inspired the intimate kisses? Her heart thumped at the thought that played over and over in her mind: He had kissed her because he wanted to kiss her, and she had kissed him for the same reason.

Thad pushed Jill gently in the swing. After kissing her, he needed to think. He loved her! He was totally, recklessly, helplessly in love with sassy little Jill—a girl he had known all her life. This love had crept up on him and had sunk deeply into his heart and mind from the night he saw her on the street corner swinging her fist at the nose of a roughneck who was teasing her. *Sweet, spunky little cuss!*

What he was feeling for her was a cherishing kind of love that made him want to be with her every minute of the day and night, both mentally and physically. He wanted to hold her in his arms, plant his children in her warm, fertile body, keep her happy and safe by his side forever.

He swore.

What did he have to offer her but a few hundred dollars sewn in an old coat and the dream of having his own farm?

Unconsciously, Thad's eyes had been focused on a light spot in the bushes at the edge of the playground. Then suddenly his mind cleared as if a shadow had passed from it.

Someone was watching them.

The light spot against the green of the bush moved. It was a man's shirt. Thad continued to swing Jill, his eyes never leaving the man watching them. Anger sent his pulse racing. The low-life bastard had been watching while Thad kissed her.

"Thad." Jill spoke his name softly when the swing brought her near him. "Is that someone standing over there by the bushes?"

"Yes, it is, sweetheart. I'm watching him." When the man moved along the bushes toward the road, Thad's eyes followed.

"Let's go," she said in a frightened whisper.

Thad's arm snaked around her waist and stopped the swing. She slid off the seat. His arm went around her and held her to him while his eyes searched the dark area for the man in the light-colored shirt.

"I don't see him. Do you?" he whispered, his lips close to her ear.

"He went around that last bush by the road while you were stopping the swing. I didn't notice him until he moved along the bushes. Who do you think it was?"

"My guess is that he's some young lad getting his juice up by peeking in windows and spying on couples." Thad didn't really think that, but he wanted to reassure her.

"He could be the killer, too. Let's go back."

"I should have stayed closer to town. The

next time we go out walking, I'll bring my pistol."

With his arm around her and hers around him, they walked quickly down the middle of the road toward town. Thad's eyes continued to scan the area around him for the man who had spied on them, and he scolded himself for putting Jill in possible danger.

Jill was pondering Thad's kiss. She didn't know what to make of it. Had he kissed her because he had special feelings for her, or did he do it just to see if he could?

As soon as Thad and Jill were out of hearing distance, Joe chuckled. "Now, don't that beat all?"

"I guess it would, if I knew what you were talking about." Radna sat down in the place Jill had just vacated.

"Old Thad has fallen hook, line and sinker for my little sister." He laughed again. "Who'da thought it? They've known each other all their lives. He used to tease her by saying 'Jill the pill fell down the hill.' She'd throw cobs at him."

"Do you mind?"

"Hell, no. I think it's great. She'll give him

a merry time. She's got enough spunk for a dozen girls."

"She was mad as a wet hen the night he got here. Lord, she ripped him up one side and down the other. She'll not admit that she likes him." Radna's musical laugh rang out. "She's a stubborn little dickens and I like her a hell of a lot."

"She's had a soft spot for Thad for a long time."

"It doesn't show," Radna insisted.

"She might not act like it, but she's had one since he saved her from a man who was trying to rape her."

"She hasn't mentioned . . . anything like that to me," Justine said.

"The family doesn't talk about it. A man had been raping girls in our town for several years. He caught Jill in the woods on her way home from the field. According to what he said, he'd been waiting for a chance at her. He wrapped a scarf around her head, threw her on the ground and had ripped open the top of her dress when Thad got there.

"He was riding down the path on his horse and heard her cry out. He was just a kid. He managed to get to her before . . . it was too late. He jumped on the man, fought him. They rolled under Thad's horse and the frightened horse stomped the man. He died a few hours later.

"For Jill's sake and for the sake of the man's wife, the rape thing was never known outside our family and Thad's. The police chief and the doctor were there when the man was dying. He told them that he had at least eighteen children from the girls he had raped over the years."

"He should have been hanged," Justine said heatedly.

"He would have been, if the horse hadn't done him in. Pa would have strung him up on the spot even if he was a town merchant and on the city council."

A pleasant half hour passed while Joe told his aunt about the neighborhood ball games they had back on the farm in Missouri and about Jack's baseball ambitions. He reminisced about the pretty woman, posing as a widow, who came to stay with the family.

"We kids were all afraid Pa would marry her."

"Did he want to?" Justine asked.

"I don't know. Before it got that far, her

husband came to take her home," Joe said with a laugh. "We were mighty glad to see the last of her."

Justine smiled at Joe, enjoying the story he was telling, then her eyes went past him and a look of horror came over her face.

"Oh, no! I shouldn't have come out here. Take me in. Please take me in!"

Joe followed her eyes to the steps to see Lloyd Madison bound up onto the porch, a friendly smile on his face.

Chapter 15

"Well, well. What do we have here?" Lloyd, with a wide smile on his face, stepped up on the porch and came to sit on the railing near where Justine sat with Joe and Radna beside her. "Hello, Justine, Joe." He ignored Radna and Blue.

"I want to go in." Justine's voice was low and strained.

"Don't let me run you off, Justine. It's a nice night and your family is gathered around you." He breathed in deeply. "This fresh, clean air will be good for you."

"As if you care what's good for me," Justine murmured and turned her head, refusing to look at him.

"I saw Jill walk off with that big, dark fellow that's been hanging around here, the one who claims he found the murdered woman. You should be careful who your sister walks out with, Joe. Especially now that there's been a murder in town."

"Are you saying that Thad had something to do with that?"

"He found the body. In a criminal investigation, the husband of a slain woman or the one who finds her body is always the first on the list of suspects. In this case, instead of a husband, it will be the lover, Hunter Westfall."

"Horse hockey!"

"Don't be crude," Lloyd said sharply, and he looked at Radna with undisguised disgust.

Unfazed, Radna said, "How come you know so damn much?" Her hand rested on Justine's trembling arm. She was aware that Blue had moved up off the steps and had sat down beside her, but she kept her dark, bright eyes on Lloyd.

"My father was a lawyer and later a judge. Right, Justine?" Lloyd spoke with cold deliberation, his eyes on Justine. "He taught me a lot about not letting people push me and giving as good as or more than I got. He taught me about criminal justice, about the sorry side of life, which unfortunately he had come to know about, because of white trash, firsthand. He insisted that I take a course in criminal investigation while I was in law school."

"Does the sheriff know this? If you're so good, you should offer your services to him and the man sent up from the city." Joe uttered the sarcastic words with a pleasant smile on his face.

Lloyd laughed. "You know how that goes. Big-city police officer has to be the big dog in this investigation. He's not going to let a small-town lawyer tell him anything." Lloyd had not taken his eyes off Justine. He spoke with his head tilted so that the side of his face with the birthmark was toward her. "You must be getting better, Justine. You're looking especially lovely tonight."

"Liar!" Justine blurted.

"Now, why do you say that?"

"You know why, damn you. Get away from me!"

"Move on, Madison. You're upsetting her." Joe's voice was strong and censorious.

"It certainly isn't my intention to upset her. I've known her for years and I'm really concerned for her—"

"Bullshit!" Justine almost shouted.

"Now, now, Justine. Such crude language coming from such a pretty lady! When you were young, I bet you made the swords of many lonely old men stand at attention. Huh?"

"I don't know what's going on here, but I don't like it," Joe said. "Move on, Madison, or I'll move you."

"Come, now, Joe, I'm interested in Justine's welfare the same as you are."

"You're interested in seeing me six feet under," Justine blurted.

Lloyd ignored the outburst and continued to speak to Joe.

"A person in her condition is bound to have delusions now and then." He tapped the side of his head with his forefinger. "I'm sorry to have to say that it's only going to get worse."

"Listen to me, you despicable ass." Radna shot up off the bench to stand protectively beside Justine. "She's not delusional. It's clear that you're out to make her life as miserable as you can. Get the hell away from her and stay away."

Lloyd laughed. "Radna, you continue to surprise me. *Despicable* and *delusional* are ten-dollar words. Did you learn them at that government school they set up to teach colored and Indian kids the difference between daylight and dark?"

"Yeah, they taught me that, and how to recognize a horse's ass when I met one." There was a sting in her voice.

Lloyd's laugh was loud and long.

"She's got a lot of spunk for a little colored gal. Don't you think so, Joe? I swear. Times are changing so fast I can hardly keep up with them. Coloreds and Indians used to know their place."

Blue got to his feet and stood in front of Justine. "You takin' her in now, Joe? I'll give ya a hand." He bent down as if to adjust Justine's feet. Instead he swiftly hooked his arm beneath Lloyd's legs and tipped him backward over the porch rail.

"Hey!" Lloyd's cry was one of fear and surprise.

"Uh-oh." Blue looked down at the man sprawled on his back amid the cannas. "Gotta be careful of these porch railin's. A feller can fall off 'em mighty easy."

Radna let out a peal of musical laughter. Even Justine smiled. A grin spread across

Joe's handsome face. He reached down and lifted his aunt in his arms.

"Wasn't that worth seeing, Aunt?" he said on his way to the door. "I wouldn't have missed it for a horse."

"Tell Mr. Blue to watch his back." Justine's voice trembled.

"Blue can take care of himself." Joe chuckled. "Madison is lucky he just got dumped in the flower bed. Blue can be rougher than a cob when he's riled. He's as strong as an ox and as ornery as one on locoweed."

Joe carried his aunt through the hotel lobby, where several guests were sitting in the big padded chairs reading or smoking. All were interested in the young man carrying the older woman so gently.

"*He'll* get even," Justine said worriedly as they started down the hall to her room.

"Don't worry. Blue knows what he's doing. It was the *little colored gal* thing and the slur on the Indian school that set him off. He's pretty mild-mannered until he thinks he's being made the goat. Then watch out. The fur will fly and he's likely to hurt someone."

"But Blue will be the one to be hurt," Justine said urgently. "Or . . . killed. You don't know *him.*"

"And you do?"

"Yes, I do," she said firmly. "*He's* crazy mean and vindictive. *He'll* get even if it takes . . . years."

Radna held open the door to Justine's room as Joe carried his aunt inside and placed her gently on the bed.

"Thank you," she whispered wearily.

"It was my pleasure."

"Joe, will you and Blue bring down the daybed from the room in the attic? I'm staying in here tonight." Radna was removing Justine's shoes.

"You don't need to stay in here with me."

"I think I do, and I'm going to." Radna's firm voice cut off Justine's protest.

"We'll bring it down, but first I'd better get back to the porch and make sure Blue doesn't lift the big-shot lawyer's hair with his scalping knife."

Justine spoke as soon as Joe closed the door. "What am I going to do, Radna? *He's* got something in mind. I wouldn't be surprised that *he* burned down his own house so *he'd* have an excuse to come here."

"Right now, you're going to get a good

night's sleep. I got another bottle of booze today. The doctor said it was good for you to have a drink at bedtime."

"I'm such a bother to everyone."

"Horse hockey. I can remember when I said the same thing to you. You said, and I quote: 'Bother, my skinny ass, Radna. What are friends for?'"

"That was different. You had been so badly beaten, I was afraid you'd not live."

"But I did. Shows you how stubborn I am. I'd have lain in the back alley and died if not for you. So don't be giving me any of that *bother* shit. Here, let me get that housecoat off you and the pins out of your hair."

"*He* despises me. I can see it in his eyes. When *he* came here I was able to get around and *he* wasn't so bold. Now I'm helpless."

"I wouldn't say that. With three big men looking out for you, you're far from help-less." Radna chuckled. "Wasn't that Blue a caution? He tipped that smart-mouthed buzzard over the rail before he could bat an eye. Too bad it didn't break his dang-blasted neck."

"*He'll* get even. *He'll* have Blue arrested on some trumped-up charge or else put a knife in his ribs or pay someone to do it. The judge was rich. I imagine he left it all to *him*."

"We won't worry about it now. If you're settled for a while, I'm going out to see about that daybed. I'll leave the light on and lock the door, but I'll keep an eye on it anyway. I'll be back with the booze. Might even have a snort myself."

"Aren't you going out tonight?"

"No, I'm staying right here. I'll go out tomorrow. The sheriff is so busy looking for the rest of that woman, he'll not be bothering about me."

"Be careful, Radna. *He'll* hurt you if *he* gets the chance."

"I'm aware of that. I carry a pistol in my pocket and a knife in my garter."

Justine's eyes went to the bureau and the picture of her late husband.

"Ralph would have known what to do about *him*. Ralph was the kindest person I ever knew. Kind and generous to a fault. He'd give you the shirt off his back if you needed it. Oh, he wasn't so good with money, but he made up for it in a hundred other ways." Justine's eyes swung back to her friend standing beside the door. "Go on,

Radna, dear. You don't have to fear that I'll get up and run off."

Jill and Thad paused on the porch steps. Joe and Blue were standing in front of Lloyd Madison, blocking his way to the door of the lobby.

"She doesn't want to see or talk to you. If you come near her, you'll find your jaws unhinged and your mouth flopping open like a fish out of water. I suggest you find another place to stay." Joe's voice was loud and stern.

"Are you threatening me?"

"I didn't hear anyone threatening you. Did you, Blue?"

"Nay. Me just dumb Indian."

"I've paid for a month, I'll stay a month. Try to get me out and I'll take her to court. I could file so many lawsuits that the court costs would take everything she's got."

"You'd do that?"

"If I have to."

"You're a real shit heel."

"Yeah, I am, and proud of it." He stepped around Joe and Blue and went into the hotel, crossed the lobby and climbed the stairs to his room.

"What's going on?" Thad asked.

"The smart-mouthed bastard was needling Aunt Justine. Blue tipped him over the railing. He landed on his butt in the flower bed. Lost his eyeglasses. Worse luck, he found them."

Thad slapped Blue on the back. "Good goin', ole hoss. I owe you one."

Joe continued, "Now he's threatening to have Blue jailed for assault and to file a court case against Aunt Justine if we try to get him out of here."

"Can he do that?" Jill asked.

"I don't know who his witnesses would be because we didn't see anything. Did we, Blue?"

"I dunno. I just—"

"Dumb Indian." Thad hit Blue on the shoulder again.

"He's as mad as a peed-on snake," Joe said. "Not that I care how damn mad he gets. I told him if he came around Aunt Justine again, I'd unhinge his flapping jaw."

"Is Aunt Justine all right?"

"Radna's with her. Aunt Justine thinks Madison will do something to Blue."

Blue snorted with disgust. "It'd take more

than a scrawny two-bit mouthpiece like him to do me in."

Jill expressed her opinion of Lloyd emphatically. "He gives me the shivers, and not because of that mark on his face."

"Radna wants us to bring a daybed down from the attic. She's going to sleep in Aunt Justine's room." Jill's hold on Thad's hand had not gone unnoticed by Joe, but wisely he realized that now wasn't the time to tease them about it.

Jill released Thad's hand and led the way into the hotel lobby. She went to the desk to speak to Mr. and Mrs. Evans.

"It's a slow night, miss. But the train came in a half an hour ago. We should get a few more."

"I'll be in the kitchen or in my aunt's room if you need me."

Officer Hurt came into the lobby as Jill was leaving the desk. With him was a dapper young man wearing a black suit and a red-patterned tie. A gray felt hat sat tilted on his head. Showing beneath the hat brim was thick black hair. He appeared to be what some folks might call a "dandy."

"Good evening."

"Evening, miss." Officer Hurt put his fingers to the brim of his Stetson. He was a man with a long upper body and short legs. His iron-gray hair and the lines in his face put his age in the late forties. "This is my friend and fellow officer from the city, D. A. Bryce."

"How do you do?" Jill extended her hand.

"Very well, ma'am."

"Do you need a room?" Jill asked, nodding toward the heavy suitcase the man had left inside the door. *Officer Hurt did say he was a police officer. But he didn't look old enough.*

"Yes, ma'am."

"For how long?"

"For as long as I'm here," Officer Hurt said.

Jill gestured toward the desk. "Welcome to Rainwater, Mr. Bryce. Mr. Evans will help you."

"Thank you, ma'am."

While his friend was signing the register, Officer Hurt asked, "Does the hotel have a laundry service, miss?"

"Yes, we do. If you have things to be washed, leave the bundle on your bed. Mrs. Cole will be here tomorrow. She'll take it home and bring it back the next day. Do you want your shirts heavily starched?"

"No, ma'am. Lightly starched front and collar. Ready to go up, Jelly?" he said to the young officer.

Jill watched the men climb the stairs, then went down the hallway to the kitchen. Radna was helping Joe and Blue maneuver the daybed through the doorway into Justine's room.

"I'm sleeping in with Justine," Radna explained, unaware that Joe had already mentioned this to Jill.

"I could have slept here with her," Jill offered.

"We'll take turns. Set the bed there by the bureau. Before I go to bed, I'll shove it up next to the door."

"Yes, ma'am," both men said in unison.

"Mr. Blue," Justine called.

"You don't need to be calling me mister, ma'am," Blue said when he approached the bed.

"I want to thank you for what you did and to tell you to be careful. Watch your back. *He's* got the devil right in him, and I'm not talking about the mark on his face. *He* has no conscience, no compassion, no feelings

for anyone at all. He dislikes Radna because she's Indian and she's close to me.
I'm afraid *he'll* do . . . something to her and
now to you because of what you did."

"Don't worry, ma'am. I may not have run
into his kind before, but I'll not underesti-
mate him. I'll not turn my back to him and
we'll watch to see that he doesn't harm
Radna. Although I think that feisty little
twister-tail can take care of herself." Blue
added the last when he became aware
Radna was listening. His dark eyes twinkled
when he heard a grunt of disgust, then a
whispered obscene word.

"Thank you." Justine closed her eyes
wearily. Blue patted the limp hand that lay
by her side and then, ignoring Radna, hurried from the room.

When Blue entered the kitchen, Thad was
at the icebox chipping ice to put in the tea
glasses Jill had set on the table.

"I can't let you out of my sight five minutes before you're in trouble," Thad said
with his back to Blue. "Why did you have to
pick a fight with that nice, friendly man?
Didn't anyone tell you that he's one of the
town's leading citizens?"

"Nice man my . . . my rear end!" Blue snorted.

"You've gone soft, Blue. Soft. As long as you were at it, you could have given him something to remember you by. A few missing teeth, perhaps, or a broken arm would have put the message across. Couldn't you think of anything more to do than dump him in a nice, soft flower bed, for God's sake?"

"There were ladies present."

"It hasn't stopped you before. Remember that flapper you were chasing down in Tulsa, the one with the big headlights? You were—"

"All right, all right. Next time I'll step on his glasses!"

"Thad!" Jill scolded. "Stop teasing Blue and pour the tea."

"If you'll come here and give me a kiss."

Without waiting for an answer, he reached for her, grabbed her around the waist and swung her off her feet. She yipped in surprise.

"What's got into you tonight?" she asked between giggles after he had kissed her soundly.

"You know," he whispered in her ear before he set her on her feet.

"Hey, there, boy." Joe came in through the back door. "Stop manhandling my little sister."

"Tend to your own business, farm boy."

"Get fresh with her again and there'll be a shotgun wedding before you can say *scat.*" Joe hit Thad on the shoulder with his hat.

Jill's face turned a bright red. Thad turned her loose and swung at Joe. The two men began scuffling around the kitchen like a couple of frisky puppies. They almost upset a kitchen chair, then bumped into the table.

"Joe! Thad! Stop it before you break something. You'll turn the table over. Blue, make them stop," Jill pleaded when the scuffling continued.

"I'm not getting between those two clabberheads." Blue sat down at the table and reached for a glass of iced tea. "Old Thad's been bit by a bug. He's going to be a hard dog to keep under the porch for a while."

"What do you mean?"

"Don't listen to him, honey." Thad stepped away from Joe and pressed Jill down in a chair. "He's jealous because he didn't see you first."

"I was sure a herd of buffalo had come through." Radna stood in the doorway. Her small feet were planted on the floor, her hands on her hips. "I could hear you in Justine's room with the door closed."

"Sorry," Joe said with a sheepish look on his face. "I went out to get our bedrolls and found Thad messing around with my little sister. Missouri men protect their little sisters from mashers and lechers and fast men who have designs on the virtues of young girls," he added seriously.

"For crying out loud, Joe. I'm not your *little* sister," Jill protested.

"I'll get you for this, Joe," Thad said in a loud whisper.

"Land-a-livin'!" Radna rolled her eyes to the ceiling. "Is it always like this?" She directed her question to Blue.

"Pretty much."

"It's too thick in here for me. I'm going to the porch for a while. Keep an eye on Justine's door." As she walked past Joe, she placed the door key on the table.

Blue stood up and followed Radna. "I was just going out to the porch to get away from all this hullabaloo myself."

"Miss Radna." Joe made a false attempt

to get up. "I'd better come and keep an eye on Blue. He's been known to be grabby. He has as many hands as a centipede has legs when he's around a pretty lady."

"Sit." Blue's heavy hand settled on Joe's shoulder. "Stick your snout out that door and it will be amputated immediately," he threatened as he followed Radna out the door.

"Joe, did you ever hear Blue spouting such big words as he's been doin' lately?"

"He's showing off."

"Well, it sure as heck isn't to impress you or me. And if he's got any sense at all, he knows that Jill's taken."

"Jill's taken? She hasn't said anything to me about it. Who is he? I'll want to give that bird the eagle eye just like Pa would do if he was here."

"Don't worry, little . . . brother." Thad hit Joe on the shoulder. "I intend to see that our Jill gets the best man in this town, in the state of Oklahoma. Hell, in the whole United States."

"And you know who that is?"

"Damn right I do, and so do you."

Chapter 16

"I didn't ask for your company." Radna sat on the dark end of the back porch smoking a cigarette.

"You didn't have to. I knew you wanted me to come out." Blue sat down beside her, pulled a pipe from his pocket and packed the bowl with tobacco.

"Jesus, my beads! You're such an arrogant jackass. Know that?"

"Yeah." He spoke with the pipe between his teeth and held a lit match to the bowl, giving her a view of his classic Indian profile.

"Why did you come out? If you came thinking that I'm going to sleep with you, you can get that thought out of your head."

"Horse hockey!" he said with a chuckle. "You've got a big opinion of yourself. I'm choosy about who I sleep with. You're too bony for my taste. I like meat on my squaws."

"Ha! Big brave chief hasn't the guts to say he doesn't sleep with coloreds!"

He turned to peer at her through the darkness and saw that she had turned her face away.

"You hold that little dab of colored blood up like a damn shield. If I wanted you for my woman, it wouldn't amount to a dribble of shit if every drop of blood in your skinny body was colored."

She turned to look at him. "Liar."

"I'm a lot of things, but a liar isn't one of them."

"Most of the time you sound more white than Indian."

"It's a white man's world, little thorny rose. If you can't beat 'em, you join 'em."

"Rose? Ha! Shows what you know about me."

"It fits. I've seen scraggly vines growing along a fence line that were so thorny you couldn't touch the scrawny little rose . . . that is, if you wanted to."

"Try touching me, you dumb Indian, and I'll lay a fist up alongside your head."

Blue grunted a reply.

After a long silence, Radna asked, "How long are you staying around here?"

"Long enough to see if you're as feisty in bed as you are out of it."

"Then you'd better get a job. Before that happens you'll starve to death."

Blue puffed on his pipe. Radna dropped her cigarette and smashed it into the ground with the toe of her shoe.

"What do you know about that loud-mouth I tossed in the bushes?" he asked.

"He's a lawyer."

"What's he to Mrs. Byers?"

"That's all you'll get from me. If you want to know more, ask her."

"Where did he come from?"

"What are you? A detective?"

"No, dumb Indian."

"Dumb like a fox." Radna scoffed.

"I heard about a fellow like him over near Joplin. Crazy mean, they said. Hated Indians and coloreds."

"I've not heard of Lloyd being mean to anyone. He's got some folks here in town eating out of his hand." Radna stood up. "I'm going to bed."

"Suits me." Blue got to his feet. "Where'll we go?"

"Forget it, Chief. You'll not use your war club in my bed."

Radna flounced up onto the porch and through the kitchen door. Blue sat back down on the edge of the porch, a grin softening his Indian features.

It was going to be a hot, windless day.

From the doorway of his office, Sheriff Page saw Clarence Hurt, the Oklahoma City officer, coming down the street. A nattily dressed young man walked beside him. Even in the dusty Oklahoma heat he looked as if he had just stepped out of a bandbox. Wearing light gray trousers, a dark suit coat, a striped bow tie and with a gray billed cap sitting at an angle on his head, he looked as out of place among the booted, overalled roustabouts on the street as a tulip in a tomato patch.

"Christ, I hope he isn't the brainy sharpshooter Hurt was expecting. All I need is a smart-mouthed, duded-up kid to kick out of the way." Muttering to himself, the sheriff went to sit at his desk. He was tired in mind and in body, and his temper was getting short. Pressure from all sides was on him to find Carsie Bakken's killer.

"Morning, Sheriff," Officer Hurt said when he entered the office.

"Morning," Page muttered, his eyes on the man who followed Hurt into the office.

"Meet Jelly Bryce, Sheriff."

"Howdy." Sheriff Page stood up and offered his hand.

Jesus, this wet-eared kid couldn't be the one Hurt said could drop a quarter from waist high and shoot a hole in it before it hit the ground. He looked like a goldfish-gulping college kid.

"It's a pleasure to meet you, Sheriff."

"You might not think so after you've been here awhile." The sheriff growled the reply and sank back down in his chair.

Lord, what was Hurt thinking of? The kid was still wet behind the ears.

"Call me Jelly, Sheriff." The boy hung his cap on the hall tree in the corner. His hair was black and thick.

"Anything new?" Hurt asked.

"The breed we were holding is clear. My deputy got a statement from Junior Fields at the pool hall that he was in there all night, the night the woman was killed. I let him out this morning and told him to get his ass out of town after he paid the doc for taking care of the finger he cut off," Sheriff Page said. "For all we know now, the woman walked out of Hunter Westfall's house and dropped into a well."

"The colored woman said that she heard a car. I don't believe that she was killed in a car. It would have been too messy." Officer Hurt sat down, lifted a booted foot to rest an ankle on his knee, then continued. "So she was taken someplace nearby and killed. But where? Where is her suitcase? Westfall said she had several pieces of good jewelry and had taken them with her."

"I have verified that Westfall was where he said he was." The sheriff shared this information with Jelly out of respect for the Oklahoma City officer. "He was at a town meeting, then on the street settling a dispute between his men and later walking out with the girl who runs the hotel. He returned home at around eleven o'clock. The colored couple who work for him verified that. They were too scared of me to lie."

"Have you questioned Westfall's neighbors? Did any of them see anything or hear the car?" Jelly stood with his back to the wall, one knee bent, the sole of his highly polished shoe against the wall.

Sheriff Page answered with an impatient look on his face. "It's been damn near a week since we found her. Of course we've questioned Westfall's neighbors. They claim to have seen nothing, and I believe them. We searched the area for the rest of the woman. Men who volunteered to help with the hunt have dwindled to zero. The only clue we'll get is when we find her head, if we find it."

Jelly Bryce spoke to Officer Hurt. "Sheriff seems to be on top of things. Why did you want me to come up here?"

"Because this is a bizarre case, and we just might need someone with your talent, Jelly."

"Until then, I think I'll just mosey on up-town and see the sights."

"Good idea." The sheriff mumbled the words, but Officer Hurt heard them. Hurt waited until Jelly had left the office before he spoke.

"Don't be deceived by the boy's looks and sell him short, Sheriff. The officers in the city gave him the name Jelly Bean. It stuck. His name is D.A., but he's known as

Jelly Bryce. He can draw and shoot faster than the eye can follow. The first day on the job he killed a man who had drawn on him."

"Shitfire! I don't need a gun-happy kid mixing it up with the tough oil field workers in this town."

"He can handle himself. He hits what he shoots at ninety-nine percent of the time."

"He might be all right in the city. But here he stands out like a shithouse in the moonlight."

"The shithouse might come in handy," Officer Hurt said irritably. "Now let's go over the information we have."

Laura arrived to do the end-of-the-week washing and had lifted Mary Pat over the chicken wire fence when Joe came out onto the back porch. The toddler, squatting in the yard, was spooning dirt into a tin cup. She grinned up at her mother for approval.

Laura clapped her hands. "You're a big girl to do that. Oh—" she exclaimed and jumped back when Joe moved up beside her.

"Sorry. I didn't mean to scare you. I'm Joe Jones. Jill's brother."

Laura's large violet eyes stayed on him as

she continued to back away, her mouth still forming an O. When the screen door slammed, she glanced at the porch and then back as if she expected the stranger to pounce on her.

"If there's a pretty woman around, I know where to find you." Thad spoke to Joe, then came to bend over the fence where the child played. Recognizing him, the little girl laughed and lifted her arms for him to take her. "Come here, little sweetheart. You know a good man when you see one." He swung the child up in his arms. "Isn't she a beauty?" he said to Joe.

"Yeah. Hello, little puddin' pie." Joe held out a finger and a small hand came out to grasp it.

"Don't let this Missouri clodhopper scare you, ma'am," Thad said to Laura. "He's harmless. Joe, this is Mrs. Hopper."

"How do you do, ma'am?"

"I wasn't scared of you. Just surprised. Mama said you were here." Laura watched the two big men with her daughter and marveled at how gentle they were.

"Fertile had her pups last night," Thad announced with pride. "Joe, get one to show Mary Pat."

"Not on your life. That hound tried to bite me this morning. I'm not touchin' her pups. I'll hold the baby, you get the pup. Come here, little pretty thing."

"Coward." Thad laughingly handed the baby over to Joe. She went to him willingly and patted his face with her dirty little hands.

Thad went to the end of the porch and knelt down. Fertile, in a nest of old blankets, was nursing six wiggly puppies.

"Let me show off one of your babies, girl. We won't hurt it and I'll bring it right back."

Thad reached in and pulled out a bundle of white fur. Cradling it in his arms, he reached for Mary Pat's little hand. Very gently he stroked the child's tiny fingertips over the downy back of the puppy. The little girl squealed in delight. Suddenly her small fingers tightened on the puppy's fur.

"Be gentle, honey. He's a little baby dog." Thad gently loosened the tiny fingers. "I'd better take him back to his mama."

When Thad returned, he lifted Mary Pat from Joe's arms and swung the giggling child around before he set her down inside the fence.

"I saw a pile of sand at the lumberyard. I'll

get some nice clean sand, darlin', so you'll not have to play in that old dirt." Thad looked up to see Joe staring at Laura's profile. "Get the car, Joe. I'll get an old washtub out of the wash house."

"It was nice meeting you, ma'am." Joe put his fingers to the brim of his straw hat.

Laura nodded, then said to Thad, "You don't have to get sand. Mrs. Byers might not like it."

"She won't care. All little girls should have a sand pile." He went into the wash house. "Let me know if the washer acts up," he said when he came out carrying an old dented tub.

Laura stood in the doorway of the wash house and watched them leave. After being married to Bradley, she had been sure that she never wanted anything to do with men again. But after meeting Joe and Thad, she wasn't so sure.

"A tub of sand is mighty heavy. We'd have been better off getting a couple of buckets," Joe said as he started the car.

Thad grinned. "I can handle it if you can. Laura's been tying the little tyke in the wagon while she worked. I put up the chicken wire so the kid would have a place to play."

Joe nodded. "That's a new one."

"You think I was playin' up to Laura? I did it for the little girl."

"What happened to Laura's man?"

"He fell off a derrick and was killed. From what Radna said, he wasn't much of a husband."

"With her looks, I'm surprised men aren't lining up at the door."

"Yeah, she's a looker."

"You interested?"

"Nope. I've picked out my woman."

"Does Jill know it?"

"Not yet."

"We used to tease her about you."

"I've got to change her way of thinking about me."

Joe laughed. "Then stop calling her *little sister.*"

"I've already done that."

"If I was ready to settle down, it wouldn't be in a place like Rainwater. I've kind of got a hankering to go back home and farm. A farmer might not have much cash money, but he's always got plenty to eat."

"Giving up the thought of our buying a ranch together?" Thad asked.

"Pushing steers instead of a plow sounds good, but I know more about farming than I do about ranching. The one thing I do know is that I don't want to live in a city or in a boomtown like this one."

"Getting homesick?"

"A little, I reckon." Joe grinned sheepishly. "What about you?"

"You know the old saying: 'There's no place like home.'"

"Does Jill want to go home?"

"I think so." Thad's green eyes, serious now, turned to those of his lifelong friend. "I've got six hundred dollars. Guess you know where to find it if something happens to me."

"In the lining of your old brown coat?"

"Yeah."

"I've not got quite that much. We should put it in a bank someplace."

"Not according to Blue. He believes money should either be in your pocket or in land."

"I'm thinking of asking Evan to look around for some land up around Fertile."

"You've been thinking about this for a while?"

"Yeah. Wages are good here, but what good are they if you can't settle someplace and put your feet down? We've been on the move since we left home. I'd like to have my own bed to sleep in, eat at my own table—"

"Have your own woman?"

"I've thought of it, but haven't found the right one yet."

"How about Laura Hopper?"

"I'm not sure I want a woman who's so damn beautiful. I'd have to lock her up to keep men away from her."

"It isn't her fault that she's pretty."

"No, it isn't. I want to love the woman I take for a wife like Evan loves Julie and like Corbin Appleby loves his Annabel."

"If you got to know Laura, you might fall for her in spite of the fact that she's so sinfully pretty."

"We can't go home for a while, maybe months. Meanwhile, I need a job. One of us at the hotel during the day is enough."

"Jill won't leave here as long as her aunt needs her, so we're stuck here for a while."

"I'm still going to write to Evan and ask

him to look around." Joe steered the car around the corner and pulled up alongside the lumberyard.

"Are you still wanting a partner?" Thad made no move to get out of the car.

"I've thought of asking you. It would take quite a bit of land to support two families."

"You're going to have one?"

"A family? Damn right. Someday. I need kids to take care of me in my old age."

"Our combined money should buy a pretty good chunk, especially if I can get another job helping to put out a fire."

"We don't need money that bad," Joe said sternly. "That was a fool thing for you to do."

"How so? I knew what I was doing."

"You could have been blown to smithereens and I'd have lost a partner."

"I wasn't going to let that happen if I could help it. Lord, I've been looking out for you for so long, I don't think you can hack it by yourself," Thad teased.

"Horsecock! Who took care of you when you got fired for telling the boss he was a stupid asshole and if shit were brains he'd be governor?"

Thad laughed. "I'd forgotten about that."

"Let's see what Evan comes up with. Who knows, I might be looking at your ugly face every day for the next forty years."

Joe got out of the car and reached for the tub.

Chapter 17

Laura was nervous about the evening ahead. She had been scolding herself all day for not being more forceful and telling Hunter Westfall not to come back.

Her mother was upset with her and rightfully so.

"What were you thinking of? He's coming here for one reason only. He knows we're as poor as Job's turkey and he thinks to buy his way into your bed."

"Then he'll be disappointed."

"That murdered woman had been staying with him. No decent single man has a woman who isn't a relative come stay with him. Some say she was a whore. It's what folks will think of you if you're seen with him."

"I'll know it isn't true and so will you."

"It'll hurt your chances of getting a decent man."

"I don't want a man, Mama. I've told you that."

"It isn't natural for a woman to live her life alone."

"I'm not alone. I have you and Mary Pat."

"I worry about what will happen to you when I'm gone. I won't always be here."

"None of us will, Mama. I hope to live long enough to see Mary Pat on her own. It's all I ask."

"I don't want him in the house."

"I'll talk to him on the porch and tell him not to come back."

"Lordy mercy. There are times when I wish you were ugly as a mud fence."

Laura laughed, stretched her mouth with her thumbs, crossed her eyes and wiggled her fingers. "Like this?"

Mrs. Cole couldn't help but smile at her daughter's antics. "Jill's brother is a nice-looking man. He's kind and as sweet as he can be. He carried Mrs. Byers to the kitchen so she could visit with Radna while she worked. He would know how to treat a decent girl. Why don't you set your cap for him? Laws honey, you could have any man in this town. All you'd have to do is beckon."

"Are you trying to get rid of me?"

"No. You've got to be careful and not make the same mistake you made with Bradley."

"He raped me, Mama. But I'm not sorry. I got Mary Pat out of it."

"I know, honey. I'm sorry I brought it up. I'm worried about Hunter Westfall coming here. He's not a marrying man, just takes his pleasure from women and doesn't give a hoot and a holler about any of them. Every single woman in town and some of the married ones have been after him."

"Not me and not Jill."

"She walked off with him Saturday night."

"Radna said she did it to prove to Thad she'd do as she pleased." Laura giggled like the young girl she was. "Radna thinks Jill's in love with Thad."

"It was nice of him to fix the pen and a sand pile for Mary Pat."

"Mary Pat's stuck on him and squeals every time she sees him."

"You like him, don't you? You could beat Jill's time with him if you set your mind to it."

"I wouldn't do such a thing, Mama! Heavens! You wouldn't want me to."

"You're right, honey, I wouldn't." Mrs. Cole hung the wet dish towel on the handle of the oven door. "I've got to iron the lawman's shirts tonight so I can take them back in the morning."

"I wish he'd catch the monster who killed that woman."

"Some think it was Hunter Westfall."

"If the sheriff thought that, Mr. Westfall would be in jail."

"When he gets here, I'll be right here in the kitchen with your daddy's old shotgun. If he makes one false move, he'll get both barrels."

The ironing board had a permanent position in Mrs. Cole's kitchen. She cleared it off and set up the iron. Earlier she had sprinkled the shirts with water, rolled them tightly and placed them in the ironing basket.

Laura filled a bucket from the water tap in the kitchen.

"I'll put this in the washtub on the porch and let Mary Pat splash in it for a while before I put her to bed."

"When is Mr. Big Shot coming?"

"I suspect about dark. Don't worry, Mama. He won't stay long."

Hunter Westfall had spent most of the morning in his office going over figures for the amusement park while the electric fan on the floor stirred the hot, dry air.

Earlier he had heard from the sheriff that the decision had been made to bury Carsie's body immediately. When and if the head was found, the sheriff explained, the coffin would have to be dug up and opened.

Hunter had gone home to fetch Dinah and Casper for the short graveside service. The three of them were the only people in town who had known her. The sheriff, Officer Hurt and the young officer he had brought up from the city also attended.

Hunter had a brief conversation with the three officers after the burial. They told him that there had been no new developments in the search for Carsie's killer.

"Watch yourself," Sheriff Page warned. "Someone is spreading the rumor that you're the killer."

"What's the basis of the rumor? You've

checked out my movements on the night in question."

"The rumor is that the colored folks who work for you are lying and that you were away most of the night."

"Do they think Miss Jones lied about me being with her? Plenty of people saw me on the street. If they think Dinah and Casper are lying, they don't know them very well. Who's behind the rumors? I'll have a talk with him. Better yet, I'll have him talk to Dinah and Casper."

"My advice is to stay away from him. You'd just be stirring the pot."

"Can't you at least tell me who started the talk?"

"I see no harm in that. It's public knowledge. Lloyd Madison is keeping the talk going. I've no way of knowing who started it, but I suspect it was him." The sheriff explained to the other two officers that Madison was one of the two attorneys in town.

"I'm not surprised," Hunter said. "He's been against everything that I've tried to do for the town since the day he came here."

"Had you known him before?"

"No. Never saw him. I'd remember it if I did. He's breeding discontent among the workers by telling them that the oil companies are taking advantage of them and the ranchers in the area. He doesn't stop to think that the oil companies create the jobs for those who are spending money in town."

"If he's the man with the blood-red mark on his face, he was at the soda fountain in the drugstore talking about the big operators paying slave wages to the workers and how the oil companies are destroying the land." The young officer spoke for the first time.

"That isn't true," Hunter said quickly. "We pay the same wages as the companies in Tulsa and Oklahoma City, and as for destroying the land—the ranchers lease to us because they want the money."

"Did he know who you were, Jelly?" Hurt asked the young officer.

"I'm sure he did. He was on the hotel porch when we left this morning. I got the feeling he was talking for my benefit."

"Do as you please about talking to Madison, Mr. Westfall," Sheriff Page said. "But if I were you, I'd avoid him as much as possible. He's a smooth talker, the kind who can stir up folks against you. A bunch of liquored-up roustabouts can get pretty ugly, pretty quick."

"I don't want any trouble with Madison, never have. He's got a chip on his shoulder where I'm concerned and I'll be damned if I know why. I'm surprised he hasn't blamed me for burning down his house." Hunter drew a paper from his pocket. "I've made a list of things I knew Miss Bakken had with her: clothes, jewelry, a mirror and brush set I had given to her and the make of the suitcase. It was a dark tapestry with brass fixtures."

"Was the jewelry valuable?"

"Some of it was. Miss Bakken had some wealthy friends."

Back in his office, while working on the figures, Hunter thought briefly about the conversation with the officers, then the memory of Laura Hopper's lovely violet eyes and the promise of seeing her again wreaked havoc on his concentration.

He leaned back in his chair, steepled his fingers, considered his life up to now and realized that the things that really mattered were missing. The only family he had ever known had been his mother, who, he guessed, had loved him in her own peculiar way.

As far as he knew, she had never had a lasting relationship—not even with the father he had known for a short time. Men had floated in and out of her life, just as women now floated in and out of his. Although not fabulously wealthy, he and his mother had been well fixed because of the money his mother had inherited from her father.

Life had been easy for Hunter. He had not had to work his way through school, as had some of his classmates. He had enlisted in the army when he was eighteen, but the war was over before he finished his training. He went back to college. After graduation, he left school with a healthy bank account he had inherited when his mother died in a boating accident.

Striking out on his own, he discovered that he had a shrewd business head and that making money was an exciting hobby. That and sexual gratification had been his life up to now.

In his entire life he had never known a closeness with anyone other than Dinah and Casper. They had been with his mother and then with him after she died. In the past he'd had glimpses of family life when he let himself be friends with classmates, and later with some of his employees. He often felt a twinge of envy when observing the devotion of wives and children but dismissed the feeling.

He hadn't fully realized what was missing in his life . . . until now.

Since Carsie's death, he had come face-to-face with his own mortality. Sitting at his desk, staring out the window, Hunter suddenly had a fierce yearning to see Laura again, talk to her, learn what she liked and what she didn't like and have her know him as a man. He wanted to share her dreams for the future and have her know his.

Instinctively he knew that she was a woman who would love a man for himself alone and not for what he could give her. He longed for the kind of love he had only read about in the classics.

Hunter got up from his desk and, with a nod toward the two employees in the office, put on his hat and went out the door.

"What's got into him?" the bookkeeper asked.

"He's got a lot on his mind. The murder of

that woman has knocked the props from under him."

"Do you think he did it?"

"No. I'd stake my life on it," Perry Reade said forcefully.

"The talk is that he did."

"I don't care about the talk! I've worked for him for six years. He hasn't even shot a jackrabbit. His one weakness, that I can see, is that he likes to screw women. Hell, there isn't a man in town who doesn't like to do that. The difference is that Hunter has the money to buy that pleasure. If he hadn't wanted Carsie Bakken anymore, he would have sent her on her way as he has done the others."

"The town is getting stirred up. The killer had better be found soon or there could be a lynching."

"Mistah Hunter, what yo doin' home dis early? I ain't even started yo dinner."

"That's all right, Dinah. It's too hot for a heavy dinner. How about a sandwich and a cold glass of tea in about an hour? I'll turn on the fan in my room and lie down for a while."

Hunter went up the stairs. Instead of going to his room, he opened the door to the room Carsie had used. The fragrance of her perfume still hung in the hot air. Rather than bringing forth the image of luscious breasts, a soft belly and a triangle of soft tight curls as it usually did, it made him slightly nauseated. He went quickly to the windows and opened them. He propped the door open with a chair, then went down the hall to the bathroom and turned on the water to fill the large clawfoot bathtub.

After shedding his clothes, he stepped into the tub and began to scrub. He didn't understand this sudden desire to cleanse himself. In fact, it was more than a desire. It was a need, and he was compelled to satisfy it. He just knew he had to wash away as much filth from his life as possible before he called on Laura. After scrubbing every inch of his body, he washed his hair, then sat in the water, thinking.

"Mistah Hunter? Yo all right in dere?" Dinah's worried voice came through the closed door.

"I'm all right, Dinah."

"Yo don't never take no bath 'fore supper."

"I . . . ah . . . wanted to cool off. I'll be out in a minute."

He heard Dinah mumbling as she went down the hall to the stairs. Hunter got out of the tub, reached for a large fluffy towel and dried himself. After wrapping it around him, he went across the hall to his room and searched in the drawers of his bureau for clean underwear and socks.

When he went downstairs he was wearing a pair of freshly washed but worn cord trousers and a blue shirt open at the neck with sleeves rolled up to his elbow. He had given a lot of thought about what to wear when he called on Laura. He didn't want her to see him as the head of the oil company or the owner of various other businesses. Most of all, he didn't want to appear as the richest man in town. He wanted to be just a man who had finished a day's work, calling on a woman he was interested in.

He ate the egg salad sandwich and the sliced cantaloupe, thankful that Dinah stayed in the kitchen while he ate. He knew that she and Casper were concerned for him. On Casper's daily trips uptown he must have heard the rumors.

Hunter took his glass of iced tea to the

front porch and sat down in the porch swing to wait until it was time to walk down the street to Laura's house.

When finally the sun settled for the night, Hunter rose to take his tea glass back into the house. Lloyd Madison's Ford roadster was coming down the street. As it approached, Hunter wondered about the man who disliked him so much. The car passed, with Madison looking toward the house. Hunter raised his hand to see if the lawyer would respond. He didn't.

In the hope that Madison would be out of the area when he went to Laura's, Hunter waited until dusk to leave the house. His palms were damp, but his mouth was dry. The tightness in his chest was the result of his anxiety as well as the anticipation of seeing Laura again.

The hope for a different life he harbored was surely the emotional backlash from Carsie's murder. Hell! He was reaching for the moon. He had always been alone and would always be alone except for Dinah and Casper. He was half ashamed of his naïveté, his secret need, his quiet desperation. The thought crossed his mind that he should turn around and go back home.

But he kept walking.

Hunter was not confident about his ability to explain to her or to himself why, after two conversations with Laura, he was obsessed with the desire to come here. When he reached the house, a light shone from the kitchen window and squeals of childish laughter came from the back. He went around the house and stood, silently taking in the scene on the back porch.

Laura's daughter sat in a washtub, splashing happily. With a washcloth in her hand, Laura jumped back from the tub.

"You little rascal! You're getting me wet." There was laughter in her voice.

"Ma-ma." The child squealed and pounded on the water with her small hands, spraying it out onto the porch.

"Mama is going to snatch you out of there if you don't calm down and let me wash you," Laura threatened.

"Ma-ma!" Mary Pat continued to splash happily.

"I guess you deserve a little fun. It was hot today, wasn't it, sugar?" Laura crooned and backed away. It was then she saw Hunter standing at the end of the porch. "Oh, my goodness—"

"I scared you again," he said quickly. "I'm sorry. I heard the baby laughing and I knew where to find . . ." His voice diminished to softness, then faded completely.

"I can't talk to you now. I've got to give Mary Pat a bath and put her to bed."

"I understand. I'll not get in the way."

He walked toward the tub, smiling down at the beautiful little girl. Mary Pat thought he was someone else to play with her. Laughing at him, she hit the water with her hands, splashing it up onto his shirt and into his face.

He laughed.

Laura gasped. "She'll get you wet."

"I'll dry." He sat down on the edge of the porch beside the tub. "This is a treat for me." He lifted his eyes to Laura. The front of her dress was wet, her bare feet snuggled in the grass growing beside the porch, her glorious hair tangled about her face. Hunter thought she was beautiful, beyond beautiful. But it went deeper than that. Her violet eyes shone with warmth and kindness, love for her child and . . . apprehension.

"I don't want you to be afraid of me. I'll go if you want me to, but I'd like to stay." When she said nothing, he retreated into the safety of silence until a splash of water hit him in the face. His laugh rang out. "You want to play, do you?"

Hunter took a folded handkerchief from his pocket, dipped it in the water and draped it over the child's head.

"Gone, gone," he said, then jerked it off her head. "There she is!"

Mary Pat squealed with laughter, clearly enjoying the attention of the man. He draped the handkerchief over her head again.

"Gone, gone."

"On, on," she echoed.

"There she is!" When he jerked the handkerchief from her head, she grabbed it and slapped it in the water.

"You've started something." Laura stood beside the tub holding the washcloth.

"On, on." The baby put the wet handkerchief on her head.

Laura's merry laugh rang out. "It didn't take her long to catch on to that."

"She's a humdinger," Hunter said of the daughter, but he couldn't take his eyes off the mother. She was so slender and delicate. Yet he instinctively knew that she would be as fierce as a cornered cat if her child was in danger. This was motherhood as it was meant to be.

"It's a game Dinah played with her little girl." Hunter found his voice.

"I didn't know she had a little girl."

"It was a long time ago. During the war."

"She's never mentioned her. Does she live around here?"

"She died during the influenza epidemic."

"Mother's folks died then, too."

Laura took Hunter's handkerchief from Mary Pat, wrung it out and handed it to him. After wiping the washcloth over the little girl's face, she placed it on the rim of the tub and attempted to lift Mary Pat out of the water. The child had other ideas. She shrieked and held out her arms to Hunter.

"No, no, sugar. Come to Mama. I'll dry you and get you ready for bed."

Mary Pat's face crumpled. She let out a piercing cry; tears appeared and rolled down her face. She held her arms out to Hunter. At first he didn't understand that she wanted him to take her. When he did, his heart leaped in a surge of gladness. He reached out and lifted the dripping baby from the water. She wrapped her little arms around his neck, snuggled against him and laid her wet little head on his shoulder.

Never in his life had he experienced such a joy. Had he been able to feel anything except the wonder of the moment, he would have felt the water from the baby's wet little body soaking his shirt and running down over his trousers. With his hand beneath her bare little bottom, he closed his eyes and hugged the child to him, wishing to savor every second of this wonderful experience.

"She's just discovered that there are people in the world besides her mama and grandma," Laura said by way of an apology. "Thad spoils her. He's the man who came to work at the hotel. Every time she sees him, she squeals and he picks her up." Laura couldn't take her eyes from Hunter's face. She was dismayed by the expression of love and longing that she saw there. He held her child as if she were the most precious thing in the world. "You'll be wet through," she said lamely.

On hearing Thad's name, Hunter had felt a sharp pang of jealousy but hurriedly crowded it out of his mind. He wanted nothing to spoil this wonderful moment.

"I don't care how wet I get."

Laura held up a towel and Hunter could do nothing but hand the child over to her. She folded the baby in the towel, stepped up onto the porch and went into the house without saying a word.

Chapter 18

She hadn't told him to leave.

Hunter waited anxiously beside the porch for a minute or two, then walked out into the yard. With shaky fingers he lit a cigarette, drew the smoke deep into his lungs and looked toward the lit kitchen window. Mrs. Cole, Laura's mother, was at the ironing board. She had murmured something to Laura when Laura went into the house. Hunter hadn't been able to make out the words, but there was no mistaking the tone of her voice. It was disapproving.

After what seemed an eternity to Hunter, Laura came out of the house. Ignoring him, she picked up a bucket and dipped it into the water in the tub. Hunter threw his cigarette to the ground, stepped on it and went to the porch as she was lifting the bucket. He took it from her hand.

"Where do you want this?"

"On the Rose of Sharon bush."

"Which one is that?"

He followed Laura's pointed finger and dumped the water on a bush beside the clothesline pole. When he returned to the porch, Laura had dragged the tub closer to the edge. Without words, he grasped the other handle of the tub and they carried it to the bush. Then he took it from her and carefully poured the water on the shrub.

"Where does this go?" Hunter asked after the tub was emptied.

"On the nail on the porch."

Hunter hung up the tub and turned to see that Laura hadn't followed him to the porch. In the semidarkness he could see her standing beside the bush. She had made no attempt to make herself presentable. Her dress was still wet, her feet still bare. Her hair was a tangled mass of curls around her white face. In quick strides, he crossed the yard to her.

"You've got to go," she said as soon as he reached her. "And . . . don't come back."

She turned her head and stared toward the house.

"Why? What have I done?"

"You make my mother nervous."

"She's heard the rumors that I may have killed that woman?"

"That . . . and more."

"I swear to God, Laura, I didn't kill that woman. If the sheriff thought I did, he'd have me in jail."

"Folks think you did."

"I can't help what folks think. I've never killed anything but a deer, and the look in the animal's eyes before I shot it haunted me for weeks."

"Why did you come here? There isn't enough money in the world to make me go to bed with you." Unsmiling, she stared into the night.

"I don't know if I have the ability to explain to you why I came here, why I looked forward to it since last night. I swear that it was not to pay you to go to bed with me," he said, unaware that there was a pleading tone in his voice.

"Men swear to a lot of things. Most of the time it doesn't mean anything."

"I mean it, Laura. May God strike me

dead if I'm lying. Can't you think of me as just a man who enjoys your company and that of your little girl?" he asked desperately. "I've never had a child lift her little arms to me, wanting me to hold her. I will treasure that moment for as long as I live."

"You've got plenty of women to choose from," she said stubbornly. "Rich men don't waste time with poor girls unless they want something rich girls won't give them."

"You think I'm here because I want something?"

"Don't you?"

"I admit that I do, Laura. I want to be with you and Mary Pat. I want to get to know you and have you know me."

"There's not much for us to talk about, Mr. Westfall. I wash clothes for a living, while you—"

"Don't hold it against me because I have money. Please, Laura," he said quickly. "I'm a flesh-and-blood man who hurts and bleeds and gets lonely the same as any man. I just want to come here, talk to you, tell you my dreams and hear about yours. That's all."

"I don't have anything to talk to you about," she said again in a quiet, resigned voice. "I've not been anywhere. I've never been out of Oklahoma. I've not had much schooling. My daddy moved from town to town looking for work."

"You can tell me about Mary Pat. I'll tell you about growing up with Dinah and Casper. They were about the only family I had. We can talk about the weather," Hunter added with a smile. He sensed that she was relenting.

Laura looked up at the millions of stars that blazed from horizon to horizon, beautiful but unreachable, shedding little light in the small yard where they stood.

"I'll not hurt you, nor will I bother you with my presence if you don't want me here. I'll go if you tell me to go, but I want to stay. Lord God! I've never wanted anything so badly in all my life."

"Mama would worry if I went off in the dark with you."

"I understand that. Both of you need to be extra careful right now. Don't go outside the house alone at night. Promise me you won't." When she didn't answer, he asked, "Can we sit on the front porch?"

Hunter held his breath waiting for her to answer. While she hesitated, his empty, lonely heart skipped a beat, then thudded painfully.

"Go around to the front. I'll go through the house and tell Mama where we are so she'll not worry."

The man who stood amid the hollyhocks that surrounded the outhouse strained his ears to hear the words that passed between Laura and Hunter Westfall.

The son-of-a-bitch has been here for the second night in a row. He's being the nice guy, playing with the kid, emptying the water—

Lloyd Madison lifted a hand to the birthmark on his face. He had a habit of fingering the mark when he was angry or anxious, as another man would crack his knuckles or whistle through his teeth. He didn't have to be reminded of the mark. He was never unaware of it or of whom he blamed for its being there.

He walked along the lot line of the property adjoining Mrs. Cole's. The lot, including the house that sat in the middle of it, was for sale. Although he had no intentions of buying it, he would pretend that he did should he be discovered lurking around. He fumed as he made his way back to his car, parked several blocks away.

He had chuckled when Laura Hopper went into the lit kitchen, spoke to her mother and Westfall had walked around the house. He had thought she had sent him on his way. But moving toward the street so that he could watch Westfall, he had seen her come out onto the front porch and sit down beside him in the swing.

Goddamn!

When he first had come to town, he had heard about the beautiful widow who washed clothes for a living. It was said that she was prettier than any movie star and that it was a mystery why she chose to labor over a washtub when half the men in town would fight over the chance to take care of her. Most of the men seemed to have a grudging respect for her and only a few talked of getting in her pants.

When Lloyd first saw her, he had been stunned.

God, she was beautiful. Haughty and beautiful. The old judge would have said that she had class. Dressed in the right clothes, and as Laura *Madison,* his wife, they would create a sensation wherever they went. Of course, he'd mused, he'd have to arrange to separate her from that damn kid, but that wouldn't be too hard to do.

With his hopes high, thinking that she would jump at the chance to marry a lawyer, he had gone to the house where Laura lived with her mother on the pretext of hiring them to do his laundry. She had refused coolly, telling him that they had all the customers they could handle and referring him to a woman who lived on the other side of town. When he attempted to linger and carry on a friendly conversation with her, she had practically closed the door in his face.

Nasty little bitch didn't know what she was missing.

It was evening.

At the supper table Thad was in one of his teasing moods. As usual, Joe was his target.

"It beats all I ever saw. When he saw Laura Hopper, his mouth dropped almost to his knees. It was like he'd been hit upside the head with a fence post." Thad passed the bowl of fried potatoes to Jill before helping himself. "He stood there with his tongue hanging out like a dog that'd run five miles without a drop of water. I thought I'd have to set him on fire to get his attention."

"If I remember right, your eyes bugged like a bullfrog's when you first saw her." Radna's remark filled the silence. Joe gave her a grateful smile before he answered Thad.

"You're just jealous because she paid more attention to me than to you." Joe reached for the bread platter. "The boy can't stand not to have a woman's full attention," he explained to Radna. "It was that way back in high school. Just let a girl look at me and he was hot for her. He hasn't changed a bit. Poor Mrs. Hopper had to walk over or around him all day to get her work done."

" 'Can I empty the tub for you, Mrs. Hopper?' " Thad's attempt to mimic Joe's voice brought a chuckle even from Blue. " 'May I please carry the clothes basket, Mrs. Hopper? Is the machine working all right? It's squeaking a little. I'll run and get the oil can and fix it.' "

"You had your chance. You got here before I did," Joe retorted. "I'm just trying to make up for lost time. I didn't get a chance to fix the washing machine or make a playpen for her little girl."

Thad's eyes sought Jill's, but she looked aside.

The teasing between Joe and Thad continued during the meal, with Blue and Radna chiming in from time to time. When they finished eating, Jill and Radna carried the dishes to the dishpan. Thad pushed back his chair.

"You cooked supper, Radna. Jill and I will wash the dishes, but first . . ." He took Jill's hand and tugged. He pulled her across the kitchen and out onto the back porch. Light coming through the kitchen door made a ribbon across the porch floor. He backed her out of the light and against the wall. "Honey—"

"Why did you pull me out here?" Jill tried to wiggle away from him, but he held her.

"Because I've not been alone with you all day."

"I work here. Remember?" She pushed on his hard body, but he wouldn't budge.

"And because I wanted to kiss you—"

"Just because I let you last night doesn't mean—"

"I wanted it so bad I could taste you all day. I've waited and waited—"

"Sounds to me like you had good company while you waited. One time doesn't give you the right to kiss me whenever you get the notion."

"It's been a long day. I'm not waiting any longer." He lowered his head and kissed the corner of her mouth. Her breath stopped. He trailed his lips down to her chin, then up to cover hers, deepening the kiss until Jill's head was swimming and her heart thumped painfully.

"Tell me you've been waiting for this, little love," he whispered against her lips and continued playing with them, letting his tongue slide back and forth until she opened her mouth. He kissed her long and deep, using his tongue to probe and stroke. Then his teeth nipped at her lower lip, sending a quick surge of excitement swimming in her blood.

"Thad . . . we shouldn't—" Her breathing slowed like a woman in a deep sleep.

"Yes, we should. Put your arms around my neck." He spoke softly, his lips close to her ear, and fought to keep his hands from caressing the sides of the soft breasts pressed to his chest.

As if in a trance, Jill lifted her arms and wrapped them around his neck. A groan came from deep inside him. His hands went up and down her back and around her waist. He wanted to feel every inch of her. Her skin was warm, soft. The scent of woman filled his senses. He felt the little tremors that passed through the sweet curves pressed to his.

As his mouth devoured hers, Jill allowed herself the luxury of being held so tightly that she could feel a rock-hard part of him pressed to her belly. Being a farm girl, she knew what it was, and gloried in the fact she had this effect on him. Somewhere in the corner of her consciousness she was aware that he was trembling violently.

"Sweetheart. My little . . . love . . ." Thad lifted his mouth and buried his face in the curve of her neck. His breath was coming in low, throaty whimpers. "I shouldn't have kissed you like that. I got carried away by my . . . wanting you." His mouth moved to hers as if he couldn't stay away.

She turned her head so that her mouth

could reach his again. Her lips clung, wet and hungry. Suddenly his hands moved to her shoulders and he held her away from him. He looked down into her face. Embarrassed by her wanton reaction to his kiss, she couldn't look at him.

"Jill, look at me. Did that mean as much to you as it did to me?"

"What do you mean?" She looked up as far as his mouth. "I don't go around kissing every man I meet."

"Am I special to you, Jill? Am I?"

"Of course you are. I've known you all my life . . . almost." She kept her eyes lowered.

He sighed and his shoulders sagged. "It's too soon for you, isn't it?"

"Too soon for what? I'm twenty years old, Thad. I've been kissed before." Pride caused her to add, "Lots of times."

"When? Where? Who?"

"None of your business. I've not asked you who you've kissed."

"Never again." Thad's hands gripped her shoulders tightly. "No one kisses you from now on but me. Get that, Jill?" His voice was so harsh it surprised her. Her eyes went up to his. He was glaring down at her.

"You can't . . . tell me what to do."

"I can and I will."

"You don't own me, Thad."

"I want to. Oh, honey, you're tying me in knots."

He touched his lips to hers. Tenderness was the last thing she expected after his harsh words. His kisses were soft, sweet. His lips asked nothing but to be allowed to caress hers. His hands moved from her shoulders to wrap her securely against him.

"I'm sorry if I was too rough with you, sweetheart. It drives me wild to think of you with someone else."

"You weren't too rough. I'm not a fragile flower."

"Thank God." His arms moved down to her waist. He bent, clasped her to him and lifted her up to whirl her around. Her arms hooked around his neck as he continued to spin her around. He took a step and whirled again as if dancing to music only he could hear.

"Thad! Put me down."

"No."

"No?"

"We're dancing."

"*You're* dancing. I'm just going along for the ride. Put me down."

"No. I like dancing with you."

"Thad, you idiot, put me down."

"Not until you kiss me."

"I can't. You're squeezing the breath out of me."

"If I put you down, will you kiss me?"

"Oh, all right."

He stopped and let her body slide down his until her feet reached the floor. The palms of her hands came up to frame his face. Her lips passed over his with a feather touch.

"Oh, no. Sweet as that was, I've got to have more."

"That's cheating, Thad. I filled my part of the bargain."

"That was a baby kiss. Kiss me like you mean it."

"You didn't tell me what kind of a kiss." Jill's heart was pounding with happiness.

"I can't tell you. I'll have to show you."

Wrapped in his arms, she gloried in the lips that captured hers. They were soft and supple and sipped at hers, moving over them with infinite care, as though he feared she might vanish before he could drink his fill. Her lips parted as she felt his tongue gliding along them, slipping between them teasingly but not breaching them completely. Unaware that her lips opened to admit him, she suddenly realized that he was inside her mouth, molding his lips with hers in a kiss that sent pleasure roaring through her.

Lost in a haze of desire, Thad tasted, explored and enjoyed the mouth beneath his, until a heavy hand was placed on his shoulder.

"Unhand her, you masher!" Joe's voice broke into the trance they had fallen into. "Do you want me to poke him in the nose, Sis?"

"No, thanks." Jill pulled away from Thad, but he kept his arms around her. "I can do that myself."

Thad swore. "You are the stinkingest friend a man ever had. Always showing up at the wrong time."

"Mr. Evans wants to see Jill. Something about putting an extra cot in a room. I thought if I waited until you stopped kissing her, I'd be here all night."

"You take care of it." Thad held on to Jill when she tried to pull away.

"Thad! I've got to go. I work here."

"Don't go in. I'm just getting warmed up, honey."

"That's what I'm afraid of." She hit him on the chest with the back of her hand and, laughing happily, slipped through the door and into the kitchen.

Thad sat down on the edge of the porch. The dog came out and waited patiently for him to scratch her head.

"You'd better get back under there and take care of your babies, girl. Did you eat all those good scraps I brought from the butcher shop? You'll have more tomorrow."

Joe sat down beside Thad, and the dog went back under the porch.

"I'm crazy about her," Thad said.

"Jill or the dog?"

"What do you think?"

"What're you going to do about it?"

"Marry her, if she'll have me."

"Have you asked her?"

"Hell, no! She hasn't got used to the idea that I'm more than just a friend."

"Looked to me like you were doing a pretty good job convincing her. I don't kiss my friends like that."

"You don't have any female friends."

"Jill's no dumbbell. She's got to know that you're nuts about her."

"She thinks I'm nuts about all girls, thanks to your big mouth."

Joe got to his feet, stretched his tall frame and stepped up on the porch.

"Good. I'll go give her a few more details about your recent amorous adventures. I'm not sure I want you for a brother-in-law, anyhow. It might ruin our friendship."

"And I just might smash all your vital organs. I'd be sorry, but I'd do it."

Thad sat on the end of the dark porch for a few minutes, waiting for his erection to go down before he went back into the kitchen.

Chapter 19

Joe had wiped out the dishpan and was slipping it under the dry sink when Radna came into the kitchen. Her look of surprise was comical.

"Holy ghost! You did the dishes?"

"Yeah. Me and the boy, here," Joe said. "Blue's too high-toned to do the cleanup. He only cooks."

"It takes no brains to wash a few pots." Blue sat at the table reading a *Police Gazette.*

"You boys are jim-dandies. I might have to marry both of you."

"I thought you were my girl," Thad teased.

"I'm thinking that I'm about to lose you to Jill. Where is she, by the way?"

"A couple came in with a girl that isn't

quite right," Thad explained. "Blue and I carried a cot to their room. Jill's putting sheets on it."

"Justine's asleep." Radna placed the key to Justine's room on the table. "Keep an ear open while Jill's busy, will you? I'm going to turn in early and catch up on my sleep. Tell her that I'll take a turn with Justine sometime after midnight."

"Has Madison come in?" Thad asked.

"If he has, he went up to his room. He's not in the lobby and he's not on the porch. I checked." Radna went into her room.

Blue's sharp ears heard the soft sound of a bolt sliding into place after she closed the door. Without appearing to hurry, he set aside his magazine and quietly went down the hall, through the lobby and out into the night.

As soon as Radna bolted the door, she pulled off her skirt and blouse, drew a pair of boy's bib overalls and a shirt from under the mattress on her bed and dressed quickly. After piling her hair on the top of her head, she twisted the thick mass into a knot, secured it with hairpins and covered it with an old brown billed cap.

From a wooden box beneath the bed,

she took a silver-handled pistol and several bullets. The pistol went into the bib of her overalls, the bullets into her pocket. She tossed over her shoulder the sack she had brought to her room earlier, raised the window and slipped out into the night.

Walking as if she were a boy going home or on an errand, she kicked a rock or swung the sack as she followed the route through the streets where she would be less likely to be noticed. Ten minutes later, she was out on the Oklahoma prairie. Slowing her pace, knowing that she had a long walk, and not wishing to wear herself out before she got there, she walked steadily toward the horizon.

The gentle wind whispered over the face of the land. Radna loved being alone out on the prairie at night. A half moon was coming up into a sky blanketed with a million brittle stars. The quiet was absolute. She liked to think of the time when her ancestors rode their ponies over these unblemished prairies, taking only what was necessary to survive.

How did the world get so messed up?

The last half mile of her trek was in a dry creek bed. She had made the trip many times. Uncertain of what she would find, she was always leery when she approached the old shack. Radna stopped a dozen yards away and peered into the darkness, looking for a small flicker of light from a lantern or a candle.

Seeing nothing but blackness, she lowered the sack to the ground and took the pistol from the bib of her overalls. Pursing her lips, she whistled softly, waited and repeated the signal. Finally her signal was returned, and minutes later a dim light appeared in the darkness.

Radna returned the pistol to the bib and climbed up out of the creek bed. She walked along a narrow path, slipped into a dense growth of straggly blackjack, and there it was, a small shack made from discarded weathered boards. It blended so well with its surroundings that one might pass within ten feet and not realize it was there.

The door was pushed back against the wall of the shack and through the opening Radna could see a man sitting on an old canvas cot. His hair was long, black and tied at his nape with a thong. His clothes were ragged and dusty but otherwise clean.

His skin was dark, almost mahogany. He was clutching a long-necked bottle.

"You're drunk, Ramon. Where did you get the whiskey?" Radna spoke as soon as she stepped inside the shack and set the cloth bag on a bench.

"Bootlegger. Where else?"

"You risked going to town to get whiskey?"

"You wouldn't bring me any." He glared at her, shrugged his shoulders and took a drink from his bottle.

"No, I wouldn't," Radna spat out angrily. "I'm trying to keep your stupid neck from being stretched. I brought you some damn food."

"What're ya mad about?"

"I'm mad because you're drinking and because you went to town."

"I didn't go to Rainwater."

"Where?"

"Curly Bill knew a place where some fellers hid their booze."

"I swear, Ramon. Curly Bill is nothing but trouble. I was hoping you'd get yourself straightened out enough to hop a freight and get out of Oklahoma."

"I could do that if I had some money."

"The town is still stirred up over that woman who was murdered."

"It doesn't take much to stir up that town." He shrugged and took another drink from his bottle. "They'll find a breed to pin it on. Everybody knows breeds are crazy for white puss."

His indifference caused Radna's blood to run cold. "Two marshals came up from the city. They're staying at the hotel."

Ramon's lips curled in a sneer. "Never heard of a city marshal yet who could find his own ass."

"The woman was cut up."

"You told me that." His black eyes were almost shocking in their intensity. "You're thinkin' that I did it?"

"Did you?"

"Might of. I scalp me a white woman every day or two." He laughed and combed his straight black hair back with his fingers.

"This isn't a joking matter, Ramon." Radna looked away before he could see the tears that came to her eyes. "They're looking for someone handy with a knife."

"They'll not find anyone handier than me. All I got to do all day is sit here and toss this pig-sticker." He palmed a thin-bladed knife and, quicker than the eye could follow, sank it into the center of a target he had fastened to the wall. "When you comin' back?"

"I don't know when I can get away again."

"If I had some money, I'd get out of your hair."

"If you had some money, you'd buy whiskey."

"I got the whiskey because I'm sick of sittin' out here," he said with exaggerated patience.

"You should have thought of that before you got into the fight with that man on the rig."

"He started it. I took his slurs until I'd had a bellyful."

"You could have used your fists instead of a knife."

"Nobody calls me a goddamn breed whose mother fucked dogs and goats!" His voice rose angrily as he stood.

"You should have stayed away or ignored him."

Ramon was a small man, not much taller than Radna. His shoulder-length hair was streaked with gray, and his Indian features took on a wolflike expression when he jutted his face close to hers.

"I hope the bastard dies."

"It's lucky for you that he didn't," Radna said softly.

"I'd not cry about it either way."

"You've got to get away from here. They're combing the country for the killer of that woman. There's a big reward. I'm surprised they haven't come on to this place."

"I'll leave soon."

"Ramon, I've got to ask you: Did you come to town the night the woman was killed?"

"And if I did?"

"Did you see anything? She was buried beside the road about a mile out of town."

"You told me that."

"Damn you, Ramon. Did you see anything? You've got eyes like a night owl."

"You wantin' me to go marchin' in and tell the sheriff I saw someone buryin' a white puss along the road? You crazy? They'd string me up before I could say Geronimo."

"I've got to go."

"Rad? Thanks for coming. I'll leave soon. Curly Bill says he'll go with me to Colorado.

I could use some money. It's the last time I'll ask."

"I'll be back day after tomorrow."

"Rad? You're all I've got."

"No, Ramon. You've got Curly Bill and the whiskey bottle."

Radna went out the door and hurried along the path, tears almost blinding her. When she reached the steep sandy bank, she slid down it on her rump, jumped up and hurried down the dry creek bed until she came to a downed log. She sat down, rested her head on her drawn-up knees and released the flood of tears from beneath her burning eyelids.

She cried for Ramon with the brilliant wasted mind and for a society that made it difficult for him to live in either the white world or the Indian. She cried for Justine, the dearest friend she had in the world. She cried for herself because this was a place where there was no one to hear, no one to see, no one to know.

She had almost cried herself out when a voice came out of the darkness.

"Are you 'bout through bawlin'?"

Radna held her breath, waiting, hoping that the voice she'd heard had been her imagination. She raised her head even as her hand was digging into the bib of her overalls for the pistol. Although she saw no more than the outline of a powerful body against the sky, she knew him.

"It isn't smart sitting out here by your-self."

"It's no business of yours what I do."

"Yeah, it is. I don't want that cooking chore back at the hotel. I've got my own fish to fry."

"Then go fry them."

"You goin' to shoot me?"

"I might. You followed me," she accused huskily, gripping the pistol.

"Wasn't hard. More like following a team of mules down a muddy road."

Radna got to her feet. "Why?"

"I didn't have anything else to do and felt like taking a walk."

"You were listening?"

"Of course. I wasn't walking all the way out here to miss out on the good stuff."

"You low-down dirty skunk! Now that you know, what are you going to do about it?"

" 'Bout what? Your secret lover hidin' out from the sheriff? Humm . . . is there a re-ward?"

"If you turn him in, I'll cut your heart out!"

"Ouch! You're always wantin' to hurt me."

"Get out of my way." She pushed on the body in front of her, but he didn't move. Instead he reached for her cap and pulled it off her head.

"I don't like that thing on your head. You look like a boy."

"You dumb Indian! That's the idea. Give it to me. I don't care if you like it or not."

"Sure you do. You want to look pretty for me."

"Damn you, Randolph," she snarled. "Give me the damn cap."

"No. And hush your swearing."

"Why did you follow me?"

" 'Cause your butt looked cute in those overalls."

"You . . . horse's ass!" she yelled. "Can't you be serious about anything?" His little cackle of laughter caused her to lose her reason. "You . . . big dumb stupid Indian!" She balled her fists, swung and hit him square on the jaw.

He didn't say a word or even grunt. He just stood there, hands at his sides. For a long moment they looked at each other.

"Feel better?" he asked softly.

"No! I want to . . . hit you . . . and hit you . . ." Her voice died. She shivered and shook her head, trying to deny the sobs that were gushing up out of her misery. She swayed, holding on to herself because there was no one else, until Blue's arms wrapped around her, drawing her to him, holding her gently but securely.

She leaned her small compact body trustingly against him and cried quietly for several minutes, her tears wetting his shirtfront. Blue's hands moved soothingly up and down her back while tiny shudders rippled through her. Then he felt her take a deep, ragged breath and begin to snuffle. Reaching into his back pocket, he pulled out a bandanna handkerchief and put it in her hands. She took it and wiped her face while still leaning against him.

"Do you love him so much?"

"Yes. There's a strong bond between us. He'd die for me, and there's so little I can do for him."

"You're risking a lot, coming out here alone."

"He's going away."

"I heard. To Colorado with Curly Bill."

"I may never see him again." Her voice was laced with despair.

"Is he worth all these tears?" Blue asked softly and wiped his thumb across her wet cheeks.

"To me, he is."

"Is he your husband?"

"No!" She shook her head, making her hair come loose from the hairpins and drift down her back. "He's my brother . . . my twin."

Blue made a helpless sound. "Ah, little thorny rose." His low and gentle voice caused sudden tears to burn her eyes. "I had a sister once. You remind me of her, frisky as a young colt and with more spunk than brains." He spoke calm words and stroked the back of her neck. At a gentle pressure, she leaned her forehead against his chest.

"Ramon is terribly smart. He could do anything he set his mind to. But . . . he hates being a breed," she said, her mouth against his shirt. "It's killing him!"

He didn't speak for a long moment. When he did, it was softly and close to her ear.

"Every man has to kill his own snakes, Radna."

It was the first time she had heard him speak her name. Tension drained out of her. It had been so long since she'd had anyone to lean on, anyone to understand. She lifted her head and looked at this man she had known for such a short time, and felt as if she had known him forever.

"Careful, Randolph. I might get to liking you."

"Christ on a horse! I can't let that happen." He put his hands on her shoulders and moved her away from him.

"I said *might.* That's a long way from *will.* You just caught me at a weak moment."

"Little thorny rose, you're makin' me as randy as a billy goat." A smile tugged at the corner of his mouth. "We'd better get back to the bright lights before I ravish you."

"Ravish? Ha! You'd have a fight on your hands."

"I'd expect no less. It'd be icing on the cake."

Blue put his arm across her shoulders and they began walking back toward town.

Chapter 20

Jill stayed at the desk with Elmer and Rose Evans until Thad came through the lobby and stopped to say that he was going up-town for a while. Jill was glad. She needed time to sort out her feelings after the wild passionate kisses they had shared on the porch. She wanted to believe the things he had whispered in her ear, but she didn't dare.

Joe had been lying on Thad's cot in the hallway when Jill went to her room for her nightdress and a house robe before going to her aunt's room to sleep.

"I wish I knew why Aunt Justine is so afraid of Madison," Joe said, when he gave his sister the key to Justine's door.

"She's more afraid of him now than when I first arrived. It may be that she feels more helpless now that she doesn't even try to lift her hands anymore."

"It must be terrible to have a mind as sharp as a tack and not be able to control your own body. It would be like being in a tight cage."

"She's a lot worse than she was a month ago. She could stand alone then, and I could help her to her chair. Now Radna and I together can hardly lift her. It's as if her life is draining out of her."

"You're good with her, Sis. I'm proud of you."

Later, Jill lay on the cot in her aunt's room and listened to Justine muttering in her sleep. It was stifling hot in the room. Justine hadn't wanted the windows open, although Jill had assured her the screens were firmly latched.

"He could slit the screen and be in here before you know it. I don't care much for myself . . . it would be a relief, in a way. But I don't want him to hurt you, Jill, and he would," Justine had said worriedly.

Now that her aunt was asleep, Jill crept across the room and raised the windows. She sat down and let the slight breeze cool her damp skin. Hugging herself, she remembered the whispered words and the kisses she had shared with Thad a few short hours ago. Just thinking about it set her heart to fluttering.

A feeling of disquiet settled over her.

Jill drew a deep breath against the pain of remembering that he'd not said one word about loving her, just that she was *his* girl. That didn't mean a thing. He'd been telling her that since she was ten years old. Thad had always teased, ever ready to spin a tall tale, charming one and all. It was possible he was doing that now and she was taking the attention he was paying to her too seriously.

She leaned her head on the windowsill, gazed out at the starlit sky and wondered if she should ask Joe what he thought Thad's intentions were. She knew that she wouldn't ask him because she was afraid of what he might say.

Jill longed to be back home with her family. But in the back of her mind was the thought that if they were back in Fertile, Thad would forget that he had kissed her and called her his "little love" and once again she would be Joe's kid sister.

Oh, Lord, would she be able to stand

seeing him with another girl . . . perhaps have to go to his wedding, then see the babies he had made with someone else? Of course, she would endure it. She would have no choice in the matter unless she chose to move to another town.

Jill had not realized it until now, but she might have fallen a little bit in love with the boy that night in the woods when he saved her from the man who would have raped and possibly killed her. Thad had held her in his arms and covered her naked breasts with her shirt as if she were his little sister.

Here in Rainwater, he still treated her like a kid except when he felt the urge to play with her emotions. She shouldn't have allowed him to kiss her that night on the school ground, and what had happened on the back porch had definitely been a mistake that must not happen again.

Thad Taylor, I'll not be another one of the stupid girls who you can charm right out of their drawers!

Thad sat on a stool at the bar and listened to the talk swirling around him. The drink he had bought was little more than watered-down beer. But it was what was legally served. He hadn't been in town long enough for the bartender to serve him the good stuff he kept under the counter. Thad didn't really care; he wasn't much of a drinker anyway.

A mustached drummer down from Kansas City was enjoying the attention he was getting by telling how folks in the city carried their booze.

"Most everyone has a hip flask," he said. "Some carry their liquor in fake books, coconut shells and hot water bottles. One fellow got caught with two boxes of eggs. He'd drained them and refilled the shells with liquor. American ingenuity is having a heyday."

The Oklahoma City policeman sat at a table playing a game of solitaire. Thad wondered how many in the bar knew he was an officer, sworn to uphold the law. He must be aware that occasionally the bartender reached under the bar to fill a glass for a certain customer. With his fancy coat, vest and spit-polished shoes, Jelly Bryce looked more like a rich college boy than a police officer.

"I heard that back in 'twenty, right after Prohibition became law, Billy Sunday, the

Bible thumper, had a mock funeral for 'John Barleycorn.' Now, don't that just chap yore ass?"

One after the other the avid listeners spoke up.

"It just ain't goin' to work. The gover'ment can't afford all them revenue agents it takes to enforce the law. It's breeding more gangsters than a dog's got fleas."

"I been hearing about them fellers who'd drink things like lemon extract and denatured alcohol till they get jakeleg or go crazy."

"What's denatured alcohol?" someone asked.

"It's ruined booze, is all I know."

"It's alcohol with kerosene or something like that in it."

"The law forces the poor man to drink that rotgut. It keeps him from having a decent drink." Lloyd Madison had come into the bar and was standing beside the door. All eyes turned to him.

"The law doesn't *force* a man to drink," Thad said loud enough for all to hear.

"A poor man is entitled to a drink as well as the rich man, my friend." Lloyd looked directly at Thad, then spoke to the room in general. "My bet is that Hunter Westfall is drinking damn good whiskey."

"How you know that?" The bartender swiped a wet rag over the bar.

"Didn't say I knew it. Said I'd bet on it."

"Yeah? Whatta you drink, Mr. Madison?" Thad asked.

Lloyd's eyes honed in on Thad again and narrowed. When he spoke, his voice was patient, as if he were talking to a child.

"I never let alcohol pass my lips except for medicinal purposes. It's against my religion."

"Is that so? What else goes against your religion?"

"I try to live by the Ten Commandments, sir."

"Humm— I commend you, Mr. Madison. I really do. With so much wickedness in the world, it is gratifying to find a man who lives by the teachings of the good Lord."

It was obvious to only a few men listening that the big dark man on the barstool was baiting the slender man with the mark on his face. Jelly Bryce never missed a word or a play as he placed a black jack on a red queen.

Lloyd's temper flared. He just barely

stopped his hand from reaching up to stroke the red mass on his face as he was wont to do when he was irritated.

Hayseed bastard! You may be bigger than I am, but I'm a hell of a lot smarter.

"I try, sir. I use the law to help keep the workers in this town from being taken advantage of by the rich and powerful. I need the Lord on my side, for it is a formidable task."

"And we appreciate it, Mr. Madison." After the roustabout spoke, there was a murmur of approval from the men in the bar.

"I know you do, Mr. Sample." Lloyd worked his hands down in his pants pockets. "I'll work for you men as long as there's a breath in me. You can count on it."

"Ain't another man in this town carin' if we get a decent wage but you, Mr. Madison."

"I wouldn't go that far, Oscar," the bartender said tersely, then angrily slapped the rag down on the bar.

"The barkeep's right, Oscar." Lloyd raised his voice so all could hear. "A few of the smaller operators want to pay you decent wages, but they have to stay in line with the big operators or be run out of business."

"That shit-faced Westfall is rakin' in the money off the sweat of our brow." The voice came from the back of the room.

"Yeah. He's livin' high on the hog, all right."

"Now, wait a minute," the bartender said. "Mr. Westfall is furnishin' ya with a job. He's riskin' his money. Don't that count for somethin'?"

"Precious little risk he's taking," Lloyd replied smoothly. "We may not have to worry about him much longer."

"Why is that?"

"I'm not at liberty to say at this time." Lloyd gave Oscar a shy grin.

"Ya think he killed that woman, don't ya?"

Lloyd laughed. "A man can get in trouble accusing another man of murder without proof. I'll wait for the sheriff and the marshals to dig up the evidence, then we'll talk about it. Meanwhile, I've got to keep my opinions to myself so I'm free to help you fellows."

"Don't seem like them marshals is in any hurry to catch the killer. Just lollygagging around playing cards and such while a murderer runs loose is what they're doin'. Go by the jail any day and the sheriff's sittin' in there with his feet on the desk."

"They're doing the best they can. Meanwhile, we'll all hang in here together, look after our womenfolk and put as much pressure as we can on the companies in hopes they'll come around to our way of thinking and pay a decent wage—that is, if they want to keep producing. That means Westfall, if he still has a company when this is over."

Thad looked at the floor to keep his eyes from rolling to the ceiling, showing his absolute disgust. The conniving son-of-a-bitch was playing these men like the strings on a violin—slyly working them up against Westfall—and they were too dumb to realize it. This was definitely a side of Lloyd Madison he'd not seen before. He wondered what they would think if he told them how Madison tormented Mrs. Byers and how scared she was of him.

They'd not believe it.

Thad set his glass on the bar and stood up. It was time for him to get out of here before he said something that could possibly start a riot.

"Leaving, Mr. Taylor?" Lloyd asked.

"Yeah. If the shit gets any deeper in here, I may not be able to get out."

"Whatta . . . ya mean?" the man called Oscar spoke up belligerently.

"Just a little joke between me and Mr. Madison, friend. Nothing to get riled over." Thad put his hand on the man's shoulder in a friendly manner as he passed him, but he kept his eyes on Madison until he went out the door.

Thad half expected Lloyd to follow him out, but it was the young marshal from the city who fell in step with him as he headed for the hotel.

"Need a little fresh air, do you?"

"That and a pair of high boots."

"The shit was getting pretty deep." Jelly Bryce spoke with a drawl somewhat like Blue's.

"Son-of-a-bitch could talk his way out of a damn gunnysack."

"He's smooth. Knows what strings to pull."

"I wanted to hit the bastard, but I was afraid I'd start a riot."

"Why does Madison have his hooks out for Westfall?"

"Hell, I don't know. I've worked in fields

for the past four years. Westfall pays as good as any and a little better than some."

"What's Madison done to get your back up?"

Thad looked at the young officer. He'd heard that he wasn't very brainy but a fast shooter. They crossed the street and stepped up onto the boardwalk that fronted the hotel before Thad spoke.

"I don't like the son-of-a-bitch. He's as full of shit as a young robin and as phony as a wooden nickel."

"What do you mean?"

"You saw how he was with the men in the bar. He'll be looking out for their welfare as long as he breathes? Bullshit! His religion doesn't allow him to drink? Again, bullshit!"

"I thought that was stretching things a mite."

"There's something going on between him and Mrs. Byers. The poor woman is scared to death of him. She even wants the door to her room kept locked at night. She's afraid he'll come in."

"Mrs. Byers, the owner of the hotel? I understood that she was bedfast."

"She is. He manages to get to her once in a while and needles her about something only the two of them know. The last time we took her to the porch, he needled her until my Indian friend tossed him backwards off the porch rail. Madison was shook up a bit and madder than a peed-on snake. I might have to bust his head."

"How about a game of checkers?" Jelly asked as they went up the hotel steps to the porch.

"Sounds good to me. There's a board set up in the lobby."

Thad decided that he liked Jelly Bryce. Liked him a lot. He was good company, never bragged and had a dry sense of humor. Whoever said he was low on brainpower hadn't talked to him much.

They had played four games and were on the fifth to break the tie when Lloyd Madison came through the lobby. He paused to pass a few words with the man at the desk before going up to his room.

Thad's eyes followed him up the stairs. He grinned at Jelly when he saw the officer watching him.

"How come he's living in a hotel?"

"His house burned down."

"Oh, yeah. I heard about that."

"It's a good thing he went on upstairs. If

he'd gone toward the family living quarters, my friend back there would've torn his head off. We take turns sleeping beside Mrs. Byers's door."

"I've noticed the two of you never leave here at the same time."

Thad lifted his brows. "Well, now. Aren't you observant?"

"It's my job."

Thad made a move on the board, looked up and saw Blue coming across the lobby. "Howdy. Where you been?"

"I went on a rampage out on the prairie. Took a few white scalps," Blue answered casually.

"Meet Jelly Bryce, Blue."

"Met him. Howdy, Jelly."

"Howdy, Blue. Been back to Mountain View lately?"

"Not for a spell. Been too busy keepin' two knot-heads out of trouble. How's your grandpa doin'?"

"Died last year, Blue."

"Sorry to hear it."

"He was old and I think he wanted to go."

"Hell of a good man, your grandpa. Never had the slightest urge to scalp him."

Thad moved a piece on the board and

jumped two of Jelly's pieces. "Hell's bells, Blue, you never told me you knew Jelly Bryce."

"You didn't ask me. If I told you everything I know, boy, it'd take me a hundred years working my mouth day and night and you'd still be as dumb as a pile of horseshit."

"Bull-foot," Thad snorted.

"I'm going to bed." Blue headed for the stairs. "Just had a long walk."

"Hey, Blue," Jelly called. "I'd like to take you up on the offer to drive me out of town so I get in a little practice."

"Sure, Jelly. How about in the morning? I plan to go out on the prairie. I got business to do out there."

"You going to set up a factory to make arrowheads, Blue?" Thad asked.

"No. I'm going to call on the spirits of my ancestors and pay my respects. I may need their help and I've got to stay in good with them."

"He likes to play the dumb Indian," Thad said to Jelly after Blue left them.

"I know. He did that for me once in a dive in Oklahoma City. Helped me catch a crook."

"How long have you known him?"

"A long time. My grandpa knew Ocie Bluefeather, Blue's grandpa."

"Blue doesn't talk much about his family."

"Blue came from good stock and is smart as all get-out. He could be president of a university or anything else if he set his mind to it."

"Joe and I found that out the first few months we were out here. We met him on an oil rig down by Ponca. I'd opened my big mouth when I should have kept it shut. Joe and I were jumped by six of the crew. They might have killed us if Blue hadn't dealt himself in."

"It's a lucky man who has Randolph Blue-feather for a friend." Jelly sat back and studied the board. "Heard you helped put out a couple of derrick fires."

"Yeah. Down near Chandler."

"Dangerous work."

"Money is good. You have to use a little common sense is all. Damn!" Thad exclaimed, "You skunked me. How are you at cribbage?"

"Not worth a damn."

"How about a game tomorrow night?"

Chapter 21

"Jill, wait."

Thad came out of Justine's room. His hand fastened on to Jill's arm and stopped her as she hurried down the hall to the stairs with clean towels for the rooms on the second floor.

"I'm busy, Thad. I've got to hurry and get back to the front desk."

"What's the matter, honey? You've been avoiding me for the last two days."

"I'm not avoiding you. I've got work to do." She pulled on her arm, but he refused to release it.

"I don't want you going upstairs alone when Madison is in the hotel."

"Then you can stay down here, be the lookout, and alert me when he comes in. Can you hoot like an owl, quack like a duck or whistle like a bird?" she asked with raised brows.

"Don't get smart, Jill." Thad's green eyes turned frosty. "The man is dangerous. I've crossed him a time or two. I'm afraid that he'll hurt you to spite me."

"Aunt Justine has been saying all along that he was dangerous. Why are you just now believing it?"

"I have my reasons. Wait until Mrs. Cole comes before you go upstairs to make the beds if I'm not here. Even if I am here, the two of you stay together."

"Let go of my arm, Thad."

"Starting tomorrow, Joe and Blue will be working on the pipeline. We drew straws to see which one of us would stay here this week. We've set it up with the boss to take turns as long as two are working at one time."

"Let me guess," she said irritably. "You were the lucky one."

"I thought so at first. Now I'm not so sure. What's got your back up? Surely it wasn't because I kissed you. You didn't seem to mind at the time. Remember telling me that you'd been kissed many times?"

"And it's true, I have. Let me go, Thad. I

can't stop my work each and every time you get bored and want to indulge in a little flirtation."

"For the past couple of days you've treated me like I'm the skunk at the picnic. I don't like it, Jill. The only time I see you is at mealtime, and you act like I don't exist. Did you hate what we did on the back porch so much that you can't even look at me?"

"You flatter yourself, Thad." Jill rolled her eyes toward the ceiling and hoped that her nonchalant attitude was convincing. "I'll admit that you're good at bowling a girl over. But why wouldn't you be, with the practice you've had? Now let go of me so I can get the beds made."

A sound like a growl came from his throat. "I ought to . . . shake you."

"I'm not surprised that you'd try that. It must be a blow to your pride to find a girl who isn't impressed with your sweet words and flirty ways."

Jill looked up into the cold ruthlessness of Thad's green eyes and realized that she had provoked him into a towering rage. She attempted to take a step back, but his hands on her upper arms held her as if she were stuck to the floor. His unblinking green eyes on her face chilled her blood.

"Be careful what you say, Jill. It may come back to bite you." His soft, velvety voice was as threatening as if he'd shouted. "You want me . . . maybe not as much as I want you right now, but you will. You know you're my girl. You liked what we did on the porch. You're just too stubborn to admit it."

When he advanced a step, she retreated a step and suddenly her back was to the wall. He loomed over her. He released her arms and when she sidled sideways, his hands shot out and flattened against the wall on either side of her shoulders, imprisoning her within his arms.

"Stand still." He pushed the towels aside when she tried to use them as a wedge between them. "Now tell me, little wildcat. What put the burr under your tail?" He spoke the words very precisely, leaning so close that his nose was almost touching hers. His shoulders and chest were like another wall in front of her.

"I shouldn't have let you kiss me. I thought it was fun, but you're taking it too seriously." Jill was proud of herself for being able to speak calmly even though her heart was about to jump out of her chest.

"Fun, huh?" His eyes widened with fury; dark color ran up his neck to his face. "You think kissing me was just . . . fun?"

"Of course. You thought so, too, or you wouldn't have been so persistent."

"If you think kissing me was *fun,* wait until I get you in bed. I'll make you crazy for me." He bent his head and moved his mouth warmly against her.

"Don't." She turned her head to avoid his lips. "I don't appreciate such . . . talk." Words stuck in her throat, but she managed to say, "It . . . will never happen!"

"It will happen, sweetheart. I'd bet my life on it." He removed a hand from the wall and, with his palm resting lightly against the peak of her breast, moved it in a circling motion against her nipple. Instantly it was a hard little knot rolling against his palm. He smiled down into her eyes. "See how easy it is to make you want me?"

"Let me go, Thad, or I'll yell for Radna."

"No, you won't. You know it would upset your aunt, and besides, Radna went uptown for a minute. That's why I was with Justine." A chuckle came from deep in his chest. His eyes were like shiny green pools. He continued to rub his palm over her hard nipple. "You can protest all you want, sweetheart, but you want me. I can feel the evidence under my palm." He bent his head slightly and kissed her nose.

Her face was fiery red. She grabbed his wrist and tried to push his hand away. Her strength was nothing against his. She looked helplessly up at him. Her eyes widened and filled with tears.

"Don't," she whispered. "Please—"

Thad's grin faded the instant he saw the tears.

"Ah . . . damn, honey. Don't cry, please. I'm sorry. You just make me . . . crazy."

As soon as Thad's hand fell away from her, Jill bent and swooped up the towels and ran down the hall to the stairs.

"Jill, sweetheart—"

Praying that he wouldn't come after her, Jill hurried up the stairs and into the lava-tory room after flipping the sign to OCCUPIED. She closed and latched the door, then sank down on the toilet seat. She covered her face with her hands and groaned in mortifi-cation. Her nerves were jangling and she was physically shaking.

Thad cared no more for her than he did a common slut or he'd not have touched her the way he had or said hateful things. Joe said he was used to getting any girl he wanted. He was irritated because she wasn't falling in line.

When she thought her legs would support her, she got up, went to the basin and splashed water on her face. She had to talk to Joe, but how could she tell him about Thad flirting with her without letting him know how gullible she had been and how miserable she was now?

During the noon meal, Blue announced that he wanted the car for the afternoon.

"There's something out on the prairie I want to show Miss Radna."

Radna looked up and fixed Blue with a cold stare.

"I'm not going anywhere with you, Randolph. I'm going to pick beans this afternoon. Thad'll be here to keep an eye on Justine and on Jill, too, if I'm not mistaken."

"You can pick beans after we get back. Pass the butter."

"Listen, you pigheaded Indian, I'm not going anywhere with you. Rose Evans said they had more beans than they could use and that I could pick all I wanted. I'm doing it this afternoon."

"Eat your dinner. Joe said he'd feed Mrs. Byers and wash up the dishes," Blue said without looking up from his plate.

"When did I say . . . that? Ouch. You kicked me." Joe reached under the table to rub his leg. "Julie cooked fresh green beans and cornbread when we were back home on the farm. She'd cook them with bacon or salt pork."

"And put new potatoes in with them," Thad added. "You may as well give up, Radna. Blue probably wants to show you the Kickapoo camp where as a boy he had a white buffalo for a pet."

"Do you drive, Radna? No?" Joe winked at Thad. "Well, drive anyway. If you've never been behind the wheel, you'll still be a better driver than Blue."

"Remember the time, Joe, when Blue took a shortcut through the farmer's yard and scattered a flock of geese? Feathers flew. The farmer cussed. We yelled for Blue to stop. He did . . . but only because the farmer's daughter was taking a bath in the horse tank."

"Yeah. She was buck-naked."

"And so ugly she'da stopped a freight train," Blue added. "I thought he'd just sheared a nanny goat and was washing her off."

Radna looked from one to the other, rolled her eyes, shook her head and got up to put food on a plate.

"I'll feed Justine. One of you go relieve Jill so she can come eat."

Thad looked pointedly at Joe. Joe tried to ignore him, then sighed and got up from the table.

"I'll do it, or I'll never hear the last of it," he muttered and followed Radna out of the kitchen.

"Don't you have something to do?" Thad asked Blue.

"No. I want to stay and hear you try to sweet-talk the young lady out of being mad at you."

"Go fix the car or something. If you're taking Radna in it, you'd better get rid of that dirty magazine."

"I doubt there's anything in it she's not seen before. I want to stay and hear what you've got to say to Jill. I might learn a few cuss words."

"Dammit, Blue. I swear that someday I'm going to knock your block off."

"You're always saying that. I'm ashamed of you. You'd hurt me, after all the times I've pulled your tail out of the fire? That's gratitude for you." Jill came into the room. Blue picked up a biscuit and got to his feet. "I'd better get out while I can."

"You don't need to leave on my account, Blue. I won't be here but a few minutes."

"If I don't go, Thad will knock my block off." Blue let the screen door slam behind him. He sat down on the edge of the porch and called to Fertile.

Jill filled her plate without looking in Thad's direction. While she was chipping ice for her tea, Thad came up silently behind her. She didn't know he was there until she felt his hands on her shoulders.

"I'm sorry I made you cry. You believe me, don't you? I was just so damn mad and frustrated, I acted the fool."

"Think nothing of it. Worrying over Aunt Justine causes me to cry easily these days." Jill tried to shrug his hands from her shoulders. For a full two minutes it seemed she couldn't breathe. There wasn't enough room in her chest. She wanted to appear nonchalant, unaffected. Actually her bones had turned to jelly and her muscles to mush. "It's all right. Honest. Forget it. I have."

Jill moved out from under his hands, buttered a biscuit and placed it alongside the helping of okra, cooked with tomatoes and onions. Since coming to Oklahoma she'd acquired a taste for it and black-eyed peas.

"I'll take my plate back to the front counter—"

"Joe's out there. Sit in here with me."

"Laura and her mother went home for dinner. She'll be back soon to take the wash off the lines."

"What has Laura coming back got to do with me?"

Jill filled her glass with tea from the pitcher and placed a fork on her plate. She picked up the plate and the glass before she turned to look at him.

"You can amuse yourself by flirting with her. Laura should present a real challenge. Every man in town has been after her. You could be the lucky one."

Thad didn't say anything for a long moment. His green eyes held hers. Was it hurt she saw there in the instant before he grinned?

"You're right, little sis. I could strike pay-dirt with Laura. She's a very nice girl and pretty, too."

"Yes, she is. Good luck."

"Go on out to the front desk and tell Joe to get back here and help me with the dishes. Then I'll see if I can give Laura a hand."

Jill's knees were shaking and her heart pounding as if she had run five miles. She walked carefully back down the hallway to the lobby, trying to hold her dinner plate steady. Skeeter Ridge leaned on the counter talking to Joe.

Jill ignored Skeeter and placed her plate on a table behind the screen.

"Why didn't you eat in the kitchen?" Joe asked when she came to stand beside him.

"I was told to tell you to come back and help clean up," she said. "Aunt Justine is having her dinner," she added to Skeeter. She had never overcome her dislike for him. He came almost every day to visit her aunt.

"I'll wait."

"It might be a long wait," Jill said irritably.

"Don't matter. I ain't got nothin' else to do."

"That's obvious."

"Go on back there and eat," Joe said when Skeeter ambled away to sit in a chair beside the window. "Maybe it'll sweeten your temper a bit."

"There's nothing wrong with my temper."

"You've been like a bear with a sore tail for several days. I thought you and Thad had something going."

"You thought wrong," she snapped. "I've more pride than to be one of a herd of women running after him. He can go jump in the lake as far as I'm concerned."

Joe laughed. "Sis, do you know how far he'd have to go to find a lake?"

"It couldn't be far enough to suit me."

She went behind the screen, sank down on the couch and automatically began eating but not tasting what she put in her mouth. What was she going to do? Oh, Lord, if she could just get away for a little while, walk out somewhere by herself where she could think.

When she went back to the front desk, Skeeter was walking down the hallway toward Justine's room.

"What does Aunt Justine see in him?"

"They are old friends. Skeeter said he knew her husband."

"More than likely, he's trying to get a handout."

"I don't think so. He seems really concerned for her."

"Well, I wouldn't trust him as far as I could throw him."

Joe studied her set profile. "You're getting cynical, Sis."

"This place is wearing me down." She looked at him and tears sprang into her eyes. "I want to go home, Joe."

"Ah, honey. I know. I can tell." He put his arms around her and she leaned her face against his shirt. "If you think you can't stick it out, I'll put you on the train. Thad and I will stay here until . . . the end."

"Oh, no!" she said quickly. "I'll not leave Aunt Justine. I just get down in the dumps sometimes."

"There's not much here in the way of entertainment. Why don't you get Thad to take you for a drive around the countryside? There are some big ranches out there on the prairie."

"I'll not go anywhere with that big . . . windbag."

"Whoa. You two have a fight?" Joe asked, knowing that it was obvious they had. His blond head was bent over hers; his arms were around her, rocking her gently.

"No. I just—"

"Hello. What do we have here?" Lloyd Madison had come in and neither one of them had noticed. "Is big brother wiping away little sister's tears, or is it a . . . lovers' quarrel?"

Joe's arms dropped from around Jill and he turned. His cold eyes honed in on Lloyd's grinning face.

"What do you mean by that?" Joe spoke softly, but the muted fury in his voice came through loud and clear.

"Taylor led me to think she belonged to him. Are the two of you sharing her?"

"She's my sister! You'd better watch your goddamn mouth, or you'll be carrying your ass in a sling." Joe was so angry, his voice was raspy.

"You can say she's your sister, your aunt or your mother if it makes you happy." Lloyd held his hands up, palms out, in a gesture of surrender and backed away, laughing. "Some folks in this town wouldn't understand it, but I've been around a bit more than most."

"Are you insinuating what I think you are?" Danger glittered in Joe's blue eyes.

"Not insinuating anything, my friend. Just merely making an observation."

"Let's get one thing straight. I'm not your friend. Another thing, if I hear one word said about my sister, I'll come after you and put your ass up between your shoulders before I leave."

The grin left Lloyd's face. "There's something you'd better get straight, Joe, before you give a second thought about jumping me. All I'd have to do is whisper in someone's ear that you're carrying on an incestuous relationship with your sister and a half hundred men in this town would be ready to tear you apart the minute I said the word. Don't mess with me. Understand?" His eyes reflected his hatred as he turned and walked slowly up the stairs.

"Joe." Jill pulled on his arm until he finally looked at her. "I didn't understand all of what he said. He thinks you and I are . . . sweethearts? That's ridiculous. He knows that I'm your sister."

"Yes, he knows you're my sister, but down in his dirty mind he wants to believe we're sweethearts," he finished in a cold choked voice.

"That . . . that's sick!" Jill managed to say.

"He doesn't really believe it. He just wants other people to believe it so he can cause trouble for us."

Jill shivered. "He scares me."

"Be careful. Don't let him get you alone." Joe's face was creased with worry. "I'm going to talk to Thad and Blue. I think there should be two of us here with you women all the time."

"Aunt Justine thinks he wants to kill her."

"Has she ever given you a reason?"

"No, but from little things I've picked up, I think she knew him before she came here."

"It would have had to be a long time ago. She's been here since before the war."

"Joe, I don't want you to give up your job. You want to earn as much as you can."

"Not when it means leaving you here where that crazy fool can get at you. Why don't you go help Thad in the kitchen? I don't want to leave you here at the desk with Madison upstairs."

"Isn't Radna there?"

"Blue was going to take her for a drive. He'd die before he admitted it, but he likes her. I've not seen him this interested in a woman before."

Radna stepped up onto the running board and got into the car. Blue was already seated behind the wheel.

"All right, Randolph, where are we going?"

"Out to say good-bye to Ramon."

"Are you out of your mind? We could be followed."

"I'll know it if we are. We'll stop and get in the backseat. They'll think we drove out there to diddle." He lifted his brows when he glanced at her.

"You've got a nasty mind, Randolph."

"Is there anything you want to take to Ramon?"

Without saying a word, she got out of the car and went into the back of the hotel. When she came out, she had an old felt hat on her head and something cradled in a scarf she had slung over her shoulder. Without a word, she climbed onto the seat and looked straight ahead.

Blue started the car, turned around in the

middle of the street and headed out toward the vast prairie. The town was almost out of sight before Radna spoke.

"That young policeman from the city was in the kitchen talking to Thad. He might ask Thad where we're going."

"I told him."

"Oh, my God," Radna shouted. "Stop this car, you fool!"

"Why? We're not there yet."

"If they've arrested Ramon, I'll cut your heart out!" She bellowed the threat, so infuriated her eyes darted wildly about.

"Sheesh!" he snorted. "You're always wanting to cut somebody. I've never known such a vicious woman."

"You're about to find out how vicious I am, you black-hearted son-of-a-bitch."

"Climb down off your thorny high horse, Rose. Jelly said the best thing to do for Ramon was to get him out of the country. I showed him where Ramon was hiding out when we came the other morning. He laughed. Said the yahoos up here couldn't find their asses with both hands."

Radna was so angry she choked with it. She balled her fist, ready to swing. Blue's hand darted out and grabbed her wrist.

"Don't hit me, Rose. I might run into a tree and you'd have to walk."

"You . . . you . . . horse's ass. There isn't a tree within a mile."

"True. But one might spring up. And don't shout, Rose. Someone might hear you." He turned to her and Radna saw deviltry, as well as something warm, glittering in the dark depths of his eyes.

She went perfectly still. For a moment she couldn't breathe, then a shout of laughter suddenly bubbled out of her. She laughed, gasped, laughed again, until tears spurted in her eyes. She leaned back, her hat tilted over her face. She laughed so hard she had to hold her stomach. Finally she sat up straight, moved close to Blue, tilted her head so that she could look into his face.

"Randolph Bluefeather, you're the cat's meow. I'd kiss you, but I'm afraid you'd run into a tree."

Blue's stony face creased in a grin. "Hell, Rose, there isn't a tree within a mile."

Radna was quiet on the way back to town. She had cried when she told her brother good-bye and for a little while after they got back in the car.

"He'll be all right." Blue's voice broke the silence. "He's got more horse sense than you give him credit for."

"I might never see him again."

"He said he'd send you a postcard from Colorado."

"What was on the paper you gave him?"

"The address of a man I know who'll give him a job."

"How do you know he won't let you down? And why'd you give him money?"

"I don't know for sure, but I'm reasonably sure he'll not let me down. I gave him money because a man can't get far on what you gave him."

"It was all I had, for God's sake."

"I realize that. He'll pay me back. Now, are you going to bawl all the way to town?"

"I'm *not* bawling."

"That's good to know. I've never diddled a woman while she was bawling. They're usually happy as larks."

Radna made a muffled sound of frustration. "I'm not going to diddle, screw, fornicate or anything else with you, Randolph."

"Why not?" Deviltry was dancing in his

eyes again. "There's no one else out here for you to diddle with."

Her lips twitched at the corners as she shook her head from side to side. His cajoling suggestions were having the effect he wanted.

"You're a horny son-of-a-bitch, Randolph, but no, thanks."

"All right," he said with resignation. "But folks back at the hotel are going to be mighty disappointed. They're sure that's what we came out here on the prairie to do."

Radna's familiar laughter rang out. She moved over close to him, placed her hand on his thigh and left it there until they drove into town.

Chapter 22

Hunter Westfall had never been happier in his life. Laura, Mary Pat and even Mrs. Cole were gradually beginning to accept him. When he went to the house, he was careful to wear clothes that had been through numerous washings, and never did he step on their pride by offering them anything of material value.

One evening he had put a stick of candy in his shirt pocket. Mary Pat had discovered it when he picked her up. Now she ran to him whenever she saw him and searched his pockets for the treat. The feeling of her trusting little arms around his neck had been so overwhelmingly wonderful that he'd squeezed his eyes tightly shut to savor the moment. When he opened them, Laura was looking at him with a quizzical look on her face.

He was surprised to discover that he enjoyed helping Laura coop up the chickens, take the clothes off the line and empty the wash water. One evening he nailed a board over a hole in their chicken house when Laura expressed alarm that a fox or a weasel might get in. He suppressed the urge to offer to send a man down to build her a good tight pen.

Lord, he'd give Laura the world if he could. He hated knowing that she made her living by bending over a washtub. He wished that he had the right to buy her a washing machine like the one they used at the hotel. But if he had that right, she wouldn't be washing clothes, even with a machine.

Hunter had gone beyond thinking of her as a heart-stoppingly beautiful woman. She was beautiful, yes, but she had inner qualities that were equally as beautiful. She was pure, sweet, the epitome of motherhood. He had never even known anyone remotely like her.

Yet during the four evenings he had spent with her, he had never as much as held her hand and had only touched her in passing. At night when he dreamed about her, his sex would become so hard, he'd roll over and lie on it to keep from touching it.

Hunter Westfall, the richest man in Rainwater, was totally, stupidly, irretrievably in love with Laura Hopper, the laundress.

"Yo goin' to call on Miss Laura t'night?"

"Yes, but if anyone other than Perry Reade from the office comes looking for me, don't tell them where I am."

Hunter had gone to the kitchen after he'd finished his meal. Dinah and Casper were sitting at the kitchen table eating their supper. Hunter poured himself a cup of coffee, sat down and looked at their worried faces.

"Don't worry that I'm going to do something to hurt Laura. I'm in love with her. I love being with her and her little girl. I'd marry her tomorrow if she'd have me."

"Ah . . . law, Mistah Hunter," Dinah exclaimed fearfully. "Dat girl ain't use to such as yo do wid dem other women dat come here."

"I know that." Hunter cupped his coffee mug with his hands. "I'd lose her if I tried to take her to bed, Dinah. I wish to God I could take back the last ten years of my life and start fresh with her. I'm tired of meaningless sex, bored with neurotic, money-hungry women and completely disgusted with the life I've been living. I'm not half good enough for Laura, but it doesn't keep me from wanting her."

"Yo is a good man, Mistah Hunter. Ain't nobody tellin' me yo ain't." Casper was a man of few words, but when he spoke up, it was strongly. "I ain't never heared of a mean thin' yo ever done."

"Thank you, Casper. Unfortunately, some wouldn't agree with you. Lloyd Madison is still out there trying to stir up my men against me. He'll sway some of them into thinking that I'm a greedy bastard. I've inquired around. We pay as well as any company in the state. I don't know what else to do."

"Yo is doin' more'n most," Casper said. "I hear dat what yo pay is what's makin' dem other oil fellers pay more."

"I'm careful to pay the men who do dangerous work as much as the company can afford and still make a profit. I wish I had been as careful with my personal affairs as I have with business. I took my pleasure with available ladies like a kid in a candy store. Now that I've met a girl that I love, I'm afraid she'll turn away from me when she finds out."

"Dat girl ain't no fool, Mistah Hunter. She knows how yo been dallyin' with dem womenfolk. She come here with yo shirts when Miss Carsie was here. Miss Carsie, she took one look at Miss Laura, seed how pretty her was an' let her know yo was her man."

"Was Carsie mean to her?" Hunter asked sharply.

"She sho wasn't nice."

Hunter groaned. "I wish I'd known that. I'd have sent her packing. That girl and her baby mean the world to me."

Later, as he walked down the street toward Laura's house, Hunter thought about that conversation. He still hadn't convinced Dinah that he was finished with the life he had lived before. He wanted her to know that he didn't view Laura purely as a sexual object. He saw her as a sweet woman he wanted to be with for the rest of his life. He wanted to be a father to her daughter and for her to be the mother of his children.

Hunter tried not to hurry as he neared the

house. He had looked forward to the evening since he awakened that morning. The closer he came to the house, the faster his feet moved and the faster his heart beat. He went around to the back of the house as he had done the first time he came to call. Tonight Laura was in the garden and Mary Pat was playing in the dirt nearby.

As soon as Hunter rounded the house, he stopped, cupped his mouth with his hands and hooted like an owl. It was a noise he'd made one night that had delighted the child. Mary Pat saw him and squealed. She got to her feet and toddled across the yard to meet him as fast as her chubby little legs could carry her.

His heart flooding with happiness, Hunter squatted down on his heels and opened his arms.

"Come on, sweetheart. Come on." His face wore a broad smile. He had eyes only for the child. When she reached him, he enclosed her in his arms and stood up. "How's my girl?" he whispered and nuzzled his nose in her neck. She giggled and searched in his pockets for the treat that she knew she would find there.

Hunter carried her, sitting on his arm,

across the yard to where Laura was picking beans. He squatted down on his heels again and set the child on his thigh while he took the paper wrapping off the candy stick.

"You're spoiling her." Laura paused to watch her daughter suck on the candy.

Hunter looked up. His eyes, alight with pure happiness, met Laura's astonishing violet ones. He took a couple of deep breaths before he could speak.

"I love spoiling her," he blurted. He hugged the child closer. Mary Pat reached up and patted his cheek with her little hand. "I've looked forward to this all day," he said with such sincerity that Laura had to believe him.

"She's getting you all sticky and dirty. Her diaper is wet and she's been sitting in the dirt."

He laughed with undeniable delight. "I'll wash. Do you need some help?"

"This is my last row. I've got two buckets of beans. Tonight I'll snap them after I get Mary to bed. Mama and I will can them in the morning."

"I'll help you snap them."

Laura laughed. "You've never snapped a bean in your life."

"No. But I know how. I've watched Dinah. She's an expert bean snapper." Hunter stood up. Mary Pat, sitting on his arm, laid her cheek against his shoulder while sucking happily on the candy stick. He bent until he could reach the handle of one of the buckets of beans and carried it to the porch.

"Evening, Mr. Westfall." Mrs. Cole opened the door leading to the kitchen.

"Evening, ma'am."

"Come to Grandma, sugar. I'll wash you and get you ready for bed." Mrs. Cole held out her arms. Mary Pat shook her head and burrowed her face into the curve of Hunter's neck. "Come on, honey. You're getting Mr. Westfall sticky."

"I don't mind. It's such a treat to hold her." Hunter's face reflected his pleasure as his smiling eyes met Mrs. Cole's over the child's head. He spoke gently to the little girl in his arms. "Sweetheart, you'd better go to your grandma. After you're ready for bed, maybe she'll let us swing in the porch swing until you go to sleep."

"Swing?" Large violet eyes, so like her

mother's, looked at him. "Swing." She wiggled to get down.

Although reluctant to release the small warm body of the child, Hunter handed her over to Mrs. Cole.

"We'll swing after you get washed, if it's all right with your grandma."

"Swing, swing," Mary Pat chanted happily as her grandmother carried her into the house.

Hunter wet his handkerchief at the pump and washed his sticky face, neck and hands. Laura pumped water into a tub to wash the beans.

"It looks like storm clouds in the southwest," he remarked.

"They were there last night, too. That's why I picked the beans tonight. A strong wind will lay the vines down and make them much harder to pick."

"This is tornado season. Do you go to the cellar when it storms?"

"Yes, but I hate going down there. Mama and I found a snake in there once."

"I'd better go down and take a look around. You may need to use it. Do you have a lantern?"

"In the kitchen. I'll get it." Laura stepped

off the wooden platform surrounding the pump. "Ouch. The darned cockleburs." She stood on one foot and reached back to grab the pump handle for support. Hunter was there.

"Here, hold on to me." After she was steady, he lifted her foot in his hand. It was narrow and slender and sun-browned. He found the burr on the ball of her foot and yanked it out. He ran his thumb over the bottom of her foot, searching for more stickers. "That's it. Watch when you put your foot down."

"I knew the burrs were there. I just didn't think."

Laura was surprised at how easily Hunter had slipped into their lives. She didn't know when she had first begun to look forward to his visits and to think of him as just a nice man and not Hunter Westfall, who lived in a big house and owned oil wells and companies.

Laura had no doubt about Hunter's sincere affection for Mary Pat. His face reflected his pleasure when he was holding her, and her daughter adored him. Even her mother was beginning to be more comfortable around him.

When he came to the house in the evenings, he didn't expect her to stop her work and usually joined in to help her. Afterward they would sit in the porch swing and talk about many things. He told her about his childhood and that after his mother died, Dinah and Casper were the nearest to family he had. He amused her by talking about places he had been and explained that a geologist he met in Oklahoma City had convinced him to lease and drill on the land around Rainwater.

He never touched her or asked personal questions but listened intently to anything she had to say about herself or Mary Pat. She liked him. She just wished that he wasn't rich.

Laura lit the lantern and went with Hunter to the slanting cellar door. He lifted it and laid it back. Then, taking the lantern, he went down the crude wooden steps to the dirt floor of the cellar. The walls and ceiling were of rough planking. A bench stood against one wall; several gunnysacks littered the floor.

"See anything?" Hunter turned to see that Laura had descended to the bottom step. She had a garden hoe in her hand.

"If anything is down here, it's under the gunnysacks. Give me the hoe and hold the lantern."

Hunter lifted first one gunnysack and then another. When he began to lift the last sack, he saw movement.

"Go back up the steps, Laura," he said quickly. Then, making sure she was safely away but holding the lantern so that he could see, he carefully lifted the sack with the hoe and uncovered a snake. Its head was raised to strike and the horny segments on the end of its tail vibrated to produce a rattling sound.

"Oh . . . oh—"

"Hold the lantern steady, honey." Hunter was totally unaware, as was Laura, of the endearment. He had moved between her and the snake. He aimed the hoe and brought it down with such force that the blade cut the snake in half. The parts writhed on the dirt floor.

"Oh . . . oh—" Laura shuddered.

"It's dead. Leave the lantern on the steps and go back to the house. I'll take care of it."

"I'll help—"

"No, I'll do it. I'll get the sacks out of here,

so there will be nothing for another one to hide under."

Later, after Hunter had cleared the cellar of the dead snake and the sacks, he lowered the slanting wooden door and went to where Laura waited on the porch.

"My daddy always said that snakes travel in pairs."

"I've heard that, too. If you have to go to the cellar, look around well before you step off the stairs."

Laura turned when she heard the screen door open. "Mama, Hunter killed a big old rattler in the cellar."

"Oh, my. I hope we don't have to go down there."

"I hope you don't, either, but if a snake is there, he'll be in plain sight," Hunter said. "There's nothing there now for one to get under. I piled the gunnysacks out by the chicken house."

Mary Pat, in her nightdress, was holding her arms out for Hunter to take her. His heart swelled. He looked for permission to Mrs. Cole.

"May I swing with her for a while?"

"I should put her in her bed. She's getting

too attached to you, Mr. Westfall." Mrs. Cole's face creased with a frown.

"And you object to that?" he asked, suddenly feeling like he'd been kicked in the stomach.

"She won't understand when you stop coming here."

Hunter looked at Laura standing on the end of the porch. He didn't want to ask the question but knew he must.

"Laura, do you want me to stay away?"

Her large expressive eyes looked directly into his. "You'll stop . . . sometime. The newness of coming here will wear off—"

Mary Pat began to howl and squirm in her grandmother's arms. "Swing," she screamed.

"I'm sorry if I've caused you distress."

"It isn't that. We've enjoyed your visits." Laura had to raise her voice to be heard over her daughter's screams.

"I'm not asking anything of you, Laura."

"I . . . know—"

Mary Pat's wails continued, her mouth open, tears running down her cheeks. She stretched her arms toward Hunter. He looked from Laura to her mother, an expression of uncertainty on his face. He had never been so miserable in his life.

Suddenly Mrs. Cole thrust the child in his arms. Mary Pat wrapped her arms around his neck. He held her tightly, pressed her wet face to his neck and scarcely heard the words Mrs. Cole uttered.

"Take her, but if you break her heart, I'll damn you forever."

"Now, now, little sweetheart," he crooned to the child. "Don't cry." Disregarding the two women watching, he kissed the little girl's wet cheek and patted her back. "Stop crying and we'll go swing." He stepped off the porch to go around the house to the front.

"Come through the house, Mr. Westfall," Mrs. Cole said and opened the screen door.

Hunter looked at her in surprise. This was the first time he had been invited into the house.

"Thank you," he murmured.

The house was small. A little more than a dozen strides and he was across the kitchen, into a bedroom and out the front door to the porch. As he sat down in the swing, he was aware that Laura had followed him and stood just outside the front door.

"I wouldn't hurt her for anything in the world, Laura."

"She hasn't known many men, and none as she knows you."

"I've not known many little girls, and none as precious as Mary." Their eyes caught and held, the only sound being the squeaking of the chains holding the swing. "Can you sit down for a while?"

"I'm dirty from the garden and I've got to snap the beans."

"I'll help after the baby goes to sleep."

"You don't need to."

"I want to."

"Why . . . do you come here?"

"I . . . like being with you and . . . Mary. I didn't realize how empty my life was until I met you . . . and Mary."

"You've got a big house and money and oil wells—"

"They mean nothing. I'm hungry for someone to like me for myself. Mary likes me and she doesn't know I have those things. I was hoping that you'd forget the things I have and like me for myself."

"Sometimes I do forget them, but . . ."

"But what, Laura?"

"But I don't understand why you like to come here. I've told you that I'll not go—"

"I'll not ask that of you," he said quickly. "It means a lot to me to come here and for a little while be a part of your life and Mary's."

"You could go anywhere—to the city, ride on a train, see a picture show—"

"I've done those things, and believe me, Laura, it didn't give me anywhere near the pleasure that I get from holding this little girl and knowing that she wants me to hold her."

"You'll get tired of us."

"Are you tired of me?" The second the words left his mouth, he wished them back. He held his breath waiting for her answer.

"Mary Pat and I look forward to seeing you. Mama still thinks that . . . ah . . . you come here because the men uptown talk about me."

"I've not heard a word about you that is in any way insulting. If I did, someone would lose a few teeth."

"The baby is asleep. I'll put her in her bed."

*   *   *

Hunter and Laura sat on the back porch and in the light from the lantern snapped the beans. Hunter told her about his enlistment in the army during the war, his training to be a medic and that although he was glad when the war ended, he had wanted to go. Just seventeen, he'd lied about his age. When his mother found out, she had been furious.

"I still think it was one of the best things I've ever done. I learned discipline and responsibility. I learned to care for my fellow man."

When they finished with the beans, they carried the tub of water to the honeysuckle bush and afterward Hunter hung the tub on the nail on the porch. It was time for him to go, but he lingered.

"Will you can the beans before you go to work in the morning?"

"I don't work tomorrow. Mama does. She'll help me until it's time for her to leave."

"Are you ever bothered by . . . anyone when you're here alone?"

"Not often."

"If you are, let me know. And . . . be careful." They had moved to the side of the house. "Will you?" he insisted. Unthinking, his hand clutched her shoulders.

She nodded. His mind suddenly snapped alive and he realized that he was holding her and pulling her toward him.

"Oh, Jesus! I swore that I'd not touch you," he whispered anxiously. "God help me! I'd give ten years of my life to kiss you . . . just once."

"Ten years?" She lifted her chin and stared up at him with wide eyes.

"It would be worth it."

"I'd not charge you . . . that much." The words came out on a mere breath, and he wasn't sure that he'd heard them correctly.

He continued to look down into her face, conscious that she might feel dwarfed by his hovering over her.

"May I? Please."

She nodded and he gently drew her to him, his arms sliding around her. Her body went slack, pressing softly against him. Her hands slid over his ribs and clasped behind his back.

"Sweetheart." He lowered his head, savoring the feel of her breath on his mouth before his lips danced with incredible lightness over hers. He trembled with the desire to crush her to him and drink long and hard from her sweet mouth, but he held himself in check.

Whatever the future held, he had this!

When she didn't draw away after the kiss, he pressed his lips to hers again, longer this time, and felt the slight movement of her soft mouth beneath his. The feelings that swamped him were not sexual and not like anything he'd ever felt before. He wanted to love, protect and care for this woman for the rest of his life.

"Sweetheart," he murmured again, his voice hoarse. She pushed gently against his chest and he let his arms fall from around her. He took her hands and held them against his heart in agony that she would tell him not to come back.

Her soft voice came out of the darkness.

"Would you like to come to supper some night? It wouldn't be anything fancy."

"You mean it? Really mean it?" The smile that broke over Hunter's face was so genuine and so beautiful that Laura stared.

"Of course I mean it." There was laughter in her voice.

"You bet. Just say when."

"Saturday night. I don't work that day."

"I'll be here." He squeezed her hands, then dropped them. "Thank you. Thank you, Laura." He turned to walk away and turned back. "Good night. Kiss Mary for me."

The man in the car parked on the side street behind a clump of blackjack had been waiting since dark for Hunter to leave Laura's house. His resentment of the man who had everything he wanted to have escalated. When he finally saw him walking up the road, he pounded on the steering wheel with his fist. He was so angry that spittle leaked from the corner of his mouth.

A low animal-like sound came from his throat. He swore viciously, uttering every filthy word that had ever been imprinted in his mind, and continued to speak as if he were talking to another person in the car.

"Son-of-a-bitch goes there every other night. Goddamn bastard isn't going there to talk and play pattycake with that damn kid. He's screwing Laura! He's screwing Laura," he said again, louder this time.

"They'll both get what they deserve. I'll hold that kid up by the heels and smash her head against a tree trunk. It'll split like a melon. Then I'll screw that stuck-up bitch until her damn eyeballs pop out. She'll wish to God she'd not been so snotty with me.

"Damn Westfall. Damn lucky son-of-a-bitch. Every damn thing goes his way. All he's got to do is snap his fingers and he makes money hand over fist. People in town treat him as if his ass was gold plated. Women fall all over him, but not for long. I've got a card to play that will really cook his goose."

He started the car to move it when he could no longer see Hunter walking down the road. The car inched forward, then turned the corner. He could see the object of his hatred ahead of him walking along the side of the road.

Suddenly he was engulfed with an unreasonable, uncontrollable fury. Blood rushed to his face. He felt as if his head would burst. With a cry of rage, he pressed his foot down on the gas pedal, gripped the steering wheel with both hands and aimed the car at his hated enemy.

Hunter, walking along the dark road happily reliving the kiss he'd shared with Laura and the miracle of being invited to dinner,

had heard the purring of the car motor behind him, but was unaware that it was bear-
ing down on him until it was no more than a
few yards away. He glanced over his shoulder and saw it, without headlights, coming
fast, aiming at him. He threw himself toward
the side of the road, but it was too late.

The front fender of the car struck him. He
felt a searing pain in his hip and thigh as he
was flung into the dense thicket of thorny
bushes that grew along the edge of a vacant lot. The wind was knocked out of him.
He lay still, half dazed, but aware that whoever was driving that car had tried to kill
him. He felt blood trickling down the side of
his face but knew that was not his most serious injury.

Lord, he hoped that his thigh was not
broken. He'd be a sitting duck for whoever
ran him down if he came back to finish the
job.

Hunter looked around for something with
which to defend himself. His hand grasped
a small branch he could use as a club. It
wasn't stout, but it would have to do. Placing the club beside him, he explored his hip
and thigh.

Who in hell had tried to kill him?

He straightened his leg, moved his hip joint. Thank God there were no broken bones! He lay quietly, listening for the sound of the car. Time passed slowly. His mind cleared.

Had the driver been waiting for him? If so, the man knew that he had been at Laura's. Half the single men in town had called on her at one time or another. It was logical that one of them, desperately in love with her and jealous of him, had run him down. He would think about it later. His only thought now should be to get home.

When he thought it safe to leave the thicket, he rolled to his side and, after several agonizing attempts, got to his feet. He stood swaying until his head cleared, then, after looking up and down the road for the car, began the painful journey home.

Chapter 23

Justine wished to God that she could die. But dear Lord, it was unthinkable that her life would be taken by Lloyd Nathan Madison.

She lay in her bed looking at the ceiling. Never had she dreamed that when she left this world, she would leave it as helpless as the day she entered it. The body she had lived in all these years was old and useless, but her mind screamed that on the inside she was still young, still had her pride and an aching heart.

Fate had dealt her a double blow. Along with this paralyzing illness, fate had given her what she had yearned for, for more than twenty-five years. Now she wished to God that her desire had not been fulfilled. The disappointment was almost more than she could bear. She remembered the saying "Be careful what you wish for."

Tears trickled from the corners of her eyes. She didn't often allow herself the luxury of self-pity. Through a blur of tears she looked to the bureau, where her husband, Ralph, in a jaunty straw hat, smiled at her.

"Say something, Ralph. Talk to me."

"Sure, babe. What'a you want to talk about?"

"I'm ugly and useless, Ralph."

"Never. You're still the prettiest little sugarplum in the state of Oklahoma."

"Damn you, Ralph. Don't lie to me. I'm a sight and you know it! I look like I've been run hard and put up wet." She sniffed back tears.

"But still sassy. Smile for me, darlin'."

"I've not had much to smile about. It's been hard without you, Ralph."

"You did all right. You ran the best whorehouse in the Cherokee Strip. I was proud of you."

"It wasn't a whorehouse, Ralph. It was a rooming house for young ladies."

"If you say so." He chuckled. *"How about you and me havin' a party, sugarplum?"* The

face in the picture winked at her. *"That always made you smile."*

"In the afternoon? In broad daylight?"

"We've done it before. Remember that time in the buggy coming up from Claremore?"

"We were on the prairie. A man on horseback came toward us and you, you horny rascal, wouldn't let me up off your lap."

"He thought I was teaching you to drive the team."

"He'd have been an idiot to have thought that. You'd wrapped the reins around the brake handle and your hands were under my skirts."

"I remember every delicious minute of it, babe."

"Oh, so do I, Ralph, darlin'."

"Aunt Justine?" The door opened and Jill came into the room. "I was sure I heard someone talking in here. Are you all right?"

"I'm all right, honey."

"I wish you'd let me leave the door open so a breeze could swish through here. Lloyd isn't here."

"Leave it open. If *he* comes, *he* comes. I'm tired of fighting him."

"You'll not be left alone. Radna has gone

to the garden, but I'll keep a close watch. By the way, Mr. Ridge is here to see you."

"It sounds funny to hear you call Skeeter Mr. Ridge."

"He isn't my favorite person, you know."

"I know, but he's been a good friend."

Jill stepped to the door and beckoned, then stepped aside so Skeeter Ridge could come into the room.

"Hello, Skeeter. Close the door, Jill. Skeeter isn't going to jump into bed with me."

"Don't be too sure," Skeeter grumbled, as he squeezed past Jill to reach the chair beside the bed.

"Would you like a glass of tea, Aunt? The man at the drugstore gave Joe some paper straws he thought you could use and he said to tell you hello."

"That would be Gary Rowe. He used to come here often . . . to see a girl who boarded here." When Skeeter raised his brows, Justine said, "It's true, Skeeter. Her name was Elizabeth, but we called her Beth. She had beautiful red hair."

"I never said anythin'," Skeeter grumbled.

"Bring a glass of tea for Skeeter, Jill. He'll help me with mine."

After Jill had delivered the iced tea, she closed the door and stood for a minute in the hallway. With a worried frown on her face, she went back to the front desk and stood beside the screen that separated the desk from the couch behind it. She was sure that she had heard her aunt talking to someone in the room, but when she opened the door, no one was there.

When an arm snaked around her waist and pulled her behind the screen, she let out a little squeak of surprise and lashed out with her arms.

"Shh . . . It's me. I'm sorry if I scared you." Thad's voice was close to her ear. His arms came around her from behind, pulling her tightly against his chest.

"Let go of me. What the heck do you think you're doing?" She stood stiffly in his embrace. Her hands folded over his as she tried to pry his arms from around her.

"I'm going to talk to you. You haven't given me a chance for three days and I'm about to go out of my mind."

"Talk, but turn me loose, Thad. I have work to do."

"I can't talk to you while you work." His lips were rubbing the soft skin beneath her ear. His breath was warm on her cheek. "Sweetheart, you smell so good. Is that Blue Waltz perfume you're wearing?"

"No, it's furniture polish, and I'm not your sweetheart!" She tried to move her head to avoid the small nibbling bites he was making along her jaw.

"Yes, you are."

"Thad! You're being . . . ridiculous!"

"Why are you mad at me? You liked my kisses that night on the back porch. Since then you've avoided me like I'd been sprayed by a skunk." His teeth nipped her earlobe. "And don't you dare say they were *fun* or I'll bite a chunk out of you," he teased.

"Let me go, Thad, or I'll tell Joe and he'll mop the floor with you."

"No, he won't. He knows my intentions are honorable." He held her possessively and repeated her name in a whispered chant, his lips moving against her ear. "Jill, Jill, darlin' Jill. Loosen up a little bit, honey."

"Stop it!"

He folded first one of her arms and then the other across her waist and then held tightly to her hands, pulling her arms and his snugly up under her breasts, his knuck-les nudging the undersides.

"I'm crazy about you, honey." His tongue tickled the corner of her lips.

"Ha! You've had a lot of practice saying that."

"I've never said it before. If you don't en-joy being like this with me, then why is your heart beating so fast?"

"Because I'm . . . scared!"

"You'll have to think of something better than that, because you're not scared of me. You know that I'd die before I'd hurt you or let anyone else hurt you."

"There are different kinds . . . of hurt. I'm not going to let you hurt my . . . heart." Her breath was so clogged in her lungs she thought they would burst from it.

"Why do you think I want to hurt you? I want to love you and I want you to love me."

"I don't! I won't!" Her breath was sob-bing. "The man I give my heart to will want me and only me. Ten thousand beautiful women could strip naked in front of him and he'd still want me!"

"You think I wouldn't? Ah, sweetheart, you don't know me at all."

Thad's fingers moved a fraction and the tips raked lightly back and forth across the tip of her breast. Her nipple was instantly a small hard knot beneath her gingham dress. The sensation of pleasure was so intense that Jill's toes lifted and she rocked back on her heels. He continued to stroke, sending shafts of warm desire through her. It was even more intense than when he touched her breast the other day.

"Does that feel good, honey? It feels so good to have you in my arms. Someday my mouth is going to be where my fingers are right now."

Heaven help her! She didn't want his fingers to stop their tender torment. Her head drooped. Shame brought tears to her eyes and they fell onto the hand on her breast.

"My God!" he groaned. "You're crying." He turned her quickly toward him and wrapped her protectively in his arms. "I didn't mean to make you cry. Please, don't. Ah . . . sweet girl, I'm so desperate to have you want me that, at times, I don't use good sense. I'm trying to prove to you that you do have feelings for me. That you respond to my touch." He pressed her cheek to his shoulder, his lips moving over her hair.

"Where's my sassy girl?" he whispered. "I want my mouthy Jill back. Hit me, kick me, yell at me." His palms framed her face and turned it up to his. "Oh, Lord. I've gone about this all wrong—" His thumbs wiped at the tears on her cheeks.

"If I'd fallen all over you and chased you, you wouldn't want me." Her words came out in gasps.

"How do you know that? If you'd just chase me a little bit, I'd be the happiest man in the world."

"I'll not do it!" Her voice was firm again. "I'll not run with the herd."

"I'm going to knock Joe's teeth out for telling you that. But first I'm going to kiss you."

His face was very close. Jill looked up at him, up at the square chin and high cheekbones, up into green eyes that gleamed down at her from beneath drooping lids. She met his gaze and read his hunger for her. She saw, not a flirting, devil-may-care Thad, but her Thad. Serious, tender, loving. A man far more dangerous to her peace of mind. Her heartbeat quickened.

"No!"

"Yes."

His lips lowered to hers. Her eyes were open. She saw his close when his lips brushed hers. The touch was gentle, sweet, so sweet that she could almost believe that he really cared for her and that she was not just a mere challenge to his ego. His lips sipped at the tears on her cheeks. He was breathing hard. She felt the strong thump of his heart.

"Your mouth is so . . . sweet. Sweetheart, believe me. I've been miserable these last few days."

As soon as he uttered the words, he lifted his head, instantly alert. Jill heard the squeak of the screen door and footsteps crossing the lobby.

"Stay here. I'll take care of it," Thad whispered. His hands caressed her arms before he put her away from him. As soon as he stepped from behind the screen, she sank down on the couch.

"Where's Jill?" Lloyd Madison's voice was hostile, and it brought Jill to her feet.

"*Miss Jones* is busy," Thad answered with equal hostility.

"Well, never mind. I really came to see Mrs. Byers."

"She's busy, too."

"Yeah? Doing what? Counting the fly-specks on the ceiling?"

"It's none of your business what she's doing. You can't see her."

"And who's going to stop me?" Lloyd moved toward the hall that ran alongside the stairs as Jill darted from behind the screen.

"I am," Thad said calmly, and he moved swiftly to block Lloyd's path. "She doesn't want to see you."

"She will have to tell me that. I've spoken to the sheriff and laid down my case about you people keeping my client prisoner here. I'm to report back to him if you should refuse to let me see her."

"She isn't your client."

Lloyd turned when he heard Jill's voice. "Ah . . . there you are, darlin'. I'm sorry I had to leave early this morning and miss our little . . . ah . . . tryst." He winked at her. "I've been horny all day."

"What . . . are you talking about?" Jill stammered.

Lloyd frowned. "Doesn't he know?" He jerked his head toward Thad.

"Know what?"

"About you and me, darlin'."

"You're crazy as a bedbug. There is no *you and me,* you stinking horse's patoot!"

Lloyd gave her a tolerant smile. "I understand why you're mad, honey, and I'm sorry I disappointed you. I'll explain it to you tonight when you come to my room. Meanwhile, I need to see Mrs. Byers."

Leaving Jill with her mouth agape, he started down the hallway and ran up against Thad. Appalled by the crazy things Lloyd had said, Jill was almost frightened by the look of pure rage on Thad's face. His hand shot out and fastened to the front of Lloyd's shirt, almost lifting the lighter man off the floor. The muscles in his forearm bulged; his jaw was clenched and jutted forward.

"Stay away from Mrs. Byers," Thad snarled.

"This is assault, you know," Lloyd said calmly. "Turn me loose or you'll find yourself up before a judge who will throw your sorry ass in jail."

Thad ignored the threat and started backing Lloyd toward the stairs. "Get your things and get out of this hotel."

"You've no authority to put me out. Ask Justine if she wants this property tied up for months, even years, in a legal court battle. I can take this building and everything in it just like that." He snapped his fingers. "If you don't believe me, ask that doddering old fool Bernie Shepard. Even a country lawyer knows that much about the law."

Thad shoved him and he stumbled back. "Stay away from Mrs. Byers and stay away from Jill or I'll catch you out some dark night and beat the holy shit out of you."

"Do that. It would be worth it to send you to jail."

"Your word would carry no more weight than mine, and I'd have a dozen people who'd lie for me just because they hate your damn guts."

"You think you're pretty smart, but I've got influence in this town and in this state. You don't know who you've come up against."

"Yes, I do. I've come up against a crazy coward, who likes to play his little sick games with a helpless woman."

"Helpless? In her day that woman was about as helpless as a den of rattlesnakes." There was scorn in Lloyd's voice. His face darkened with anger.

"That was then. This is now. She's under

my protection, and I'll break both your goddamn legs if that's what it takes to keep you
away from her."

Lloyd laughed. "When you don't have
brains, you must resort to violence. It's
been that way all down through the ages."
He went slowly up the stairs without looking
back.

Thad waited until he was out of sight before he spoke. "Go to the kitchen, Jill, and
stay there until that bastard leaves."

"Skeeter Ridge is with Aunt Justine."

Thad passed her and went behind the
desk. "Where's Radna?"

"In Elmer's garden picking cucumbers
and okra."

"Go to the kitchen," he said curtly. "I
don't want you out here when he comes
back down."

"He's crazy, isn't he?"

"Jill, will you please go to the kitchen?"
Thad said impatiently.

"Why don't you want me out here? Do
you believe what he said?"

Thad swore viciously. The single word he
uttered was ugly and very filthy. His voice
was more normal than his face. Murder was
there in his eyes, in the set of his jaw, in the

redness beneath his sun-baked skin. Jill had never seen him look like this, and it scared her. Their eyes met.

"You are the most irritating woman God ever created. Can't you do as you're told just this one time?"

"I'm going."

Thad was acting as if he believed Lloyd Madison's lies! How could he believe that of her?

On trembling legs she walked down the hall past her aunt's room. She heard the low murmur of voices and was grateful for Skeeter's presence because it allowed her time to hide out in the kitchen and put her scattered, confused thoughts in some kind of order.

She was disgusted with herself for crying. Good Lord! When she was with Thad, her pride went out the window. She wasn't a *crier*! Thad would be sure to tell Joe and Blue, and she would be teased about it. Months from now, in some other oil town, Thad would be bragging about how he'd made the little *wildcat* in Rainwater cry.

Dammit, she'd not cry again and she'd not engage in a brief flirtation with him.

So that was that!

She bent over and dried her eyes on the hem of her apron, straightened her shoulders and wished to God she could go five minutes without thinking about him.

Chapter 24

"Don't fuss, Dinah. I'm all right."

"Yo ain't no such, Mistah Hunter. Yore hip and leg pert' near black as mine. Yo is hurtin'. Ain't no use yo tellin' me yo ain't."

"I'll admit that I hurt if it'll make you feel better, but I'm not using that walking stick you dug out of the attic. I'll not give the bastard who ran me down the pleasure of seeing me use it."

"Yo is stubborn as a mule, but guess if yo wasn't, yo would still be layin' out dere 'side of de road in dem bushes."

"I'm going to the office as usual. Did you call and tell Perry that I'd be a little late?"

"I tol' him. Mistah Hunter, somebody ain't likin' yo to be callin' on Miss Laura."

"It could be that someone doesn't like the way I do business."

"Laws! Yo been doin' business in dis town pert' nigh five years 'nd ain't no cars run yo down. Yo be careful yo don't brin' no hurt down on dat girl."

"Good Lord! I hadn't thought of that."

Hunter walked the three blocks to the sheriff's office, his leg and hip hurting every step of the way. His mind was occupied with the possibility that Laura, Mary Pat and Mrs. Cole could be at risk because of their friendship with him. He would have to tell them of the possibility. What if they told him not to come back? But what if harm came to one of them because of him? *Oh, God. Don't let that happen! They are so very precious to me.*

Hunter forced himself not to limp until he passed through the door and saw that the only person in the office was Sheriff Page.

"Morning, Sheriff."

"Howdy. Have a seat."

"Thanks, but I'll stand."

"Suit yourself."

"I was hit by a car last night, Sheriff, and it hurts like hell to sit down."

"Yeah? How'd that happen?"

Hunter made the telling brief.

"Could have been he didn't see you," Sheriff Page said when he finished.

"He saw me. It wasn't an accident, Sheriff. The car was without lights. He meant to run me down."

"Have you had trouble with any of the men who work for you?"

"I've got more than fifty men working for me in one capacity or another. The only ones who are dissatisfied are the ones Lloyd Madison is stirring up against me. Much to his disappointment, there are damn few who swallow the lies he puts out."

"Lloyd means well. He just goes about it with too much enthusiasm."

"Yeah? Well, I realize there isn't much you can do about a car running me down on a dark night, but I thought I should report it anyway. I'd rather it not be noised around for the time being."

"Do you mind telling me why you were walking along that road at that time of night?"

"No, I don't mind. I had called on a friend."

"Humm—the only house on the end of

that street is the one where Laura Hopper lives with her mother."

"So?"

"You'd been there?"

"What do you think, Sheriff?"

"I've got a couple of thoughts on the subject. One is that Laura Hopper is a nice woman. The other one is that if I found out that she was being forced, either by threats or otherwise, into letting some horny son-of-a-gun call on her, I'd not take kindly to it."

"I agree with both of those thoughts. I've called on Laura five times." He held up five fingers. Each time, except the first time, by invitation. "I'm invited there to supper Saturday night. Hell and high water won't keep me from going."

"Does she know about Miss Bakken?"

"She knows that she was murdered."

"I mean, does she know that she was your . . . whore?"

"I don't like that word, Sheriff. Carsie wasn't a whore. She was a mistress to a lot of men. Me, on occasion. I've not discussed that part of my life with Laura."

"A woman, even a good one like Laura

who has next to nothing, can be dazzled by a man with your money."

Hunter's face reddened. "I resent that."

"Resent it all you want. It's true. She's a decent woman, Westfall."

"I know that."

"Then why are you hanging around her?"

"That's none of your business." Hunter's angry eyes blazed into those of the sheriff. "I came in here to report that I'd been run down, not to be lectured." Still holding the sheriff's eyes, he said, "Anything new on Carsie's case?"

"Nothing. Officer Hurt and Jelly Bryce went back to the city. Bryce will be back in a day or two. Whoever killed Miss Bakken was pretty damn smart. I'd not be surprised if he's done this before. Hurt will put out the word to see if there's been anything like it the past few years."

"It's strange that a woman could be murdered in this town and no one see or hear a thing. Have you found any of her belongings?"

"Not a scrap."

"If any more attempts are made on my life, I'll let you know." Hunter went to the door, turned and leveled his gaze on the sheriff. "I'll do my best to see that they are only *attempts.* From now on, I'll be carrying a gun."

"Don't blame you. Good day, Westfall."

Hunter nodded and left the office. His hip was killing him; nevertheless, he walked up the street to his office without a limp. By the time he reached the door, sweat was running down the side of his face. He looked across the street to see Lloyd Madison come out of his office and amble off down the sidewalk toward the hotel. *Righteous son-of-a-bitch.*

"Perry, do you know where Madison keeps his car?" Hunter asked as soon as he entered his office.

"No, but I can probably find out."

"This isn't to leave this office. Last night someone tried to run me down. I'm betting it was Madison."

"Were you hurt?"

"Hell, yes, I was hurt. I've a solid bruise down one side of my body and every one of my bones aches. I was lucky to see the car in time to jump to the side. The fender hit me a glancing blow. I doubt there's any damage to the car, but if you find Madison's car, take a look at the front left fender."

"Why do you think it was him?"

"Who else hates me enough to kill me?"

"I'm not sure he hates you. I think he's ambitious to build a name for himself. Maybe he wants to run for mayor."

The door opened and a man wearing a pair of greasy overalls came in.

"Hello, George."

"Howdy, Mr. Westfall."

"What brings you to town?"

"We're down to nine hundred and sixty feet on the number four well and broke a bit. Part of it fell in the well. We're having a hell of a time getting it out. Another bit is on the way. But that isn't why I came in. Someone poured sand in the motor of our water pump. Shot it all to hell. We've got to have a new one before we can start drilling again."

"Goddammit," Hunter swore.

"That's not all. The valve on the water pump on number two is leaking. The son-of-a-bitch didn't just take a notion to leak. It had help, 'cause I checked it a couple days ago."

"Got any idea who's behind it?"

"There's a couple of soreheads working on number six. It isn't any of the men on number four. They're as put out about this as we are. They don't want to lose the work."

George stood on first one foot, then the other. He was plainly nervous that he'd be blamed for the mishaps.

"While you wait for the bit to be replaced on number four and the motor on the water pump, place the men that you're sure are loyal among the other wells. Tell them to keep their eyes open and to especially watch the water pumps."

"If we catch the son-of-a-bitch who damaged that pump, there won't be enough left of him to scrape off the floor," George growled.

"Have you hired any new men?"

"Yeah. I gave the names to Perry."

"Joe Jones, R. Bluefeather and Thad Taylor," Perry said when Hunter looked his way. "They're staying at the hotel."

"Jones? Is that the brother of the girl who is taking care of Mrs. Byers?"

George answered, "Yes, he said something about that. Only two of them will work at any one time. One stays at the hotel and two work laying pipe. They want to switch off once in a while. It's fine with me as long as the work gets done. Jones and the Indian are working now. They know their stuff and are damn good workers. Taylor is the one who found the murdered woman."

"I saw him the other night at the pool hall." This came from Conrad, the bookkeeper. "Big, dark-haired fellow. He was baiting Madison and enjoying it. It was plain there's no love lost between the two of them. Taylor left with that jelly bean policeman from the city."

"He's the one that helped put out the fire down at Marlow. I recognized the name right away. Not many fellows named Thad," George said, then added, "He's got guts a mile long."

"I wonder why one of them stays at the hotel."

"Probably keeping an eye on that feisty little girl who is supposed to be running the place." George slapped his hat down on his head. "I was on the street the night Taylor came wading in among a bunch of rowdy roustabouts to take her back to the hotel. Lord, she was as mad as a rattler with its tail tied in a knot."

After George had left, Hunter leaned against the wall, attempting to relieve his aching hip.

"Go over to the house and get the car, Perry. I'm going to have to ride in it to get back home."

Joe and Blue came back to the hotel, tired and dirty. After a bath and a change of clothes, they came to the supper table.

"It's a treat to have a bath when I get home from work," Joe said as he sat down at the table. "Before we came to Rainwater, we bathed in a creek if there was one handy. At times it was icy cold."

"You washed at the pump at home. That water was cold springwater. Julie wouldn't let you sit down at the table until your face and hands were clean and you'd combed your hair." Jill placed a plate of cornbread squares on the table.

"Yeah. Habits are hard to break. Where's Thad?"

"I don't know."

"Isn't he coming to supper?"

"I don't know. Can't you eat without him?"

"I can," Blue said. "Pass the cornbread."

"Lloyd Madison tried to go to Aunt Justine's room today." Jill dropped that bit of news after they were all seated. She had al-

ready given Radna a word-for-word rundown.

"Thad stopped him?"

"Yes, and Lloyd said that he'd reported to
the sheriff that we were holding Aunt Justine prisoner and wouldn't let him see her."

"Thad talked to the sheriff." Radna
tossed her long black braid over her shoulder. "That took care of that. Lloyd was bluff-
ing. He hadn't complained to the sheriff."

Jill mulled over whether or not to tell what
Lloyd had said concerning her, but she
couldn't find the words. The decision was
made for her when Radna and Blue began
their usual sparring. Thad would tell Joe.
Her brother wouldn't believe she had been
meeting Lloyd, even if Thad did.

Jill set aside food for Thad while Radna
filled a plate and went in to feed Justine.
Blue went out onto the back porch to
smoke his pipe, and for the first time in a
couple of days, Jill was alone with her
brother.

"More tea, Joe? There's plenty of ice left
and the ice man comes tomorrow."

"I would like more, thanks. It was a hot
one out there today."

Jill chipped ice and poured tea from the

pitcher. She placed it in front of him on the table, then sat down.

"Tell me what happened today," Joe said before she could say anything. "Radna didn't tell it all."

"There's a bit more. Lloyd is the most evil, conniving person I've ever met. Remember what he said about you and me? Evil and crazy. He looked me straight in the eye and told me he was sorry he hadn't been able to meet me this morning and said that he'd explain when I came to his room tonight. He talked as if I had been meeting him for . . . you know. And Thad stood right there, not saying a word. He believed him."

"Thad isn't that stupid."

"He believed him, Joe. That is why he was so angry. He told me to go to the kitchen and said that I was the most irritating girl he'd ever met."

"He's crazy about you, Sis. I've not seen him like this before, and I've known him a long time."

"He can't stand it because I'm not chasing after him. You said he had girls running after him all the time. I remember how it was back home. Most girls, young or old, would have given their eyeteeth to have him notice them."

"That's true. Thad never had trouble getting girls. Are you holding that against him? Would you have noticed him if he'd been ugly as a mud fence?"

"He's like a brother to me and that is all." Jill spoke deliberately slowly and tilted her chin defiantly.

Joe looked at the ceiling: "Yeah, sure. You're—" He cut off his words when Thad came in the kitchen door. "It's about time you showed up. Jill was about to feed your supper to the dog."

"I had things to do."

"Like what?"

"I went to see Bernie Shepard, Justine's lawyer. I asked him about getting Madison out of the hotel. He said it could be done, but it would take a while. By then his month's rent would be up and we could refuse to let him take a room again, using an excuse like the hotel was full or we were going to do some painting." Thad glanced at Jill and then away. She placed his food on the table and poured him some tea. "Thanks," he said without taking his eyes off his plate. "We'll have to put up with Madison for another ten days."

Thinking that she wouldn't be noticed, Jill slipped out onto the back porch. Aware of every move she made, Thad lifted his fork to his mouth, hesitated, then returned it to his plate.

Seeing Thad glance at the door, Joe dropped some news into the silence that followed. "She thinks that you believed she was meeting Madison in his room."

Thad looked dumbfounded. "She . . . what? Where did she get a stupid idea like that?"

"Ask her. She said you were mad and told her to go to the kitchen."

"I was mad, but not at her. Good Lord! I knew he was lying. I wouldn't insult her by even asking her about it. I didn't want her there when he came back downstairs because I planned to beat him to death with my fists."

"You should tell her that."

"I can't talk to her anymore. She doesn't want anything to do with me. She's made that plain as the nose on her face. I've been on my knees for darn near a week and it's enough. Hell, I've got my pride, too. No woman is going to lead me around by the nose."

Joe laughed. "So is that all there is?"

"I don't know. I'm tired of walking around with my heart on my sleeve waiting for her to give me a kind word. It's too damn humiliating."

Joe threw up his hands. "Hell and damnation! Swallow your pride. Tell her you love her and that you'll beat the holy shit out of Madison if he comes near her. You've had enough women after you to have learned something."

"Do you want to keep your nose on your face?"

"Do you want to go out with Blue tomorrow? I can stay here for a day or two until things between you and Jill cool down."

"Good idea." A knowing look came over Thad's face. "Oh, I get it. Tomorrow is the day Laura is here. Are you making any progress with her?"

"I've not tried. I don't think it would do me any good."

"For God's sake. Try, man. She's as pretty as they come and as nice as they get."

"Then why don't you try your luck?"

"I've got other things on my mind."

Joe got up and slapped his friend on the back. "You're losing your touch, bud. You can't even reel in my little sis, who has been nuts about you all her life. Shoot, I remember when I had to carry a club to keep the girls off you."

"The problem is your big mouth," Thad protested. "I should get up and beat hell out of you. For old times' sake."

"Come on, then." Joe's mouth curved in a wide, reckless grin. "We haven't had a good fistfight since I whipped you over eating the last of the cookies Julie sent me."

"It'd be too easy this time. I owe you one. Your damn exaggerations about me and women have ruined things for me with Jill."

"Cheer up, bud. She's crazy about you. You just don't know how to handle women. Now, if you'd just listen to the master . . ." On seeing the angry gleam in Thad's eyes, Joe paused and ran his tongue over the edge of his teeth. He really wanted to keep all of them.

Thad got up from the table to take his empty plate to the dishpan, plowed his elbow into Joe's gut in passing and enjoyed the grunt that followed.

"Want to go uptown and hang around the pool hall?"

"It'd be more fun to stay here and watch you and Jill snarl at each other. I'm putting my money on my little sis. She'll have a ring in your nose before you know it." With a self-deprecating smile, Joe thumped his friend on the back, then went out onto the porch.

Thad stomped off toward the lobby, his misery wrapped around him like a winter coat.

Chapter 25

Hunter rapped gently on the back door. Through the window he could see Mrs. Cole at the ironing board and Laura sitting at the kitchen table mending a shirt. He had waited until it was fully dark before approaching the small house at the end of the road. Casper had driven him part of the way and would wait for him to return to the car.

"Who is it?" He heard the anxiety in Laura's voice and feared that she might be angry because he had come without an invitation.

"Hunter, Laura. I'm sorry to come at this time of night unannounced, but there is something important I need to tell you."

"What is it? What's wrong?" He heard the rasp of the lock before the door was opened.

"May I come in for a minute? I'd like for your mother to hear this."

Laura moved back and Hunter stepped into the kitchen and propped himself back against the door as soon as it was closed. He took off his hat and held it against his thigh. Mrs. Cole had turned the iron up on end and moved away from the ironing board. Her face was creased with a worried frown, her hands clenched in the pockets of her apron.

"When I left here last night, I was run down by a car."

"Oh, my goodness!" Laura gasped, her hand going to her throat.

"I saw it in time to dive to the side of the road. Only the fender hit me. I'm all right except for bruises and being sore as the dickens. It wasn't an accident. The driver of the car aimed it right at me."

"Do you have any idea who it was?" Mrs. Cole asked.

"I've made enemies. A man in business, especially my kind of business, is bound to have, but I never thought that any one of them wanted to kill me. I spoke to the sheriff. He asked if I had been here, because I was just a short distance from your house.

He wasn't too pleased when I said that I had been."

"Why would he care?" Laura asked.

"He thinks that whoever ran me down knew that I was here and waited for me to leave. What I came to say, Laura, is if I have put all of you in danger, I'm sorry. I will do anything in my power to protect you. If you agree, I'll have a man watch the house day and night—"

"No. We don't want that," Mrs. Cole said.

"Will you let me have a telephone put in so that if you need me you can call?"

"No." Laura spoke quickly.

"I understand your reluctance. Please don't think that my motives are any other than to keep you safe. If anything happened to you, Mary Pat or your mother, I'm not sure that I'd be able to handle it. I've enjoyed coming here. I can't put into words what it has meant to me."

"We'll be careful."

"May I leave this with you?" Hunter took a pistol and a small box of shells from his pocket. "Put it on a shelf someplace where you can get to it, and don't hesitate to use it if someone is trying to break into the house, because they are not coming in to steal the cookstove. They want to hurt you to get back at me."

Mrs. Cole took the gun, turned it aside and checked to see if it was loaded. She handled it as if she knew how.

"Thank you. I'll put it here in the cabinet. Laura and I both know how to handle a gun. My husband made sure of that."

"Be on your guard even if someone you know comes here. And don't go out onto the porch or to the outbuildings after dark."

"We haven't done that since the woman was killed."

"I would have never come here if I had thought there was the slightest chance that someone would try to hurt you because of me."

"Being run down by the car could have nothing to do with us," Laura said gently. "It could be someone . . . who doesn't like you because . . . because . . ." She couldn't bring herself to say because he was rich.

Hunter finished for her: "Because of the oil wells."

"Sit down, Mr. Westfall," Mrs. Cole invited. "I'll make coffee."

"Thank you, ma'am. But the truth is, I could hardly endure sitting in the car long enough for Casper to bring me down here. He let me out on the other side of the vacant house and I walked across the field."

Laura saw the dark smudges beneath his eyes, the white streaks on each side of his mouth and the careful way he held himself erect. She knew that he was in pain.

"Ma'am, may I talk to Laura for a minute on the porch?" Hunter's eyes were on Laura, but he spoke to Mrs. Cole.

"It's up to Laura."

Laura opened the door.

"Good night, Mrs. Cole."

"Be careful, Mr. Westfall."

Hunter waited for Laura, then followed her out the door. She walked to the end of the porch, out of the light from the window, before she turned to him. Her voice was quavery.

"You're hurting and you've got to walk back across that field."

On hearing the concern in her voice, Hunter reached out and took her hand.

"I'm afraid that my coming here has brought you to the attention of someone who may hurt you or the baby or your mother. Dear Lord, Laura. I couldn't . . . bear it if that happens." His voice broke. He stumbled over the words that came pouring from his mouth. "Laura, sweetheart, I'm so a-afraid for you that . . . that it's making me sick."

"Don't be afraid. We'll be all right." She clasped the hand holding hers in both her hands and brought it up between them. Her eyes met his and words that he never intended to say came tumbling from him like water from a dam.

"Sweet, sweet woman. I can't describe what I feel for you because I don't have the words. What I'm trying to say, Laura, is that what I feel is wonderful, strange, different from anything I've ever felt before. I can't tell you why I feel this way. It's just there inside me as if it had always been there, as if you'd always been there, or as if I'd been waiting for you to be there. It's crazy, sweetheart. The first time I saw your face, I knew that you were everything that is sweet and good. Far too good for a man like me. But, dear God! I can't keep myself from wanting you."

The more he talked, the more he feared that he would never be able to find the right words. His voice trailed. He fell into silence.

She didn't speak, as if she knew that in spite of his silence, he wasn't finished.

"I don't know why I'm telling you this now. I had planned to keep my feelings to myself for fear that you'd not want me to come here again. I don't expect you to feel anything in return and I'll not speak of it again."

He retreated to the safety of silence, but didn't linger, for fear that he would lose the will to break it.

"I'm sorry if I've embarrassed you." He raised the hands clasping hers to his lips and kissed her knuckles. "Does this change anything between us? Am I still invited to supper on Saturday night?" There was desperation in his voice.

"If you still want to come."

She leaned toward him, silently inviting. His arms enfolded her slowly, as if he were afraid she would push him away. She turned her face to his shoulder and leaned against him. They stood there, pressed together, not speaking, merely drinking in the closeness of each other. She put her arms around him. He buried his face in her hair, kissing it, murmuring her name softly.

"Laura, Laura, you make me weak."

Unaware that she was smiling, Laura lifted her head to look at him. He couldn't prevent his mouth from closing over hers. She stopped smiling with her lips, but smiles danced through her blood. The kiss was long and sweet. He felt the slow, subtle yielding of her lips and body. It aroused him unbearably. His heart thundered wildly against hers.

Terribly afraid of being too rough with her, he lifted his head, leaned back against the wall of the house and cuddled her against him. Her arms moved to encircle his neck. He looked deeply into her eyes, and what he saw there melted his heart.

"I'm trying to be . . . gentle. . . ."

Laughter bubbled up within her.

"Don't look so scared. I won't break," she whispered. Her breath on his face was warm and fragrant, just before she fit her lips to his in a sweet and gentle kiss.

"Oh, Lord." His eyes on her face were wet and gleaming in the moonlight. "If I could sing, I would. If I could fly, I'd snatch you up and fly away with you." He pushed the hair back from her temples. "I thought sure I'd ruined things."

"I have to think about what you said.

We're not at all suited, you know." She pressed her parted lips to his again. He ran his fingers through her dark curls to the nape of her neck and gently massaged it.

"You suit me, sweetheart. I'd not change one thing about you. But *I'll* change. I'll make myself into whatever you want me to be." He murmured against her lips and kissed them again and again, not daring to press too hard and kiss too passionately, for fear of scaring her. The tip of his tongue stroked her upper lip. "Let's just take it one day at a time. My main concern now is that you, Mary Pat and your mother are safe."

"Whoever tried to run you over will try again. I'll worry about you."

"Honey, I've never heard sweeter words," he whispered, unable to believe that he'd heard them. "No one has ever worried about me but Dinah and Casper."

"I'll worry. Mama will worry, too. She likes you. Mary Pat thinks you're grand."

"How about Laura? Does she like me . . . a little bit?"

"She'd not be here kissing you if she didn't."

"This is worth being hit by a dozen cars!"

he exclaimed and placed soft kisses on her wet lips.

He could have stood there forever if not for the pain in his hip and leg. The thought came to him that he still had to cross that rough field to reach the car where Casper waited.

"I should go, but I don't want to. Promise that you and your mother will stay together. When she goes to the hotel, go with her, or come stay with Dinah. She would fuss over you and the baby. I don't like you being here alone."

"We'll see. Don't worry. Mama and I have been taking care of ourselves for quite a while."

Hunter stepped off the porch still holding her hand. He lifted it to his lips, gently kissed the palm, then walked out into the dark yard toward the field. He scarcely felt the pain in his leg and hip for the happiness in his heart.

Laura, his precious Laura, cared something for him. It might not be love now, but he had hope. If she would let him, he would cherish her for a lifetime.

*   *   *

Thad spent a miserable night on the cot in the hallway, but it was not any more miserable than the previous nights, only that this night seemed longer. A lot longer. After his talk with Joe, he had about made up his mind to try and talk to Jill again. When he had approached her in the lobby, she went down the hallway to her aunt's room and closed the door. That took care of that.

He had sat in the kitchen while Radna sliced cucumbers and put them to soak in salt water. Blue was there. Those two spent quite a lot of time together. Radna was good for Blue, and he for her. They seemed to speak the same language. At times the barbs they flung at each other made a person uncomfortable. But they had an understanding, and that was all that mattered. Tonight, after Radna finished in the kitchen, they walked off into the darkness together.

Thad was worried about Lloyd Madison. It was his opinion that the man was unbalanced, mean and manipulative. Joe had told him about Lloyd hinting that he and Jill were lovers. Thad's blood boiled on hearing that and he longed to plant his fist in the man's face. He hadn't believed for an instant that Jill was meeting that madman in his room. It was so ridiculous that he hadn't thought it worth reassuring Jill.

Now, in the light of dawn, he got up, dressed and folded the canvas cot. After he put it away, he headed for the outhouse behind the hotel, which he used most of the time instead of the small lavatory at the end of the hall.

As soon as he walked out onto the porch, he lifted his head to sniff the air. He stepped off the porch, looked toward the south and saw great clouds of black, greasy smoke boiling skyward against a horizon streaked with the rays of the rising sun.

Oil fire! He'd seen several during the past few years. Somewhere out there on the prairie a well or a tank was burning wild, hurling thousands of cubic feet of gas or oil upward in a raging sheet of hell. There was a tank farm nearby with dozens of tanks filled with oil. If the fire spread and reached the flow tanks, the entire area could go up in flames.

Thad hit the porch running and didn't stop until he was on the second floor of the hotel, flinging open the door to Joe and Blue's room. The door bounced back

against the wall. Both men reared up in
bed.

"What the hell—" Blue sputtered.

"Oil fire! Let's go! They'll need all the experienced help they can get to keep it from
reaching the tank farm, if it hasn't already."

Blue bounced out of bed, naked as a
plucked chicken, and pulled on his britches.

"I'm going," Thad said. "One of you will
have to stay here with the women. It would
be just like Madison to take advantage of a
situation like this."

"I'm with you." Blue was putting on his
shoes.

"Guess that leaves you, Joe," Thad said.
"Come on, Blue. I'll go get the car started."

"Hell," Joe grumbled as he hurried after
them down the stairs.

Jill had come to the doorway of her room
when she heard the commotion.

"What's going on?"

"An oil well is on fire," Joe said. "Thad
and Blue are going out to help."

"Don't they want breakfast . . . or coffee?"

"No time."

Thad started to walk past her, then
paused, snaked an arm around her waist

and jerked her up close. His mouth came down on hers, fast and strong. The force of it left her reeling and helpless to resist her own answering need. Her lips softened and parted as she tumbled deaf and blind into a kiss that went on and on. His mouth worked on hers, frantic and impatient.

When he lifted his head, green eyes beneath heavily lashed lids stared down into hers as if daring her to deny what was between them. His arm dropped from around her. She staggered back against the wall and stood there until she heard the back screen door slam.

He was gone.

As Thad and Blue neared the burning oil well, a rising wind whipped choking clouds of dust across the plains to mingle with the smoke. The derrick and engine house were a twisted mass of red flames. Cars were parked back along the road; men stood gawking, but no one seemed to be doing anything.

Fifty yards from the burning inferno, Thad slammed on the brakes. He recognized George Hinkle, the head driller, standing with a group of grim-faced men. They were apparently oblivious to the danger they were in. Thad knew instantly that the heat from the fire could cause the overflow tank to explode. If so, the men would be scalded with burning oil. He jumped from the car and plowed through lakes of water from a leaky water pump to yell at the men.

"Stay back!" he shouted. "Stay back from the tank. I've seen them explode from the heat."

The urgency in his voice set the men to running. A minute later the tank exploded, sending spraying flaming oil in all directions, igniting pools of it on the water.

"Jesus! Jesus!" George said again and again. "If we'd been standing there—"

"Get shovels, boards, anything to heap dirt and keep the burning oil from traveling on the water to another tank," Thad shouted as Blue ran to get shovels from the back of their car.

Working desperately to build a dirt dam, a dozen men dug into the red Oklahoma soil. Small pools of burning oil floated on the water. As soon as they dammed up one area, they shifted to another. George worked alongside Thad. Men from other drilling companies gathered along the road to watch. A few brought shovels and pitched in to help. A dozen others stood around watching.

"Mr. Westfall will be out as soon as he knows when the fire crew will be here. I hear you've had some experience in putting out fires," George said to Thad.

"Not much. I've helped a time or two when steam was used to put out a fire while the wellhead was capped. Who did Westfall call?"

"Jim Hovelson out of Tulsa."

"He's got a good team," Thad said. "It'll take him a couple hours to get here."

"Mr. Westfall was farsighted enough to see that we've got the best boilers made."

"Hell of a time to have a leak in your water tank."

"I'm thinking that leak didn't just happen this time."

Thad swore. "Did the leak cut your water supply so that you couldn't get enough mud in the well?"

"I've no way of knowing. We had a five-man crew. The derrick man, firemen and two floor men got off. The driller didn't make it off the derrick." George swore. "He was a damn good man."

"Could the fire have been set?"

"I don't think so. My men wouldn't have let anyone they didn't know near the derrick. The most frequent cause of an oil well fire is when a geological formation is struck by the drilling bit, inducing a higher pressure than the weight of the long column of drilling mud. We just put in a new bit."

"How far down were you?"

"A thousand feet into blue shale. We may have hit a gas pressure, and the weight of the drilling mud wasn't enough to keep it from blowing."

"Mr. Westfall has enemies among the small wildcatters. Stirred up, no doubt, by Lloyd Madison."

"Yeah, the bastard."

The heat from the towering fire and the burning tank scorched the faces of the men trying to contain the water to keep the oil and the fire from spreading. The thick black greasy smoke made it difficult to breathe.

"All we can do is try to keep the fire from spreading to the next tank," George said. The oilman's face was set in hard lines. The big rawboned hand dropped from the shovel to form a tight fist.

"Usually men from other companies will

pitch in to help when there's an emergency." Thad glanced at a group of men
watching the frantic effort they were making
to keep the fire contained.

"Madison has done a good job turning
the men against Westfall."

"Do you know why?"

"No. The rumor is that when Madison first
came to Rainwater, he wanted Westfall's legal work and to be cozy with him, includin'
sharin' his female company. Madison was
put out when it didn't happen. He then began working on the roustabouts to organize
for higher pay and shorter hours." George
snorted. "They should go work down
around Healdton and they'll see how good
they have it here. I'll compare Westfall's pay
with any in the state."

"Seems like Madison's gone to a lot of
trouble to get back at a man who didn't
want to have him over for dinner."

"Yeah, well, some of us think Madison
isn't playing with a full deck most of the
time."

"I'll go along with that."

Having surrounded the pool of water with
a high dirt bank, the weary men stopped to

lean on their shovels. Their fire-reddened faces glistened with sweat.

"Some fire ya got here, George."

As soon as the man spoke, Thad recognized him as one of the men in the pool hall the night he was there with Jelly Bryce and had the little set-to with Madison.

"Yeah, Sample. It cost the life of a good man, a man with a woman and two kids. If I find out the valve on that water pump was stripped intentionally, I know who to come looking for."

"Hey, now! You accusin' me?"

"If the shoe fits—"

"Gawddammit! I don't know nothin' bout how this fire got started or how your water pump fizzled."

"You don't know jack-shit, Sample. All you know is what that shyster lawyer feeds you, and you don't have the brains to think for yourself."

"If you're not going to work, get the hell out of the way." Thad brought his shovel up and pressed it against the man's chest and pushed him back.

"Don't ya be pushin' me, ya hayseed," Oscar Sample sputtered. "Mr. Madison said ya ain't nothin' but a hanger-on hopin' to get some pussy from that gal at the hotel."

Thad dropped the shovel and hit him. His fist smashed into the man's face. Sample took several stumbling backward steps before he hit the ground. Blood spurted from his broken nose.

"Open your mouth again and I'll string your guts from here to Tulsa. If you know what's good for you, you'll get the hell away from here while you've got legs to carry you."

Sample scrambled to his feet and backed away out of Thad's reach.

"You'll not get away with this. We're goin' to organize. Then all of ya will be fixed good." A couple of men came forward and stood beside Oscar Sample.

Blue moved up beside Thad. "There's only three of them, Thad. It ain't hardly worth gettin' dirty for. I can take two of them if you're tired."

"Naw. We've got more important things to do. I'll meet this piece of horseshit some night. It'll be just him and me, and after I've finished with him, he'll have a new asshole and be wearing a diaper for the rest of his life."

"Ouch!" Blue said and picked up his shovel.

"Now, listen here, all a ya," George shouted when more men hurried up to support Sample. "If there's any trouble, I'll see ya all in jail."

One of them whispered something. They looked back down the road, then backed away, taking Oscar Sample with them.

"Shit a brick, George, you messed it up," Blue said. "I wanted to hit someone."

"Save it for Madison. He's the one that's got these poor fools stirred up."

The sheriff was trying to steer his car down the road now clogged with cars, trucks, boys on bicycles and men on horseback. Sightseers from town were out in full force. Black greasy smoke continued to billow from the well and the tank. The men were putting out small grass fires.

"The wind is changing. Watch that second tank. Jesus! Someone tell those people to get the hell back," Thad said loudly.

The sheriff, Jelly Bryce and Hunter Westfall got out of the sheriff's car. Hunter, ignoring the jeers from Oscar Sample and his cronies, hurried over to George.

"Jim Hovelson and his crew will be here within the hour. Anyone hurt?"

"Payne Caldwell, the driller. I couldn't find him when I got here. He may have been on the crown board when the well went up."

"Ah, law. I'm sorry about that." There was genuine sorrow on Hunter's face.

"Any idea how it started?"

"No. But whoever caused the leak in the water tank had a hand in it. The valve is stripped. We couldn't pump enough mud. Lord God, but I wish I'd shut down the well."

Hunter put his hand on George's shoulder. "You had no way of knowing. Don't blame yourself."

"Having any trouble with those boys?" Sheriff Page asked with a jerk of his head toward Oscar Sample and the men who had jeered Hunter.

"Not now."

"Figured they was Madison men. I'll keep an eye on 'em."

Thad and Blue moved away to join the men throwing dirt on small grass fires.

"Some folks don't have the brains of a flea," Thad said and paused to view the throng of townfolk. "Look at them, letting those kids run all over." He motioned to a group of small boys playing in the road. "They think this is a picnic."

Ten minutes later the second tank exploded, spraying flaming oil in all directions, igniting pools of water and numerous grass fires. A blasting rush of air slammed Thad to his knees. When he came up again he heard a woman screaming.

"Bobby! Bobby!"

Thad looked over his shoulder and terror clutched at him. Running desperately through a spreading pool of water, his face distorted with terror, was a young boy no more than five or six. And racing along over the oil-soaked water were leaping tongues of fire reaching out for him.

"Bobby!" His mother's voice was hysterical.

Terrified by the searing flames that surrounded him, the boy, possessed by fear and indecision, was running in circles.

"This way, boy! This way!" Racing against near-hopeless odds, Thad ran toward the boy, water splashing his pant legs with every step; his booted feet seemed heavy, awkward, as if each weighed a hundred pounds. A single glance told him that the boy's short stubby legs would never take him beyond the reach of those leaping flames in time. On the other hand, there was a chance—one chance in a hundred—that he might be able to grab him and out-run the fire.

"Here, boy!" Thad's voice was choked and strangled. "This way!"

The sound of Thad's voice must have driven some of the terror from the lad's mind, for he turned and stumbled toward him.

"Papa!" he screamed. "Papa!"

"Run, boy!" Thad's booted feet sank in the mud of the soggy ground. Fear for the boy gave him the extra speed he needed. He reached the boy and scooped him into his arms.

The small, squat corrugated tin that covered the water well seemed miles away as he headed for it. When he reached it, he dropped to the ground behind the shelter, covering the boy's small body with his big one.

Jill, I love you! The thought screamed in Thad's mind as the living wall of flame swept over and around the well covering to fizzle out on the muddy ground beyond.

Thad felt the searing agony of the flames, heard the boy cry out. From far away he could hear a woman's hysterical cries: "Bobby! My God! Oh, my God!"

He was sucked down into a vortex of darkness for only a few seconds, then Blue was beside him, tearing the burning shirt off his back. As soon as he could, he rolled off the boy and Blue helped him up.

Jelly Bryce lifted the boy up and carried him toward his mother.

"Is the boy . . . all right?" Thad gasped. Needles of pain were stabbing his back with relentless precision.

"Yeah," Blue growled. "But you ain't."

Chapter 26

Joe moved restlessly from the backyard, where he watched the billowing black smoke, to the front porch, where he saw the people streaming by on their way to get a better view of the fire. He knew more than most the danger of an oil well fire and was worried for Thad and Blue.

Elmer had told him that Lloyd Madison had come down shortly after Thad and Blue left the hotel. Without even a morning greeting, he had walked quickly through the lobby, across the porch and up the street toward his office.

The night clerk and his wife had agreed to stay on throughout the day. One of them would man the desk while the other napped on the couch behind the screen. Joe was glad to have them there to help him keep an eye on Madison as well as take care of the morning checkouts.

Jill and Radna were worried about Justine. This morning her speech was slurred; she had a strange vacant look in her eyes and she had swallowed only a few bites of her breakfast. Not wanting to use the telephone and alert everyone listening in on the line, Radna had gone down to fetch the doctor, only to find that he was out delivering a baby. She had left word for him to come to the hotel as soon as he returned.

When Mrs. Cole came to work, Laura and Mary Pat were with her, even though it wasn't wash day. Laura volunteered to take over the chore of canning the cucumbers Radna had sliced the night before. After putting her daughter in the playpen Thad had built for her beside the wash house, she rinsed the slices to remove the salt and packed them in the jars Radna had scalded the night before. A mixture of pickling spices, sugar and vinegar was heating on the stove.

Laura and Joe conversed while she worked. She was sincerely concerned for Justine. She knew, too, the danger of an oil well fire and understood Joe's worry for his friends. Mrs. Cole had not given a reason why Laura and Mary Pat had come to work with her. Considering Justine's condition this morning and the oil fire, neither Jill nor Radna had thought to ask. They were grateful for Laura's help.

When the hot spiced vinegar came to a boil, Laura wrapped a dish towel around a Mason jar filled with cucumber slices and ladled it into the jar. After filling it, she screwed on a zinc lid and set it on the table to cool. Before filling another jar, she looked out the door to where Mary Pat played in the sand pile.

Her heart jumped into her throat. A man was leaning over the fence and was lifting her daughter up into his arms. Laura dropped the dish towel and ran out the door, allowing the screen door to slam behind her.

Lloyd Madison turned and smiled.

"Hello, Laura. The baby has grown since I saw her last."

"Give her to me." Laura reached to take the child. Lloyd turned, keeping Mary Pat out of her reach. The baby began to cry.

"I'll hold her. You are a pretty thing," he said to the child. "Almost as pretty as your mama. Another twelve to fifteen years, you and your mama can open up a real whore-house. I bet there's not another in the state of Oklahoma with a working mother and daughter."

"Give her to me!"

"I went by your house, Laura. Not open for business during the day? Well, I knew that if you weren't at home, you'd be here." Lloyd walked toward the wash house. Mary Pat began to scream in earnest.

"Stop! Give me my baby!" Laura ran after him, yelling at the top of her voice.

"Don't get in a snit, Laura. I'll take her in here out of the sun and play with her for a while. You want to play with me, don't you, baby doll?" Lloyd spoke calmly, completely ignoring the baby's cries.

"Give her to me," Laura screamed and beat on his back with her fists.

He turned suddenly and lifted a hand as if to hit her. "Stop it, you . . . shitty slut," he snarled and shoved her away. "You are a slut. Any woman who would fuck Hunter Westfall is a . . . shitty . . . trashy slut! He's poked his pecker into hundreds of sluts just like you. You'll find out what happens to a woman's *kids* when she plays fast and loose with me."

"Hey! Hey!" Jill's yell mingled with cries from Laura and her daughter.

Jill had been in her aunt's room when she heard the back door slam and, thinking it strange, went to investigate. At the door she saw Lloyd Madison with Laura's little girl in his arms and Laura screaming and running after him. Without another thought, Jill was on her way out the door. She grabbed the mop as she crossed the porch.

Lloyd was going into the wash house, Laura's hands fastened to his shirt trying to pull him back. As soon as Jill reached them, she swung the mop handle with all her strength. Crack! The heavy wooden handle connected solidly with the side of Lloyd's head. The blow knocked his head against the doorframe, cutting his ear. He staggered, then he righted himself, turned and shoved Laura to her knees. She was up in an instant and when his hand went to his ear, she grabbed Mary Pat from his arms.

His fury now was directed at Jill.

"Bitch!" he yelled, holding the side of his head where blood trickled down through his fingers from his bloody ear. "You'll pay for this." His eyes were bright with anger, his lips curled in a snarl. He was like a snarling wolf ready to spring.

"I'm not afraid of your threats." Jill stood her ground, ready to swing the mop handle again. "Get away from here or I'll hit you again."

"Slut! Whore!" He pulled a handkerchief from his pocket and pressed it to his head. He looked past Jill to the porch, then turned and walked quickly around the hotel to the street.

Joe jumped from the porch and hurried to them. "What happened?"

Laura was sobbing and clutching the baby to her. Mary Pat had quieted now that she was with her mother. Jill had her arms around both of them.

"That polecat had Mary Pat and wouldn't let go of her."

"He . . . he was going to . . . take her in the wash house." It was difficult for Laura to get enough air in her lungs to talk. She hugged the little girl so tight, the child was wiggling to get down. "He just kept holding her and turning so I couldn't grab her."

"I whacked him a good one up alongside

the head," Jill exclaimed. "I doubt it knocked any sense in him."

"That awful man called me nasty names and said nasty things," Laura blurted. "He said . . . he said he'd been to my house and . . . and came here looking for us. Hunter told me not to stay at home by myself."

"Mr. Westfall told you?" Jill asked.

"Someone ran him down with a car near our house."

"Deliberately?"

"He thinks so. He also thinks whoever did it may try to hurt us . . . to get back at him."

"I didn't know you were that friendly with Mr. Westfall."

"He comes to the house. He's really a nice man." Laura's tone was defensive.

Oh, Lord. Sweet little Laura has fallen for Hunter Westfall's smooth talk, thought Jill.

"I wasn't really afraid of Lloyd Madison at first," Jill confessed to her brother. "But now . . . he's getting stranger and stranger."

"Come on back to the kitchen," Joe said, herding the women before him. "I don't think Madison would be foolish enough to come back in through the front door, but I need to make sure."

*   *   *

It was a half hour before noon when Blue stopped the old topless touring car on the street beside the hotel. Seconds later, he stuck his head in the kitchen. Joe was moving jars of hot pickles to a shelf. Jill and Laura were cleaning up.

"Joe, Thad's been burned. Jill, call the doctor."

Blue's words hit Jill like a blow in the stomach and robbed her of speech. It was several seconds before she could expel a breath.

"The doctor's here . . . with Aunt Justine."

Joe shot past her out the door. Her breath had clogged her throat and her heart had jumped out of rhythm. She ran to the end of the porch to see Jelly Bryce, the Oklahoma City policeman, and Blue helping Thad out of the car. He was shirtless, his face dark with smoke, his back . . . oh, dear God . . . his back . . .

Jill ran to her aunt's room and jerked open the door. She could hardly breathe for the tide of panic that rose in her throat— Thad, her Thad! People died from burns, even minor ones, if they got infected.

"Doctor, don't leave. Thad's been burned. They're bringing him in." With dread making her sick to her stomach, she went to her room and jerked off the quilt she used for a spread and smoothed the sheets. "In here," she yelled when she heard them come into the kitchen.

"No," Thad said when they led him into Jill's room. She stood in the corner with her hand over her mouth. Their eyes met for an instant. "Set up my cot, Joe."

Jill almost cried out when she saw the raised blisters on his shoulders and back.

"Lie down, Thad. The doctor's here."

"No. She won't want me here."

"You stubborn, muleheaded jackass," Jill shouted. "Lie down on that damn bed or I'll . . . I'll pull every damn hair out of your stupid hard head!"

"Hush your swearing," Thad growled. "Someone ought to paddle your behind," he muttered and sank face down on the bed.

Jill burst into tears and ran from the room. Seeing the grimace of pain on Thad's face cut through her like a knife. By the time Jelly and Blue had returned to the kitchen, she was dabbing at her wet eyes.

"Thanks for bringing him home, Mr. Bryce," Jill managed to say. "Laura and I are about to put the noon meal on the table. Please stay."

"Thanks, ma'am. It's a treat to have a home-cooked meal." Jelly eyed the pretty girl sitting in the chair with the small child on her lap.

"This is Laura Hopper. Laura, Mr. Bryce is a policeman."

Laura nodded but refused to look at him.

"I want my thanks," Blue grumbled. "I drove the car."

"Thanks, Blue." To Blue's surprise, Jill gave him a quick kiss on the cheek.

"Where's Radna?"

"She's with Aunt Justine. The doctor said my aunt has had a stroke."

Joe came in. "I need a clean wet cloth to cover his back. The doctor said wet it with water from the teakettle."

Jill opened a drawer and took out a clean thin flour sack, one they used to dry dishes. She held it over the sink while Joe poured water over it. The water had cooled enough that Joe could squeeze out the excess and hurry from the room.

Minutes later he was back. "The doctor wants me to get some things from the drugstore. Keep an eye out, Blue, and make sure Madison goes to his room if he comes in the hotel. He picked up Laura's baby this morning and wouldn't give her back. Jill clobbered him with the mop handle." He grinned. "She'll tell you about it."

"Is the doctor with Thad?" Jill asked.

"He's dividing his time between him and Aunt Justine. I've got to go get this stuff."

"Tell Blue and Mr. Bryce about what happened, Laura. I'll be right back."

Forgetting how bashful Laura was and how uncomfortable she would be when left alone with the two men, Jill went down the hall to her room and looked in. Thad was lying on his stomach across the end of her bed. The wet cloth covered his back and shoulders and a sheet lay over him from his waist to his knees. The sharp smell of smoke drifted up from the muddy boots and britches that lay in a heap on the floor.

His face was turned away from the door.

She went quietly into the room, knelt down and removed his black socks, noting that a hole in the toe of one had been closed with white thread.

"Thanks," he murmured.

Tears rolled down her cheeks when she saw the singed hair and the red blistered flesh on his neck. She moved to the other side of the bed and sank down on her knees. His smoke-darkened face lay against the white sheet.

"Thad? Is there anything I can do?" Her fingers stroked his unruly dark hair back over his ear.

On hearing her voice, he stopped breathing. Then green eyes were looking at her from between his thick dark lashes. Although her eyes were swimming in tears, she saw the concern in his. He said nothing for a long while. When he finally spoke, it was in a husky whisper.

"I hate it when you cry."

"I can't help it." Her fingers continued to stroke his hair.

"I'm filthy dirty. I don't want you to see me . . . like this."

"You look wonderful to me."

"I'm getting your bed dirty." His lips barely moved as he spoke.

"Would you feel better if I washed your face?" Her small hand reached to cover his where it lay on the white sheet.

"If I had a washcloth I could do it."

Jill left the room and returned with a basin and a cloth. She placed it on the floor beside the bed and dipped the cloth in the warm water. She gently washed the greasy smoke from his face. The cloth caught in the whiskers as she smoothed it over his chin and his cheeks. His eyes remained closed until she finished.

"Feel better?"

"Uh-huh."

She washed his hands with the wet cloth and placed them back on the bed. Thad watched her. When she stood up with the basin, he was sure that she would leave the room. But she set it on the bureau and came back to sink down on the floor beside the bed.

"Joe's gone to the drugstore to get something to ease the pain. Is it very bad?" Her hand sought his where it lay on the bed.

"Not . . . so bad . . . now." He turned his hand over and gripped hers tightly.

"I wish I could take the pain away."

She laid her head on the bed beside his. Then, as if she had no control over her actions, her lips brushed his in a kiss so gentle that it was over in an instant.

"What does that mean?" he asked in a choked whisper.

"It means that I don't care . . . if you get

my bed dirty, or if you have a dozen women chasing after you. I'm so glad you're here and safe, where I can take care of you. You're mine for . . . now."

Oh, God, I ache for you. I love you so damn much.

"You're just saying that because . . . because you're feeling sorry for me."

"Yes, I'm sorry you're hurt, you . . . you dumbbell!" she said almost angrily. "But I've got more sense than to tell a man that I love him . . . just because he's hurt. There, I've said it!" A thin thread of panic ran through her. She lifted her head so that she could look at him. Her blue eyes, full of defiance, met his. "Now you can add my name to the list of all your other women and . . . laugh because the stupid little farm girl that's been crazy about you all her life has admitted that she loves you."

Damn the pain in her heart that was causing tears to fill her eyes!

"Jill, Jill," he whispered and lifted his head off the bed. "Sweet girl, the first day I came to Rainwater you took over my heart. Damn! I wish I could get up and hold you. Come closer, honey, so I can kiss you."

A stubble of beard scraped her chin as

she fit her mouth to his. He didn't just kiss her; he stroked, nibbled, coaxed her lips apart with light sweet kisses. After a long and delicious moment, she backed away slightly to take a breath, then her mouth returned to his again as if it were cool, sweet water and she were dying of thirst.

His free hand moved to the back of her head, his fingers forked through her hair. When she ended the kiss and moved, he didn't try to hold her. He feasted his eyes on her face. Hungrily, they inspected every detail.

"Why didn't you tell me this days ago? I've been through hell—"

"My pride wouldn't let me." Her fingers stroked his lips. "It's gone now. I've not a shred of pride left. I just had to tell you, even if you . . . if you just want to add me to your string." The tears that filled her eyes made them look like twin stars.

"I'm going to beat Joe senseless for telling you that. I think I've always known that you and I would be together someday, raise a family, grow old together. When will you marry me?"

She took a gasping breath. "I don't know. I've got to think—"

"You said you loved me. Didn't you mean it?" he asked with something like panic in his voice.

"I meant it . . . with all my heart."

"I love you, too," he said simply.

She could see the anguish in his eyes and swallowed dryly, feeling the frantic clamor of her throbbing pulse. Was he saying that because she cried? Go slowly, she warned her leaping heart. Did he really mean it?

"We can talk about it . . . later."

"Is this a dream?" She heard his voice quaver.

"I'm awake. Are you?" Too moved to form more words, she could only kiss his lips, again and again. "I'll always love you," she whispered.

His laugh was low, intimate, joyous. He pressed on the back of her head to bring her lips to his again.

"And I love you. . . ." The words were muttered against her lips.

So much tenderness was in the timbre of his voice that Jill almost cried again. She choked back the sobs and smiled at him. Her fingers stroked his cheeks, feeling the rough drag of his whiskers. She traced his eyebrows and trailed her fingers over his lips. He remained still, his eyes devouring her face.

"I never imagined it would be like this. Me, flat on my stomach, not daring to move lest I break open the skin on my back. I want to pick you up, run away with you and love you until we're both so old we can't get up out of a chair."

"When that time comes, I'll be sitting on your lap and you won't have to get up out of a chair," she teased and kissed his eyes shut. Then her lips sought his and opened over his mouth with drugged sweetness. Closing her eyes, she reveled in the feel of his lips moving under hers and the strong fingers stroking the nape of her neck.

"My patient seems to be in good hands."

Jill lifted her head to see Dr. Russell coming into the room. A grinning Joe was behind him. Red-faced, she scrambled to her feet. Thad refused to let go of her hand even though she pulled on it.

The doctor came to the bed. "Let's see what we've got here. Young lady, if you can get your hand back, I'd like you to bring me some things from the kitchen. I stuck my head in there a while ago and told Laura what I was going to need. The water should be cool by now."

After the doctor had dressed the burns on Thad's back and shoulders with the salve from the drugstore, he gave instructions to Jill.

"He's lucky the burns aren't any deeper than they are. He should heal fast if he doesn't stretch and break open the skin. Keep it covered tonight. Tomorrow take off the cover so the air can get to it. If he runs the slightest temperature, call me. It could mean an infection."

"I need to get up," Thad protested.

"Too bad," the doctor said without a trace of sympathy. "Stay right there. I'll not have my reputation ruined because I let a puny little old burn kill my patient. I'll be back in the morning."

Jill followed the doctor out of the room. Thad twisted his head so that he could see Joe.

"Shut the door, Joe. I've got to pee so bad I'm about to bust."

"That so? I didn't think men in love had to do things as ordinary as pee."

"Don't be smart. I'm hungry, too. I haven't had a bite to eat all day."

"Worked up an appetite, did you? Kissin' does that to a fellow."

"When I get up from here, I'm going to stomp your sorry hide into the ground."

"It takes a brave man to threaten me when he knows that I'll not hit him when he's down." Joe brought the chamber pot and set it beside the bed.

"She loves me," Thad said after he had used the pot and scooted back up onto the bed.

"She's dumber than I thought."

"I'm going to marry her as soon as I get out of this bed."

"I don't know about that. You'll have to get permission from her nearest male relative. You'd better start buttering him up."

"You put a kink in this, Joe Jones, and I'll go through your guts like a hot chili pepper."

"I'm ready to bargain."

"What've I got you want?"

"Your half of the car."

"I'd rather kiss a dead moose's ass than give you my half of the car," Thad sputtered.

"Jill will be delighted to hear that," Joe

said in a superior tone and left the room. He was grinning.

"Come back here, you pig-ugly—"

Thad thought that he was shouting, but he was only whispering, and his voice faded. The medicine the doctor had given him was kicking in. His eyes drifted shut and he fell into a deep sleep.

Chapter 27

Jelly Bryce walked into the sheriff's office and hung his hat on the peg beside the door.

"You missed a good meal, Sheriff. The ladies at the hotel invited me to dinner. We had fried potatoes, green beans, turnip greens cooked with side pork and corn-bread."

"That's what happens when you're young and pretty. No one offers to feed me turnip greens and cornbread."

"Some of us have all the luck, Sheriff."

"How is Taylor doing?"

"All right. The doctor gave him something to make him sleep. Is the kid all right?"

"Judge Broers said so. The kid's his grandson."

"I hope he realizes what a chance Taylor

took to save the boy. I didn't think that he and the kid had a snowball's chance in hell to outrun that fire. When Blue and I got to them, he was just coming around, still holding on to the kid. Must have blacked out for a minute."

"A well fire will happen once in a while. The valve on the water tank is another matter. Westfall's man swears someone stripped the threads on the valve."

"Blue and I went back out to the well after we brought Taylor in. Hovelson and his men are there. They'll have the fire put out by night. The burning tank is another matter. They were getting ready to knock a hole in the bottom to drain out the oil."

"Is Westfall still out there?"

"Yeah. The man don't mind getting dirty. He picked up a shovel and worked even though he was hurting like hell."

The sheriff leaned back in his chair. "Westfall's got the idea in his head that it was Madison who run him down with his car."

"Did he see him?"

"No, and my deputy didn't find any damage to the car."

"Madison is acting strange." Jelly related

the story Laura told him and Blue about Madison grabbing her little girl. He had to grin when he told the part about Jill cracking Madison on the head with the mop handle. "That little gal has spunk she hasn't used yet."

"Folks are still stirred up about the murder of that woman and any little thing sets them off. Laura and Miss Jones may have got carried away. Madison doesn't strike me as a man who would act the way they say he did."

"I believe them. Madison said some pretty nasty things to the mother of the little girl. She didn't tell us that part. Joe's sister told him and he told us. My old friend Bluefeather was ready to go scalp him."

"I'll call Madison in for a talk and get his side of the story."

"I saw him driving out of town just now."

"Going out to the fire?"

"Guess so."

"I'll catch him later. How long will you be staying?"

"They'll pull me off the Carsie Bakken case in a week unless we come up with a reason for me to stay."

"Hell, I've run into a dead end. The case has me stumped."

"Whoever killed that woman and cut her up was no dummy. We've found none of her belongings, nor the place where he butchered her. He has her head hidden away for a reason. My bet is that he's holding it for his trump card."

"Maybe the sick bastard likes to look at it." A grimace came over the sheriff's tired face and he shook his shaggy head. "I hate like hell to think a lunatic may get away with killing a woman in my town."

It was evening.

Radna had not left Justine's bedside. Her dearest friend was dying and there was nothing she could do. The doctor had said that Justine could go at any time, and Radna was going to make sure that when that time came, Justine would not be alone.

"He was . . . mean even as a little boy. The devil is in him," Justine said in a voice so low and slurred that Radna had to bend close to hear her. For the past few hours Justine's eyes had been fixed on the ceiling above her bed. She had been silent until now.

"Yes." Radna knew to whom she was referring. "But it's not your fault."

"I wish I could be sure. I dreamed about his coming and telling me that he didn't blame me. Now I wish to God he hadn't found me. My dream turned into a nightmare."

"The old judge drilled it into him that it was your fault. He made him the way he is."

"It's too late for him to hurt me. I'm dying anyway." Justine's limp hand lay in Radna's. "I don't want him to hurt you or Jill. He will if he gets the chance."

"He'll not get the chance. Don't worry."

"When I'm gone, he'll turn his hate to someone else. I want you and Jill to leave here just as soon as you can."

"We will. Jill will go back to Missouri with Joe and Thad. She'll marry Thad. He'll take care of her."

"And . . . you?"

"I'll not be alone. Don't worry."

"Ralph understood about Lloyd. He went with me to see him. He was on the lawn in front of the big house. We saw him kick a little puppy. Later that night, Ralph went back and found the puppy under a bush.

We kept the little thing for a few days . . . then it died."

"Ralph was crazy about you."

"I wish you had a good man."

Blue had come silently into the room and stood behind Radna with his hand on her shoulder. She hoped that he hadn't understood Justine's slurred words. He bent his head to her ear.

"I'm taking Mrs. Cole and Laura home to do chicken chores and get a few things. Joe asked them to spend the night here. Can they use your room? You can sleep with me."

"Holy cow, Randolph. You've got a one-track mind. Where's Joe?"

"He'll be around."

"Hurry back. I feel better when you're here."

"I knew you loved me. When are you moving into my teepee?"

"When you're old and gray and your beard is down to your knees. Now get going, Romeo, so you can get back."

"Me Indian. Me don't have beard."

"You catch on fast, Randolph."

Radna felt him leave, although she didn't hear a sound. The man was sneaky and as quiet as a ghost . . . but he was truly one of the smartest men she had ever known, kind, witty and as dependable as a rock. Why couldn't she have met a man like him years ago?

But, Radna thought now, if he'd been as dumb as a stump, she would still have a soft spot for him because of his help and treatment of her brother. It was such a relief not to worry about Ramon being sent to prison or killed, because he wouldn't have given himself up without a fight.

Radna was terribly afraid that she was getting too fond of Randolph Bluefeather and would suffer when he left with Thad and Joe. She didn't want that. She'd seen what love could do to a woman. Justine was still grieving for her Ralph.

Blue was forever trying to get her in bed, she mused. One of these nights she'd let him succeed. A woman could tell a lot about a man's character when he was between the sheets.

It was near dark when Mrs. Cole came to sit with Justine while Radna ate her supper.

"How is she?"

"She hasn't opened her eyes for hours, but she is breathing steadily."

"Poor soul." Mrs. Cole clicked her tongue. "I'm sure she's tired of being sick."

When Radna reached the kitchen, she went directly to the sink to wash. Laura was putting the food on the table. Blue was sitting in a chair holding Mary Pat. The child was playing with an amulet that hung on a cord around his neck.

"Joe went to the front desk so Elmer and Rose could come eat their supper. Jill took a plate to Thad." Laura smiled with her eyes. "She's taking good care of him."

"It's good of you and your mother to stay and help us." Radna dried her face and hung the towel on the hook.

"We were not looking forward to going home to that dark house."

"Because of Lloyd Madison?"

"Him or . . . someone else. I know Mr. Madison has a room . . . here in the hotel, but Joe said that he and Mr. Blue would be here."

"If the bastard makes a move toward this babe, it'll be his last," Blue said with such conviction that Radna turned to look at him. His face was dead serious, and she knew he meant what he had said.

Throughout the evening Blue lingered in

the kitchen or the back hall. Joe prowled from the hall to the lobby, stopping occasionally to chat with a hotel guest or with Elmer and Rose at the desk, constantly on the lookout for Lloyd Madison.

Mary Pat fussed when Laura stood her on a chair beside the sink, washed her and slipped her nightdress over her head. As soon as Laura put her on her feet, the child made a beeline for Blue and climbed up into his lap.

"Mary—" Laura scolded. Then, "You don't have to hold her. It's time she was in bed."

"Laura?" Hunter Westfall was standing in the doorway of the kitchen. "I went to the house—"

Mary Pat squealed, wiggled off Blue's lap and ran to Hunter. He scooped her up into his arms and hugged her. The child giggled happily and wound her arms around his neck.

"How's my little sweetheart?" he murmured and nuzzled her cheek with his nose. "I went to the house," he said again, his eyes on Laura. "I came here thinking this would be the only place you'd be. They told me at the desk that you were back here."

"This is . . . Mr. Bluefeather," Laura stammered, indicating Blue with a wave of her hand.

"Howdy." Blue got to his feet and offered his hand.

"Glad to meet you," Hunter replied and took it. "I saw you today at the well." As soon as he finished speaking, his eyes went to Laura.

"He took us home to look after the chickens. We're staying to help out. Mrs. Byers took a turn for the worse. And . . . Jill is taking care of Thad," Laura explained.

Hunter's eyes went back to Blue. "Thanks. I'm glad they didn't go back alone. Mrs. Byers is worse?"

When Laura didn't answer, Blue spoke up. "Doctor said she could go at any time."

"And Taylor? Were his burns severe?"

"Bad enough, but the doctor seems to think they'll heal fast."

"I'm relieved to hear that. He didn't hesitate. He jumped right in the middle of that fire to get the boy. I owe the two of you for getting right out there. George said if not for your warning about the possibility of the tank exploding, more men would have been killed or badly injured."

Blue shrugged. "You owe us nothing. A man does what he can do at the time."

"Well, I want you to know that I appreciate what you did. I'll tell Taylor as soon as I can see him."

Watching Hunter closely, Blue asked bluntly, "Is Laura your woman?"

Hunter heard Laura gasp at the blunt words. His eyes met and held Blue's stare.

"She is, if she'll have me," he said firmly.

"Good. Look after her and the babe while I'm gone. If Madison comes near them, smash his nuts with that hammer over there. If you've not got the stomach, call me. It'll be my pleasure to do it." Blue walked from the kitchen.

In the silence following Blue's departure, Hunter looked at Laura's red face. He longed to ease her embarrassment but didn't know how.

"Can we go out onto the porch?"

She nodded and headed for the door. Carrying Mary Pat, Hunter followed her. They sat down on the edge of the platform porch. Thad's dog came from under it, sniffed and went back to her litter. Hunter settled Mary Pat in his lap and covered her small bare feet with her long nightdress.

The child leaned contentedly against him and yawned. He put his arm around Laura, pulled her close and pressed her head to his shoulder.

"My two girls," he whispered and brushed his mouth across Laura's forehead. "I almost died when I got to your house and you weren't there. I hardly took a breath until I got here and found my two girls safe." He placed a gentle kiss on her lips. "Lord help me! I love you, Laura. I love both of you so damn much."

"I knew you'd find us."

"Kiss me, honey, then tell me what Blue-feather was talking about."

She offered her mouth. He kissed her softly time and again, then pulled her lower lip between his teeth and worried it with his tongue for a long, wonderful minute before he released it and kissed her hard.

"In just a short time you and this little tyke have become my whole life. Loving the two of you is the most wonderful thing that's ever happened to me. I feel like I could move mountains and change the course of rivers if the two of you were waiting for me."

"I've dreamed of someone loving me like

that." Her words came on the expulsion of a breath.

"Sweetheart, I swear it's true. I'll spend the rest of my life taking care of you, if you'll let me."

"It's too soon to talk about . . . that."

"I know, and I'll not rush you. Now, I want to know what Bluefeather was talking about."

"I didn't want you to know. You've got enough to worry about . . . with your oil well burning and someone running you down—"

"The well has been capped, honey. The tank fire is under control."

"But . . . you've lost—"

"Yes, but I'm not concerned with that now. I want to know if Madison has bothered you."

Laura told him briefly what had happened that morning, leaving out the filthy words Madison spewed at her and the fact that he had shoved her down.

"He had to know that if he hurt Mary Pat, he would pay for it. Jill and Joe were here. He mentioned your name a couple of times. I think he was warning me to keep you away or he'd hurt Mary Pat."

Hunter was so angry he didn't speak for a

minute or two. His arm tightened around her and words far too obscene for her ears flooded his mind.

"He'll not get close to you or this baby again. If he does, I'll kill him." Hunter paused to steady his voice. "Are you going to keep me away?" The agony in his voice caused her to lift her fingers to his cheek.

"Not as long as you want to come."

"That will be forever. Ah, sweetheart. I hate having brought this down on you. I'll tell the sheriff what happened. He knows that I think Madison was in the car that ran me down."

"Jelly Bryce, the policeman from the city, was here when I told Mr. Blue. He's not much older than I am, but Mr. Blue said that he was plenty smart and if anyone could figure Mr. Madison out, he could."

"Up until now, I thought Madison a misguided man trying to make himself look good by being on the side of the underdog. Now I think something else is driving him. If he bothers you again, I'll run him clear out of the state if I have to."

"Be careful. Oh, please be careful—"

"I'll go to the sheriff, and if he doesn't do

anything, I'll go to the governor and ask to have Madison investigated."

"He'd listen to you?"

"Sweetheart, money talks. It's sad but true. If I donated a chunk of money to his reelection campaign, he'd at least listen. But first I'll talk to the sheriff."

"Sheriff, I'm sorry that Mrs. Hopper got the wrong impression."

Lloyd leaned back in his chair and shook his head. He longed to finger the mark on his face. Instead, he folded his thumb over his fingers and cracked his knuckles.

"What were you thinking, man? You scared the woman half to death."

"The little girl was alone in the yard, Sheriff. I was concerned for her. I picked her up, thinking her mother was in the wash house. A woman came running at me. I didn't know that she was the child's mother, so naturally I wouldn't turn a helpless child over to a hysterical woman."

"Did you talk nasty to Mrs. Hopper? Did you call her a slut?" Sheriff Page eyed Lloyd closely.

"Sheriff!" Lloyd straightened in his chair, indignation on his face. "How can you even

suggest such a thing? I was taught to respect women. All women."

"I'm only repeating what I was told."

"Whoever told you that is a . . . a liar, or
terribly misinformed. I tried to calm a hysterical woman. Then another woman came
up behind me and hit me with . . . something. It was such a shock. I just stood there
with my mouth open for a minute, then
walked away. As I was leaving, I realized
that my ear was bloody." Lloyd clutched his
hands tightly together to keep them off his
face.

"Sheriff," he said and managed to make
his eyes appear to be tear-wet, a skill he
had learned while in law school, "I've got a
million things on my mind. Harming a little
child would not even occur to me."

"Mrs. Hopper evidently thinks otherwise."

"I'm sorry about that." Lloyd bit his lips
and looked out the window as if he were
struggling to make a decision. "Sheriff, I've
a problem more serious than Mrs. Hopper's
accusation." After a small awkward silence,
he continued: "I'd like to tell you about it, if I
may?" The sheriff nodded. Lloyd began to
talk, softly, hesitantly.

"I didn't come to Rainwater by accident. I

came because someone I'd been searching for was here. You can't know how elated I was when I stepped off the train thinking, at long last, after years of searching, that I was going to see the one who gave me life. My mother." Lloyd paused to judge the sheriff's reaction and was not disappointed. The weathered face reflected surprise.

"Mother left me and my father when I was a few weeks old. She was just a young girl and the mark on my face repulsed her. My father was older, settled, a judge. No doubt she was bored and longed for a more exciting life with a younger man.

"She was not happy to see me, Sheriff Page. Although she didn't say so, I'm sure she was ashamed of my face. She had made a life here in Rainwater, and having a son my age, a son with a disfigurement, was an embarrassment to her."

"Hold on, Madison. Who are you talking about?"

"Justine Byers, Sheriff. She's my mother and dear to me, even though she doesn't publicly acknowledge me." Lloyd paused and turned toward the window as if needing time to compose himself. "During the time I've been here, I've tried to see her more times than I can count. Each time she has been less than cordial. The last time I tried to talk to her, one of the hangers-on at the hotel knocked me off the porch railing. I landed on my back. The only hurt I suffered was to my pride." He laughed nervously.

"Why are you telling me this? There's no law been broken here."

"I'm telling you, Sheriff, because my mother is dying. I want to see her before she goes, and her niece and nephew won't let me near her room. Can't you do something to help me?" Lloyd pleaded, his eyes tearing again.

"What do you want me to do?"

"Go to the hotel with me and tell Joe and Jill Jones that I have more right to be with her during her last hours than they have. I want to see my mother!"

"Jesus! You're putting me between a rock and a hard place. This is a family affair."

"What possible harm can there be in my going in to see her? She's had a stroke. The doctor said she could go at any time. Please, Sheriff. This is my last chance to see my mother."

"I'll walk down there with you, but I have no authority. I want you to understand that."

"I'm a lawyer. I know you can't force them to let me see her. Just your presence could be enough to make them see reason."

"I'll meet you out front. I've got to make sure my deputy is here."

When Lloyd went out the front door, the sheriff pushed open the door to the back room. Jelly Bryce and his deputy, Gus Franklin, were standing just inside the door. Both were staring at him. Jelly had a disgusted look on his face.

"Holy cow! I've got to hand it to the man, he can really dish out the horseshit. He's a first-class liar, too. He should go on the stage. He'd give Will Rogers a run for his money."

"You were listening?"

"I came in the back door, saw you were busy and stayed out of sight. Couldn't help but hear, even if that drunk back there is yelling bloody murder."

"Hellfire, Jelly. I've known Madison for six months or more. He's been straight as a string. I don't think he meant to hurt the little girl, and I've no reason to disbelieve him when he says Mrs. Byers is his mother."

"When he shows up at that hotel and tries to see Mrs. Byers, there'll be trouble."

"Did you know that she was his mother?"

"Lord, no! I don't think anyone else knows it, either. Blue says she's scared to death of him. She's helpless and afraid he'll kill her. I've not known Blue to exaggerate. He says Madison harasses Mrs. Byers about things that only the two of them know about. I trust Blue's instincts. He's the one who knocked him off the porch railing."

"I've known Madison longer than I've known that Indian."

"Then you're going along with Madison?" Jelly asked.

"Stick around, Gus," the sheriff said in answer to Jelly's question. "I shouldn't be gone long. If that drunk back there gets any louder, throw a bucket of water on him."

"He'd not mind that a-tall," Gus drawled. "He'd not have to take no bath till Christmas."

"He'd mind it if it had a couple of scoops of fresh cow shit in it."

"Then I'd have to clean the cell, Sheriff. Can't I just whack him with a pair of brass knuckles and knock him out for a while?"

The sheriff ignored Gus's joking request and picked up his hat. After giving his deputy a warning look, he went out to meet Madison.

Jelly swore, checked the gun in the shoulder holster beneath his coat and hurried out the back door and down the dark alley toward the hotel.

Lloyd paced up and down in front of the jail with a satisfied smile, and his fingers caressed his face while he waited for the sheriff. He was extremely proud of his performance.

These yokels didn't have any idea they were dealing with a master of manipulation. He had wiggled out of more serious scrapes than this and loved the challenge of doing it! He rubbed his hands together in satisfaction. He had come out on top then, and he'd do it again.

Damn, but he enjoyed having a woman afraid of him! Beautiful Laura had about shit her drawers when he had her kid. It served her right. She should never have cozied up with Westfall.

Lloyd recognized that he might have made a mistake snatching up the kid. It was a spur-of-the-moment decision, one he now regretted. But he had been so damn mad when he went to Laura's house, found it locked up tighter than a banker's purse and discovered her gone. All of his careful planning not to be seen going out there had been wasted. He had looked forward to spending a couple of hours with her while Westfall was at the fire. After that he doubted the rich boy would have wanted the little widow.

He'd not fret about it now. He was sure that he'd get another chance at her.

Things had gone exactly the way he'd planned, except for one thing: Westfall should be in jail by now. Oh well, it could happen any day, and in the meantime he would make his presence known at the hotel. He didn't want the damn bitch to die yet. But when she did, he wanted her to slide into hell knowing just how much he despised her!

Lloyd smoothed the mark on his face. The gullible sheriff would help him. He had swallowed his story, hook, line and sinker.

God! I am good. I should have gone on the stage!

Chapter 28

Jelly was within a dozen paces of the couple sitting on the end of the porch before they saw him. The man hastily shifted the child in his arms to the woman and stood protectively in front of them.

"Evening," Jelly said pleasantly and moved into the light from the kitchen window.

"It's Mr. Bryce," Laura said quickly and tugged on the man's hand. "Mr. Bryce, this is Mr. Westfall—"

"Howdy." Hunter held out his hand. "I've seen you around, just didn't recognize you in the dark. I'm edgy after all that's happened."

"Understandable," Jelly replied and shook Hunter's hand. "Madison is coming into the front of the hotel with the sheriff. I suggest that you stay with Mrs. Hopper and the baby and keep them out of sight."

"I've a score to settle with him—"

"I understand that, but now isn't the time." Jelly stepped up onto the porch.

"Is there going to be trouble?" Hunter asked.

"Might be."

Jelly went through the kitchen to find Blue slouching beside Justine's partially open door.

"How is she?" Jelly asked.

"Conscious and talking to Radna and Jill."

"Madison is on his way here with the sheriff. He says that she's his mother and is demanding to see her."

"Holy shit!" Blue straightened. "Are you sure? He could be making it up."

"He's convinced the sheriff that he's got a right to be here. To make it legal he'd have to have a court order or have Mrs. Byers acknowledge him as her son. In that case he could take charge."

"Whata you think we should do, Jelly?"

"Keep him out of there. Stay here by the door. I'll find Joe and ask him to send someone for the doctor. That may be the one way we can keep him out."

Blue slipped into the room and placed his hand on Radna's shoulder.

Justine's eyes moved to him. "Take . . . care of her." Her voice was faint and slurred. "She's . . . dear to me."

He nodded that he understood. "She's dear to me, too." Blue bent over the bed to press the hand that lay in Radna's. "Don't worry about Radna. I'll put a hobble on her."

Jill was crying silently, her eyes lingering on her aunt's face.

"Don't cry, honey," Justine said. "I'm ready to . . . go—"

Blue motioned to Radna. They went into the hall, leaving Jill alone with her aunt.

"I don't think she'll last the night." Radna wiped her eyes with the back of her hand.

"Madison is coming here with the sheriff. Jelly just told me."

"No! Why is the sheriff coming?"

"She's Madison's mother. Did you know that?"

"Of course I knew that. I've known her for fifteen years. She told me about him years ago. She knew that he was mean and hard, but not to the extent that he is. She hasn't been the same since he came here. He broke her heart. I'll not let him make her last hours on earth miserable! I mean it, Blue, I'll kill him if I have to."

"Godamighty, Rosebud. It won't come to that."

"Jelly has gone to tell Joe. He's sending someone for the doctor. He thinks that may be a way of keeping him out. Do Jill and Joe know?"

"She told them tonight. She doesn't want *him* at her funeral."

"It'll be hard to keep him away unless we knock him out and lock him in his room." Blue put his arms around her and held her close. "When you go back in," he said, his lips against her forehead, "lock the door and don't worry. He won't come in. I promise you. Believe me?"

Radna nodded, leaned on him and wrapped her arms around his waist. It was comforting to hear the strong beat of his heart beneath her ear.

"I'm glad you're here, Randolph."

"Me, too, Rosebud. Between me and Joe and Jelly, we'll keep him out."

"Have you looked in on Thad?"

"He's sleeping. Mrs. Cole is in the kitchen

building a stew and making coffee. It's what she wanted to do. Laura and the baby are with Westfall on the back porch. He's about as crazy about her as I am about you, Rosebud."

"Still full of bull, aren't you, Randolph? Even at a time like this, your tongue is loose at both ends."

He chuckled. "That's my sassy girl." He lifted his head to listen to voices coming from the lobby. "Go on in and lock the door."

As soon as Radna slipped into the room, Blue went down the hall to the lobby. Sheriff Page was talking to Joe.

"He wants to say good-bye to his mother."

"How do you know that she's his mother, Sheriff? Are you taking his say-so?" Joe stood with his arms folded across his chest. "Madison has been needling her about this and that ever since he came here. Why hasn't he mentioned before that she's his mother?" Joe's eyes went to Lloyd.

"I told you, Sheriff, Mother was ashamed she gave birth to a child with a hideous birthmark. I've been told that some in Jefferson City, where I was born, considered it the mark of the devil. That's why she left me and never mentioned having me. I assumed Joe and Jill knew who I was. They've taken over my mother's life and her hotel. They are only a niece and nephew. I'm the next of kin, and I demand my right to be with her during her last days."

"Prove that she's your mother," Blue said.

"What's your interest in this?" Lloyd asked. He barely managed to keep his voice civil.

"Just made a reasonable request," Blue answered calmly.

"Well, keep your requests to yourself and stay out of things that are none of your business." Lloyd lifted his hand to his cheek, then dropped it quickly when he realized what he had done. He moved to walk down the hall. Blue and Joe moved in unison to block his way. "Sheriff," Lloyd said. "Tell them my rights here."

"Show me a birth certificate with Mrs. Byers's name on it and I'll make sure that you see her."

"It would take days to get my birth certificate and you know it," Lloyd sputtered. "It's in the courthouse in Jefferson City, Missouri."

"Get it. Is Justine Jones Madison listed as your mother?"

"I've never looked at it, but I'm sure she is. Why wouldn't she be?" Lloyd's face turned a brick red because he was angry; he was not uneasy about lying. "Now, listen here, Sheriff Page. She'll be dead before I can get that certificate. I'm going to see her. Now!"

"No, you're not!" Joe grabbed Lloyd's shirtfront as he tried to dart around him. "The doctor is on his way. He'll go in and see my aunt, then tell you if you can see her."

"That sounds reasonable to me," the sheriff said.

"Turn me loose, you . . . ignorant hick. I'm the next of kin here. You stand in my way and I'll swear out a warrant for your arrest."

"Then you'll have to swear out one for me, too." Blue moved in behind Joe.

"And me." Elmer, on his crutches, moved out from behind the desk.

"Make it four," Jelly said and noticed the startled look on the sheriff's face.

"Five." Mr. Boise, the barber, moved his chubby body beside Jelly's tall frame.

"Godamighty," the sheriff swore. "What's your stake in this, Boise?"

"I've known Mrs. Byers for ten years and lived in this hotel for seven. I've visited with her for many hours. If she'd had a son, she'd have mentioned it."

"That's the truth, Sheriff." Skeeter Ridge sidled out of the corner where he had sat all afternoon waiting for news of Justine. "If Justine'd had a boy, she'd a been proud of it. A little old mark on the face wouldn'ta put her off."

"Well, Sheriff, what's it going to be?" Lloyd was getting a perverse pleasure out of the confrontation. It was like being on the stage. But at times he could scarcely hold his temper. "Are you going to let this bunch, who are waiting to get their hands on my mother's hotel, keep her from spending her last hours with her child, her only child?"

"We'll see what the doctor says. He's here now." Relieved, the sheriff greeted the doctor. "Glad you're here, Doc."

"The man said it was urgent. I'd better get on back and see my patient."

"Doc, find out if she wants to see Madison. He claims he's her son, and they"—he nodded toward the group behind Joe— "claim she doesn't want to see him."

Dr. Russell glanced at Lloyd. "I never heard anything about Justine having a son."

"Just find out, will you, Doc? This is taking more time than I intended to spend on it. I've other things to do."

The gray-haired doctor, followed by Blue, went down the hall to Justine's door. Blue knocked and called to Radna.

"Open up. The doctor is here."

The doctor heard the key turn in the lock before the door opened. He stepped into the room. Blue waited beside the closed door. Joe, Jelly and the others continued to block the hallway, refusing to allow Lloyd to pass.

Lloyd used the time to berate himself for not preparing a false birth certificate. The one on file in Jefferson City listed Jane J. Madison as his mother, with the notation: *died during childbirth.* He had known since an early age that it was not true.

The servants had delighted in telling him that his mother was a slut his father had brought in to give him a son and that, after the child was born, he had thrown her out. By the time he was fifteen, Lloyd knew her real name and had kept it a guarded secret until he was old enough and had the means to punish her. He had gained a vast amount of experience during college and the years following. When he was ready he had come to Rainwater.

Justine had known him immediately and had gaped at him like a fish out of water. Her tears of so-called joy had disgusted him. He had hated her before, and seeing her had intensified that hatred. That day he had vowed to do everything he could do to make her miserable until the day she died.

The damn slut is going to die before I've had my fill of revenge. But all was not lost. He would get his revenge through his little country cousin; and when she met his *dear mother* in hell, she could tell her about it.

The clock in the lobby struck twelve midnight when Justine breathed her last. Joe, Jill and Radna were at her bedside. She had opened her eyes briefly when the doctor came into the room, bent over her and took her pulse, then closed them forever. Dr. Russell shook his head and left the room. The sheriff was waiting in the hall.

"Let her die in peace, Ira."

The sheriff nodded and went down the hall to where Lloyd waited. After a short conversation, Lloyd went up the stairs to his room.

Shortly after that Joe came into his aunt's room and softly closed the door. The three people closest to Justine waited silently for the end. The minutes melted into an hour.

It was Joe who said, "She's gone."

Jill and Radna cried softly while Joe went to fetch the doctor, who was in the kitchen drinking coffee with Jelly and Blue. When the doctor came out of Justine's room, he picked up his bag and put on his hat. Joe walked with him to the front lobby.

Skeeter Ridge sat in the chair he had occupied for the past eight hours. With a hand on his shoulder, Joe told him the news. Skeeter nodded. Without a word, he rose wearily from the chair and went out into the night.

After combing the hair of the woman who had been like a sister to her and placing her hands on her chest, Radna sat alone in the semidarkened room beside her. Blue waited, giving her time to be alone with her friend, then came in, picked Radna up and carried her to the big chair beside the window. He sat down and cuddled her on his lap. Radna let her head rest on his shoulder.

"I'm going to miss her. She was the best friend I ever had."

"Friends are treasures, sweet girl. A man is lucky if he has five good friends during his lifetime."

"I had only one and she's . . . gone."

"You've got me, Rosebud."

"You've been a big help, Randolph. I've come to depend on you. But you just want to get me in bed." She lifted her head to look at him.

"I'll not deny that. But you're a sweet little cuss, too. Go to sleep." He pressed her head to his shoulder. "You'll be worn out tomorrow; and, if I know you, you'll be right in the thick of things."

They were quiet. The only sound in the room was the ticking of the clock and occasionally low voices coming from the kitchen across the hall.

Blue was content just to hold the small woman, and being close to him helped Radna hold her grief at bay. He put his lips against her forehead, then whispered, "The wind has come up. We may be in for a storm."

Radna didn't reply. She had fallen asleep.

*   *   *

"Go lie down on Thad's cot, Sis, and get some rest."

"I don't want to leave you here alone." Jill's eyes were swollen and red-rimmed from crying.

"I'll wander in and talk to Elmer. First I want to take a look outside. The wind came up pretty fast and I've been seeing flashes of lightning. Oklahoma storms can roll in like a stampede of buffalo."

"Don't stay out long. Lloyd might come down."

"Jelly is keeping an eye on him. His room is across the hall." Joe grinned. "Before he went up, he asked Mrs. Cole for a half dozen tin cups. He said he'd line them up in front of Lloyd's door. If he came out, he was sure to kick one. Jelly is a light sleeper."

"Thad was asleep the last time I looked in on him. The medicine the doctor gave him knocked him out."

"Go on. Rest for a while. I'll wake you in the morning."

Jill tiptoed into the darkened room. A strong wind was coming in through the south window. She went to fold up the curtain and tuck it into the curtain rod.

"Honey?" It was Thad's voice.

"Did I wake you?"

"I've been awake for a while."

"Can I get you something? Water?"

"No. Come here."

"Aunt Justine is . . . gone," Jill blurted.

"Ah . . . law—" Thad raised himself up and sat on the side of the bed, bringing the sheet across his lap.

"You shouldn't . . . get up!" Jill hurried to him and knelt down on the floor between his knees.

"It's all right. I sit up every now and then when I can't lie on my belly any longer." His hands stroked her hair and brought her face up for his kiss, then pressed her head to his chest. "I'm sorry about Aunt Justine. I should have been with you."

"Radna and Blue are sitting with her. The undertaker will be here in the morning. Thank goodness she didn't have to see Lloyd again." Jill lifted her head and clasped his hands. "Thad—you won't believe this. Lloyd is her son. She told us, Joe and me, tonight. Radna has known all the while."

"Lordee, honey," he exclaimed. "That's hard to believe. Does Lloyd know that he's Justine's son?"

"Oh, yes. He blames her for that mark on his face. Radna said she went to work in a big house for a judge. He . . . used her. When Lloyd was born with the birthmark, the judge threw her out. Aunt Justine met Ralph Byers and they came here."

Jill went on to tell him about hitting Lloyd with the mop handle and about his bringing the sheriff to the hotel demanding to see his mother.

"Joe and Mr. Bryce are keeping an eye on him." She turned her face, trailed kisses along his collarbone and felt the tremors pass through him. "It's all over, Thad. I can go home soon."

"*We* can go home. You're not going without me."

"Are you sure?"

"I was never so sure of anything." He held her tightly to his naked chest. "Take off your shoes and lie down with me for a little while," he whispered to the top of her head.

"We . . . shouldn't—"

"You're tired. Let me hold you." He moved over into the middle of the bed and lay on his side. The sheet covered him from his waist to his middle thighs. The rest of him was exposed to her shy gaze.

Jill slipped off her shoes and eased down on the bed with her back to him. Thad looped an arm over her, his fingers spread over her rib cage.

"Closer," he whispered. "Closer."

She moved until her back was snug against his chest, cradled in the bend made by his thighs pressed to the backs of hers. She drew in a deep, long breath before she could utter a word.

"Joe . . . might come in."

"We're doing nothing wrong, sweetheart. You're tired and I'm holding you." His cheek rested against her hair, his breath warm on her ear, when he whispered, "Don't you like it here with me?"

"You know I do."

His hand moved from her rib cage down to slide over her belly, then up to slip beneath and around her breast. She grabbed his wrist to pull his hand away.

"Let me touch you here." His fingers tightened. "I know it's all I can have . . . for now."

"You were hateful when you did it before."

"I'm sorry, sweetheart. I was so damn frustrated. I was trying to prove that our kisses that night meant something to you, too. This hard, sweet little knot pops right out when I touch you." His fingertips flicked lightly back and forth over her nipple.

"I'm not ... I don't ..." It was hard to carry on a conversation when his fingers were causing her heart to jump out of time, her breasts to ache and her womb to throb.

"Oh, Lord. I know that, and thank God for it," he said in a husky whisper, his lips nuzzling the soft spot beneath her ear. "Does it feel good?"

"Yes." The word came out on a breath. She was also conscious that her bottom was pressed snugly against his sex. It was rock-hard with desire.

"I can't do anything about it," he whispered urgently, knowing that she had to be aware of his arousal. "I can't help wanting you. But I can wait. When you're Jill Taylor, I'll love you all night, every night, and we won't have this"—his fingers plucked at her dress—"between us. Don't be afraid of it, honey. I'll never, never, hurt you. You're too precious to me."

"I'm not afraid. I love you."

Her soft words fired him with a new tenderness. He leaned over her, lowering his mouth to hers for a long, sweet caress.

"I love you, too, sweetheart." He lay back down. His hand slipped around her breast again, his thumb sliding back and forth across her nipple. "Go to sleep. You'll have a busy day tomorrow."

"I can't . . . with you doing that."

"Sweetheart." He turned his face into her hair and laughed happily. "I love doing it, but I'll stop so you can go to sleep."

Jill's heart was beating so hard and so fast, she was sure she'd never sleep. She felt guilty for being so gloriously, foolishly happy when her dear aunt lay dead in the next room.

Thad lay awake long after Jill's regular breathing told him that she was sleeping soundly. He wasn't sure how long he would have to wait after her aunt's funeral to marry her. He wanted to do it before they left Rainwater so he could take her home as his bride.

The wind became stronger as the prairie storm rolled in. Lightning flashed, followed by the crack of thunder. Rain came down suddenly. Not wanting to leave the girl in his arms, but knowing that the rain was coming in the window, Thad had pulled himself up to get out of bed and close it when the door opened. Joe came in. He went to the window and lowered it partway before he came to stand beside the bed.

"I don't have a shotgun, but I'll borrow one from Jelly. Looks like I'm goin' to be needin' it."

"Go away."

Joe stood a minute waiting for Thad to say something more, and when he didn't, Joe left the room, closing the door behind him.

Thad lay back down, snuggled close to the warm girl in his bed, cupped her soft breast in his hand and closed his eyes. Despite the painful burns on his back, he drifted off to sleep with a pleased smile on his face.

Chapter 29

Morning found the streets of Rainwater littered with tree limbs, shingles from the roofs of houses and business buildings, and puddles of water. Anything that wasn't tied down had been blown or battered by the vicious storm that had raced through town during the early morning hours. A few small trees had been uprooted and some signs had been ripped from buildings.

"Mistah Hunter, dat ole lean-to by de carriage house was blowed down by de wind."

"Any other damage?" Hunter was at the kitchen table eating his breakfast when Casper came in with the news.

"Jist tree limbs and dat board fence out back. Hit was goin' ta go down anyhow."

"Don't try to do the cleanup by yourself, Casper. Get the man who cleans out the septic tank to help you. He has a truck and can haul it away."

"I do dat. We needs to use some of dem boards fo' kindlin'."

"Save some big stuff fo' my cookstove," Dinah instructed.

"Yo knows dat I will." Casper cast an impatient glance at his wife and headed for the door.

"Will ya be here for noonin'?" Dinah asked.

"I don't think so. I'm going out to the well this morning. On second thought, I probably won't be, so don't plan on it."

"Den I think I scrub dis floor. It be dry 'fore yo 'nd Casper come trackin' in on it."

Hunter left the house as soon as he finished his breakfast. He was eager to see Laura but was relieved that she wasn't at the house when he stopped there. He fed her chickens and filled their water trough. His next stop was at the sheriff's office.

Sheriff Page was talking to Jelly Bryce.

"Because Mrs. Byers was his mother, he says he has a claim to the hotel. He'll have to work it out with Bernie Shepard, Mrs. Byers's attorney. Thank God I don't have to deal with that." He looked up when Hunter pushed open the door.

"Morning," Hunter said as soon as he entered the office.

The sheriff grunted a reply.

"Morning." Jelly grinned. "The sheriff's not in the best of moods this morning."

"Then I'm afraid I'm going to add to his distress. What are you going to do about Lloyd Madison's attack on Laura Hopper and her little girl?"

"So it's an attack now? Pretty soon it'll be kidnapping or rape."

"This is serious," Hunter snapped. "I don't appreciate your making light of it."

"Hellfire, Westfall. What do you want me to do?"

"Arrest him!"

"I've not a shred of evidence that he intended to harm them." Sheriff Page didn't mention that Lloyd had pointed this out to him. "He's the one with the injury, if you can call it that. He's got a knot on one side of his head and his ear is cut on the other side. He's thinking of filing charges against Jill Jones for assault."

"So you're not going to do anything?"

"Folks would be up in arms if I arrested

him on the say-so of a couple of hysterical women. Like it or not, he's some kind of hero to some of the folks in this town." The sheriff sank down heavily in his chair. "I've told him to stay away from Laura Hopper and Jill Jones."

"And if he doesn't?"

"I'll handle it when the time comes."

"You've put your cards on the table, Sheriff, so I'll put down mine. If Lloyd Madison as much as touches Laura Hopper or her little girl, I will kill him just as I would a coiled rattler."

"If you do that, Westfall, it'll be murder and I'll be after you."

"I'm aware of that, but it doesn't change a thing. You've not had much luck catching the one who murdered Carsie."

Hunter strode out the door, anger making him forget his sore hip and leg. He drove to the hotel and parked his car on the side street. Laura and Mary Pat were coming out the back door. Mary Pat saw him and tried to break away from her mother.

Hunter hurried to the edge of the porch and scooped the child up in his arms. His shining eyes met Laura's before he nuzzled his face in the baby's neck and set her to giggling. Mary Pat prowled his pockets, found the candy stick and hit him on the nose with it. Hunter laughed, made a blowing sound against her neck and set her on her feet.

"I stopped at the house and fed your chickens."

"Thank you."

"Are you staying here today?"

"I'm helping in the kitchen. The undertaker came at daylight, and the word is out about Mrs. Byers. Folks are bringing food."

"I'm glad you'll be here. I'm going out to the well, but I'll come back here around sundown. If you want to go home for a while, I can take you."

"Mr. Blue offered."

"I wish you'd consider staying at my house with Dinah."

"No. I can't do that." She shook her head.

"All right. 'Bye, honey. Be careful."

"You, too."

Hunter drove away with a worried frown on his face. He didn't want to leave her. In just a few short weeks, his priorities had changed so drastically that he resented the time he had to spend looking out for his business interests.

He disliked having to depend on Blue-feather and Joe Jones to protect her when he was the one responsible for her and the baby being in danger in the first place. The time had come to call in favors from high places. He had never expected to do that for personal reasons, but he had to do something about Lloyd Madison.

During the morning, an almost steady stream of Justine's friends came to the hotel to pay their respects; some left food or bouquets of garden flowers. Jill and Joe accepted the condolences. Radna stayed in the background, choosing to relieve Mrs. Cole of the cleaning chores so that she could accept the gifts of food that were piling up on the kitchen table.

After the burns on his back were dressed, Thad insisted on moving around with a loose shirt hanging from his shoulders. Shortly before noon, Rose Evans came to the kitchen to tell Thad that he had visitors. Puzzled as to who they might be, he followed her back to the lobby.

A woman and a small boy stood just inside the door. As he approached, the woman burst into tears. The boy, looking as uncomfortable as Thad felt, looked first at his mother, then held his hand out to Thad.

"Thank you," he murmured.

"You're welcome," Thad replied, taking the small hand in his.

"Are ya hurt bad?"

"Naw. Not much. I'll be good as new in a day or two. You all right?"

The boy nodded, then, after a poke by his mother, said, "Yes, sir."

"Lady Luck was riding with us, Bobby. Did you learn anything about staying away from fire?"

"Yes, sir. And . . . I learned to mind my mama when she says not to do something."

"That's a good thing to know. Don't forget it. Mamas usually know what's right."

"I'll never, ever, be able to thank you enough for what you did." The woman's eyes teared up again.

"No thanks are necessary. I just happened to be at the right place."

"May I . . . give you a hug?"

"Well, now . . . I've never turned down a hug by a pretty lady in my life. My mama would be plumb ashamed of me if I did. The only thing is . . . be careful of my back."

"A kiss, then?"

"Sounds good." Thad bent down and the woman placed a kiss on his cheek.

"You're a real hero, Mr. Taylor. You've given my little boy his life. I pray that he'll grow up to be as fine a man as you are."

"Ma'am, you should want the boy to shoot a mite higher than that, but I thank you for saying so."

As Thad watched them leave, he felt a small warm hand wiggle into his. Jill looked tired. She was wearing one of her Sunday dresses. Her shiny blond hair was held back on one side with a barrette. His heart thudded with pride when he looked at her.

"You are a hero." Her blue eyes smiled into his.

"You heard that, huh?"

"Saw her kiss you, too. If she'd been ten years younger, I'd have been on her like a bee on a honeypot."

"Jealous? I like that."

"Don't get a swelled head, Thad Taylor."

"Yes, ma'am. Let's go get something to eat. There's enough food back there to feed an army."

Whenever possible, the sheriff went home for dinner. Being in the quiet house with his wife of twenty-two years had the calming effect that he needed. Especially today. When he returned, Gus, his deputy, left for his noon meal.

Alone in the office, the sheriff leaned back in his chair and rested his booted feet on the corner of the desk. He had plenty to think about. He had an unsolved murder on his hands, and the young lawyer who most folks considered a decent, churchgoing young man was acting strange. Half the mothers in town were trying to hook him for their daughters. The sheriff just didn't know what to make of it.

Where there's smoke, there's fire.

Recalling the saying, the sheriff began to think that it might not be too far-fetched, after all, that it could have been Madison who had tried to run down Hunter Westfall. For months, now, the young lawyer had done everything he could to discredit the man who provided most of the jobs for the citizens of Rainwater.

Laura had been frightened by what happened at the wash house; but with only the two women's word against Madison's, the complaint would go nowhere. The man swore he meant the child no harm. Thank

God he didn't have to deal with his claim to be the son of Justine Byers. That would be up to Judge Broers.

"Where you been?" The sheriff squinted at Jelly when he came in and hung his hat on the rack.

"At Martha's. You can get a better meal here for less money than in the city." Jelly took off his coat and carefully hung it over the back of a chair. "Madison was holding court at the café. He's blaming Westfall for the death of the driller. He says poor equipment and unsafe practices cost the man his life."

"Bullshit!" Sheriff Page snorted. "I'm not crazy about Westfall, I think he's a queer duck; but drilling is a dangerous job, and anyone who chooses to do it knows the risks. Did Madison have anything to say about Justine Byers?"

"Not a word. Some of the folks made a remark or two about her passing on, but he didn't say anything."

"I was sure he'd be out spreading the story about being her son." The sheriff's feet hit the floor. "What the hell!"

An old truck stopped in front of the office so fast the front wheel came up onto the walk. A skinny, bald man was out of the truck in an instant and came barreling through the door.

"Sheriff . . . Sher-iff—" He was out of breath and his eyes were rolling. "I . . . I . . . found it."

The sheriff was on his feet. "What the hell you talkin' about, Robinson?"

"The . . . the . . . head!" he gasped.

"You found the woman's head? Where?"

"At Westfall's. Casper came to get me. Said Mr. Westfall wanted me to help haul off the roof from an old shed that blowed down."

"Casper's the colored man who works for Westfall?"

"Yes. He helped me load up the roof and showed me some big stuff to load. He said he'd saw up some of the planks for the cookstove. I prowled around the stack he told to leave and I saw . . . this gunnysack. I pulled it out and looked—"

"Where was Casper?"

"His woman called and he went off somewhere. He didn't want me to mess with the pile. He kept sayin' that he'd tend to it. Jesus, Sheriff, I never saw anythin' so awful.

After I puked, I came here as fast as I could."

"You left it there?"

"Hell, yes! I ain't touchin' it."

"Come on, Jelly, this might be the break we've been waiting for."

Robinson led the way in his old truck to the back of the Westfall property where the shed had stood. The skinny man looked fearfully about, then went to a pile of boards and pointed to a brown-stained gunnysack.

"Jesus!" Sheriff Page gagged when he saw what was inside. Bugs and maggots were crawling all over it. One ear had a gold loop earring attached to it. The blond hair was stiff with blood. "Want to see?" he asked Jelly.

"No, thanks. I'll take your word for it."

The sheriff carried the bag to his car and placed it on the floor of the backseat.

"Is this where you found it?"

"Just about."

"What did the colored man say about that pile of boards?"

"Said leave them alone. Said it a time or two."

"Go on home, Robinson. Keep this under your hat for a while."

"Are ya goin' to arrest that murderin' nigger?"

"Why do you say that?"

"Ain't it plain to ya? He knowed it was there."

"Maybe. The law will handle it."

"I get the reward, don't I?"

"I would think so. Go on, now. Keep this under your hat. I'll be in touch."

The sheriff and Jelly waited until Robinson had left before they approached the house. They stepped up onto the porch and knocked on the back door. A neat woman with a smooth coffee-colored face came to the door.

"How do," she said politely.

"Is Casper here?"

"Nawsah. He gone to de icehouse." A worried frown came over her face when she saw the star on the sheriff's shirt. "Be there somethin' I can do?"

"No. Is this him coming, pulling the wagon?"

"Yassah."

The sheriff and Jelly stepped back. Casper approached the back door with a puzzled look on his face. His eyes went from the men at the door to Dinah.

"Go on in, Casper," Sheriff Page said. "Get the ice in the box, then come out. We want to talk to you."

"Yassah." Casper sank a pair of ice tongs in the block of ice and lifted the fifty-pound chunk out of the wagon. His wife held open the door and he carried it into the kitchen. He came out almost immediately.

"Let's walk out to where the shed blew down last night, Casper, and have a little talk."

"Yassah."

Casper walked along beside them until they reached the sheriff's car. The sheriff stopped and leaned against the side of it.

"The shed blew down in the big wind, did it?"

"Yassah. We be cleanin' up de mess."

"Rudy Robinson been helpin' you?"

"Yassah."

"Rudy said you didn't want him to bother with that stack of boards over there. Is that right?"

"Yassah. Dinah want 'em for de cook-stove."

"Did you notice a gunnysack under the boards?"

"Nawsah."

Sheriff Page reached into the car and pulled out the gunnysack. "Take a look, Casper. Have you ever seen anything like that?"

Casper peered into the sack, then reared back in shock. His eyes rolled, his hands came out as if to ward off the ghastly sight. He staggered back a step.

"Law-ssy! Ah, Law-ssy!"

"You didn't know that was in the shed?"

"Nawsah, nawsah, nawsah!"

"Didn't you ever go into the shed? Didn't you smell anything?"

"Nawsah. I don' go in dey shed fo' a long time."

"Why not?"

"Dey was a big ol' rattler in der. Nothin' in der I need."

"How do you think that sack got in there?"

"I don' know, sah. I don' know."

"It's the head of that woman who stayed here with Mr. Westfall. You know that, don't you?"

"Yassah." Casper was so shaken that he put his hand on the car to steady himself.

"What time will Mr. Westfall get home?"

"Sup-pertime."

"I'll be back to talk to you some more about this."

As Jelly and the sheriff drove away from Hunter Westfall's house, Jelly spoke for the first time since they had left the office.

"Poor cuss. He was so shocked, it wouldn't have surprised me if he'd taken off running."

"You don't think he knew it was there?"

"Hell, no!"

"He could be protecting Westfall."

"Could be, but not likely. If he knew it was there, he'd not have gone off and left Robinson out there by himself. And if he or Westfall had put it there, they would have moved it as soon as the shed blew down."

"My thoughts exactly. But who planted it there?"

"Somebody who hates Westfall."

By suppertime the sheriff and his deputy had all the trouble they could handle. Rudy Robinson had made the rounds of the domino parlors and pool halls, telling what he had found in Westfall's shed. The news swept the town like a prairie fire.

Rudy was the man of the hour.

He told his story over and over, and each

time he embellished it. Casper, Westfall's colored man, had tried to keep him from finding the sack. But, according to Rudy, he had become suspicious about a gunnysack Casper had tried to hide beneath some boards. It wasn't until Casper was called away that Rudy was able to dig under the pile of lumber to see what he was hiding and go for the sheriff.

The remarks from the crowd of listeners surprised even Rudy:

Westfall and his colored man are in it together.

Yeah, it was Westfall's whore's head. He probably butchered her in that shed.

I thought there was something fishy about him bringing them colored folk here to live with him.

The nigger probably did Westfall's dirty work. He wouldn't want to get his hands dirty.

We ought to hang the son-of-a-bitch!

Don't it beat all what rich folks can get away with.

Comments such as these were roiling the townspeople to a fevered pitch as Lloyd Madison moved among them:

We don't want to jump the gun here.

Every man is entitled to a fair trial no matter how guilty we think he is.

The sheriff will want to make sure before he makes an arrest.

No, I don't believe in mob rule, but in this case—

Oh, my God. Have you heard that Westfall is courting Laura Hopper? She could be next.

She's a sly one. Could of helped him.

It's sad, but true, that once a killer gets a taste of killing he never stops.

Someone should warn that poor girl.

The sheriff should take her into custody for safekeeping.

Poor girl, my foot. You know what they say about birds of a feather.

Yeah, especially birds with deep pockets. Hee, hee, hee.

On hearing the remarks, Lloyd knew that he was using just the right words to whip up the crowd without seeming to do so. Unconsciously, he caressed the mark on his face. This was turning out far better than he had expected.

On his return from the telephone office where he had called Clarence Hurt, his superior in the Oklahoma City Police Department, Jelly mingled with the men on the street, listened to the remarks and hurried back to the sheriff's office.

Conrad Burke, the bookkeeper from Westfall Drilling, was talking to the sheriff.

"As soon as we heard the talk on the street, we locked up. Perry Reade has gone out to the field to find Mr. Westfall. That idiot Rudy Robinson is telling everyone who will listen that Casper Ellis killed Carsie Bakken and hid her head in that old shed."

"The stupid son-of-a-bitch!" The sheriff cursed loud and long, then looked at Jelly. "What did you find out?"

"Out on the street? It's like the man says. The roustabouts and loafers are gathering on every street corner. Madison is putting his two cents' worth in. On the pretext of trying to calm them down, he's adding fuel to the fire. He thinks you should bring in Laura Hopper."

"What the hell for?"

"He planted two seeds in the minds of the gullible. She could have helped Westfall kill the woman, or she's in danger of him killing her."

"Christ on a horse! Aren't they using any common sense?"

"Don't look like it. Could be trouble before the night's over. Clarence is catching the night train. He'll be here early in the morning with some interesting information. It's all he'd say."

The sheriff sank down in his chair. Why in hell had he decided to become a lawman? He wouldn't be having all this grief if he were a barber or a meat cutter.

Chapter 30

As soon as Perry Reade found Hunter and gave him a quick rundown on what was going on in town, Hunter began to issue orders with the precision of a drill sergeant. Thirty minutes later, he drove into town followed by two truckloads of armed men. He stopped at the sheriff's office.

"Have you arrested Casper?" he demanded as soon as he cleared the door.

"No." The sheriff got to his feet. "But the dead woman's head was found in your shed, and Rudy Robinson seems to think that your man Casper was trying to hide it."

"That's bullshit!" Hunter shouted. "I've known Casper all my life. He wouldn't hurt a flea. Rudy Robinson is an ignorant, stupid fool!"

"That may be, but right now he's got the

ears of every man in town, and I've got to worry about a lynch mob."

"No lynch mob will ever get their hands on Casper. I've got fifteen armed men out there who are as loyal to me as Madison's men are to him."

"Why are you bringing him into this?"

"You know why. He'll be out there stirring the men up, egging them on. I'll tell you this now, Sheriff: I'll shoot any man who lays a hand on Casper."

"If you try to take the law into your hands, you'll find yourself in my jail."

"I'll not sit by and let a mob, stirred up by a rabble-rouser like Madison, harm a good and decent man. If you can't protect him, I can."

"You'd best be thinking of yourself. The talk is the two of you did it together."

"Talk is cheap, Sheriff. If you had as much as a smidgen of evidence against me, you'd have arrested me. I'm going home. My men and I will be guarding Casper and you'd better get to finding out who really killed Carsie and planted her head in my shed." Hunter turned toward Jelly Bryce. "I'd like to speak to you, Bryce." He waited on the sidewalk for Jelly to join him.

"Hell of a mess, isn't it?" Jelly said casually.

"I've a favor to ask. You know the situation with Laura Hopper and her little girl. They're at the hotel. I'm afraid that they'll be hurt because of me. I'll forever be in your debt if you'll go down there and persuade her to come to my house. Whoever is after me just might harm Laura or Mary Pat because they know that I'm fond of them."

"I'll tell her. But the woman's got a mind of her own."

"Tell her that if she can't come to me, I'll leave my men to guard Casper and come to her. Take my car. I'll ride with the men in one of the trucks."

On reaching the house, Hunter left George Hinkle in charge of the men and hurried inside. Dinah and Casper sat at the kitchen table. Dinah jumped up when he came in; her face was wet with tears. Hunter went to her and enfolded her in his arms.

"What's this? My Dinah bawling like a baby and no supper ready?" he chided gently.

"Mistah Conrad, he says dey think Casper—"

"We know better, don't we? Don't worry, now. Dry your tears. Nothing will happen to Casper. I've got fifteen men out there who'll see to it."

"I neber hide nothin', Mistah Hunter—"

"I know you didn't. This is all a misunderstanding and will be cleared up. Meanwhile, there are hungry men out there who've not had supper. Dinah, how about you and Casper rustling up something? Not one of those men has ever eaten a biscuit as good as yours. Let's give them a treat."

"I make up a batch, an' fry up some ham an' make redeye gravy." Dinah dried her eyes on the end of her apron. "Casper, fire up my cookstove."

After laying a reassuring hand on Casper's shoulder, Hunter went to the porch to wait for Jelly Bryce. George Hinkle came from around the house, his rifle in his hand.

"According to Bryce, the town's pretty stirred up. There could be trouble before the night's over. I'll double the wages for tonight, but there'll be no hard feelings if you or any of the men walk away."

"We ain't walkin', double pay or not."

"Have you stopped to think that you may

be defending a murderer? Folks seem to think I or Casper killed Miss Bakken."

George laughed. "Been workin' for ya for nigh on five years now. Reckon if'n ya or Casper was a killer, it'd showed up 'fore now."

"Thanks, George. Dinah is fixing supper for the men. We'll eat in shifts."

Hunter paced up and down the porch. When his car turned the corner down the street, he strained his eyes to see if Jelly Bryce was alone. As it neared, he felt a vast relief. Laura was with him. He left the porch and was in the drive waiting when the car stopped. He opened the door.

"Thank God, you're here. I've been so worried. Come to me, sweetheart." He lifted Mary Pat off Laura's lap. She went to him eagerly. "Did you bring your things?"

"Only what we had with us."

"Where's your mother? She didn't go back to the house, did she?" he asked anxiously.

"She stayed at the hotel."

After Laura got out of the car, Hunter pulled her close to him and looked over her head at Jelly.

"Much obliged, Bryce. George will take you back unless you want to stay awhile."

"Thanks, but I think I'll take a stroll through town and see what's going on."

"Tell the sheriff to keep that rabble away from here, because if they come, he knows what they'll get."

"Yeah, well, hang in here tonight. Things usually look better in the morning."

Hunter, carrying Mary Pat, led Laura into the house. She stood beside the door, her eyes roaming over the rich furnishings in the house. Seeing the uncertainty on her face, Hunter slipped an arm around her waist and drew her close, the baby between them.

"Honey, I'm still the same man who sat on your porch and helped you snap beans."

Her eyes moved from a gold-framed picture on the wall to the rich carpet on the floor, then to his. The tenderness, the concern, the love were there in his eyes. Her insides melted.

"My sweet and wonderful Laura. Give yourself a chance to know me here in my house." Hunter brought her hand to his lips. "No one will ever love you the way I do."

Laura tilted her head against his shoulder

for just a moment, then looked up at him. Her eyes were shining, her smile beautiful. She believed him. She rose up on her toes and lifted her mouth for his kiss.

The hotel guests—two salesmen, a single man waiting to be picked up by a nearby ranch owner, a couple on their way to Kansas City to visit their daughter, and a man waiting to take the morning train— were understandably nervous as night fell.

After a meal at Martha's, they returned to sit on the porch or in the hotel lobby. Joe moved among them, reassuring them that they were perfectly safe, that the sheriff had everything under control.

From the porch of the hotel they could hear the raised voices of the men gathered in groups along the street discussing the latest news. No one had as yet come forward who was willing to lead them to act in an unlawful manner.

Blue stayed in the kitchen with Nettie Cole and Radna in case Lloyd or some of the rowdies might come in the back door. Jill joined Thad on the front porch.

"It's strange without Aunt Justine here,"

she said. "I keep thinking I should go back to her room and see about her."

"I wonder why she never said anything about Madison being her son."

"Radna said she was ashamed. He blamed her for the mark on his face, yet he seems proud of it. Aunt Justine had wished for many years that someday she would see her son again. But at their first meeting, Radna said, he broke her heart, and she was never the same after that."

"I'll be glad for us to leave this place, honey. When the field plays out, a boom-town dies a slow death. And I don't like the feeling of always looking over my shoulder."

"You'd not feel that way if not for Lloyd."

"He's got a following here, even if they are a bunch of brainless mush-heads who can't think for themselves."

"We can't go until a decision has been made about what's to be done with the hotel. I can't just go off and leave it."

"Madison will try to get it."

"Aunt Justine didn't want him to have it. She told Radna to sell it when she was gone."

"I hope your aunt had an airtight will."

"Do you realize that Lloyd being Aunt Justine's son makes him my cousin?"

"Scary thought, isn't it?"

"His month here is up day after tomorrow."

"I'll be delighted to tell him to leave. But enough about him." With an arm across her shoulders, Thad pulled her close to him.

"Careful of your back," she cautioned.

"Don't worry, honey. It's much better—hardly hurts at all now. Have you decided how long we have to wait before we can get married?"

"Aunt Justine would say, don't wait. But I'm thinking it would be nice to be married back home among our families and friends."

"That would take weeks," he complained. "You and Julie would spend days fussing with dresses and flowers and doodads. You'd not have any time for me."

"What's a few weeks when we'll have a lifetime to be together? We'll have to decide where to live—"

"Why can't we be married here? Someone might steal you away from me." He brushed light kisses on her temple.

Jill laughed. "Sure. Did you see that line

of men wanting to marry me?" He caught her earlobe between his teeth. "Thad! Stop. Someone will see."

"Unhand my sister, you cad!"

Thad looked up at Joe. "You again? Why don't you go lie down in the road and let a car or a wagon run over you?"

"I'd get all wet and . . . muddy."

"We've decided to wait until we get home to be married." Jill smiled.

Thad frowned. "I didn't decide, you did. They've got perfectly good, decent preachers here in Rainwater. I don't understand why we have to wait."

"You don't have to understand it, you clobberhead. Just get in the harness and do as you're told," Joe said. "You might as well get used to it. By the time we get back to Fertile, you'll be dancing a jig and whistling 'Dixie' every time she snaps her fingers."

"But honeybunch," Thad protested as he put a kiss on Jill's nose, "I can't even carry a tune."

Jill laughed, then sobered quickly. "It isn't right for us to be sitting out here laughing, with Aunt Justine up at the funeral parlor."

"I didn't know her as well as you did, Sis.

But I think she'd want you to be happy and planning your wedding."

"Yes, she would. Do you and Thad have good shirts to wear to the funeral tomorrow?"

"Yes, and Mrs. Cole has offered to iron them for us." Joe went to stand by the porch steps. "I think I'll walk uptown and see which way the wind is blowing. Guard the front door, lover boy. If you're so in love you can't handle it, call Blue." Joe went down the steps to the walk.

"I hate him . . . sometimes," Thad said, wrapping both arms around Jill. "I'd beat him up, but he's going to be my brother-in-law and I'm going to have to get along with him."

Much to the relief of Sheriff Page and his deputy, the night passed without the expected eruption of mob violence. By midnight the streets held only a few of the diehard rowdies, too drunk to do anything but argue and brag. The sheriff didn't bother to arrest them.

Jelly Bryce was at the depot to meet the morning train bringing Officer Hurt from Oklahoma City. Ignoring the curious glances they received, the two officers greeted each other.

"How's it goin', Jelly?"

"Thought we'd run into a dead end until yesterday."

"We have a break in this case. I'd planned to come up here today even before you called. I'll wait and tell you and Sheriff Page at the same time. Did you alert the folks at the hotel that I'd need a room?"

"No, but we can go by and tell them now. I'm using the sheriff's car and the sheriff's gas."

Officer Hurt checked into the hotel. Later, after leaving his suitcase in his room, and carrying a leather folder, he and Jelly entered the sheriff's office through the back door. Red-eyed and weary, the sheriff greeted him.

"I understand things could have gotten out of hand here last night," Hurt said as the two men shook hands.

"Yeah. We've got a few hotheads. Most of it was all blow. But you never know what a crowd like that will do." Sheriff Page led the way to the front office and pulled up chairs for the two men before he sank into the old leather chair behind his desk.

"I've got a few things here I think you'll be interested in," Officer Hurt began. "When I went back to the city, I sent word to people I knew in the surrounding states about the crime here and asked if anyone knew of anything similar happening in their area.

"The other day I heard from a friend of mine who's with the police department in Springfield, Missouri. And what he had to say rang a bell.

"A few years ago, the dismembered body of a young woman was found in a shallow ditch alongside a well-used road outside of town. It was covered with a thin layer of brush, as if the killer had wanted her to be found. She was all there except for her head. It's never been found.

"Now, here is the sticker, or coincidence, whichever you want to call it. The body was identified as that of a young college student who had been missing for several weeks. While checking into her background, it was discovered that she had gone out a few times with a young fellow enrolled at Drury College. He had been living in a small house on the edge of town. A few days after he graduated, his house burned to the ground and he left town to go to law school."

The sheriff had not uttered a sound since the officer had started talking. He leaned back in his chair, his hands folded over his stomach. At the officer's next words the sheriff's head snapped up and his hands gripped the arms of the chair.

"The young man, a brilliant student, had a red mark the shape of the palm of a hand on his face."

"Godamighty!" The skin of Sheriff Page's weathered face had paled. "Godamighty," he said again in a hoarse whisper. He was visibly stunned. His hamlike fists balled and unballed. "How many men do you know with a mark like that?"

"Only one. I never mentioned that there was a man here with an unusual mark on his face. Or that right after the murder his house burned to the ground. In the second telegram, my friend sent me the name of their suspect." Officer Hurt took a yellow square of paper out of his folder and placed it on the desk in front of the sheriff.

Sheriff Page stared down at the paper for several minutes before he spoke.

"I don't have a thing to tie him to what

happened here. If I brought him in for ques-
tioning and accused him, I'd be run out of
town."

"Now that we suspect who committed
the crime, we'll have to work on getting him
to give himself away, or the son-of-a-bitch
will get away with butchering that woman.
He burned his house down to hide the
bloody mess just like he did in Springfield."
Officer Hurt retrieved the telegram and put
it back in his folder.

"Dad-blast it!" the sheriff snorted. "I can't
believe this. He's the last one I'd have suspected. If he's the one, he's fooled a lot of
folks, including me."

"Don't let it get to you. He fooled the de-
tectives over in Springfield, too. He was a
popular young man around town, a favorite
of the professors, president of his class. He
even helped in the search for the girl. They
suspected him but couldn't lay a finger on
him. He checked out clean as a whistle."

"He was in here the other day claiming to
be the son of the woman who owned the
hotel, and I believed him. Hell, now I don't
know what to believe. Mrs. Byers will be
buried this afternoon. I plan to be there because he may kick up a fuss."

"Sheriff." Jelly spoke up for the first time. "You told me yesterday that the head found out at Westfall's had an earring."

"Yeah, it did."

"Where is it now?"

"The head? I took it to the undertaker. Ernest will bury it with the rest of her."

"What about the earring?"

"Still on it. Now that I think about it, there might have been one in each ear. It was about the size of a nickel and had a little doodad hanging from it. I hope never to have to look on anything like that again."

"Did you tell the undertaker to remove the earrings?"

"Didn't think about it."

"Would he have buried it already or shown it to anyone?"

"I doubt it. He has respect for a dead body. Besides, he's been busy with Mrs. Byers. What are you thinking?"

"I'm thinking that this is one smart guy we're dealing with. Like in Springfield, he didn't leave a trail, so let's make one. It's a shot in the dark, but it might work."

For the next half hour, Officer Hurt, Jelly and the sheriff sat huddled around the desk talking strategy. When they were finally satisfied with a plan, the sheriff slipped out the back door of the jail and headed for the funeral parlor. Jelly went to the hotel to borrow a garden rake and Officer Hurt went to the mercantile to speak to Mayor Henshaw.

Chapter 31

The funeral service for Justine Byers was the largest one ever held in Rainwater. Most of the merchants in town closed their shops for a couple of hours in the afternoon to enable them to pay their respects. The Baptist church overflowed and fifty or more mourners waited outside to follow the casket to the cemetery, where Justine would be buried beside her beloved Ralph.

Radna refused to go inside the church and no amount of coaxing could change her mind. Jill insisted until Thad took her aside and explained that because of Radna's colored blood she feared her presence would be remarked on by some of the others, so she chose to wait in the car with Blue. Jill, Joe and Thad were the only occupants of the front row of seats reserved for family until Lloyd Madison came in and took a seat beside Joe.

Jill fumed. The nerve of the man!

When the service was over, Jill, along with her brother and Thad, climbed into the car with Blue and Radna to follow the same horse-drawn hearse that had carried Justine's husband, Ralph, to the cemetery.

At the grave site, Jill and Joe prodded Radna to move to the front and take her place with the family during the brief prayer service. Across the grave, Lloyd Madison, in a dark suit and sparkling white shirt, stood with his head bowed, a black felt hat in his hand, ignoring the curious stares of the mourners gathered around the grave.

The preacher made an announcement at the start of the service.

"The family, Joe and Jill Jones and Miss Radna Beau, a close friend of Mrs. Byers, invite you to take refreshments on the veranda of the hotel, to reminisce about the life of Justine Byers, who had such an influence on this community."

Robbed of logical thought, Jill stood stupefied during the graveside service. Thad held tightly to her hand.

When the minister nodded to them, Jill

and Joe stooped and picked up a handful of soil and sprinkled it on the casket. Across from them, Lloyd also stooped and took a handful of soil.

"Good-bye, Mother." Lloyd spoke in a loud, clear voice so that all present could hear. "I'm sorry that, at the last, I never got to tell you the depth of my feelings for you." He held his hand over the casket. When he opened it, amid the handful of dirt that cascaded down was a small stone that bounced with a hollow thudding sound and rolled off the coffin.

When the service ended, Lloyd stood beside the grave shaking hands with those who came forward.

"I'm sorry I couldn't claim her as my mother while she was alive. She didn't want to acknowledge me, and I respected her wishes.

"Why? Well, she was always deeply ashamed that she had given birth to a child so badly disfigured.

"No, I didn't blame her. I loved her. . . ."

Knowing that Jill was about to explode and that she would create a scene, Thad tried to steer her toward the car. She resisted until she saw that Blue had moved up to be with Radna. Blindly, Jill accepted the condolences of friends and acquaintances of her aunt as they made their way to the car. She spotted Skeeter Ridge standing alone beside a tall granite marker. He was clean-shaven, and he wore a pair of dark trousers and a white shirt. She hardly recognized him.

"Mr. Ridge," Jill said as they approached. "We'd be pleased if you would come back to the hotel for refreshments. Aunt Justine always looked forward to your visits."

"I'll come," he muttered without looking at her.

When they walked away, Thad leaned down and murmured, "Did you see the handful of flowers he was holding behind his back? He's waiting until everyone leaves."

On the fringe of the crowd Laura stood beside Hunter Westfall. He was holding Mary Pat. They looked very much like a family. Ignoring the curious looks cast their way, Hunter clasped Laura's elbow and they went back to his car.

A table with desserts, coffee and iced tea was set up on the veranda. Mrs. Cole and Martha, from the restaurant across the street, were seeing to it. Nothing needed Jill's immediate attention. She sank down on a kitchen chair.

Her time in Rainwater was almost over. She would never regret coming here. Here she and Thad had discovered their love; here she had learned to tolerate a lifestyle that was different from hers. Here she had discovered once again what it meant to lose someone you love.

But she was homesick. She wanted to go home.

Jelly Bryce and Officer Hurt, with their police badges prominently displayed on their shirts, raked through the ashes and burned timbers of Lloyd's house. Cars slowed; men on horseback and people coming from Justine Byers's funeral paused. A few, including Mayor Henshaw, came up to the foundation of the burned-out house to watch.

"What's going on here?" the mayor asked.

"Lookin' to see what we can find," Officer Hurt replied. "Had a tip we might find something, but it doesn't look very promising."

"This is Mr. Madison's place." The man

who spoke wore the clothes of an oil field worker. "Are you lookin' for somethin' for him?"

"You might say that."

There were three people besides the mayor standing close by when Jelly, pulling his rake through the ashes, suddenly stopped and lifted the rake.

"Hey, Chief, come look at this."

"What'd you find?" Officer Hurt dropped his spade. The mayor stepped up onto the foundation to get a look at what was caught on the tine of the rake. "It's an earring with a doodad hanging on it."

"Shitfire! It's like the one on the head that—" Jelly cut off his words.

"You reckon that tip that came from Springfield was right about him?" Hurt asked.

"Looks like it. I swear that I saw the mate to this on the head that was found yesterday."

"How'd it get here?" The question came from a man in the greasy overalls.

"It sure as hell didn't walk in here all by its lonesome. Holy shit! He did the same thing in Springfield, to cover up what he did to that woman—"

"Hush, Jelly!" Officer Hurt said sharply.

"Sorry, Clarence. I got carried away."

The man in overalls backed quickly away.

"Keep this under your hat, hear?" Mayor Henshaw said sharply.

"Yeah, sure." The man kept walking.

"He can hardly wait to get uptown to tell it," the mayor said as soon as the man was out of hearing distance.

"This may turn out better than we expected," Jelly said. "It may force Madison to make a move."

"Thanks, Mayor. With you being here, he can't accuse us of planting the earring. Now we sit back and see what happens."

"I never would have suspected him of being anything but what he appeared to be: a nice young lawyer working to better the conditions of the field workers. But the similarity between what happened here and what happened in Springfield is just too close to ignore."

"We couldn't get a conviction on similarity. If we tried, he'd turn around and sue us. We've got to get him to make a move. Thanks again, Mayor. Having that fellow show up takes some of the heat off you. By the way, who is he?"

"I can't recall right off, but he's one of those in Madison's pocket."

"We'll wait a little while, then go looking for Mr. Madison."

Lloyd sat behind his desk and listened to what the man Oscar Sample had brought in had to say. Not a flicker of the anxiety he was feeling showed on his face.

"That's about it, Mr. Madison. I never believed a word of what they was sayin'. The mayor told me to keep it under my hat, but I knew I had to tell you 'cause they're plottin' somethin' that smells."

"You were right to go to Oscar. He's a good friend of mine and knows what I'm trying to do for the men and their families."

"They're doin' this 'cause you want to organize the workers and get more money for them," Oscar said angrily.

"You are more than likely right. I can't think of any other reason why they would concoct such a cock-and-bull story to be rid of me. I'm going to have to defend myself, and I'll need the help of my friends.

"I'll have to leave town until things quiet down and they find the real killer of that woman. Here are the keys to my car. It would help me a lot if you would bring it to the alley behind the hotel. I'll slip over there and pick up a few things. I'll get in touch with you from time to time and you can tell me when it's safe to come back."

"We understand. You can depend on us, Mr. Madison."

After the men had left the office, Lloyd jumped up and started shoving papers in a leather case. It paid to cultivate men in *low* places. His dear papa had taught him that. The news they had brought was surprising.

Dammit to hell! How had he lost that damn earring? And how had he missed it when he raked through the ashes and picked up the metal from the suitcase and a few other trinkets that hadn't burned? And how had they found out about Springfield?

None of what had happened a month ago had been planned. He had been passing Westfall's house, on his way to see if by chance he could catch Laura Hopper going or coming from the outhouse, when the woman came out carrying a suitcase.

The rest was as easy as falling off a log. He'd stopped, introduced himself and asked her if she needed help. When she said she'd appreciate a ride to the depot, he'd told her there wasn't another train until after midnight and the depot wasn't a place for a lady alone this time of night. He had invited her to stay at his "mother's" house until train time.

When they reached his house, "Mother" had gone to visit a sick friend. After a couple of drinks of one-hundred-proof whiskey, the woman was in a talkative mood.

In Westfall's bedroom, she had found a notepad he used to jot down things he wanted to remember to do. At the head of the list was a note to tell Perry Reade to get a train ticket for Carsie early the next morning. The original plan had been that she stay another week. That he was tired of her so soon and was sending her off the next morning without even discussing it with her had made her so furious that she had packed up and left the house.

He hadn't planned to kill Westfall's bitch, Lloyd thought now. The opportunity had fallen into his lap and he hadn't been able to resist it. After a kill he would ride on a cloud of euphoria for months and lately had craved the feeling again. He didn't regret a minute of it. It had been just as wonderful as the first time, when he was twelve years old and had taken that dirty little brat to the shed. The old man had burned down the shed, given him a good beating and made him promise not to do it again. Ha! A lot he knew!

He might, he decided now, after he got out of this mess—and he was confident he would—go to one of the South American countries, where he could live like a king on what money he had.

Lloyd was aware that he had made mistakes. He should not have picked up Laura Hopper's brat at the hotel. But hell, the desire to get even with the bitch for choosing Westfall over him had been too great. The hick-town sheriff had swallowed his explanation.

Another mistake was hiding the woman's head too well. He had wanted it found two or three days after the body was found, while the town was still riled up against Westfall. A third mistake was losing the earring. They were mistakes he would not make again. What was done, was done.

He had to get over to the hotel, pick up a few things and get out of this one-horse town. Thank God he'd been able to get a key to the upper back door. Stupid fools had thought to keep it locked so they would know when he was in the hotel. He had used it many times. The only trick was getting up the outside stairs without being seen.

There were so many people milling around on the veranda and in the hotel lobby that at times Jill had to turn sideways to get through the crowd. Thad had insisted on helping to carry cakes, pies, tea and ice from the kitchen until an elbow had poked him in the back. He had been unable to choke back a gasp of pain. On hearing it, Jill asserted her rights as his future wife to order him to her bedroom to lie down for a while.

After removing his shirt, Thad flopped down on his stomach on the bed.

"Stay with me for a while."

"I wish I could." Resisting the desire to linger with him, Jill gave him a tender kiss and left the room.

Dreading to go back among the chattering, gossipy crowd, and needing a few minutes by herself, she went out onto the back porch and sat down in the shade. Fertile, the spotted dog, came out from under the porch and waited for Jill to scratch her head.

"I don't know what Thad will do with you and all those pups when we leave. But don't worry, he'll not leave until he finds you a home," Jill said to the dog.

"Aunt Justine would be pleased that so many showed up at her funeral. I didn't know what in the world we were going to do with all those cakes and pies. Would you believe it, Fertile, they are almost gone? Blue had to go for more ice for the tea." Jill stroked the dog's head.

"Mr. Shepard told Joe that he'd be here in the morning to tell us what was in Aunt Justine's will. I just want it over so we can go home."

Jill looked up when Skeeter Ridge came around the side of the hotel. He jerked his cap off his head as he approached her.

"Ya ain't ort to be out here by yoreself."

"Why not?" Jill liked the man slightly more than when they first met, but he still irritated her.

"Madison went up the back stairs a while ago."

"But . . . that door is locked and has been since he moved in."

"Pshaw!" Skeeter snorted. "He's been going in and out of it all along."

Jill jumped to her feet. "Why in tarnation didn't you say so?"

"I told Justine."

"She never said anything."

"She said not to bother ya, that what would be, would be. She's gone now. He can't hurt her no more."

"I've got to tell Joe. I wish I'd let Thad nail that door shut when he wanted to."

Skeeter walked back around the hotel to the front. He didn't tell the young miss that Oscar Sample had driven Madison's car up the alley and left it behind the wash house. Lloyd was up to something. He'd just have to watch and see what it was.

Upstairs, Lloyd hurriedly packed what he wanted to take with him, stuck his .44-caliber revolver in his belt beneath his coat and went to the door at the end of the hall to see if his car was in the alley.

When he didn't see it, he swore and went back to his room. He'd told the idiot to leave the car in the alley. Lord, he was tired of kowtowing to a bunch of stupid laborers. He would wait five more minutes and go down the back stairs. If the car wasn't there, he'd wait in the alley.

By the time Jill reached the lobby, the crowd had begun to thin out. She went out onto the veranda. Radna was gathering up the used Dixie cups that had been sent over by Mr. Rowe, the druggist. Nettie Cole was carrying the empty cake plates back to the kitchen to be washed and returned to the owners.

"Where's Joe?" Jill asked Radna.

"The last time I saw him, he was in the lobby."

Jill returned to the lobby and met Joe coming down the hall from the family rooms.

"Lloyd is upstairs. He came up the outside stairway."

"I thought that door was locked. I've been watching for him to come in. He's got more guts than an army mule. Did you hear what he was saying at the cemetery?"

"He's crazy, Joe. I'll be glad to leave this place."

"We'll know in the morning when Mr. Shepard comes to tell us what Aunt Justine wanted done. We can leave the hotel in his hands and go home."

"It can't be too soon to suit me." She turned to speak to the sheriff and Mr. Hurt, who had come in and stopped at the desk. "The dessert table has been taken down, but there's cake and pie in the kitchen."

"We didn't come for dessert, miss. Is Madison here?"

"No," Elmer said.

"Yes," Jill said quickly. Then, to Elmer: "He came up the back outside stairs. Skeeter Ridge saw him."

"Same room?" the Oklahoma City officer asked. At a nod from Jill, he and the sheriff took the stairs two at a time to reach the upper floor. Jelly took a post at the bottom of the stairs.

"What's going on, Jelly?" Joe asked.

"They have a few questions to ask Madison."

A hard rap sounded on the upstairs door. "It's Sheriff Page, Madison."

"I'm not dressed, Sheriff."

"I want to ask you something about Mrs. Byers."

"I'll come down to the office in an hour or so."

"Madison, I know that you took a suitcase from your office and your car is waiting in the alley behind the hotel. Are you going somewhere?"

Silence.

"Madison?" Sheriff Page rapped on the door again. "We want to talk to you. Open the door."

Silence.

"We're coming in one way or the other. Open the door and save yourself some trouble."

The sheriff lifted his hand to rap on the door again.

Bang! The shot that came through the door missed the sheriff's head by inches and passed through the door across the hall. Both Sheriff Page and Officer Hurt darted to the side of the door.

"Godamighty! I hope there isn't anyone in that room." As they drew their weapons, they heard the sliding of a heavy object.

"He isn't coming out. He's barricading the door with the bureau."

The sound of the shot had rocketed throughout the hotel. Jelly bounded up the stairs to see the two officers hovering on each side of the door. Officer Hurt waved him back.

"That was foolish, Madison," Officer Hurt

shouted. "You've got to come out some-time."

Bang! Another shot came through the wooden door.

Down the hall, a door opened. A man stuck his head out. The sheriff waved him back in. The door slammed shut.

"Is there anyone else up here?"

"I'll go ask." Jelly started back down the stairs.

"I didn't expect this. He's gone crazy." Sheriff Page pulled a handkerchief from his pocket and wiped the sweat off his face.

Jelly didn't have to ask. Joe was standing on the stairs halfway up to the second floor.

"One man in room seven. The rest of the rooms are empty."

"What's under that front room?" Jelly asked, going down into the lobby. Joe followed.

"The desk and part of the lobby."

"Clear everyone out. You never know what a desperate man with a gun will do. He might shoot through the floor."

The sound of the shots had awakened Thad. He had come barreling into the lobby shirtless and now stood with his arms around Jill, who was shaking uncontrollably.

"Folks," Joe said. "Mr. Madison has gone berserk and is shooting through the door. We don't know what is going to happen, but we sure don't want anyone to get hurt. To be on the safe side, I'll take you out the back way: down the hallway and through the kitchen. The window upstairs looks down on the street."

"Why was the sheriff coming to see him?" Jill asked Jelly from the shelter of Thad's arms.

"He was going to talk to him about the murder of Carsie Bakken."

"Oh, my goodness. Does he think he killed her?"

"He's as sure as he can be without actually seeing him do it."

Jelly went up the stairs and Jill turned her face to Thad's bare shoulder.

"He killed that woman we found. Cut her up—"

"Good Lord! He's been living right here in the hotel all this time." Thad's arms tightened and he buried his lips in her hair. "Justine must have known or sensed that he was capable of killing."

Blue stepped out on the veranda to look around for Radna. When he had last seen her, she had been helping Martha carry dishes across the street to the restaurant. He spied her there, standing in the doorway, and waved frantically for her to stay where she was. She didn't see him. She was laughing over her shoulder at Martha as she came out the door and started across the street to the hotel.

Radna had just stepped off the walk when a shot rang out. The bullet dug into the oil-packed road a foot ahead of her. Startled, she paused and looked around. A second bullet, followed closely behind the first, struck her. Her legs buckled and she fell.

A third shot rang out. The small body sprawling in the street jerked when the bullet hit.

Blue, with a bellow of rage, leaped off the porch and dashed out into the street. As he bent low to scoop Radna up in his arms, he felt the breeze from another bullet pass over his head. He ran a zigzag pattern to the side of the restaurant, thanking God the shooter was such a poor shot that several succeeding shots missed them.

"Who shot me?" Radna was breathing

fast, her hand reaching for the wound in her thigh.

"Madison. He's in the upstairs window at the hotel."

"Why . . . ?"

" 'Cause he's backed into a corner."

"Well, you've been wantin' to carry me off to bed."

"Not this way. I've got to get you to the doctor." Blue kept walking as if she weighed no more than one of Fertile's pups.

"Wait." Martha stepped out of the back of the restaurant. "Is she hurt bad? Who shot her?"

Blue shook his head. "That son-of-a-bitch Madison shot her."

"Lloyd shot her? Why'd he do that?" Martha drew up Radna's skirt. Blood had soaked the skirt and was dripping on the ground. She whipped a dish towel from over her shoulder and wrapped it tightly around Radna's thigh.

"I'll call the doctor and tell him you're on the way. The office is a block down and—"

"I know where it is."

"Why'd ya come get me, Randolph?"

" 'Cause . . . I'm dumb Indian."

Radna gritted her teeth. Blue knew she

was suffering terribly from the wound in her thigh and from the one in her shoulder. The front of her dress was soaked with blood.

Don't die on me, Rosebud. I've not loved a woman before.

"After this, I . . . just might fall in love with you—"

"That'd be mighty kind of you, thorny Rosebud. Now be quiet, unless you want to say again what you just said."

Chapter 32

The news swept through town like a tornado. Lloyd Madison was holed up in the hotel shooting out the window.

Oscar Sample and his friend were standing on the street corner when a boy ran by shouting the news.

"Ah, law! Somethin's gone wrong. Come on, we gotta help him." Oscar grabbed the arm of his friend and they hurried toward the hotel.

A car was parked in the middle of the street to stop traffic from going past the hotel. Deputy Franklin was telling the crowd that had gathered to stay back. "A shooter is in a upstairs room at the hotel. He shot a woman on the street and is shooting at anything that moves."

"Why're they doin' that to Mr. Madison for?" Oscar asked belligerently.

"Stay back. The sheriff will take care of it."

"Take care of it, my hind leg! He pushed him and he's too scared to come out." Oscar turned to the crowd. "Ain't any of ya goin' to help him? He's the only one stickin' up for us." Oscar looked around at the workers who had just come in from the field. "He ain't done nothin' wrong. They're framin' him, is what they're doin', to get him out of town so the big oil companies can take over."

"Use your head, Oscar," the deputy said. "He just shot a woman on the street."

"He was pushed to do it. He won't shoot me. I'm goin' to stand by him if none of ya ain't. He'll come out and explain it all if I ask him to." Oscar motioned for his friend to follow. The man hesitated, then followed Oscar down the street.

"Oscar, I don't think we ort to go—"

"Cowards is what they are. Mr. Madison's been working to make things better for us and none of 'em would lift a hand to help him."

"They said he shot a woman." The man looked fearfully up at the hotel room.

"We're his friends. He wouldn't shoot—"

Oscar never finished what he was going to say. A bullet caught him in the chest and he crumpled to the ground.

"Oh, God! Oh, God!" The other man ran screaming, but a second bullet caught him in the back and he fell face first onto the hard-packed road.

In the hotel, Jelly took the stairs two at a time and squatted down beside Officer Hurt.

"He's shot two men on the street."

"Kill 'em?"

"I'm not sure. He's using a .44. I can tell by the sound of it."

"He isn't coming out now. He's gone too far."

At that moment, two more shots came through the door.

They could hear Lloyd laughing. Then he shouted, "I got two boxes of shells, Judge, and I'm going to use them all. You said I'd not amount to a dribble of shit. You dried-up old bastard! I've got a whole town waiting to watch me blow your ugly head off."

"The judge? Does he think I'm his pa?"

"Who knows what he's thinking? He's gone berserk."

"What did you ever do, Judge, besides send some penny-ante crook to jail?" Lloyd was shouting again. "Oh, yeah, you tried to screw the maids. But you couldn't get your tally-whacker to work." More shrill laughter. "I did it for you, disgusting as it was, so they'd know I could do something the self-righteous old judge couldn't do."

A series of gunshots came from the room. None came through the door.

"He's shooting out the window again, or . . . through the floor."

"Mo-ther. Dear, trashy strumpet! I cut you up and I'll do it again and again and again." The laughter that followed was chilling.

"He's out of his mind," Sheriff Page whispered.

"What do you want me to do?" Jelly asked.

"I don't see a way out of this, do you, Hurt?"

"If I could get on the roof of the restaurant across the street, I could get a shot at him through the window," Jelly said.

"And he could get a shot at you."

"Not if I can get behind the false front above the restaurant before he sees me."

"Then you'd better take off those fancy white pants."

Jelly smiled. "I'll change and get my rifle."

When Jelly came out of his room, he was wearing a pair of dark pants and carrying his rifle. He motioned to Hurt and went out the back door and down the outside stairs that hugged the side of the hotel.

Officer Hurt beckoned to Joe at the bottom of the stairs.

"Jelly is going to try to get on the roof of the restaurant across the street," he whispered when Joe was beside him. "Watch, and when you get a glimpse of him, let me know. We'll try to get Madison's attention so Jelly can get in place."

Joe nodded and scurried back downstairs and over to where Thad, with a loose shirt over his shoulders, stood in a far corner with Jill, the Evanses and Nettie Cole.

"Jelly is going to get on the roof of the restaurant so he can get a shot at him through the window."

"Through the window? That's a long shot." Thad held tightly to Jill, stroking the nape of her neck, trying to keep her calm.

"Blue said he was good. The best he'd ever seen," Joe answered.

The telephone rang. Almost immediately shots came through the floor.

"He does that every time," Jill said. "I wish the operator would stop ringing. I'm worried about Radna."

"Blue will take care of her, honey," Thad said.

"She could be dead."

"Don't think that."

"I thought he was strange-acting, but to kill that woman . . . and cut her up—"

"Jelly said that they think he did the same thing in Springfield."

"He's crazy. He's got to be. I'm glad Laura and the baby are safe with Mr. Westfall." Nettie Cole clasped her work-worn hands and went over to stand beside Skeeter Ridge, who sat quietly in a chair in the corner.

On the side of the restaurant, out of sight of the upstairs window, Thad got a glimpse of two men attempting to boost Jelly to the roof. He signaled to Joe. Joe relayed the silent message.

"Madison," the sheriff called. "Let's talk about this. Did you know the Bakken woman? It was smart of you to burn down your house so we couldn't find where you'd cut her up."

"Of course it was, you fool. It was a bloody mess. The judge burned down the back shed where I cut—" Two shots came through the door. "I killed that whoring bitch we buried today. I cut her black heart out."

The sheriff shook his head at Hurt. "Why did you do that, Lloyd?"

"The judge told me to. He said, Find the bitch and kill her. I practiced on a cat, then a dog, then when I was twelve I—" He laughed. "You'd like for me to tell you what I did, wouldn't you? I'm not going to. The judge said never, never, never say that I did it. They caught a bum and hung him."

"Sweet Jesus," the sheriff whispered. "He's a lunatic and I never suspected a thing."

Joe scooted up the stairs. "Jelly got across the roof."

Six rapid shots and the sound of shattered glass came from inside the room. The sheriff looked at Joe.

"How many windows in that room?"

"Two on the front and one on the side."

"Let's hope he goes by one on the front."

Joe went back down to the lobby as Hunter Westfall came in from the back.

"Laura is worried about her mother." Hunter went directly to Mrs. Cole. "Are you all right?"

"I'm all right. Laura and the baby?"

"They're at my house with Dinah. I left two men there with them."

"I'm glad she isn't here."

"I went by the doctor's office." Hunter turned to Jill and the others. "Bluefeather said for me to tell you that Radna was shot in the shoulder and the thigh. She lost a lot of blood, but she's conscious and the doctor thinks she will be all right. He's now working on the man who was shot in the back. He managed to crawl to the side of the street, where a couple of fellows ran out and dragged him out of the line of fire. He's in bad shape."

"Were they not able to get to the other man?" Joe asked.

"They're sure that he's dead."

Thad groaned. "That was Sample, the one I belted out at the oil fire. He thought the sun rose and set in the man who killed him."

"I hope Jelly gets Lloyd before he kills anyone else." Joe took up his position beside the window where he could see the roof of the restaurant across the street.

In the upstairs hallway, the sheriff wiped the sweat from his face and spoke to Hurt. "How good a shot is this Jelly?"

"He hits what he aims at ninety-nine percent of the time."

The sheriff whistled through his teeth. He cocked his head toward the door. "Let's hope this doesn't fall into that one percent."

"It won't. He—" Hurt's words were cut off by the sound of more shots coming from the room.

"Jesus! He's used up a lot of bullets."

Suddenly they heard a different sound. A heavy thud. Seconds later, Joe bounded up the steps.

"Jelly's standing up with his arms raised. He's coming down off the roof."

"It means that he got him." Hurt stood on his cramped legs. "Thank God."

"Are you sure?"

"I'm sure. Jelly wouldn't be coming off that roof if he wasn't sure. Got a key, Joe?"

It took three men to push the heavy bureau aside so that the sheriff could squeeze into the room. Lloyd Madison lay dead on the floor, a bullet in his heart.

A week later, Jill, Thad and Joe stood on the platform waiting for the train that would take them to Kansas City, where they would transfer to another train for St. Joseph. There, Jill and Joe's brother-in-law, Evan Johnson, would meet them and take them home to Fertile.

Blue had brought them to the station in the car that Thad and Joe insisted on leaving with him.

"As soon as Radna is well enough, bring her and come to Fertile. Among our families there will be plenty of places to stay." Joe's face was all smiles.

"But don't drive," Thad said seriously. "Jill wants Radna to get there in one piece."

"We're talking about going to Colorado. Now that Radna's got money from the hotel, I've got to help her spend it."

The three men clasped hands. "Thanks, Blue, for everything." Joe choked up.

"Yeah, Blue, you dumb Indian." Thad cuffed him on the back. "At times you were a pain in the ass, but I'd not have missed knowing you for the world."

"Keep your tail out of a crack. Listen to the girl. She seems to have more sense than both of you." Blue's voice wasn't quite as steady as he wanted it to be.

Jill went to the edge of the platform to say good-bye to Laura, who arrived with Hunter and Mary Pat. She hugged the shy girl.

"I'm going to miss you, Laura. I hope you and Mary Pat have a happy life."

"They will, if I have anything to say about it." Hunter, holding Mary Pat with one arm, put his other arm around Laura.

"Fertile is about fifty miles east of St. Joseph. If you get up that way, please come to see us."

"Have you set a date for the wedding?"

Jill laughed happily. "Thad's giving me three weeks from the day we arrive home and not a day more."

"Don't worry about Radna. Mama will take care of her until she can get around," said Laura.

"Aunt Justine would be glad that you bought the hotel, Mr. Westfall, and that Mrs.

Cole will be running it. Nettie knows a lot more about it than I did when I came here."

Thad came to Jill and put his arm around her. "Honey, the train is coming and there's someone else you should say good-bye to." He tilted his head toward the station house, where a familiar figure was leaning against the wall.

"'Bye, Laura. 'Bye, Mary Pat and Mr. Westfall." She kissed Laura and the baby on the cheeks. Thad shook hands with Hunter and Laura.

Jill found her eyes filled with tears as she approached Skeeter Ridge.

"I'm going to kiss you whether you like it or not," she said gruffly and pecked him on the cheek. "If not for you, we'd not have known Lloyd had gone up to his room and he might have escaped and gone on to kill someone else. Besides, you can't be all bad. Aunt Justine liked you."

"You're kinda like Justine was . . . twenty years ago."

"That's the nicest thing you could say. Keep your eye on the hotel, hear? Aunt Justine would want you to help Mrs. Cole if she needs it."

Jill hurried away. Thad shook hands with Skeeter and followed.

The train came to a screeching halt, the iron wheels grating on the rails. The conductor stepped down and placed a stool beside the steps.

"All aboard!"

Jill made a dash for Blue and wrapped her arms around his waist.

"Come to Fertile, Blue. Please come and bring Radna."

"Might just do that. By then those two clabberheads will need straightening out again."

"'Bye, Blue." She kissed his cheek. "'Bye Elmer, Rose, Skeeter, Laura, Mary Pat, and Mr. Westfall. 'Bye, everybody."

Thad steered Jill up the steps and into the half-filled railroad car. Joe stored their suitcases in the compartment at the end of the car and came to where Thad was waiting for Jill to be seated. He gave Joe a sour look.

"Go sit in the next car. I want to sit with my girl without any interference from you."

"Get smart with me," Joe said in a loud whisper, "and I'll tell these folks about your connection with Al Capone and the Valentine's Day Massacre."

"Sit down, Joe," Jill said sternly. "Behave, now, or I'll take both of you back to the insane asylum."

The other passengers turned their heads toward the small girl giving strict orders to the two young men. They saw the one still standing move obediently to a seat several rows behind the other two.

The train lurched. Jill waved to those on the platform. When they were out of sight, she settled back in her seat and took off her hat.

"Good-bye, Rainwater." She reached for Thad's hand. "Did Blue mean it when he said he would help Radna spend the money from the hotel?" she asked with a worried frown.

"Don't worry about Radna, honey. Blue's probably got more money than Hunter Westfall. He inherited a pile of it from his father and his grandfather, and he's got an interest in a big hotel in Oklahoma City. He's far from broke."

"For goodness' sake. Then why was he working in the oil fields?"

"Because he wanted to. Randolph Frazier

Bluefeather is a very special man. He plays the dumb Indian if he wants to, and lays pipeline in an oil field if he wants to. He's been lonely. Radna is the first woman I've known of who can hold her own with him. He's crazy about her. They'll be good together."

"Well for goodness' sake," Jill said again. "I'm glad he fell in love with her. She hasn't had an easy life."

"Are you going to let me help you spend the two hundred dollars your aunt left you in her will?"

"If you'll let me help you spend the fifty dollars you got from Mr. Westfall for what you did the day of the fire."

"I'll have to think on that. You're getting pretty sassy." He put his arm around her. "I'm going to take you in hand after we're married—in more ways than one." He cupped his hand as if to fit it around her breast and nuzzled her ear with his nose.

"Thad Taylor! You're the limit!" Jill whispered as she grabbed his wrist to hold his hand away from her breast.

"But . . . sugarpuss, I want to . . ." His mouth curved in a happy smile, his eyes teasing her.

"And I want you to. But not now. Not here." Then she turned, threw her arms around his neck and kissed him full on the mouth. "Oh, Thad! We're going home!"

He chuckled and tightened his arm around her. "Yes, sweetheart, we're going home."

Author's Note

The oil town of Rainwater, Oklahoma, as well as the characters in this story, are imaginary, with the exception of Clarence Hurt and D. A. "Jelly" Bryce. Hurt and Bryce were Oklahoma City police officers in 1929.

Jelly Bryce became legendary among lawmen of the Southwest as possibly the best sharpshooter the FBI ever had. When a hostage standoff with a dangerous killer occurred, Jelly would be called in. He was reputed to be accurate ninety-nine percent of the time.

Bryce grew up along a creek bank with a rifle in his hand. In 1926, just out of high school, Jelly was planning to enroll at the University of Oklahoma when he heard of a pistol contest, with a prize of a hundred dollars in gold. He entered the contest, won and was asked by Night Chief Clarence Hurt to join the Oklahoma City police as a detective. He was twenty years old.

Bryce was always a fancy dresser, usually favoring white slacks, shirt and either a vest or a sweater. Shortly after joining the force, he shot a crook who then looked up at him and said, "I can't believe I was killed by a jelly bean." Following the remark, Bryce quickly became known as "Jelly," a name he grew to like.

Jelly Bryce was an easygoing, relaxed, friendly man. He was well liked by everyone who worked with him and extremely intelligent. Gifted with what seemed to the average man as supernatural eyesight, he claimed to see a bullet when it left his gun and his eyes could follow its trajectory to the target. That, Jelly said, was why he could do the things he did. He could hit a Mexican peso thrown through the air with a .22 and he never, ever missed.

During the twenties and thirties, the indestructible lawman killed nineteen men. In 1974, he died in his sleep of a heart attack. He had a clear conscience. He had never killed anyone he didn't have to kill in order to save a life.

If you would like to know more about Jelly Bryce, take a look at *Jelly Bryce, the FBI's Legendary Sharpshooter,* by K. B. Chaffin.

In 1927 the Oklahoma City oil field was discovered and soon became the largest in the nation.

By 1929, forty major producing oil fields were spread across Oklahoma. Boomtowns sprang up on the prairies. That same year, in October, the stock market crashed—the beginning of the Great Depression.

Dorothy Garlock